GODSRAIN

OTHER PATHFINDER TITLES BY LIANE MERCIEL

Nightglass
Nightblade
Hellknight

The Shroud of Four Silences

Pathfinder®

GODSRAIN

Liane Merciel

Cover illustration by Mirco Paganessi. Cover design by Sonja Morris.
Cartography and interior illustration by James Nalepa.

Published by Paizo Inc.
15902 Woodinville-Redmond Rd NE, Suite B
Woodinville, WA 98072-4572
www.paizo.com

ISBN 978-1-64078-718-6 (trade paperback)
ISBN 978-1-64078-627-1 (eBook)

The Library of Congress Cataloging-in-Publication Data is available upon request.

For information about special discounts available for bulk purchases, sales promotions, fund-raising, and educational needs, contact Paizo Sales at sales@paizo.com.

First Softcover Edition: May 2025

Produced using ecologically sourced FSC® certified paper and soy ink.

Printed in China

FSC
www.fsc.org
MIX
Paper | Supporting responsible forestry
FSC® C013314

To Peter, Alexander, and Catherine.

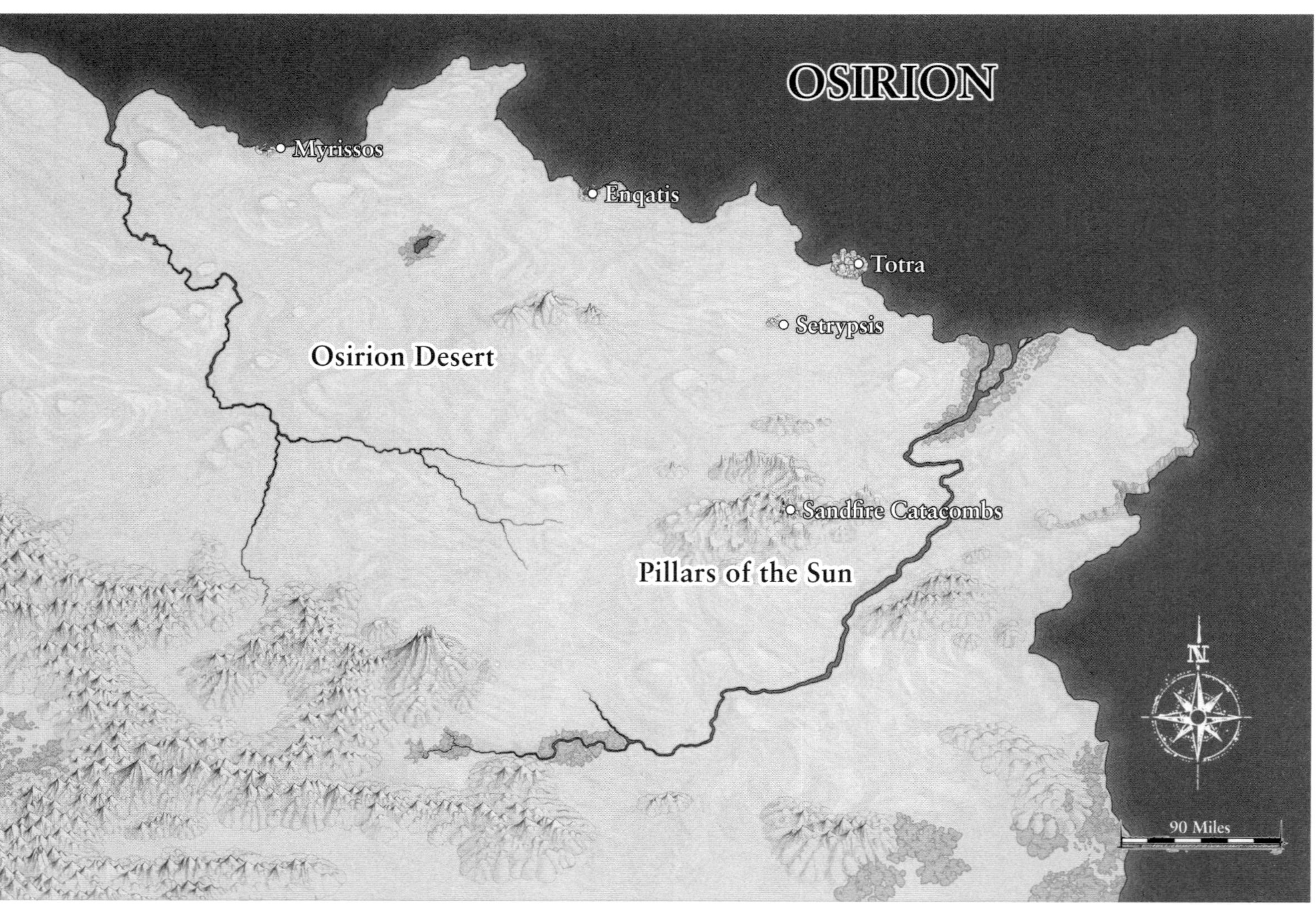
OSIRION
Myrissos
Enqatis
Totra
Setrypsis
Osirion Desert
Sandfire Catacombs
Pillars of the Sun
N
90 Miles

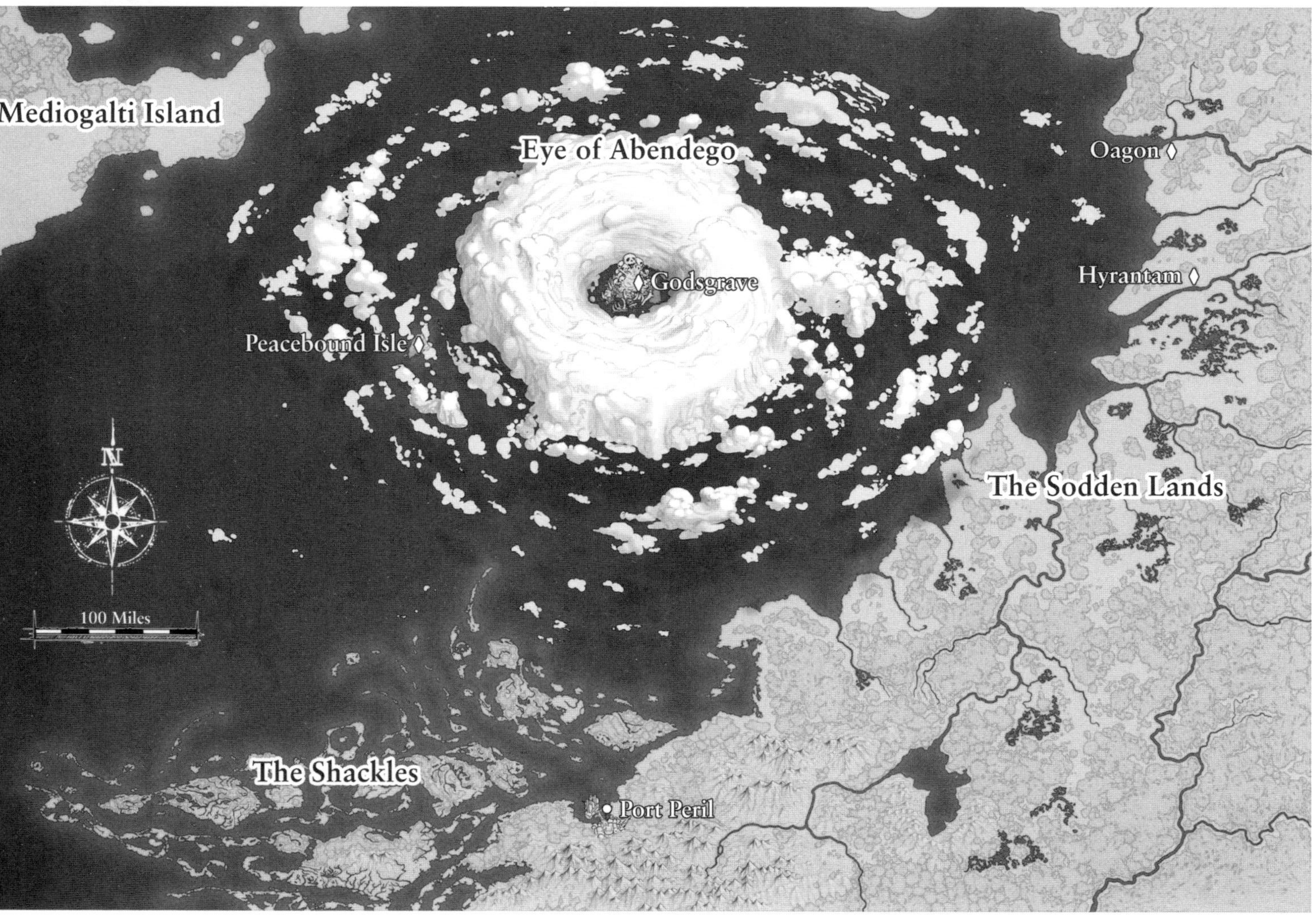
Mediogalti Island
Eye of Abendego
Oagon
Godsgrave
Hyrantam
Peacebound Isle
N
The Sodden Lands
100 Miles
The Shackles
Port Peril

PROLOGUE

In the beginning, when the multiverse was young, it was nearly devoured.

The gods forged mountains and filled oceans, planted gardens and forests, and devised animals and peoples of all description to marvel at the new-made landscapes laid before them. Gods and mortals alike were delighted by the wonder of their works, and together they celebrated the magnificence of creation.

But for one deity, alone among his kind, these marvels existed only to be destroyed.

Rovagug, the Rough Beast, was a pariah among the divine. A being of savage appetite and endless cruelty, he had neither respect nor pity for the others' works. He tore apart worlds and crushed civilizations for the sheer joy of hearing the screams, and he did not care that the other gods despised him for trampling what they had wrought. All that they had created existed, in his mind, solely so that he could have the pleasure of grinding it to blood and dust between his teeth.

The other gods soon realized that Rovagug cared nothing for any of them, would honor no agreement, and would never stop his depredations until he had consumed and ruined all the worlds they had built, all the peoples they had nurtured, and even the gods themselves.

They formed an alliance, and they went to war. With guile and strategy, powerful magic and divine strength, the gods assaulted Rovagug and his small handful of defenders.

It was a terrible battle. Worlds were devastated. Innumerable gods were slain and forgotten. But in the end, the alliance prevailed, and Rovagug was defeated.

He was not slain. None believed the Rough Beast could be slain. He was, instead, imprisoned at the center of a world named Golarion, where the seal to his captivity was locked, buried, and lost to the eons.

There it lay for ages beyond counting, while empires rose and collapsed, peoples flourished and failed, and historians believed themselves wise for knowing all that had been written.

What was not written, what lay unseen in the depths, was forgotten.

Gods, too, ascended and fell during the eons following Rovagug's banishment. Now and again, in the rarest and most terrible cataclysms, gods died.

Such events shook the world. Their ripples spread far, often in unexpected ways, and not always where anyone might see.

The last god to die had been Aroden, patron of humanity, over a century earlier. His death shattered the foundations of prophecy, and left seers unable to see into the mists of a future they had once read easily.

None knew why, or what it might mean. But, strange though it might seem, the phenomenon stirred little fear among the gods.

The world was, for the most part, calm. Mortal wars roiled across its surface, and sporadic calamities threatened, but these were as transient in their violence as summer storms. They did not worry the gods.

Nothing, they thought, would worry them anytime soon.

Chapter One
TRADING INFORMATION

"Take one bottle each night before you go to sleep," Kyra told the dazed-looking man on the bench before her, "and avoid drinking any wine or spirits until you've finished them all. If you notice the wounds becoming discolored or smelly, or you see pus soak through the bandages, come back to the chapel at once. Do you understand?"

The man nodded. "Thank you," he groaned as his brother took the bag of medicines and helped him off the patient's bench. "I'm sorry I was fool enough to end up like this. Pure stupidity and too much ale; that's all it was. Just stupidity and ale, and I'd be crippled for life without your blessing."

"The Dawnflower is glad to give it." Kyra held the man's other arm with a gold-gloved hand, gently but firmly providing her support alongside his brother's. "Sarenrae does not judge mistakes, and she honors honest regrets. If you believe that poor decisions brought you here, then all the Dawnflower asks is that you consider your future choices more carefully and avoid treading the same path again."

"I won't," the man said with a grin, clasping Kyra's hand against his shoulder. He let go with some reluctance, taking the walking stick that she offered him instead. With the aid of the stick and his brother, he managed to hobble from the chapel.

Merisiel, sitting cross-legged on a windowsill, glanced up from sharpening her knives as they passed. "Good luck," she said, flashing a smile, which both men returned uncertainly.

Then they were gone, out into the dry heat and sand of Enqatis. A wash of raucous laughter carried from a nearby ale shack as the men made their way past, and then the chapel's tattered curtains fell closed and returned Kyra and Merisiel to relative quiet.

Kyra wiped her brow, grateful that the heat of Enqatis stayed outside. She'd used a minor prayer to cool the chapel and keep the desert bugs out, primarily because it made her patients more comfortable, but also because it improved her own ability to focus on their problems. Now that she and Merisiel were alone at the end of the day, it felt a bit self-indulgent, but she wasn't ready to let it go.

"Would you mind taking down the flag?" she asked Merisiel. The little chapel wasn't a dedicated sanctuary of Sarenrae. It was a travelers' chapel, empty and unattended except for when a healer or preacher was passing through Enqatis and felt like raising a flag to signal that care was available to the town's denizens.

The quality of that care and the honesty of those who offered their services were always a gamble in such a place. Healers hoping to make money from a stint in Enqatis generally performed demonstrations in the town square before setting up shop in the chapel, but Kyra eschewed such theatrics. She wasn't there to profit.

But she wasn't there to exhaust herself, either, so she nodded gratefully when Meri came back in with the hand-stitched banner of Sarenrae tucked under one slender arm. There'd be no more patients on this day. "Thank you."

"Tired?" Meri strapped the bundled banner onto her pack and came over to give Kyra a quick kiss. "I don't blame you. The problems people have in this town… "

"The need is great."

"The need is self-inflicted." The elf shook her head with a look of mystified disapproval. "Braggarts talking themselves into knife fights, drunks swilling cheap concoctions from nameless peddlers… What do they *think* will happen? That last fellow was here because he'd swaggered up to an orc and called her—what was it?—'a big stupid horse-fearer who'd run screaming from the letters of her own name.' Pure gibberish, and he nearly lost his life for it."

"He confused her for a goblin," Kyra said, amused, "or was pretending to, for an extra bit of insult."

Merisiel snorted. "He's lucky he got off as lightly as he did. Kept all his limbs, thanks to you. But don't you get tired of trying to save people from their own mistakes?"

"Sometimes," Kyra admitted, rolling up bandages and checking the medicine bottles in her traveling kit, "but it's as I told our last patient:

Sarenrae teaches that people who make mistakes must be given the opportunity to remedy them. Regret must be met with forgiveness, or else those wounds will fester in the soul as surely as untreated ills would in the body. If I do not heal them, then they will never have that chance to make amends.

"So, even if I'm frustrated in the moment—and sometimes, yes, I am—I try to remember that the purpose of my work is not based on who my patient is today, but who they might become tomorrow.

"I remind myself, too, that I offer my prayers not only for each patient, but for those whose lives they've touched. Anyone who hurts themselves badly enough to need my help has likely hurt others along the way. Those people deserve a chance to hear remorse from the one who wronged them, and they won't get that if my patient dies."

"Or the satisfaction of exacting revenge themselves." Merisiel crossed her arms and canted her hip invitingly, a playful glint in her eye. "Calistria would approve of your methods. I suppose I shouldn't complain."

"You're welcome," Kyra said dryly. She tucked one last packet of suturing needles into a side pocket and straightened, pressing both hands to the small of her back and arching her shoulders. After a long day bent over patients, her spine felt like one long cord of knots. "Now tell me about this smuggler we're waiting for."

"Right." Merisiel twitched aside a corner of the chapel's curtain and, apparently seeing nothing, let it fall again. "His name is Itaguen. He says he's from Mediogalti Island, though there's a good chance that's a lie. What's certainly true is that he does a thriving business in illicit artifacts between Osirion and Rahadoum, and occasionally he comes across a bit of information that he can't personally use but still sees a chance to profit from."

Kyra nodded. That was the real reason she and Merisiel had come to Enqatis: to meet with this Itaguen, who claimed to have a lead on where they might find the Thurible of the Dawn.

In the proudly secular nation of Rahadoum, worship of any deity was forbidden, and had been so for generations. Religious paraphernalia was confiscated and destroyed on sight, and those who possessed it were subject to heavy fines, or worse.

Over the centuries, most artifacts of Rahadoum's old faiths had either been smuggled out or smashed. The Thurible of the Dawn, sacred to the goddess Sarenrae, was long believed to have been among the treasures lost to Rahadoum's secular zealots. But when Kyra's church learned of the possibility that the thurible still survived, and might even be traceable by a skilled operative, they'd asked her to take on the task.

She had been honored to accept and delighted that Merisiel had not only agreed to accompany her but had offered her own skills to the cause.

For almost a year, the pair had chased rumors and whispers around the Inner Sea, slowly closing in on northern Garund. Again and again, Kyra had thought they'd finally found a solid thread, only for it to dissolve into smoke as her fingers closed around it.

This time, though, she felt in her bones that it would be different. Itaguen had a real lead. Kyra couldn't articulate *how* she knew, but she did know it, with the same soul-deep certainty that she had in Sarenrae herself.

But she couldn't afford to let her confidence slide into delusion. "You're sure he's coming?" she asked Meri, not because she had any real doubts but because she needed to hear an outside voice of reason.

"No." The elf's dark eyes flashed with amusement. She would understand why Kyra was asking. "Of course I can't be sure. He'll do what he wants to do. But I think he wants to come here, yes. Why wouldn't he? We're rich and credulous, a smuggler's favorite combination. Besides, you're offering free healing. He might come just for that."

"The chapel's closed for the day," Kyra pointed out.

"Better open back up, then." Merisiel slid toward the door. Her stance relaxed into an easy slouch, one that emphasized the slim curves of her hips and the tight fit of her black leather armor. It tended to be effective in distracting people from her knives. It certainly distracted Kyra. "We have visitors."

Meri opened the door to the dry desert night, and Itaguen slipped in.

He was a large man who moved like a small one, light-footed and quick despite his cloaked bulk. *Dangerous,* Kyra thought, recognizing the strength and training that created his improbable grace.

Itaguen lowered his hood as he came into the chapel, revealing a clean-shaven brown head, sharp slitted eyes, and a small, tight mouth. He looked less like a smuggler than a hired killer, one whose victims didn't often escape. His gaze flickered over Merisiel and Kyra in turn, and Kyra felt each of them being weighed swiftly and expertly. She doubted Itaguen had missed Meri's knives or been much distracted by her pose.

"You seek the Thurible of the Dawn?" His voice was a raspy whisper, inflected with an accent that Kyra guessed was from somewhere in southern Tian Xia. It didn't sound like Mediogalti to her, but then, few from that island were inclined to betray their origins.

"We do," Kyra answered. "I was told you might be able to help us."

"I don't have it," he said, "but I know its tale." There were black stains on his teeth, and when Kyra looked closer, she saw that their surfaces had been etched with curling runes. Something about them made her uncomfortable, although she didn't recognize the script or the import of the markings.

Trying to hide her disquiet, Kyra said, "What do you know?"

The man smiled, as if he knew full well that she'd glimpsed the runes on his teeth and wanted a better look. "I know it was made by Oloris Open-Song, and that she bequeathed it to the Sun Temple of Azir upon her death. I know that it was said to have been destroyed when the Sun Temple was razed during the Oath Wars.

"And I know that is a lie, that the thurible was smuggled out of the burning city by the Chelaxian captain Arzadelle Grulios, who had seen her future self in its smoke and wished to make that vision a reality. She saved the artifact, but her family claimed the thurible for its own machinations, holding it in secret as they climbed the ranks of Cheliax's nobility.

"As House Grulios turned secretly toward diabolism, however, the thurible ceased to show them futures that they cared to see. Lord Asad the First, therefore, resolved to sell it in a private deal brokered with a baroness of Porthmos.

"He was murdered before the deal was finalized, and his house collapsed into infighting. During that chaotic time, the thurible vanished. When Asad the Second claimed victory as the new Lord Grulios, it was gone, and House Grulios could pursue it only so far without acknowledging that they'd stolen the artifact from Sarenrae's faith. And then, of course, House Thrune came to power, and it was no longer in House Grulios's interest to admit any involvement with the thurible at all.

"So the trail was lost. I assume that is as far as your temple could follow it, if indeed they were able to keep the thread that far." Itaguen's smile was small and baiting, and his eyes stayed cold above it.

Kyra dipped her head in a wary nod. If the point of Itaguen's preamble was to convince her that he was no ignorant fraud but versed in the true history of the Thurible of the Dawn, then he'd convinced her. Outside House Grulios and the temples of the Dawnflower, almost no one knew that story. Even within those organizations, Kyra doubted there were more than a dozen people, all told, who knew everything that Itaguen had just recited to her.

"I believe you know the thurible's history," she said, "but I came here to learn of its present whereabouts. What can you tell me of that?"

"That depends on what you're prepared to pay for the knowledge," Itaguen said. He leaned forward, his stare intensifying until Kyra had to consciously stop herself from taking a half step back.

She gestured to Merisiel, who produced a velvet pouch with a flick of her wrist. The elf held it over a nearby operating tray and loosened the braided strings. Gold and silver tumbled out, along with a rainbow of jewels. Brilliant diamonds in yellow and white, dark opals that shimmered like coral reefs caught in the shallows of a dreamer's sea, rubies redder than dragon's blood—all shone together on the surgeon's tray.

Itaguen didn't give the offered treasure a glance.

"My price is not in coin or gems," he said. "The Thurible of the Dawn is too great a prize to be bought so cheaply."

"Then what do you want?" Kyra asked, as Meri tensed behind her. They hadn't anticipated this.

"Information," Itaguen answered, unperturbed.

"About what?"

"The Pathfinder agent Ezren. I believe you are acquainted with him. I wish to know everything about him. His habits, his associates. Strengths." Itaguen leaned back. Leather armor creaked under his cloak, and Kyra glimpsed the hilts of sheathed knives tucked neatly along his thighs and under his shoulders. "Weaknesses."

Chapter Two
THE THOUSAND TENTS

I bet he'd drop his price if I broke his arms," Amiri said.

"I don't believe that will be necessary." Ezren eyed the merchant before them, whose complexion had gone three shades grayer at Amiri's casual suggestion. "I expect Master Tuardun is quite willing to negotiate in a civilized fashion."

"Naturally," the dwarf said, mopping his brow. Sweat glistened in the creases of his weathered skin. "Clan Aringeld would be pleased to underwrite Venture-Captain Innorai's expedition to the ruins of Hyrantam for a very reasonable percentage. Shall we say, thirty percent of finds? In exchange, we can not only assist with covering losses to life, limb"—he glanced nervously at Amiri—"and property, but with the proper outfitting of the expedition. It would be in our interest, as well as yours, to see that the venture-captain and her employees are adequately equipped for the challenges they'll face."

"Thirty percent?" Amiri scoffed. Her snort of laughter curdled into a scowl as she saw that Tuardun was serious. "Thirty percent is—"

"Entirely reasonable," Ezren interrupted smoothly, making a quick gesture for Amiri to calm down. "Thirty percent of any unclaimed finds, lucrative discoveries, or an equivalent sum as judged by a neutral arbiter. The archbanker would be acceptable as a price-setter, or a delegate he deems trustworthy. We would also rely on the church of Abadar to settle any other disputes that might arise over valuations of finds or losses." Though Ezren had little love for Abadar's church himself, he knew that was likely to be the most palatable choice to the merchant, and he wanted this deal done.

"Agreed," Tuardun said promptly, extending a heavily ringed hand for a brisk, formal shake. "The Abadarans are acceptable to us as well. I shall have copies of the agreement drawn up and sent to your lodge for review. May I invite you to our embassy in three days' time to have the signatures witnessed?"

"I accept your invitation with pleasure," Ezren said, standing to see their guest out.

When the dwarf had gone, Amiri vaulted up to sit cross-legged on Ezren's writing desk. She ignored, or was oblivious to, his disapproving frown. "Thirty percent's highway robbery. Imagine what he would've asked if I *hadn't* threatened him."

"It would have been exactly the same," Ezren replied. "He wasn't intimidated. He pretended to be so that we'd think we'd gotten a better deal. Tuardun dampened the corner of his cloth in his water goblet before he patted it onto his forehead, did you notice? He faked his sweat."

"I'll kill him," Amiri growled, uncrossing her legs and leaping into a predatory crouch.

Ezren grimaced. He'd forgotten how much Amiri hated to be deceived. He had, in fact, forgotten quite a bit about the Kellid woman; it had been a long while since they'd traveled together. But now he remembered that few things sent her into a killing rage faster than the thought that someone had tricked her, and he cursed himself for the oversight.

"Please don't," he said, as soothingly as he could manage. "He didn't actually fool us with the ruse, Amiri. He tried, it's true. But we saw right through him."

"*You* did," she corrected, but she relaxed. Her fists uncurled, the tension seeped from her shoulders, and she no longer seemed poised to snatch up her oversized sword and rush out to behead the dwarf.

"It's all the same," Ezren assured her. "Tuardun gained nothing by the subterfuge. The terms are good, and the deal is fair. There aren't many who'd be willing to underwrite an expedition to Hyrantam under any terms, let alone assist with outfitting and preparation. The Society needs him, and others like him. We can't afford you chopping him to bits. Besides, you still need to keep a low profile after that nastiness in Sothis."

That was where he'd found her, about to have her ears slit and her cheeks branded for various offenses, some of which Amiri had probably committed and others that were bald lies. The story, as best

Ezren had been able to piece it together, was that Amiri had annoyed the scion of an Osiriani noble house by besting him at a game of thrown knives, and had then compounded the insult by beating his favorite bodyguard at arm wrestling.

Unable to countenance the humiliation of having his bodyguard out-wrestled by a scrawny Kellid woman, the aristocrat had commanded the rest of his entourage to apprehend her and hold her fast for a whipping.

In response, Amiri had committed at least a half-dozen clear-cut felonies under Osiriani law. A contingent of the Sothis city guard had been called in to help and had eventually subdued her, after which the local magistrate had added another two dozen charges.

Ezren strongly suspected that at least some of those charges had come at the behest of the insulted nobleman, and that the magistrate had been motivated less by the interests of justice than by a quietly passed coin pouch or two, but it hardly mattered. Amiri had been charged, convicted, and was preparing to face punishment when he'd happened across the market square where they were heating the branding irons.

Fortunately, Ezren had friends in Sothis. After a few quick exchanges of money and promises to resolve the "misunderstanding," Amiri was released to his custody. He'd promptly made arrangements to leave Sothis, and they'd set off for the nearby port city of Totra.

It was only then that Ezren had realized he had no idea what to do with her. Left to her own devices, Amiri would surely get into another fight and end up where she'd started, or worse.

Amiri knew it too, though. And she didn't like being in debt, so she'd suggested that she hire on as Ezren's personal guard for as long as it took to work off the sum he'd spent on bribes.

The arrangement suited Ezren well enough. He hoped to find a Pathfinder expedition that could use Amiri's talents, but in the meantime, the fiction that he needed a bodyguard gave him an excuse to keep her close at hand, where he could at least try to dissuade her from pointless fights. Until he could send the Kellid off to the wilderness, where her ferocity could be more appropriately directed, it would have to do.

For now, Amiri seemed relatively calm, but Ezren knew how fragile her self-control could be. A distraction might help keep her happy.

Besides, he'd spent enough time cooped up in this office, dealing with administrative tasks and negotiations on behalf of the local branch of the Pathfinder Society. It was important work, but it did grow tedious after a time.

Collecting his cloak and snake-headed cane, Ezren went to the door. "Let's visit the bazaar before the sellers close their stalls for the night. I think the success of our negotiation calls for a bit of celebration. My treat. What would you have if you could have anything you liked?"

"Anything?" Amiri said doubtfully.

Ezren turned back toward her with a sudden twinkle in his blue eyes. "No, actually, since you ask. Not anything. *Almost* anything. Nothing too practical today. What would you want if you could have something that spoke to your small, silly whims? Something trivial. Frivolous. Even sentimental, if you dare. That's what I want you to choose today, Amiri."

She spent a moment contemplating the question. Then she said, with uncharacteristic hesitation, "I don't know if there's anything like that I want."

"Oh, there must be something," Ezren said, breezily assured. "Perhaps you won't know what it is until you see it. But these are the Thousand Tents of Totra, where every peddler and snake singer claims to know your heart's desire.

"One of them must be right, surely. We have only to find that one."

The Thousand Tents of Totra fell well shy of that number, in Ezren's estimation, but the city's main bazaar was still an impressive sight. Colorful tents unfurled along the market square like toadstools after a rain, and hawkers sang their wares with the single-minded, full-chested ferocity of bullfrogs staking out territory amid them.

Brass pendants and glowing lamps shone under every awning. Between them, braziers smoked and broad bronze pans spat as street cooks tended sizzling kebabs over the coals and flipped tiny white crabs, legs fried into battered lace, in baths of hot oil. Other vendors sold jewel-colored drinks served in fanciful glasses, cooled by flowers frozen in disks of ice, that steamed in the desert heat. There were twelve-stringed lutes with golden strings and double-headed drums finished in exotic hides, perfumes rendered from the rarest ingredients in Garund, talking birds and six-toed lizards in collars studded with glass and gems.

Amiri walked through the bazaar stiffly, eying the crowds as if she expected to find a pickpocket or brigand at every turn.

Her instincts weren't wrong, really. The Thousand Tents were notoriously rife with thieves. But Ezren had purchased a token of protection from the local thieves' guild—a little blue disk carved with the two-headed asp that they'd taken as their symbol—and wore it prominently on his left shoulder, as paying clients were told to do.

It wasn't the sort of measure he ordinarily took. Under normal circumstances, Ezren was happy to teach pickpockets a more direct lesson in choosing their targets wisely. But since he was in Amiri's company, and she was more likely to teach that lesson by tearing a thief's arms off than by stinging their fingers with a cantrip, Ezren had decided that paying the guild was the prudent course of action.

Eventually, Amiri noticed that they weren't being bothered. "You bribed them," she muttered accusingly as the crowds swirled around them.

"I requested that our shopping be undisturbed," Ezren replied, picking up a twig laden with wrinkled red dates. He handed a coin to the fruit seller's monkey and nibbled at the dates as they went on. "I won't need a guard today. You're free to think of other things instead. Such as—which of these wonders should be yours?"

Amiri took some time to answer. But, gradually, she relaxed enough to look at the vendors' wares. She accepted a skewer of spiced lizard when Ezren caught her studying it, took a curious nibble, and then finished it in three bites, after which she licked her fingers with an appreciative grunt. "Didn't think the scales could get so crispy."

"I'm pleased you enjoyed it."

The Kellid nodded, though she didn't seem to be listening. Her gaze lingered on a tent filled with clever clockwork toys and musical devices, some enchanted and others that worked by intricate machineries of gears and pegs.

One of the toys was a small, jeweled songbird, perhaps loosely modeled after a phoenix or peacock—it was hard to tell which the jeweler had intended, as the bird combined the phoenix's radiant red-

and-gold coloring and wide-spreading wings with the peacock's tail and crest—which perched on a gilded branch. Leaves of green cut glass and amethyst flowers framed the bird, and a wisp of illusion lent its feathers a shimmering scintillation.

The bird opened and closed its beak as it mimed singing a song. Ezren couldn't make out the melody from where he was standing, but it seemed to hold Amiri enraptured. The fierce barbarian listened with an expression as close to pleasure as he'd ever seen on her face, but there was an ache of sorrow in it as well.

"Do you like it?" he asked.

Amiri swallowed hard, dashing the back of a hide-gauntleted hand across her eyes before she answered. Ezren pretended he hadn't seen, feigning an intense interest in a clockwork cobra, until the Kellid had straightened and cleared her throat.

"It's fine," she said, moving on. "It reminded me of something. But I was mistaken. The song isn't what I thought it was."

Ezren moved a bit closer so he could hear the song, a romantic old Taldan standby favored by bards of the more sentimental variety. It was called "The Phoenix of My Love," or something of that sort.

"Would you like me to—" he began, reaching for his coin purse, but suddenly Amiri's head snapped up and her lip curled in a feral snarl. Before Ezren could register what had drawn the Kellid's attention, she was shoving him out of the way.

Too astonished to catch himself, Ezren stumbled back, crashing into a cart full of nuts and dried fruit. Walnuts and dates spilled around him, and the vendor cursed him roundly. The crowd scattered in a panic, shouting and knocking things over as they fled.

Amiri crouched in front of Ezren, her greatsword out and in both hands as she faced off against some unseen assailant. She growled, a harsh, wild sound that prickled the hair on the back of Ezren's neck.

"You were wrong," she snarled, planting her back foot against the ground as she prepared to lunge. "You did need a guard today. That man wants to kill you."

Chapter Three
BLOOD IN THE BAZAAR

The wizard was mumbling something behind her, but Amiri ignored it. If it were important, he'd yell. Until then, she needed to stay focused on the man in front of her.

There was something wrong with him. It wasn't the sharpened meat hook he was swinging, although that was a stupid weapon, and Amiri looked forward to slamming it into his skull at the first opportunity. It wasn't the lack of training that betrayed itself in his poorly balanced stance and clumsy swipes. She'd been attacked by plenty of untrained idiots; in fact, it was almost always the untrained idiots who came at her. People with the sense to recognize danger when they saw it rarely bothered her.

No, what was wrong with this man was something else. Something different.

He didn't blink when the sweat ran straight into his eyes. His breathing hadn't quickened, though he'd charged through a panicked crowd while flailing about with a twelve-pound steel weight in his hands. He didn't flinch, didn't jeer, didn't say a word.

He'd just attacked, and he wasn't alone. Others were converging on them, cutting their own paths through the sea of terrified people, and they, too, were mute and unblinking.

"What do you want?" Amiri snarled at the one in front of her. She already knew the answer. He wanted to kill Ezren, and he wanted to kill her because she was in the way.

But asking broke the silence, and it vented some of her apprehensions in the face of this unnatural enemy.

Magic. Magic is what's wrong with him. Amiri's following, like most Kellids, had a deep suspicion of arcane power and its wielders. To them it was incomprehensible, and therefore abhorrent, that strange formulas and mystic diagrams should be able to affect the solid reality of their world. Wizardly magic was a cosmic trick and an affront to the natural order on which their lives relied, and so those who lived in the Realm of the Mammoth Lords despised its practitioners.

Amiri had been away from her people for a long time, and she had mostly forgotten the taboos of her childhood. Arcane magic was common and accepted in the southlands, and like any frequently encountered danger, it had lost its power to overawe her by its mere presence. Amiri didn't even flinch when Ezren cast his spells around her.

But as she studied the man with the meat hook and braced her weight against the expected attack, Amiri felt the old terror well up inside. Some foul sorcery had seized this man and the others like him.

Fear wouldn't serve her. She needed anger. Rage had always been her strength, the power she could seize when she was outnumbered or overmatched. When she was angry, Amiri didn't have to be anxious or afraid or alone.

She could just be strong. Strong enough to kill anything that threatened.

Amiri reached for her anger, and welcomed it in.

"Come on and die," she growled, just before the red haze closed around her, and any further words became pointless.

The silent man came to meet her, scything his meat hook.

Amiri ducked under the strike and twisted away. Driving her greatsword's tip into the earth, she pivoted around it and came up on her attacker's other side. She slammed her elbow into the steel curve of his meat hook, redirecting the weapon's momentum so that it drove into the side of his head with a grisly crack.

It was as satisfying as she'd imagined.

She had little time to exult in her victory, though. Even as the first man fell, his companions closed in.

They, too, were silent. One wore a dirty apron speckled with blood and fish scales. Another had the crabbed posture and tar-stained hands of a lifelong sailor. They wielded mismatched, makeshift weapons with no finesse, and they moved in an uncoordinated horde.

Amiri snarled, jerked her greatsword from the ground, and threw all her weight into a sweeping blow.

She chopped through the sailor and into a woman behind him. They dropped, and others stepped over the bodies. Amiri whirled into the crowd, spinning the greatsword in an arc of death, but her heel skidded on a puddle of slime just as she was about to strike home.

Amiri stumbled to one knee. A bull-necked butcher's apprentice hacked at her with a notched cleaver. She threw her left arm up, catching the heavy blade on the thick leather wrapped around her forearm. It gouged an ugly gash in the gauntlet and skidded along Amiri's arm, shearing off skin and muscle. Pain flared across her vision, and the force of the blow drove her the rest of the way to the ground.

She managed to kick the youth's feet out from under him as she fell, taking him down with her. Amiri grabbed him around the throat, twisting. Fueled by rage, she snapped his neck with her bare hands. She flung the body aside and scrabbled to get up, but she slipped again in the filthy slime and landed eye to eye with the sailor she'd killed earlier.

Gelatinous blue bubbles spilled from the corpse's lips and the wound in his midsection. More bubbles swelled the coils of his intestines, stretching the membrane so thin that Amiri could see the blobs crowding together like fish eggs in a sac. The same bubbles choked the dead woman beside the sailor, visible through the exposed curves of her ribs.

Some of the blue orbs had ruptured, spilling out the slime upon which Amiri had slipped. It reeked of decaying seaweed and dead fish, and it left a slick coating on everything it touched.

Amiri recoiled. She planted a palm in the slime to push herself back to her knees, trying to ignore the squelch and pop of the bubbles between her fingers.

Before she could recover her feet, a red-tasseled spear came stabbing down at her. Amiri hunched her shoulders against the impact, knowing she was doomed.

But the air grew thick as jelly around the spear, dragging it almost to a halt. The sudden interference didn't slow Amiri. She jerked away from the weapon and sprang to her feet, slapping the slime off her hands as she took up her oversized sword again. The spear-wielder had just enough time to tug stupidly at his trapped weapon before she took off his head.

"You're welcome," Ezren said, leaning on his snake-headed cane.

Amiri only grunted. Her enemies were still alive, and the rage was still upon her. There was no time for talking.

She cleaved through the rest of the mob with broad, brutal strokes, crushing and tearing bodies as often as she rent them apart. With the wizard's spell slowing her enemies, it was child's play. The dead fell around her, and at last Amiri let her sword's tip slump to the ground. Her rage slipped away, leaving a bone-deep exhaustion in its wake. Breathing hard, she leaned on the massive weapon and closed her eyes.

"Amiri." Ezren's voice was tight and clipped. "Get away from there. *Now.*"

"Why—" Amiri began to ask, but then something seized her around the ankles, and she hit the ground again.

Her chin cracked against the paving stones. Black stars flared across her vision, and the taste of blood filled her mouth.

So did the stench of the rotting sea.

A semitransparent tentacle was knotted around her ankles. It was thick as her forearm and suckered like an octopus's leg, and it had emerged from the ooze that spilled from the corpses' ruptured bubbles.

Other things were emerging as well. More tentacles slithered out of the blue morass, along with thin, serrated spikes, flowering tubes that resembled gigantic sea anemones, and a ring of misshapen eyes that leaked into the surrounding sludge like eggs cracked into cake batter.

The odor of briny decomposition was overwhelming. Amiri choked back bile as she fumbled for a knife to hack away the tentacle. Clenching her abdomen, she bent her knees and pulled her legs forward, straining every muscle against the tentacle's grip.

Another inch... there. Fatigue burned the muscles of her core and thighs, but she dragged the tentacle into reach. Swiftly, Amiri slashed at it with her tusk-handled knife. The blade ripped through its jellylike skin, and stinking blue slime gushed out.

Amiri kicked it away. More tentacles came lashing out at her, trying to drag her into the tangle. A smaller concentric ring of gnashing teeth had begun to emerge within the circle of eyes. Through the teeth, Amiri glimpsed a sucker-lined throat pulsing hungrily at the creature's core.

"Do something, wizard," Amiri growled. Distrust magic she might, but she wasn't fool enough to turn down a ready weapon.

She reached for her rage, trying to will away the exhaustion that sapped the strength from her muscles, but she might as well have been trying to shove a mountain aside with her bare hands. Her weariness wouldn't budge.

Snarling, she hacked at the oncoming tentacles with her knife. "Do something!"

Lightning blasted past Amiri, raising her hair into a bristling cloud before striking the tentacled monstrosity. Its rings of teeth incandesced to a blinding azure, glowing like submerged stars through the jelly of its throat. Its gums boiled into white meat around the superheated teeth.

Instead of releasing her, however, the tentacles wrapped around Amiri froze in electrified shock for an instant and then pulled her harder toward the central maw. Fragments of baked tooth ground under her stomach and elbows as the creature dragged her through the sludge of its own body.

More lights flashed and flared over Amiri's head, but she was barely conscious of them. She clawed at the slimed cobblestones, trying to find any traction she could to pull against the creature's grip, but the jellylike sludge came up under her nails and spurted through her fingers, giving her nothing to grasp.

"Gorum split your skull and crack your bones," she spat, but if the monstrosity had either skull or bones, Amiri hadn't seen them, and she could feel its teeth grinding through the leather of her boots.

The creature's eyes passed under her as the tentacles dragged her into the maw. She looked down at the saucer-sized eyes, and they goggled back up at her, their pupils and irises wobbling. Amiri drove her elbow into the one beneath her, bursting it in a vile, wet spurt, but her satisfaction was short-lived.

Small as her movement was, it lifted her upper body slightly off the ground, and the tentacles seized their advantage to yank her into the toothy pit.

Amiri curled into as tight a ball as she could, bringing her shins up to protect her abdomen and covering her face with her forearms. She took a deep breath to fill her lungs with air and braced against the horror of being swallowed.

Even if this was the end, she was determined to fight as hard as she could until it killed her. Maybe she'd be able to knock its teeth back out through its throat. Maybe she'd wrest a rib free and use that to carve her way out.

Or maybe it would eat her and that would be that, but at the very least, Amiri was going to make sure the thing regretted its decision to swallow a Kellid alive.

The creature's mouth closed over her. Rings upon rings of muscle-driven teeth slashed at Amiri, lacerating her flesh and battering her bits of mismatched armor.

She wanted to sing a death song, but she couldn't spare the air now that she'd been swallowed. The injustice of it kindled the old familiar fire in her heart, despite her exhaustion, and gratefully, Amiri reached for her rage.

Just as she was about to give in to the battle fury, a searing flash of golden light struck the creature somewhere above her. Amiri saw the flare like a dawn glimpsed through the sea above. Its brilliance made her eyes water, even though she'd barely ventured a peek through the protection of her arms.

A thunderous impact shook the creature around her. Amiri felt the blow shudder through the gelatinous body that encased her. The distorted bass rumble of a thunderclap followed, more sensation than sound. An astonished breath puffed from her lips in slow, sticky bubbles, and then the monstrosity's body ruptured.

It spewed Amiri out in a gush of foul effluvia. The sunbaked stones of the market square were hot and dusty beneath her hands, shocking in their ordinariness. Her wet palms stuck to the stone, and it took a moment for her to muster the strength to lift her head and see who had saved her.

The ichor dripping down Amiri's face made it almost impossible to see the figure who stood silhouetted by the late afternoon sun at the market's edge. And yet there was something familiar about the stance, something that touched a chord of memory...

"Thank you," Amiri croaked.

"You're welcome," said Kyra. "I'm glad we weren't too late."

Chapter Four
CATCHING UP

Kyra?" Ezren asked, scarcely able to believe his eyes. It was too fortuitous to imagine that the Sarenite would appear just when he and Amiri were in dire need. Yet there she stood, resplendent in blue and white. "What are you doing here?"

"Saving you," Merisiel answered for her, slipping out of the shadows with a smile on her lips and a knife between her fingers. "We had an inkling you might need some help."

"A little more than an inkling," Kyra said. "We—"

Before she could finish the sentence, a thin, bald man in a yellow robe and headdress, wearing a vendor's sash on his arm, came scrambling out of an alley with two members of the Coin Guard in tow. "There!" he shouted, pointing at Ezren and Amiri. "Those are the miscreants who brought disaster to the bazaar!"

"What?" Amiri lifted her head. Blue slime dripped from her hair and oozed down her face. The barbarian still looked dazed, but her stupor was rapidly changing to irritation.

"I'm sure there's been some misunderstanding," Ezren said hastily, holding his hands out placatingly and stepping between Amiri and the trio of newcomers. "We were the victims of an unprovoked attack. Our attackers seem, in turn, to have been victims themselves. When we fought them off, they erupted into... this." He gestured to the tentacled monstrosity, whose body was rapidly dissolving into a bubbling pool of filth.

"Nonsense," the man in the yellow robe scoffed. Bangles clattered about his bony wrists as he flung his hands toward the rotting monster. Some of the bracelets were tin and glass, but others were gold, and looked heavy enough to be solid all the way through. This man, Ezren surmised, was wealthy enough for the Coin Guard to take seriously.

"They caused this disturbance, and they should be made to pay for it," the merchant insisted. "The damage to my business—to all the good businesses of the Thousand Tents of Totra!—is terrible, and it is all their fault. All their fault!"

"That is not true." Kyra drew herself up proudly, straightening her posture so that the golden emblems of Sarenrae pinned to her headscarf and affixed to her chest caught the waning sun. She put a hand to the hilt of her scimitar, not in threat, but merely to emphasize that she carried the sacred weapon by right, and with it, all the authority of the Dawnflower's chosen. "Honorable guards, this witness is mistaken. These people were merely shopping in the bazaar when they were attacked. I saw it all happen, and I will attest to this under any oath of truth you wish to administer."

"Me too," Merisiel said. The guards hardly gave her a glance, which seemed to amuse the elf greatly. She hid a lopsided smile behind one hand as they bowed stiffly to Kyra and stepped back.

"We trust your word, honored lady," one of the Coin Guards said. "If you would be willing to give a signed statement at the guardhouse, that should settle the matter."

The yellow-robed man's face soured, but he made no further protest. Muttering something that might have been a half-hearted apology, he slipped back into the alley from which he'd come.

Kyra and Merisiel shared a glance. The elf nodded and melted into the shadows. Ezren guessed that she was following the merchant, although he couldn't actually see her well enough to be sure. Somehow, between the market square and the alley's mouth, the elf had vanished.

"Let's go make our statements for the Coin Guard," Kyra said to the others, offering a clean handkerchief for Amiri to wipe away the slime. "After that, I think, we'd better sit down and talk."

"I don't recognize your description of this Itaguen, and I can think of no reason why such a man would want to kill me," Ezren said slowly, after they'd finished giving their accounts to the Coin Guard and reconvened in the villa he'd rented to conduct his Pathfinder business in Totra.

Amiri sat on the floor, bandaging her wounds in silence, while Kyra and Ezren talked. It was late afternoon, and they were all tired, but

Kyra's description of the peculiar encounter she'd had in Enqatis had filled Ezren with a restless energy.

He wanted to know who'd tried to kill him, and why. "I've made my share of enemies over the years, and no few of them have been wealthy and powerful enough to hire such agents. But none stands out as a likelier suspect than the others."

Kyra nodded without looking back. The Sarenite was gazing out through the only window that offered a vantage over the villa's garden, past the courtyard walls, into the public streets of Totra. It was a quiet neighborhood, without much in the way of street life to observe, but the view had held the cleric fast since she'd arrived.

"He claimed to be from Mediogalti, but Merisiel thought that might not be true. Still, whether or not he hails from that infamous island, I do believe he was a hired killer. Had he held his own grudge against you, he would not have needed to ask us for information. His questions were those of a man who had never personally met you."

"Or they were meant to create that impression," Ezren said.

Kyra conceded the point with a shrug. "It is possible. I don't think he cared much about deceiving us, though. He did not hide his motives in seeking information about you, and he made no effort to conceal the markings on his teeth. Indeed, I had the impression that he was proud of all those things, and amused that we should know them."

"Markings on his teeth?" Ezren lifted a bushy white eyebrow.

"Runes, or sigils. I believe they were enchanted in place, rather than being carved or inked by ordinary means. As I said, he seemed almost proud of them and did not care that I tried to study the markings." Kyra turned away from the window, perhaps a bit reluctantly, and took a curled paper from one of her belt pouches.

She brought the paper over to Ezren and smoothed it upon his desk, showing him three runic symbols painted in blue. "I drew these from memory after he'd gone, so they may not be accurate. But this was the best I could do."

"Curious." Ezren studied the sweeping, spiraling marks. It was a profoundly inhuman script. Though he had spent decades studying all manner of languages across the known multiverse, including some that were quite literally demonic and others that were the mere unintentional residues of minds that had no concept of written or spoken speech, the sight of this one still unsettled him.

It was not as alien as some he'd seen, but that only made it more disconcerting. The sigils Kyra showed him looked like the squiggles of slug tracks, or the curlicues that an octopus might leave across a seabed as it slithered over the sand. But there were faint echoes of human scripts in the markings, as if what Ezren looked upon were some remote, nearly unrecognizable ancestor that had nevertheless spawned something that survived into his own everyday world.

"What do you make of it?" he asked, glancing up at Kyra.

"It's no fiendish script," the cleric answered, "which was my first thought. But if it were either holy or unholy in essence, I am confident I would recognize that much, even if other details might escape me. This language holds nothing of divinity in its nature. If anything, it seems almost... anathema to any language of faith."

That was an intriguing suggestion, so much so that Ezren momentarily forgot his own line of thought. He had never considered the possibility that a script itself could somehow be innately opposed to Golarion's faiths. "How so?"

Kyra shrugged, coaxing a gentle chime of gilded ornaments from her headdress. "I have not the skill to articulate it. Something in the shape of the letters, the flow of the lines... it's a feeling, an intuition, more than anything I can define in words. As one looks upon oil and knows it will not mix with water, so I knew upon seeing it that this script kept itself apart from the gods."

"Ah." Ezren tried to hide his disappointment at the answer. He respected Kyra, both for her good sense and for her skill with scimitar and scalpel, but he often found it difficult to follow her logic, especially when it came to matters of faith. So much of it was rooted in nothing more solid than emotions and beliefs. "Well, I trust your judgment in these things."

From one of his own pouches, Ezren fished out a tooth from the creature that had nearly devoured Amiri. He'd pocketed it during the confusion, hoping to study it later. Now he laid it beside the drawings Kyra had spread over his desk.

The tooth was roughly triangular, with a pronounced ridge that ran along the center and a clearly defined, textured root that flared out to either side like a whale's tail. Its two flattened faces were smooth as pearl, but the edges were covered with sawlike serrations.

Dark blue curlicues wound around the tooth in a spiral, and though they did not precisely match any of the symbols that Kyra had sketched, they were clearly drawn from the same family. Side by side, the similarities were unmistakable.

"I'd say it shows a connection between the attack in the bazaar and this Itaguen," said Ezren.

"So it does," Kyra murmured, studying the tooth. "Were the others so marked?"

"I couldn't say. I didn't get a good enough look. Amiri?"

The barbarian looked up with a scowl at the interruption, although she'd nearly finished tending her wounds. She cinched a knot over one of her bandages and ripped excess the cloth off with her teeth. "The monster's teeth were all blue, and they were all covered in slime. Beyond that, I didn't look. I was trying to keep it from chewing my face off."

"I think one tooth suffices to show the link," Ezren said. "It's too great a coincidence to imagine that they both had blue-scribed teeth by accident."

"I agree," Kyra said, with a touch of acerbity, "but I would like to study the magic that created this abomination, and I can make little of so small a sample. Can you?"

Ezren contemplated the tooth in silence, considering his answer. It did resemble a shark's tooth, but on closer examination, he thought it was flatter and broader than a natural fish's tooth, and more scalloped on the inner surface. There were hairline cracks in the root, which brightened when he passed them over a silver disk that magnified magical resonances. When he blew against the tooth's serrated edges, they split his breath into a reedy whisper that contained echoes of magic as well.

"I believe I can extract some information from it," he said. "But that would entail testing it in my laboratory, and perhaps destroying it in the process. If the loss of the specimen is acceptable—"

"I have no other use for it," Kyra said. "Do it."

Ezren nodded and dropped the tooth back into his belt pouch. He curled up Kyra's drawings and stowed them away, then cocked his head at the cleric. "Why did you come personally to warn me of Itaguen, rather than sending a message?"

"Probably they didn't expect you'd listen." Amiri snorted. "I wouldn't have. You're delusional about danger, wizard. You think there are rules in this world, and that you can protect yourself from those who'd do you harm by buying them off with pretty words or gold. But it doesn't work that way. What's bigger eats what's smaller, unless the smaller thing is quicker, luckier, or meaner. That's it. But you don't see it that way, so what's the point of trying to warn you?"

Kyra regarded the Kellid with a trace of amusement, betrayed only by a crinkle at the corners of her deep brown eyes. She glanced at the street again, clasping her forearms and running her thumbs over the holy insignia embroidered on her sleeves.

Twilight was falling, and the lamplighters were moving through the streets. Wavering specks of reflected firelight danced across the bands of gold on Kyra's regalia as the streetlamps awakened outside.

The cleric turned back to Ezren, her face somber in the shadows.

"There were two reasons that Merisiel and I decided to come in person. The first, of course, is that you were and are our friend, and we thought you might need our help. We had no way of knowing how dangerous Itaguen might be, but we guessed he might prove a serious adversary, and so he has.

"The other reason was that Itaguen offered the Thurible of the Dawn as an enticement for us to betray you. His knowledge of the thurible convinced me that he does indeed possess authentic information concerning the whereabouts of that holy relic. No one could have learned such secrets without devoting years to the hunt.

"But why, then, would he part with that information in this fashion? You will forgive me, Ezren, if I do not believe that what little we told him about you would warrant the secret of the thurible's location in return."

"I wouldn't consider my life worth trading for a long-lost divine artifact either. Not if it was a real one." Ezren waved the idea away with a chuckle. "Go on."

Kyra didn't share his mirth. She held his gaze steadily until Ezren let his smile slip away. "Several possibilities suggested themselves. One was that Itaguen did not believe we would survive our pursuit of the thurible, and so did not care if we sought it. That seemed unlikely, however, as nothing would prevent me from conveying the information to the rest of the Dawnflower's faith, and I do not believe that any hazard exists that the full might of Sarenrae's church could not overcome.

"Another possibility, which seemed more probable, was that Itaguen intended to follow close at our heels and seize the prize once we had brought it within his reach. There might be some holy ward or guardian that he was unable to bypass, but which he thought might let us through. Once we had removed the obstacle for him, he would remove us in turn.

"A third possibility was that I was wrong, and that your death might truly be worth paying such a high price. I thought this less likely, but I could not discount it entirely. It might even be possible that he meant to distract us by sending us to chase the thurible so that we would not interfere with his attack. Therefore, Merisiel and I came to warn you in person, hoping to thwart Itaguen's plans."

"For which I am grateful, as I do not believe we would have bested him without you," Ezren said. He lit the lamp on his desk and the two sconces on the walls, then bowed his head formally to Kyra. Amiri snorted again.

"It isn't over yet," Kyra cautioned. "I doubt he'll stop with this first failed strike."

"No, I wouldn't think so." Ezren rubbed the belt pouch containing the sharklike tooth. He only touched it lightly, yet the leather snagged against the serrated edges and tore so easily that the sharp little bumps threatened to bite into his thumb. Ezren pulled his hand away, unsettled. It was too easy to imagine that he could feel the thing thirsting for his blood.

"I'm still not quite sure I understand, though," he said, to take his mind off the tooth. "You came to help us, but you also came because Itaguen knew too much about the Thurible of the Dawn?"

"She wants us to help them get it, wizard," Amiri said with an impatient huff. The Kellid uncrossed her legs and sprang up to stand with feline fluidity. Though her torso was corseted with bandages, and more bound her upper arms, they didn't seem to constrain the athletic power of her movements. "They saved you from Itaguen, and now they want you to help save their trinket from him."

Kyra nodded in agreement. "Eventually. Once we're certain the threat is past."

Amiri grunted. "Fine. We're in."

"We are?" Ezren raised his eyebrows at the Kellid. He didn't disagree, but he was surprised that she was so quick to join the Sarenite's quest. As far as he knew, Amiri cared little for religion, and less for its relics. Why should she want to chase the Thurible of the Dawn?

"Of course we are." Amiri heaved her massive greatsword off the ground and thrust it back into its scabbard. "Man tried to kill us. Almost did. So I don't just want to kick his teeth in. I want to take his shiny little prize, hold it up in front of his face, and *then* kick his teeth in. Right through the back of his skull."

Chapter Five
THE MERCHANT'S TRAIL

Merisiel showed up the next morning.

She was terribly pleased with herself, Kyra saw. The elf strolled casually into Ezren's dining room at breakfast, having circumvented his wards and unlocked his doors with ease, but Kyra doubted that was the reason her wife looked so self-satisfied. Meri did love tweaking their friends' noses, but breaking into a villa wasn't nearly enough of a challenge to have her in so good a mood.

"Well?" Kyra prompted as the elf helped herself to the eggs and fresh-baked bread that Ezren's servants had laid out for them.

"I found the merchant." Meri slathered apricot jam over a slice of warm, fluffy bread, then took another piece and covered that one in a thick smear of fig preserves. Eying a basket of braided and sugared pastries, she added several to the steadily increasing pile on her plate. Clearly whatever she'd been doing all night hadn't left her with much time to eat. "Tailed him back to his office, then from there to his home. I spent the evening watching him, which was interesting. When he went to sleep, I took a look around the house, which was still more interesting. Then I doubled back to the office and looked around there too, and that was the most interesting yet."

Amiri, who'd been busily hacking a plate full of sausages into pieces that she could fit into an eviscerated loaf of bread, cast the elf an acid look. "Do you want to tell us what any of these interesting things *were*?"

"I'll get to that. First I want some breakfast. Sneaking about is hungry work, and the merchant didn't have much food. At least, none I'd want to eat." Meri took her plate to an empty seat at the table, licking jam from her fingers as she went.

"Why is that?" Ezren looked up over the top of his book. The wizard had taken only a cup of sweetened tea and a single slice of buttered toast. Kyra had the impression he didn't eat much, at least not in the mornings, and the lavish breakfast was mostly for his guests.

"All the food in his house was for show," Meri replied, catching a sugar-studded bun that threatened to topple off the heap as she sat down. She ate daintily, but with great speed, and talked in quick bursts between bites. "It looked like either he or his servant would go out to the markets every few days and buy things: a fish here, a basket of figs there. But I don't think they ate any of it. They just let it sit in the kitchen until it rotted, and then they'd throw it out and buy more. I found heaps of untouched, spoiled food in their refuse. None of it was missing a single bite."

"Odd," Kyra said. She'd finished her own cup of strong, smoky local tea. Ezren lifted the brass teapot in wordless offer, and she held out her cup for him to refill.

"That's the least of it. There are only two servants in the house: an elderly manservant and a female cook. They don't talk, either to each other or to their master. At the end of the day, when their chores are done, they go back to their rooms, lie flat on their beds, and put these odd blue sheets over their faces. The sheets are clear, but solid, like they're made of aspic. Then they just lie there, all night long, with their eyes and mouths open. I suppose they could've been sleeping, but they never tossed or turned, and I don't know how they could breathe with their noses and mouths covered."

"And the merchant?" Ezren asked, after exchanging a troubled glance with the others.

"The same." Merisiel finished her pastry, tried the tea, and pushed her cup away with a pretty little wrinkle of her nose. "Do you have any water?"

Ezren rose and poured a glass for her. Like everything else in his house, it was a piece of art: a dimpled, uneven vessel of sapphire blue, solid and surprisingly comfortable in the hand. A band of mica-brightened copper glaze ran around the rim.

Meri spent a moment admiring the gleam before she put it to her lips. "So. The merchant. He, too, slept with a sheet of jelly over his open eyes and mouth. Once I was certain he wouldn't stir, I let myself in and looked around."

"Find anything?" Amiri asked. Unable to cram any more sausage into her overstuffed sandwich, the Kellid was stabbing the remaining chunks with her dagger and eating them off the blade.

"Less than I'd hoped. I found the bowl that they used to make the jelly sheets, but I couldn't make much of it. Ugly stone thing, covered in barnacles and worm tracks. There was some writing inside the barnacle shells, but I couldn't make out what it said. The letters were tiny, and you'd have to crack the shells to get a decent view. If I'd done that, they would have known I was there, so I let it be."

Merisiel stretched her arms overhead, bending gracefully from side to side in her chair. "Sorry. Long night. Where was I?"

"Leaving the house," Kyra prompted, sipping her tea. It might not be to Meri's taste, but she liked it. The smoke-touched fragrance reminded her of her own childhood, and of the Sarenite priestesses who'd sat in a circle each afternoon, discussing poetry and politics with the villagers, after practicing swordplay on their sacred hill in the mornings.

But that was a complicated memory, and not one she wished to be distracted by at the moment. Kyra focused her attention on Merisiel, who nodded and set down her water glass.

"Right. I left the house and went to the merchant's office." The elf's pale lips pursed in a fleeting frown. "It was easy enough to slip past the guards and get in. Expensive locks and a few minor wards, but nothing that gave me any real trouble.

"I didn't see anything interesting in his ledgers. Maybe if you had time to pore over them all, you'd find more, but I was looking for something that might explain what I'd seen at the bazaar and in his house, not questionable bookkeeping.

"In one of the back rooms, though, I found an iron safe hidden behind a false shelf, and *that* was very interesting indeed." Merisiel leaned back in her chair, smug as a cat dropping a dead mouse on the doorstep. "The safe was covered with arcane sigils and gems that hummed with power, and its lock was one of the cleverest I've seen. I didn't touch it, because I wasn't sure what all that magic might do, but I'm certain it connects to the attack in the bazaar somehow. There was salt water dribbling from the bottom of the safe's door, and it had been there long enough that it had pooled into crusts of salt and rust on the floor.

"When I saw that," Meri finished, with a sharp, bright smile at Kyra and Ezren, "I thought you might like to take a look at it yourselves."

"Safe to say," Ezren agreed, stroking his neat silver-white beard. He raised his eyebrows questioningly at Kyra. "How long do you need to prepare?"

"Do you expect the merchant and his servants will sleep the same way again tonight?" Kyra asked Merisiel.

The elf shrugged, a fluid ripple in black leather. "I can't promise anything, but I think it's probable. There was a lot of uneaten food rotting in their kitchen, and the bowl looked like it had been there for a while. Whatever's going on in that house, it didn't start recently, and I don't think I left enough traces for them to suspect I was there. I don't see any reason they'd change their routine."

"And they don't stir once they're in bed?"

"No. Whatever else the jelly on their faces did, it kept them still as the dead."

"Then I believe our course is simple." Kyra touched her holy symbol, drawing strength and reassurance from Sarenrae's golden sun as she always did. "We will wait for them to sleep, and then we will learn what lies in the merchant's safe."

A flutter of excitement coursed through Kyra's stomach as she donned a gauzy black cloak and prepared to follow Merisiel through the gathering dusk. Ezren had brushed dark powder into his beard to disguise its silver and had found an uncharacteristic floppy hat that hid his features. Even Amiri had, with great reluctance, consented to leave her greatsword behind and put on a loose-fitting desert robe that gave the wiry woman the illusion of added bulk.

The companions weren't fully disguised, but hopefully they'd avoid recognition at a glance.

Night would help with that. Totra's lamplighters had come and gone, and pools of shadow spread between the lamps' golden islands of light.

Far from quieting after dark, the city blossomed into vibrant life once it was freed from the sun's blistering glare. Musicians filled the streets with a complex medley of flute, oud, and playfully slapped hand drums, their melodies and rhythms shifting from street to street as one song melded into the next. Dancers moved sinuously between them, their faces and bare arms painted in phosphorescent patterns inspired by cheetah spots and beetle wings. Some were professionals, but most were ordinary citizens drawn to the music out of the pure, simple joy of sharing a dance with friends and strangers.

Above them, people threw their windows wide to the night's cooling breezes, and the fragrances of spiced lentil stews, jasmine tea, and burning incense mingled together from house and temple. Seductive perfumes spilled from flower-draped balconies, hinting at the pleasures to be found within, and now and then a shapely limb extended from beyond the pierced wooden screens to beckon to a passerby.

It reminded Kyra of her long-lost home, and yet it was all so different. The music shared roots with the songs of her childhood, and the food was close enough to evoke a pang of memory. But no one would have danced so scandalously in the streets of her own village, and no one would have called such wanton invitations from their balconies.

Though she herself preferred to behave more modestly, Kyra wasn't offended by the more relaxed standards that prevailed in Totra. No, what unsettled her—if that was the right word—was just that this place held so many echoes of the world she'd once known.

So close, but so far.

Her village was ashes and fallen stones. Totra was vibrantly alive.

And her duty, according to the Dawnflower's teachings, was to the living.

She shook off the melancholy that always came when she thought of her village. In her distraction, she'd lost sight of Merisiel, but that wasn't surprising. The elf was almost impossible to follow in the dark.

Amiri seemed to be able to track her, though. The Kellid strode through the crowds with single-minded efficiency, ignoring the colorful lights and perfumed dancers as though none of them existed. She might have been stalking a wounded caribou across the empty tundra, so oblivious did she seem to the people around her.

At least she isn't getting angry at them. Kyra had been surprised to find the barbarian in Ezren's company. She hadn't thought he had the patience to deal with Amiri, or much tolerance for the chaos that the Kellid often brought.

But something had changed between them. Ezren seemed to regard Amiri with an almost paternal protectiveness, though he had the sense to keep it subtle enough that the Kellid didn't notice or chafe against it.

Kyra wondered what had happened, and when. What had changed between them?

Whatever it was, she was glad for it. The adventuring life was hard. Without friends, it was impossible.

Ahead, Amiri slowed and raised a hand to signal a stop. The streets were emptier here, with longer gaps between streetlights. The dancers and musicians didn't come down this way. They'd crossed into a business district, where no taverns or wine shops drew revelers, and the locals tended toward early-rising, hardworking sorts who rose and slept with the sun.

There were far fewer eyes to see them here, but that only made Kyra more conscious of how much she and her companions stood out. She huddled at the edge of a streetlight's shadow, keeping her hooded head turned into the darkness and hoping she looked innocent enough to avoid the neighbors' notice.

"She wants us to wait here while she scouts the place." The barbarian lowered her hood and peered into the night, balancing on the balls of her feet. Especially without the bulk of the greatsword across her back, she seemed a lean and hungry thing, more feral cat than bear or wolf.

The impression didn't lessen when Amiri relaxed a few minutes later. If anything, she seemed more dangerous, for it was evident then that the Kellid never fully relinquished the tension that thrummed at her core. "It's all right. We can move forward now. But be quiet."

With that, the woman hurried onward through the sleeping street. Ezren followed, moving quietly but not furtively. He held his head high and swung his walking stick with the calm authority of an upstanding citizen who had every right to be abroad in this neighborhood at night, but Kyra noticed that he never let the stick's end strike against the ground. If anyone glanced out their window to see the wizard, they'd likely notice nothing amiss, but Ezren wasn't about to make enough noise to draw them to that view.

Kyra did her best to imitate him, but she had never been adept at moving silently. She'd taken off most of her jewelry to prevent it from jangling and had tucked her golden symbol beneath the plain robes she'd worn tonight, but still it seemed that her toes found every cobblestone in the dark, and even the sound of her own breathing was uncomfortably loud in her ears.

Thankfully, no one seemed to notice. Amiri led them to an elegant old building of light-colored stone, its windows screened by shutters of pierced, sun-bleached wood. An abbreviated portico shaded the front entrance. Kyra could just make out the sliver of deeper darkness that signaled a door propped ajar.

Statues of beetle-winged lions flanked the portico. Their carved stone eyes were dark with smudges of some thick unguent that shimmered with particles of mica or silver, barely visible in the gloom.

"There was a ward here," Ezren observed in a whisper as the companions gathered in the portico. "Merisiel's disabled it, at least for the next hour or so. If we linger beyond that, we run the risk of being trapped inside, or alerting our quarry to our intrusion."

"Good to know," Kyra said. She squinted into the darkness of the opened door. "Let's be quick and find out what this merchant is hiding."

Chapter Six
A WARD AGAINST DIVINITY

As the door closed behind them, Ezren summoned a small golden light to illuminate the merchant's office. He calibrated the color to resemble a candle flame and dimmed it until it barely showed the contours of the room they were in. With luck, the shutters would suffice to conceal the light from anyone passing by outside, but if not, the glow should pass for some insomniac's candle.

Unless they know the master of this house never leaves his house at night.

Ezren suspected, however, that the merchant took pains to conceal his secret from the neighbors. Ordinary precautions, he thought, should suffice.

"Good, you're here." Merisiel's face appeared suddenly in the tiny light's glow, less than an arm's reach away. Ezren managed to keep from starting, barely, but he saw the elf's lips twitch toward a smile and knew she'd spotted his surprise.

"Come on," she said, slipping between the office's furniture and bookshelves toward the back. "The safe is this way."

Motioning for his light to float after Merisiel, Ezren followed. Kyra fell in behind him, with Amiri casting a wary eye for pursuit at their back.

Once they were safely away from the windows, Ezren brightened the light so they could better see their surroundings. The golden glow fell over racks upon racks of honeycombed shelves for scroll cases, imposing cabinets with heavy locks on every door, and racks of leatherbound ledgers that stood as mute testament to decades, if not centuries, of profitable trade.

This was no small operation. Ezren had assumed, based on Merisiel's description of the merchant's household, that he was either a junior clerk or a man of modest affairs, since a merchant running a great house in Totra would certainly have had more than two servants.

But these records, and the curios sprinkled among their shelves as trophies and adornments, spoke of a storied house whose ships sailed across the known world. Ezren spotted an ivory-ribbed fan from Imperial Lung Wa, a lion-headed spearpoint once used by the Bas'o savanna hunters, and other treasures from far-flung lands.

"Did you see any others here? Assistants? Clerks?" Ezren whispered to Merisiel. It was inconceivable that one man could run such a trading empire alone, unless it had fallen far from its original glory.

That struck him as unlikely since the offices didn't show any signs of penury or impending collapse. Those costly trophies hadn't been auctioned off to satisfy creditors, and these were obviously the company's original headquarters. The office's scroll shelves and bookcases had been built to fit their rooms and couldn't have been moved without being destroyed.

But, then, where were the other employees?

Merisiel shook her head, just once, quick and decisive. "There's no one else here. No one living, anyway."

"Very well." He didn't have to ask what she meant. Ezren had recognized the stone guardians outside immediately, and he doubted that they were the only such creations in this place. Few had as many secrets worth protecting, or as much money to protect them, as mercantile companies.

Keeping a careful eye out for any arcane signifiers that might indicate the presence of additional alarms or constructs, Ezren and the others followed Merisiel deeper into the offices.

The elf led them into a cluttered back office. Unlike the front rooms, which were meant to awe with their high ceilings, gilded showpieces, and walls full of tomes, this place spoke of an overwhelming burden of mundane work. Sheaves of paper spilled over the room's two desks and piled in dreary drifts against the walls.

Amiri glanced into the crowded room, grimaced at the claustrophobic confines, and stayed outside the door. She paced down the hall and back, a loping shadow. "I'll keep watch. Yell if you need me."

"Our merchant hid his secret behind walls of dullness," Merisiel said, stooping and clearing away the papers to reveal a section of previously buried bookshelf. A shallow puddle seeped out from the bottom, and rings of dried residue discolored the floor tiles around it. "I wouldn't have found it if not for the smell. The papers on the bottom soaked up all the water, and the ones on top stayed dry. I put it all back when I left last night, of course."

"Is it safe for me to examine?" Ezren asked, drawing his light closer. The boards at the back of the shelf were swollen and water-stained. They bowed outward, as though some enormous pressure strained against them from the other side.

"Should be. It doesn't look like anyone noticed my tampering from last night." Merisiel had gotten her tools out while Ezren looked over the shelves.

She ushered him out of the way and hooked a slim black pick into a nearly invisible crack between two boards. With a deft twist and a jerk, Merisiel popped out a metal latch. She gave it a tug, and the back of the shelf pulled away from the wall.

An iron safe stood in a recess behind it. Merisiel stood and backed away from the safe, bowing to the others with an ironic flourish as she stepped aside. "All yours."

Ezren looked at Kyra, but the cleric shook her head and didn't budge from her place near the door. "Meri said it was arcane magic. That's your field, not mine."

Grunting in acknowledgment—and because his knees protested as he lowered himself down to a crouch—Ezren put on a pair of spectacles and peered at the safe.

Scrolled patterns, reminiscent of cresting waves, wound along the safe's dark iron sides. The patterns were marred by ugly, ragged-edged holes that were scattered across them at irregular intervals. Magic thrummed throughout the entire object, but Ezren felt it pulse more intensely against his skin when he passed his palm over those pockmarked holes. Without additional testing, he couldn't tell whether the magic was responding to his presence or was simply stronger around those nodes because they held its enchantment together, but he filed the observation away.

Carved jewels and metallic sigils covered the object's front panel. The interrupted wave pattern continued there, but it changed too, spiraling inward as if sucked into a whirlpool. A complicated-looking keyhole, finished with a matte-black paint or varnish that obscured its details, sat at the center of the vortex. Ezren could make out little of that central element, except that the keyhole seemed to be covered by tight, overlapping metal scales, like leaves covering a closed thistle bud.

Ezren traced over the spirals with a fingertip, not quite touching them, but testing the arcane vibrations trapped in the interplay of metal and gem.

Diamond to focus, obsidian flakes to slash... but what is this?

Ezren's finger paused above a squiggle of porous, pumice-like stone. It was an uneven cylinder, about an inch long and partially hollowed, like an empty cocoon that had collapsed at one end. No residue was visible in the interior, but he could sense that magic permeated the stony accretion. Whatever had made this had imbued it with an arcane resonance, and the safe's creator had drawn upon that lingering magic to fuel their own enchantments. A dozen similar cocoons dotted the spiral design, three times as many as any other stone.

He pulled back, rubbed his eyes behind the spectacles, and drew out a thin wand of shaved mistletoe braided together with alchemical wire, a string from a Shelynite lyre, and a shimmering, semisubstantial hair plucked from the head of a ghost. A split crystal, half clear and half black, tipped the wand.

Ezren drew the wand in slow circles across the safe's face, pausing where he'd felt the strongest magical resonances earlier. He watched the crystal carefully, noting where the line between its transparent and opaque halves wavered, and in what direction. When the wand's strands trembled against his hand, he marked that as well.

"Curious," he said at last, rocking back on his heels. He tucked the wand beneath one arm and stood, pressing a hand to the small of his aching back. "Kyra, perhaps you'd care to take a look."

"Is it not wizardly magic?" the Sarenite asked.

"No, it is, but it is... strangely hostile to the divine." Ezren held up the wand he'd been using, plucking at the lyre string to emphasize it for the others. "This allows me to test an enchantment's affinity for certain powers, and its antipathy toward others. Analyzing the vibrations provides insight into the nature, purpose, and construction of novel spells.

"This one is, primarily, a ward against intrusion. Its enchantment is built on elemental water." He gestured to the stony cocoons that anchored the front face's spiral design. "These were dredged from the coldest depths of the sea, and they carry resonances of incredible pressure and crushing gloom. I surmise that the ward crushes those who try to force the safe open, and likely also destroys its contents with water and pressure.

"That much is straightforward. What puzzles me is that the keystones of the enchantment are so hostile to even the tiny fragment of divine magic in my wand. I can't fathom how that serves the overall function—but why else include it?"

"I do not expect to be able to learn more than you have," Kyra said with a dubious look, but she came forward in a swirl of gossamer black fabric. Along the way, she paused, with a glance at Merisiel. "Is it dangerous?"

The elf shrugged. "If I could tell you that and feel sure of it, we'd have no use for Ezren here. But as far as I can tell, it only goes off if someone fiddles with the lock or tries to force the door. Don't do that, and you should have no trouble."

"Very well." Kyra inclined her head. Ezren moved aside, and she knelt before the safe with an ease that he quietly envied.

Murmuring a soft invocation to her goddess, Kyra withdrew the golden sun symbol she'd hidden beneath her cloak. Gentle light blossomed from the Dawnflower's insignia, spreading over the safe's etched metal and jewel-studded spirals.

As soon as the light touched it, the knot of metal scales at the center of the safe blinked open. Ezren, looking over Kyra's shoulder, caught the tiny movement as the scales retracted, and glimpsed the hideous eye that they revealed.

It was soft and misshapen, like some boneless creature dredged from the depths and stripped of the pressure that had once lent structure to its form. Pinpricks of blue-green light swam through its jellied mass, illuminating the horizontal, keyhole-shaped pupil at its core. In its gelatinous hostility, it reminded him of the monster in the square that had swallowed Amiri whole.

The pupil rotated upward. It fixed on Kyra and blinked.

Toothless mouths opened in the stone cocoons mounted on the safe's front face. They let out a ululating chorus of shrieks, and then in unison they vomited up a flurry of barbed bones like miniscule harpoons. Each serrated shard was connected to its cocoon by a pulsating strand of viscera, and the mass of them reeked of rotting fish.

They hurtled into Kyra. She fell backward with a cry, throwing up an arm too late to shield herself.

At the same time, the safe shuddered from side to side as a bass vibration rocked its innards. Murky water gushed from its bottom, pushing drifts of paper before it as it flooded across the room. It, too, stank of a fouled sea.

"Kyra!" Merisiel cried, bolting forward. She lifted the cleric's head away from the water and, cradling Kyra's head in an elbow, jerked at the miniature harpoons with her other hand. They came out with clumps of flesh attached, and the elf let out a moan as she saw slimy, acidic poison dripping from their points.

Kyra didn't answer. Her body stiffened and convulsed, and her eyes rolled back white in her head.

"Help her!" Merisiel snarled at Ezren. She fumbled a potion bottle out of a thigh-strapped holder, popped the wax-sealed cork out with her thumb, and held it to Kyra's lips. "Come on, drink. Drink!"

Shocked out of his stupor, Ezren grabbed for a belt knife and slashed at the blobby strands of guts connecting the remaining bone spears to the safe. They put up a surprising resistance to his blade. The slimy coating helped them slide off the edge unscathed, and the tendrils themselves were tough as gristle. He hacked and sawed but made little progress.

"Out of the way, wizard," Amiri growled. Ezren raised his hands and threw himself to the side, narrowly avoiding the barbarian's sweeping slash.

Though Amiri had left her greatsword behind in Ezren's home, her curved knife hardly seemed any smaller in the office's close quarters. It cleaved through the ropy viscera, tearing apart the strands with brute force rather than finesse. Stinking slime spattered Kyra, Ezren, and the sodden, scattered papers around them.

Merisiel pulled Kyra free and forced the last of the bottle's contents down her throat. The cleric coughed as her wounds began to heal, though Ezren noted that the acid-eaten flesh was the slowest to knit back together. "That was... not pleasant."

"I'm sorry. I'm so sorry. I truly thought it would be safe." Merisiel's hands shook so badly that she dropped the empty bottle. She stared at it glassily, then picked it up as if she'd never seen the thing before. "You could have died."

"We can always die on these ventures," Kyra murmured with a strained smile. She sat up, wobbled to one side, and caught herself with a hand. "Thank you. With Sarenrae's blessing, I will be well now." She gripped her holy symbol again, fingers trembling, and exhaled a slow, shivery breath as she drew upon her goddess's strength to renew her own.

"We need to get out of here," Amiri said, shaking slime from her knife as she eyed the monstrous safe. Its severed strands were still twitching. Ichor dribbled from their ruptured ends, and the cocoon mouths at their bases continued to gibber and drool.

The central eye had closed, however, and Ezren had a bleak intuition that it would not open again. Whatever sentience lay behind that eye had already seen all it needed.

"She's right." Merisiel had mostly recovered her composure now that Kyra was up and talking. The elf's face remained bleak, but rather than waste any more time, she'd begun rifling through the office's books and ledgers with professional efficiency. "Too many people saw what happened at the Thousand Tents, and your disguises won't hold up if the Coin Guard starts pushing. That merchant was already out to discredit you, and now he's got enough proof to do it. Can't lean on Sarenrae's authority anymore, or the Pathfinders'. You need to get out of Totra."

"How long do we have?" Kyra asked, pushing herself back to her feet. She leaned against a half-buried desk for support, one hand pressed over her eyes, then shook her head and moved to Merisiel's side to help pick documents out of the piles.

"I don't know Totra well enough to guess when, or if, the Coin Guard might respond. The statues outside will reawaken within the hour, though." Merisiel swept her heaped papers into a satchel and cinched it shut. She tossed it to Amiri and began filling another. "We'd better be gone before that."

Suppressing his revulsion at the turn their night had taken, Ezren thrust his knife's tip under the edge of a stone cocoon and pried it, along with its limp tendrils, from the safe. "One hour. Let's make the most of it."

Chapter Seven
PIECING CLUES TOGETHER

It was a very difficult trap to find," Ezren said.

"Is that supposed to make me feel better?" Merisiel snapped. She forced herself not to wrench apart the sodden papers she was spreading over the bedside table in their cheap rented room, but her hands shook with the effort. The whole place reeked of goats and their manure, which did not improve her mood. Since fleeing Totra under cover of night, they'd traveled for days on foot before finally stopping in this wretched hamlet. Meri had been in her climbing shoes when they fled, not her walking boots, and she'd blistered both feet before she'd been able to find new boots.

That didn't make her feel any better either.

Inhale: one, two. Breathe down to the belly. Exhale: one, two, three. Inhale...

Kyra had taught her that exercise to find composure when her passions threatened to get the best of her. Merisiel closed her eyes and clung to it. *Inhale: one, two.*

Where would I be if I hadn't met her? Who *would I be?*

Who would I be if I lost her?

No. Meri couldn't let herself think that. *No.*

It was one of the unspoken truths of their relationship that the lengths of their lives were mismatched. Merisiel was an elf. Kyra was a human. Unless some stroke of disaster swept across their fates, Kyra would grow old and die long before Merisiel reached middle age.

That knowledge made every day precious, and bittersweet. Though she was young for an elf, Merisiel had already endured more loss than most humans could imagine. She'd had few friends or lovers among her own kind; she'd lived most of her years among Golarion's other quick, bright-burning peoples, and they did not endure time's toll as she did.

The loss of Kyra, when it came, would be worse than any other.

But we have today. That was what Kyra had told her from the beginning, and Merisiel had held tightly to those words. They had this day, and the next, and a handful of days beyond that, and Merisiel was determined to cherish each one.

She didn't want to lose a single one of those days. Not to anyone. Not to anything. Above all, not to a trap that she *should* have been able to spot.

"Yes, actually," Ezren said, interrupting Merisiel's thoughts. He'd been poring over the gems and dried-up mud cocoons he'd pried off the safe. Pulling off his silver-framed spectacles, he folded them into a front pocket and rubbed the bridge of his nose. "You shouldn't fault yourself for failing to see it. I didn't either. It was made to be an exceptionally subtle snare, hidden from those who had already seen the more obvious trap. Perhaps even more telling, it was set to kill servants of divinity. Clerics, priests, or blessed champions sworn to any god."

"Why?" Merisiel frowned, glancing down at the papers in her hands as if she'd find some answer in their mutilated pages. "Did he know we were coming? Was the trap aimed at *us*?"

"I don't believe so. I'll need to examine those papers to be certain, however. Have you finished laying them out?" Ezren glanced over at the bedside table, which was the only flat surface in the room not already draped with bits of wet paper.

"Just about." Merisiel eased apart the last handful of scraps and did her best to smooth them over the tabletop's chipped wood.

Setrypsis didn't cater to travelers who cared for luxury. The inn's furnishings were made for patrons who might be unfamiliar with the finer points of indoor living. The mattress held more lumps than straw, the washbasin and chamber pot were suspiciously interchangeable, and this table looked as if someone had tried to break it down for firewood—or, possibly, eat it—before the innkeeper had intervened. Spreading the fragile wet paper over the room's rough surfaces required a deft touch to keep the scraps from disintegrating any further, which was probably why Ezren had asked Merisiel to help him.

At the time, Merisiel had been vaguely flattered, but that was hours ago. Now she was thoroughly tired of it. Kyra and Amiri had been free to do whatever they liked all day, while she'd been cooped up in this dull little room, unraveling soggy bits of slime-stained paper for Ezren to study.

The prospect of learning more about the trap that had nearly killed Kyra, however, reignited her waning interest. "What are you hoping to find?"

"Whatever secrets were worth destroying in such spectacular fashion," Ezren replied. He sketched a diagram in the air with one hand, holding the other out toward the spread-out scraps. Moisture beaded on the soggy papers as if they'd been sprinkled with coarse grains of salt. As the water gathered, it rose up into the air in translucent strands and condensed into an oblong disk over the wizard's empty hand.

He pointed to the wash basin, and the globule obediently floated into it, then splashed back into shapeless water. Ezren repeated his spell a second and then a third time, drawing out all the water in the papers until every fragment was dry and the basin threatened to spill over.

Merisiel glanced over the dry scraps, but pulling the water from the paper hadn't done anything to restore the ink. The letters remained indecipherable blotches, and some of the larger fragments had shriveled and curled as they dried, so that they looked more like misshapen bowls than pages.

"I don't think your spell helped much," she said.

"I'm not finished yet." Ezren began another incantation, piecing together pages as he chanted.

It was slow, tedious work. Meri soon grew so bored that she lay flat on the floor, staring at the brown stains on the ceiling as though they were clouds drifting overhead. "Look, there's a cat being attacked by a horde of vicious mice. I think they're winning."

Ezren didn't reply. Merisiel lifted her head. The wizard wasn't paying any attention to her needling. He was, instead, absorbed in a book that had materialized out of the salvaged pages. Another book rested beside it, and a complicated-looking scroll sat beside that. Nearly all the paper scraps were gone, save for a scant handful that Ezren had laid out in a row on the bed.

"You made books?" she asked.

"No. I *restored* books. Two ledgers, specifically, and what appears to be a contract of some kind. The remainder of these pieces were separate documents—letters, deeds, I don't know what—but they were not part of these materials, and thus cannot be joined to the rest."

"What do they say?" Merisiel craned her neck for a glimpse, but all she could make out were meaningless smudges on the pages.

"Very little. I regret that my spell did not restore much of the writing. Evidently that was not an essential part of the ledgers' identities. The books were complete, as objects, before they were written upon, and so the ruined ink was not restored with the rest." Ezren turned the pages of the first ledger with a sigh of dissatisfaction. "I knew, theoretically, that this might be the case, but it was disheartening to see it proven. Nevertheless, our efforts have not been wasted."

"They haven't?" Merisiel laced her fingers around her knee and scoffed. "You just said you didn't recover any of the writing. What use is a book if you can't read the pages?"

The wizard shot her an acerbic look. "I failed to restore *most* of the writing. Some came through. Beyond that, the design and insignia of a book can tell us much in their own right." He lifted the first ledger, examining its exterior. "Would you mind gathering the others? I think we should all be present to discuss this."

"Gladly." Hopping to her feet, Merisiel went out to find them.

She had a good guess where they'd be. There wasn't much to do in Setrypsis.

The only notable feature in the region, and the only reason anyone visited, was the Dragon's Pupil, an unusual rock formation said to have been created by a fiery plume of dragon's breath in some ancient pharaoh's day. It was a needle-thin obsidian spire that bisected the sun, creating the appearance of a burning eye, for a few minutes each sunset. Local lore claimed that in such moments, those who gazed into the Dragon's Pupil could glimpse their futures, and so the formation had drawn a small but steady stream of pilgrims for centuries.

The sun beat down on Merisiel as she loped across the pilgrim's trail that led through arid hills to the Dragon's Pupil. She'd wound a white cloth about her head, partly for protection against the sun and partly to conceal the distinctive green gem that she wore on her brow, but even that light wrapping felt stifling in the afternoon heat.

Scrubby gray-green plants clung to the hillsides, but Merisiel saw none in the winding tracks between them. She would have expected plants to grow where rain gathered, however ephemerally, in a dry land.

Instead, cracked white crusts rippled across the bases of the hills, along with rocks washed down by seasonal rains. Nothing grew among the stones, and Merisiel guessed that the crystalline residue that masked them was some lethal salt, leached out by the rains or exposed by storms' scouring.

Merisiel drew up a layer of cloth to shield her mouth and nostrils, made a note to be wary of any strange odor or sensation as she breathed, and continued on her way. Golarion was rife with such hazards, ancient and new. She couldn't panic every time she encountered a reminder of that truth, and the fact that plants still grew above the white rime suggested that this one was minor indeed.

But it was a reminder, once again, that their lives in this world were fragile. That thought lingered as she spotted Amiri and Kyra on the pilgrim's path.

Putting two fingers to her lips, Merisiel blew an elderbird's trill, a signal they'd used from their earliest adventuring days.

Kyra turned, her smile apparent even across the distance. "Merisiel!"

Amiri was slower to react, but Meri had the impression that it was because the Kellid had known she was there all along and saw no reason to pretend to be surprised. More amused than annoyed—she hadn't, after all, been trying to move quietly—she hurried to close the distance.

"Ezren's finished restoring what we found in the merchant's safe," she told them. "He wants us all there to discuss what comes next."

"It's nearly sunset," Kyra said. She pointed across the sunbaked hills to a wavering blade of black glass that shimmered like a heat illusion in the distance. "We could make the Dragon's Pupil by the prophetic hour. Do you want to try?"

Amiri snorted. The barbarian had used one of Merisiel's disguising paints to temporarily bleach her hair and skin as pale as one of the Nidalese. It gave her an unearthly air, like some primordial snow creature stranded in the Osiriani heat. "No." Contempt dripped from her words. "Such things are nothing but sorcerous treachery. They show you lies about your future to fill you with fear and to blind you to the true dangers that lie in wait. Those who gird themselves against imagined foes are easy prey for real ones. I will not make myself victim to such tricks."

"I was asking Meri." Kyra laughed. She, too, had disguised herself, although only to the extent of changing into a nondescript beige tunic and trousers, and daubing paint over the facial tattoos beneath her eyes. "I know how you feel about it already."

"I don't know," Merisiel said, surprised and slightly uncomfortable to be asked. Did she *want* to glimpse her future, knowing how much sorrow was likely to lie ahead? "Do you want to look?"

Kyra shook her head. "Sarenrae will light my path as necessary to show the way. I need no other visions of the future. Faith often means walking in blindness, and trusting in the divine for what cannot be known. I would not change that, even if I believed that I could trust such sights, and I am not certain that I can."

"Then I see no reason to waste any more time on it," Merisiel said, shrugging. The Dragon's Pupil was almost invisible now, nothing more than a black gleam against the falling sun.

She looked away. She knew what her future held, and she didn't want to see it.

We have today.

Nothing else mattered.

Upstairs in the inn, Ezren lifted the first of the ledgers he'd restored and turned it so that the spine faced the others. Three signs were embossed in gold and silver upon the coffee-colored leather, and he tapped each of them in turn. The sun had sunk low outside, but the wizard's floating lights illuminated the book for their examination.

"The marks on this ledger are the emblem of House Adurguai, the sign of the Salt Cartel of Osirion, and Totra's city seal. I would wager that our merchant was the head of that mercantile house, and that he was a proud member of the Salt Cartel in Totra."

"Not exactly a risky bet," Merisiel said, unimpressed, as she leaned against the wall next to the door. "We found it in his safe."

"Perhaps not, but it confirms his identity, and might explain his hostility. I have a… history… with the Salt Cartel." Ezren opened the book and showed them the nameplate inside the front cover. "The ledger was made for Endio of House Adurguai and was meant to hold a true and accurate accounting of his business dealings. Such ledgers are common for members of the Salt Cartel, who often cloak their dealings in more palatable legal and political fictions when conducting business in nations whose laws are hostile to their endeavors. Naturally, the Salt Cartel prefers to have an accurate measure of what they're *really* doing, regardless of what might be filed in the official records of Almas or Ravounel."

"And what were they really doing?" Kyra asked. Her tone was serene, but Merisiel knew her well enough to hear the steel beneath. The Sarenite had no love for the Salt Cartel, a gang of profiteers who exploited mortal misery ruthlessly while pretending to be honest traders.

Ezren shrugged and flipped through the ledger as he held it out for their perusal. The yellow-edged pages were largely blank, stained only by vague smudges that could have been shadows as easily as ink. Nothing was legible.

About two thirds of the way through the ledger, even those indecipherable smears stopped. The remaining pages were empty, and Ezren closed the book.

"We come, next, to the scrolls," he said, putting the ledger down and holding up three furled scrolls linked by a gold ring worked into the likeness of a devil with malachite eyes, which pierced through the top corner of each sheet. "This is a devil's-knot contract from Cheliax, used when signatories do not trust each other in a matter of grave importance, and believe that magic is necessary to ensure that each party performs as promised. It holds three contracts, bound together. Each comes into effect only when the previous contract is fulfilled."

"Those have words," Amiri said abruptly. The Kellid's brow furrowed, and she scowled when Merisiel looked at her, as if she suspected Meri was surprised to hear her recognize such things. "I meant they have words we can read. The book didn't."

"Yes." Ezren said. "The contracts' enchantment did not entirely spare their physical embodiments from destruction, but it did have some protective effect. Enough for me to restore them, at least."

"What did the contracts say?" Kyra stepped forward, reaching for the scrolls. She remained in the nondescript desert garb she'd worn on the pilgrims' path that afternoon, but the familiar scent of sandalwood and incense caught Merisiel's attention as the cleric stepped past her.

Ezren cleared his throat as he handed the documents to Kyra. The pages' golden rings jangled quietly in the devil's mouth, unexpectedly melodic. "The first is a contract between Endio of House Adurguai and Itaguen Three-Eyed, in which Itaguen agrees to 'kill or cripple,' ah, me. And any of my associates that might get in the way." He coughed into a sleeve, and Merisiel thought she spotted the hint of a blush of embarrassment behind the wizard's white beard. "In exchange, the Salt Cartel agrees to provide Itaguen with transportation, translators, and a local guide to Inithyra's Orb. There are then a number of stipulations as to the speed and safety of that transportation."

"And you thought no one wanted to kill you," Amiri scoffed. She crossed her arms, flexing her shoulders and pectorals as she did so. Merisiel wasn't even sure it was intentional; it seemed to be reflexive, as if the Kellid couldn't help but flex when she felt victorious. "He'll try again, you know."

"Likely so," Ezren said dryly. "The more interesting question, in my mind, is: what is Inithyra's Orb, and what does Itaguen hope to find there?"

Merisiel shrugged. Amiri seemed annoyed to be asked. "What difference does it make? He'll never get there, not if he has to kill you first. We'll make sure he's the one who dies."

"It *is* the price for my life," Ezren said mildly. "I think it's only natural to be curious."

"Who, or what, is Curuvrakh?" Kyra asked, looking up from the chained scrolls. Her fingers framed that name, writ large in illumined letters and underlined with a slash of blood-red ink. "The second scroll specifies that this entity is also to be given passage to Inithyra's

Orb, in exchange for 'serving with all loyalty for a year and a day from the date of this signature.' The rest of the page is comprised of runes of binding. Is this creature a demon of some kind? I have never seen so many strictures used to control anything but a fiend."

"I don't know, but whatever it is, they were willing to pay a high price to secure its aid. Look at the last scroll," Ezren said.

Kyra slid the second scroll away on its ring, revealing the last page. Curious, Merisiel edged closer to read over her shoulder.

Upon reaching Inithyra's Orb, and for the duration of their journey to, on, and from that island, Curuvrakh pledges to give all requested aid to Itaguen, and to refrain from any unnecessary destruction. Should Itaguen procure the known prize with the aid of Curuvrakh, he shall have one week's uncontested possession of the prize, to do with as he wishes, except that he may not damage, destroy, or intentionally lose it. He will then pass the prize to Curuvrakh as full and complete payment for services rendered.

Each party will then leave without raising any hostility against the other.

It was signed with a flourish by Itaguen Three-Eyed, and countersigned in an indecipherable, scratchy red scrawl that might have begun with a C.

"What's it mean?" Merisiel asked.

"That we should go to Inithyra's Orb, and find the 'prize' they seek there," Ezren replied, leaning on his snake-headed staff as he straightened. "I am still alive and unbroken, so the Salt Cartel owes their co-conspirators nothing. Until Itaguen fulfills his end of the bargain, he cannot find or reach this place; if he could, he would not have agreed to those terms. Therefore, as long as I'm alive, we are probably at least somewhat ahead of them."

"How do we find it?" Amiri asked, seemingly more interested now that they were talking about taking action against their enemies.

Merisiel and Kyra exchanged a look.

"The Sandfire Catacombs," the cleric said, after a pause. "It is a repository of holy knowledge and old lore in the desert mountains.

We had planned to go there to follow up on Itaguen's information concerning the Thurible of the Dawn. It's possible that the catacomb's keepers might have information about Inithyra's Orb as well, however, or might be able to tell us who does. Given what we know about the parties who seek it, I believe they would be amenable to our cause."

Ezren nodded. "Would they permit me to accompany you?"

"I would expect so," Kyra said.

"Then I propose we split up." Ezren gestured toward Kyra and himself with the snake-headed staff. "We will go to the Sandfire Catacombs. Merisiel, I suggest, should return to Totra and see how our enemies have responded to the burglary of the merchant's offices. She was not with us during the attack at the bazaar, and although Itaguen may know her face, I doubt that Endio does. Also, now that we know more about our opponents' nature, it may be worth investigating the Salt Cartel's role in this. If they know where Inithyra's Orb is, perhaps we can simply take the information from them."

"I can do that. Doesn't matter if they know my face or not," Merisiel said with a casual shrug, drawing out a knife to clean her nails as she leaned against the wall. "They won't see me if I don't want to be seen."

"Very good. Then please learn whatever you can in Totra, if you can do so safely, and find us at the Sandfire Catacombs when you're done."

Amiri frowned. "What about me?"

"Ah." Ezren turned to the barbarian and smiled. It was a cold smile, so much so that it unnerved Meri. The wizard seldom let his anger show. His temper didn't flare hot, as hers or Amiri's did. It was an icy fury, tightly held and channeled into forms dictated by logic. "You'll come with us, of course. So that when Itaguen tries to kill me, you'll be there. And ready to kill him."

Chapter Eight
FIRST WATCH

Under other circumstances, Amiri thought, she might have enjoyed the journey out to the Sandfire Catacombs.

They rode through the wilderness on hardy, foul-tempered camels, threading a course between the poisonous Sahure Wastes to the west and the eastern floodplains where goatherds drove flocks of curly-horned beasts and farmers tended fields of beans and wheat. Kyra and Ezren didn't want to risk being recognized, and Amiri preferred solitude anyway.

Away from the rivers that were Osirion's gray-green lifeblood, the country was a sere land of wind-carved rock and blowing sand, possessed of a hostile beauty that reminded Amiri of her own homeland. Here, all was bleached pale by the sun and scorched by a withering heat, but the starkness of its shapes and the toughness of its wildlife spoke to her.

Nothing weak survived the desert. Nothing soft. Those were terms Amiri understood. As they sat around their campfires each night, shaking the dust from their white robes and sipping the water that Kyra conjured with her prayers, Amiri felt an unexpected belonging in the dry wastes of Osirion.

Yes, in another life, she might have been happy here. Content, at least.

But in this life, she was waiting for some sign of their enemies' pursuit, and so she stared hard at the rocks and sand, seeing nothing but unwilling to let her vigilance waver.

The days were hot and quiet, and the nights were cold and quiet, and hour by hour, Amiri's frustration grew. She had never really mastered the patience of the hunter, not like some in her following. Hers was a raider's soul, and she craved action.

The steep and lonely mountains known as the Pillars of the Sun held many terrors, according to Kyra. Manticores, sand drakes, and flame wyrms hunted the rocky slopes and the desert beneath them, while undead warriors with gilded bones and jackal masks guarded the tombs of dust-dead rulers in the mountains' heart.

But all Amiri saw was rocks and sand, and rocks and sand, until they came to the burning plumes of the Sandfire Catacombs.

They reached the Pillars of the Sun at dusk. As night claimed the mountains, the easternmost peak lit up in flares of golden flame, illuminating the curved walls and gold-tiled towers of a temple built in an ancient Keleshite style and dropped, incongruously, atop this remote and hostile wilderness.

"We should wait to approach in the morning," Kyra told them, tugging her recalcitrant camel to a halt. "Custom dictates that honest visitors, unless driven by desperate need, should present their faces in daylight."

"Is our need not desperate enough?" Ezren asked wryly. He was joking, Amiri thought, but only halfway. Though the wizard never voiced a complaint, he wasn't as young as the rest of them, and she'd spotted him moving stiffly in the mornings and at night. The long days in the saddle weren't easy on him. He'd probably welcome a night's rest in a real bed, especially if it came with dinner and a bath.

She didn't have much pity for him. The elders of her following endured worse.

"It's not that urgent." Amiri dismounted in a smooth, single-handed vault and led her camel toward a cleft in the foothills that she thought might make a good, sheltered camp. "No one's tried to kill you yet. We can wait."

"It would be safer in the sanctuary. Tales abound of the perils in the Pillars of the Sun," Ezren protested, following on camelback.

Amiri shrugged. "Maybe that's how they want to test us." Many Kellid followings had such tests, never announced to outsiders but well known to neighboring followings. Those who came to petition for marriages, negotiate trade agreements, or seek alliances in raids were expected to prove their worth by bringing a hard-won prize as a chieftain's gift, or arriving at an hour that indicated they'd braved fearsome distances or formidable beasts on the way.

"Do the Sarenites have such traditions?" Ezren cast a questioning look at Kyra, then cursed and grabbed at the reins as his camel stumbled in the dark. He kept his seat, but it wasn't graceful.

Kyra waited to answer until it was clear the wizard didn't need her help. Then she glanced at the points of fire burning on the mountainside, nudging her camel to follow Amiri. Unlike Ezren, the cleric held her reins loosely, trusting the animal to find its own path through the night.

"It is not the Dawnflower's nature to test her supplicants before deciding that they are deserving of her aid," she replied. "But the cults in this part of the world are old, and some keep traditions that the mainstream faith has abandoned. Still, I would say that is not the primary intent of the custom. It is merely that visitors who arrive in sunlight are thought to walk with Sarenrae's favor."

"And they want to see if we're undead," Amiri suggested, clambering over a pile of fallen boulders at the cleft's mouth. "Whenever people get worried about whether strangers can walk through sunlight, it means they've had problems with undead."

Likely the rocks had been washed there by a flash flood, which suggested they'd be in danger if it rained overnight, but she didn't taste any water on the wind. If they didn't have to worry about flooding, then the boulder wall would serve as a natural defense against potential attackers in the night.

Good. If there were undead in these mountains, they'd be ready.

Ezren looked far less enthused about the campsite than she was. He didn't seem to appreciate the value of the rocks at all. "*Must* we sleep in a field of boulders?"

"You'll thank me in the morning," Amiri said, unsaddling her camel. She slung her pack onto the ground and pulled off the camel's hair-prickled saddle blanket, draping it over a boulder to air out. "Maybe you'll be stiff and achy, but you'll be alive to be stiff and achy, and that's what counts."

"The longer I travel with you, the less convinced I become that that's true," Ezren sighed, but he got off his camel with only a few winces. Amiri had taught him some stretches to loosen up his legs and back, and she was pleased to see him dutifully practice them before he set about making the group's dinner. Soft he might be, but the wizard was willing to learn.

Neither Kyra nor Ezren was talkative after an exhausting day of travel, and Amiri wasn't the type to press for conversation. They ate a simple meal of stewed lentils and rice, followed by dates and candied nuts, and then retired to sleep.

Amiri took first watch, as usual. Early night, when the day's forbidding heat faded and the twilight hunters emerged, was the best time to observe the local wildlife. She found comfort in the rhythm of owl and beetle, mouse and bat. The foxes were scrawny and sandy-furred, and the desert hares were long-legged creatures with comically huge ears, but their dance was the same as it was in the north.

Predator and prey, hunter and hunted. Cruel, perhaps, but it was the natural way of things, and there was no duplicity in that game. No tricks. The fox and the hare knew their places.

She breathed in the dry, sweet fragrance of desert herbs opening their flowers to the moths and moonlight, and she listened to the chittering of insects trying to cram entire lives into the scant hours between blazing sun and midnight cold, and she felt a full, rare peace come upon her, as the gift of this difficult land.

When the insects' whirring stopped, and a heavier silence suffocated the night, Amiri rose soundlessly to her feet and took up her giant's blade.

She'd listened to the animals. She'd heard their warning.

Crouched low against the rocks, she crept toward the enemy in the dark.

The desert moon gleamed off the speckled gray carapace of an enormous scorpion, easily twelve feet long. Its segmented tail, hooked high over its back, ended in a hollow, broken bulb and the splintered stump of a stinger. Dark liquid dribbled from the bulb, and though the stinger looked fragile enough to shatter the next time it struck anything solid, Amiri didn't doubt it was strong enough to drive through a mammoth-hide shield.

The scorpion was undead. Its pincers were chipped and lusterless. Some of its eyes had been pecked out, and those that were left were withered clots. Gaps in its shell showed that nothing remained of its innards except a few strands of dry fiber that might have been guts or sinews or whatever musculature scorpions had. Amiri hadn't any idea; such creatures did not live in the frigid north.

She knew undead, though. Her lip curled as she took in the sight of the thing.

There was no reasoning with such a monster. It had no desires, no morals, no concept of mercy. It was a pure abomination, and that meant Amiri could slaughter it without fear of lectures from any of her companions.

Blade at the ready, she shifted her angle and made a stealthy approach, crouching between the stones for cover. Best if her companions slept through this attack. Partly that was practicality—Ezren and Kyra needed to be well rested to work their magic, whereas Amiri could easily run for a day and a night without sleep—but partly it was pride too.

She didn't like that she'd needed her friends to rescue her from the monstrosity in Totra. Of course she was grateful that they *had*, but it rankled that she'd needed it.

A warrior should be able to look after herself. Amiri was determined to remind them all that she was such a warrior, and dependent on no one.

The undead scorpion would be her proof. It rattled through the rocks ahead of her, oblivious.

Amiri waited, watching her prey draw nearer. A heap of flood-stacked rocks closed off the scorpion's right side, partly blocking the lash of its tail. The narrow passage also trammeled the creature's pincers, preventing it from turning easily or striking at an adversary behind it.

Five feet away, she could smell the musty, faintly acrid odor of the creature's husk.

Amiri knew this was her moment to strike. She shifted her grip on the greatsword's hilt, tensed into a low squat, and sprang up from the boulders to stab down at the unsuspecting scorpion.

Driven by all her weight and momentum, her giant's sword smashed into the scorpion's back, spearing it through and driving into the ground. The scorpion thrashed hard enough to fracture its own shell against the unyielding steel, but it couldn't break free. It was pinned to the earth like a butterfly fixed to a board.

Amiri released the sword and, clenching her hands together into a single fist, hammered down on the fracture lines spreading outward from her blade through the scorpion's chitin. The shell cracked wider. She grabbed its edges and pulled. As chunks came loose in her hands, she flung them away, dismantling the undead creature piece by piece.

Smaller chitinous balls rattled inside the shell. At first Amiri took them for pieces of the giant scorpion's shell, but then they uncoiled and scuttled toward her.

Babies. The scorpion must have been carrying a recently hatched brood when it died and turned. Now its offspring were undead too.

Their sharp little legs clacked against their parent's shell as they flooded toward Amiri, tiny tails swishing and jabbing at the air.

She could barely see them in the gloom, but she could guess at their deadliness. Using a curved shard of the undead scorpion's shell as a scoop, Amiri swept the verminous little creatures away. Some tumbled out of the carapace and landed on the ground, where Amiri stomped them. Others evaded her scoop and clambered up her arm, stabbing and pinching.

A shivery numbness spread from the stings. Amiri choked down a cry. Fear nipped at the edges of her mind—her people had always dreaded pestilence and poison, twin treacheries that weakened strong warriors and gave them nothing to strike back against—and she sought refuge, as she always had, in rage.

Her fears vanished into the red tide. In her rage she was invulnerable to pain, impervious to terror. The future shrank to the split seconds between an enemy's attack and her own, and that span of time could hold nothing that frightened her.

She couldn't grow old or weak or unloved. Her friends couldn't deem her worthless and leave her behind. She couldn't *need* anyone.

She could only live and die and kill. None of those things frightened Amiri.

The baby scorpions were still stinging her. Her arm swelled up so badly that the straps of her hide gauntlet bit into her flesh. Growling, Amiri smashed her forearm back and forth inside the hollow of the great scorpion's carapace, pulverizing the smaller ones' fragile bodies against its walls.

A roar welled up in her throat. Amiri had tried to stay silent earlier, but in the throes of her rage, she no longer cared. Her war cry reverberated in the chitinous drum of the great scorpion's body, and she punctuated her roar with a percussion of punches as she destroyed the last of the creature's undead spawn.

Something slammed into the small of her back and her buttocks. Amiri's forehead cracked against the scorpion's belly, blinding her with pain. A jolt of agony throbbed from the bridge of her nose; it might have broken.

Amiri twisted to peer through the opaque roof of the scorpion's shell. She could tell her left eye was going to swell shut in moments, but for now she could still see through both.

A shadow swayed through the sky, blurrily visible when it crossed the sliver of moon that reached through the rocky defile. Amiri could scarcely see it, but she knew by its rhythmic passes and the strained quaver of the scorpion's body that it had to be the undead beast's tail.

It must have been rocks that hit me. The scorpion had managed to knock enough stones loose to bring its tail forward.

Amiri lunged for cover in the only place available to her: inside the scorpion's hollow body.

She grabbed the blade of her greatsword with her right hand, hissing as the steel bit into her palm, and used it to drag herself in deeper. Using her left elbow, she smashed at the chitinous wall separating the scorpion's thorax from the rest of its abdomen, making room to fit herself inside. At the same time, she kicked both feet against the stones behind her, propelling her legs into the makeshift shelter.

The tail came jabbing down, missing her calves by inches, as Amiri jerked her legs into the scorpion's abdomen. She tucked her knees in tight against her chest. Breathing hard, she stared up through the shell, watching the tail sway over her face while shards of the pulverized baby scorpions ground into her sweaty neck.

Her greatsword remained firmly lodged in the scorpion's body, still pinning it to the earth. The weapon was useless to her in there. She had knives, but they weren't likely to do her much good at the moment.

The air was getting hotter and harder to breathe. Amiri scowled. Frustration spurred her rage to new heights, and she punched up at the scorpion's shell, not because she had any particular plan in mind but because she was angry and wanted to hit something.

Chitin cracked against her knuckles. She punched it again, widening the fissures, then shoved her fingers into the cracks and tore the shell open to let the clean night air in. The scorpion's tail swayed overhead, dripping venom, but Amiri didn't care.

She inhaled, welcoming the cool rush of wind, and then she shouted, "Stab me if you want, you bastard. Go ahead! Stab me! I killed your brood and I'll kill you too, already dead or not."

The tail came down, flashing through the dark. Amiri wrenched herself to the side, flattening her body against the curve of the scorpion's shell, and grabbed the bulb above the stinger with both hands.

Rather than try to stop it, Amiri pushed the stinger forward and away from her, redirecting it toward the gap at the base of the scorpion's neck. Then she let go, allowing the tail's momentum to plunge its stinger down.

Chitin shrilled against chitin as the undead scorpion stabbed itself. The creature's pincers beat against the neighboring rocks as it tried to free itself from the twin impalements of sword and stinger.

Amiri twisted inside the scorpion's abdomen and sprang up, shattering the remnants of its back plate across her head and shoulders. She landed hard on the tail's bulb, driving the stinger deeper. The scorpion convulsed again, then collapsed under her feet as death claimed it once more.

Breathing hard, Amiri crouched atop the hulk, alert for any movement.

None came. It was dead, truly dead.

Amiri pulled her sword from the carcass. Her anger slowly receded, letting the throbbing pain of her wounds and the ache of strained muscles surface again, like rocks revealed by a retreating tide.

She had won, but without her rage lending urgency to the battle, it seemed a meaningless victory. What had she slain, and why?

Brooding, Amiri gazed at the undead corpse. Then she climbed back onto the scorpion's shell, took hold of the tail embedded in its back, and wrenched the stinger free. She put her foot on the tail and bent it back until the segments snapped.

She held up her grisly prize. It was nearly as large as her entire torso. Threads of sinew dangled from its stump, tickling at her wrists. Ichor streaked the broken bulb and gummed the stinger.

A worthy gift, she decided, for the guardians of the Sandfire Catacombs. Perhaps it wasn't their tradition, as Kyra had said, but it was hers.

She *was* a true warrior. The scorpion's tail was proof. Whatever her following's doubts, or her own, the trophy Amiri held in her hands was testament to her skill and courage. She could fight alone, and she could win alone, and she did not need anyone else to save her.

As her muscles burned and her wounds bled, Amiri held the broken stinger over her head, and she roared.

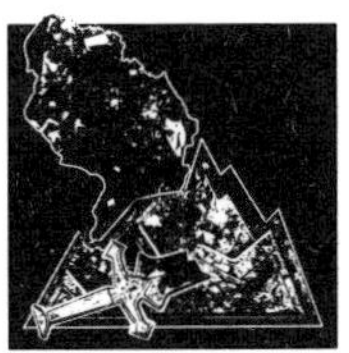

Chapter Nine
GODSRAIN

For the thousandth time, we don't *need* a trophy," Ezren said in exasperation, while Amiri set her jaw and gripped the ruined scorpion's tail tighter. "Kyra, tell her."

Kyra shook her head, trying to judge the distance to the Sandfire Catacombs' signal blazes and tiled towers, which rose above a zigzagging road that fell into shadow as the rising sun painted the mountain peaks in light.

She understood Ezren's concern, of course. There was a better-than-fair chance that the Sarenites of the Sandfire Catacombs would regard Amiri's gift as barbaric, and though she doubted that her fellow faithful would let that reaction show, she couldn't be sure. If so, it was likely to provoke a violent response from Amiri. The Kellid had always been touchy about being scorned by "civilized" folk, most of all when she'd made some effort to please them.

At the moment, however, that didn't feel like a grave concern. An ominous premonition had been troubling Kyra since she awakened, and it was only growing stronger by the moment. She didn't know *why* she was so certain that a calamity was on the horizon, but she had no doubt it was coming, and that whatever it was, it centered on her faith.

Over the years, she had learned to trust such feelings. Whether they were her own intuition or warnings sent by her goddess, they were never wrong.

"It's not important. Let her bring it if she likes." Kyra urged her camel to kneel and climbed into the saddle, holding on to the saddle horn as the animal swayed back to its feet. "We should go to the sanctuary quickly. I fear there may be trouble ahead."

Ezren frowned, but he asked no questions until he was riding behind her. Amiri scouted ahead on foot, leaving her camel to serve as the party's beast of burden. The scorpion's tail sat on its saddle, lashed into place by cords wrapped around its stinger.

"What is your concern?" the wizard murmured, once Amiri was out of earshot.

"Nothing I can name." Kyra looked up to the sky, but there was nothing to be read there. The sun burned against an endless field of pristine blue, unmarred by cloud or shadow. "You don't sense anything amiss?"

"No. But I put little trust in such suspicions, as you know. One step removed from superstition, and a short step, at that." Ezren waved toward the sanctuary's distant fires. "I'm more worried about the welcome we'll receive there."

"I don't think—" Kyra began, and then cut off as the earth shuddered beneath them.

Ezren's camel went to its knees, braying in panic, as the wizard cursed and grabbed the saddle horn to keep from tumbling off. The other two kept their feet, but their eyes rolled white with terror. The pack goods slid sideways on Amiri's beast.

Again the earth shook like a drum struck by some immense mallet. Rocks rumbled off the mountains' faces, crashing down in yellow clouds of dust. The lights of the Sandfire Catacombs winked out in deliberate lines, one by one, although the sanctuary itself had not been harmed by any of the rockfalls.

"What—" Ezren started to say, coughing, but he never finished the thought.

A flurry of long-legged brown birds raced out from a ravine ahead. Kyra had seen several such birds, racing across the rocks in search of scorpions and lizards, during their journey across the desert. They were flightless, or close to it, yet this group suddenly took wing and streaked screaming through the air. Their voices sounded human, and they cried an agonized chorus of "Woe, woe!" that Kyra winced to hear.

A mote of blackness spiraled out from the sun's heart, blotting out its light. Out of nowhere, within seconds, a full eclipse seized the sky.

Kyra thought, for a delirious instant, that she saw... fangs or claws or perhaps gnashing needles of bone... ripping at the edges of the eclipse, as though there were something *within* that darkness that strove to escape, or to consume the sun more fully than the shadow itself could. But then it was gone, leaving her unsure that she'd seen it at all.

Two figures stood illumined against the darkness. They were limned in a weak radiance that revealed their outlines and movements but gave no indication of their surroundings. All that was behind and around them was masked by the void.

One was a faceless giant in heavy plate armor, dented and scarred by battle. Dirt and soot grimed the metal. Dried blood flaked from between the gauntleted knuckles, and red mud caked the greaves. The warrior's helm was a featureless iron mask stripped of any identifying mark, but it seemed, simultaneously, to bear ghostly likenesses of every crest and insignia Kyra had ever seen.

A second figure lurked behind the armored behemoth. Smaller and slighter, it moved with arachnoid deliberation. Even in this vision, it seemed to be cloaked in shadow, and was visible only as occasional glimpses of sleek red plates crafted into an inhuman, mantis-like form—or, perhaps, merely forged to fit a body that had been alien from inception.

Gorum and Achaekek. Kyra knew them instantly, as nearly anyone in Golarion would. The Lord in Iron and the Red Assassin were among the most dreaded gods in the pantheon, for their deeds were written in blood. One claimed the allegiance of steel-clad armies and shouting barbarian hordes, while the other was the ruthlessly efficient lord of professional killers and master poisoners.

Kyra had never been able to decide which of the gods she found more terrible than the other. They were both dealers in death, givers of grief and ruin.

Yet they did not cross paths often. Why should they appear together now?

The answer came in a crimson blur. The Red Mantis struck with a matched pair of sawtooth sabres, driving them into the armored hulk with deadly sureness. Kyra couldn't imagine that Gorum's divine armor harbored any weakness, but it seemed that Achaekek could either perceive inconceivably tiny flaws, or could create them by his own divine might, for the first of his sabres cracked two of Gorum's massive plates apart, and the second bit into the gap.

There was no blood, no outcry, nothing. Gorum stiffened and then turned his helm slowly to look about, but already the Red Mantis had disappeared.

The Lord in Iron sank to one iron-clad knee. He reached up to his wound with a gauntleted hand, and Kyra felt an echoed incredulity fill her own chest as the dying god's iron fingers brushed over the hole in his armor. Gorum's glowing red eyes dimmed to embers, and then went out.

A deep rumble reverberated through Kyra's body, as if she stood in a house that had been rocked by thunder. There was a cruel snarl to it, and a faraway whisper of monstrous laughter.

The sound of that laughter sent a cold shock into Kyra's soul. An old, old dread stirred within her, something so ancient and profound that she knew at once it wasn't her own emotion. Nothing in her mortal life or experience could hold such power.

It was Sarenrae's memory, Sarenrae's fear, that she felt. Before Kyra could begin to guess what had spurred such apprehension in the Dawnflower, Gorum—and the vision—exploded.

The stricken god's armor burst into shining shards. Red and silver sparks flew from his body, faster and faster, obscuring Gorum's fallen form. The red and silver sparks flew from the rent in his armor, and gleamed wet as blood, bright as starfire, though the wound itself had been bloodless. Among them flew sharp-edged flakes of the god's armor.

Together they swirled up in a sparkling cloud. They pulled together in the eclipse's core, compacting so tightly against one another that they nearly vanished, and then they burst back outward. Red, silver, and steel-gray fragments flew outward, brilliant against the blinded sun, like a fire-flower exploding in the night.

As the whirlwind's dazzling afterimages faded, Kyra saw an emptiness where the god of war had fallen.

He was gone. Nothing remained. Only glittering sparks and shards spun above the space where, moments earlier, one of the great gods of Golarion had stood.

Kyra watched in astonishment, too shaken to move.

What does it mean? she asked Sarenrae, pleading for an answer. *What is this?*

But there was no response. No guidance came from the Dawnflower. The sun itself seemed mute and blind behind its unnatural mask.

In that moment, the gods themselves seemed to have been struck dumb by shock, and Kyra felt more perilously alone than she had ever been in her life.

Across the skies and seas of Golarion, every creature with senses to perceive it and a mind to comprehend it witnessed Gorum's death.

The vision of Achaekek's fatal blow played across the lightless, long-forgotten prisons of starving ghouls and barrow wights, illuminating the dripping walls of their miserable caverns and the bones of their mindless skeletal companions. It flashed across the submerged pearlescent palaces of the merfolk, and it flooded the dreams of those who were not awake to watch the god of war die in the heavens.

Those who could not see Gorum's death heard it, scented it, or felt it in the shrill quaverings of the universe's ley lines.

The psychic resonances shattered the high windows of cathedrals and caused schools of fish to spontaneously explode into flame. New-forged swords dripped with smoking blood as smiths pulled them from the fire. The eggs of robins and kestrels cracked in their nests, and the shrieking, half-formed hatchlings that emerged were clad in shards of iron.

All through the world, ripples of shock reverberated.

For some, they were more than ripples.

In the ever-shadowed Hungry Mountains of Ustalav, the tremors of Gorum's death shook apart a centuries-old dam, known to the villagers who lived in the valley below as the Catchment of Tangled Teeth. Local rumor had long held that some malign spirit dwelled behind the interlocking wooden teeth and snarled waterweeds that made up the dam's glowering facade, but that spirit was only a story. Or so people believed, until it sprang to life and brought doom to Ilmor's Wend.

As the Godsrain fell from the sky, the frothing weight of decades of collected rain and snowmelt came thundering down upon the hapless people of Ilmor's Wend. Within minutes, the village was gone, lost beneath a bubbling lake. If there were survivors, none were found.

Only a few woodcutters and goatherds on the slopes above were left to witness the radiant shard that fell from the stricken heavens into their valley, or to hear the terrible laugh that emanated from the monstrous dam after it had spewed out its killing flood.

They did not speak of it for weeks after the disaster. It was all they could do to salvage enough to move on. None wished to linger where so many had died, and none could shake off the memory of the catchment's awful, wooden-fanged laugh.

But in later days, as the survivors of Ilmor's Wend found themselves trying to build new lives in new towns, with little to help them back onto their feet, some reached for that memory and wove stories around it. They told tales of a treasure that fell from the sky and of the evil spirit that haunted the lake of the dead. They drew maps to their submerged valley, and they wove beads and string into protective talismans for the fortune seekers who went that way.

In Ustalav, peasants did not tempt the attention of the gods. But if the gods happened to glance their way, and the misfortune could not be avoided, then they would find ways to glean what they could from the rubble.

In Ustalav, such things were understood.

Pressed hard against the shelter of a spell-scarred rock, Kulgor stopped to catch his breath and bind the dirt-caked gash in his leg. The wind howled across the bare plains of the Felldales, whipping the poisoned Numerian dust into phantoms and rising to a shriek whenever it split around one of the rocky claws that erupted from the lifeless soil.

Kulgor coughed, pulled his cloth face covering aside, and spit out grit. The wind made it impossible to tell how close the spine dragon was. Though only a juvenile, the crystalline beast was a deadly foe, and the young warrior knew he couldn't hope to fight it off in his state. He'd barely escaped with his life the first time, and he hadn't been crippled then.

Squinting through the blowing dust, Kulgor tied a final knot in the rag binding his leg, adjusted the sand-specked cloth over his nose and mouth, and stood, leaning on his skymetal spear for support.

If he was lucky, the spine dragon had lost him in the toxic windstorm.

If he was lucky...

Above him, the sun went black. The wind fell quiet, and the raging sandstorm tumbled back to dead earth. Kulgor looked up, clenching the rag that bound his leg, and saw Gorum struck down by the Red Mantis.

Red and silver and shining shards hailed from the heavens. Kulgor, caught in awe, watched them fall with open-mouthed astonishment. He'd forgotten the pain in his leg and the threat of the spine dragon.

Gorum is dead. A god. How could it be?

The crimson and silver stars were still falling from the sky. A scarlet droplet, wet as a spring snowflake, drifted toward Kulgor's uplifted face. It fell between his eyes, settling on his brow.

Divine energy arced through him, so powerful that Kulgor thought it might have lifted his entire body off the ground. Perhaps it did; he couldn't tell. The pain in his leg vanished, and heat filled his chest. It felt like the red lightning of battle rage, but... different. Stronger. Fiercer. More enduring.

His heart was pumping so hard he thought it might break through his chest. The skymetal spear glowed in his hand, gold and incandescing blue, and gave off a scent of ozone.

The eclipse vanished. The sun returned. So did the wind and the blowing sand. But the strange fury that had gripped Kulgor did not fade.

The chime of sand grains pinging against crystalline spires was his first and only warning that the spine dragon had found him. But rather than greeting his death with dread, Kulgor sprang to his feet, readying his skymetal spear.

"Come," he snarled.

He wasn't afraid of the spine dragon anymore. He wasn't afraid of anything.

It was time, he thought, that the world learned to be afraid of him.

A hungry fish saw a crimson gleam spin through the frigid murk of the northern Okaiyo Ocean. Millennia of instinct drove it forward, and it swallowed the glowing morsel with no more thought than a dull surprise at the heat that passed through its gullet.

Little in this icy sea was warm. What had it swallowed?

The fish felt a brief, puzzling hint of something that might, in a more intelligent creature, have been worry. But it was not blessed, or cursed, with the capacity for such concerns, and it swam on through the gloom with a swish of its tail.

Minutes later, the pain came.

Iron spikes erupted from the fish's vertebrae, spiking up through its skin. Iron ribs radiated out through the spines of its fins, pulverizing the bony rays as they replaced each one. Its eyes swelled and exploded in puffs of blood and vitreous jelly, soon swept away by the sea. A raw red glow emanated from the wounds that remained.

It grew larger, and larger, and larger still.

Despite the weight of the iron that made a serrated monstrosity of its form, the fish was swifter by far than it had been before. Swifter than anything it had ever known. Swifter, and stronger.

Hungrier, too.

In the blood farms of Geb, a blind girl reached for a blade that she could not see. She had heard its silver song in her soul, and she had followed its call to a muddy corner in a half-collapsed pen where the keepers did not go. They were too big, and the pen was too wretched, for the pale ones to bother. Secrets could go unnoticed there.

Her fingers closed upon it, and she felt its promise of power and protection flow into her. She turned her unseeing gaze from side to side, hoping none had noticed her seizing that talisman of hope.

None had, or at least none took it from her. She clenched it tight in a small, trembling fist.

The pale ones who fed upon her and her family would feed no more.

Her Infernal Majestrix, Queen Abrogail II of the Thrice-Damned House of Thrune, was examining a newly commissioned diadem of white and red diamonds when the sky went black outside her study windows. A thunderous tremor shook the palace tower, throwing crystal vases to the floor in shattering spills of black and crimson roses.

Abrogail herself was nearly knocked off her feet, though she managed to catch herself with a practiced twist. She glanced across the room at Gorthoklek, her most trusted advisor, and was shocked to see a hint of fear—subtle, almost perfectly controlled, but real *fear*—on the disguised fiend's face.

Swiftly she drew upon the protective enchantments woven into nearly every piece of jewelry she wore, as well as the embroidered sigils hidden in the inner lining of her garments. Shields of arcane force sprang up around her, guarding against every foreseeable hazard, while other enchantments sharpened her reflexes, enhanced her senses, and quickened her premonitions of danger.

It was that last spell that caused her to relax, after a tense, silent moment. "There is no danger?"

"None immediate." Gorthoklek, too, had recovered. Almost. His eyes showed split pupils of black flame against burning red irises. He turned to the windows and blinked, and they returned to the calm brown that he favored in his human guise. "Not to us."

"To whom?" Abrogail asked, but then Achaekek's sawtooth blades bit into the Lord in Iron, and there was no need for her advisor to answer.

Together, struck momentarily mute, the queen and her general watched Gorum fall. When his armored body erupted into silver and red, Abrogail swallowed, feeling the world pivot under her feet. The chaos that this would cause...

But the Chelaxian queen was no stranger to crisis. Flashes of scarlet and silver danced off her circlet and the diamond-haloed rubies that hung from her ears, but a disaster reflected in her jewelry meant she still had jewelry, and all the power that came with it. She spoke calmly, willing herself back to control. "What is it?"

"A dead god's power. Fragments of Gorum's divine might, scattering across Golarion. Where they will fall, and what they will do, I cannot say." Gorthoklek shrugged, but he didn't look as composed as he sounded. Flickers of hellfire still sparked in his gaze, and his fingernails flashed into claws and back as he tapped them restlessly against the hilt of his sword. "But they will change the world."

Abrogail nodded. She'd reached the same conclusion, of course; it was too obvious to miss. The complexities would come in the details.

"Summon the nameless council." This small, secret group, without title or formal recognition at court, comprised the only counselors whom Abrogail trusted even minutely.

"All of them?" Gorthoklek prompted delicately. The membership of the nameless council often changed, as the queen's favor and disdain were infamously mercurial. He wanted to know who was to be summoned today.

Abrogail sighed, feigning annoyance that the general had to ask. "Lord-Admiral Isair Charthagnion, to discuss military implications. Arch-Minister Mirasel Tanessen, for the diplomatic perspective. Call our cousin Velenne back from Westcrown; her counsel has been valuable, even if she did make the most absurd of marriages."

"Anyone else?"

The queen pondered the matter, then smiled. Outside, the sun was black, and shards of a dead god fell from the shuddering sky, but Abrogail was back in her element. "Lord Sangreval Grulios."

The young lord had recently ascended to lead the Wiscrani branch of his house after his father's not-terribly-mysterious death. He was untested on a stage of this import, and his wife, Lady Morgan, was one of those peculiar commoners who occasionally rose to wealth and prominence entirely unjustified by her birth. But he was clever, and the Egorian branch of House Grulios was beginning to think too much of itself, and this was a good opportunity to determine whether the young lord was worth binding to her side.

The world might be shuddering through a cataclysm, and the gods themselves might be dying, but that only raised the stakes in Cheliax's great game. Now, perhaps, the Empire of Devils might have an opportunity to reclaim some of what they had lost in recent years—if they could turn this turmoil to their advantage.

"Yes," Queen Abrogail said. "Do call Lord Sangreval."

On the red planet of Akiton, a hunting party of four-armed shobhads loped across the cold crimson foothills in pursuit of an elder arabuk. They'd been tracking the spotted predator for days and knew from the size of his pawprints and the spread of his antlers that he was a magnificent specimen. Whether they captured him alive as a breeding stud or were only able to claim his pelt and crown as trophies, a successful hunt would bring glory to them all.

The eclipse of their sun astonished the shobhads, and the eruption of crimson and silver as a god was torn asunder shocked them anew. They watched in amazement as shards of red, silver, and burning steel hurtled from the heavens like wounded stars.

What calamity was this, that reached across the span of worlds?

Alarmed, the hunters conferred in a hushed but heated conference. After much debate, they decided not to abandon their pursuit and return to the tribe but to continue their chase of the arabuk.

It was an unlucky choice. A fragment of Gorum's shattered mail had struck the old arabuk between the antlers, crowning the elder with star-steel and divine might.

When the hunters came upon it, they did not escape.

The Godsrain fell at random, scattering magic in silver and red across the world. Divine droplets fell where they would, driven by nothing but blind chance and happenstance.

All save one.

One shard, guided by a deliberate hand, plunged into the Eye of Abendego. It plunged through the storm clouds and dove into the sea, hissing through unlit fathoms of brine.

There, it struck a mark buried since the dawn of time.

Mud boiled and stone cracked. Reality churned in an agony that, as yet, none witnessed.

A god's grave began to open.

Sarenrae, my goddess, where are you?

Silence met Kyra's imploring call. The metal rays of her holy symbol bit into her fingers as she clenched her hand around the Dawnflower's sign, but it was only bronze and enamel, devoid of any divine presence.

Where are you? Why have you gone?

The last of the silver and crimson stars were falling from the sky. The cloak of darkness slipped away from the sun, and the eclipse's chill relaxed its grip on the world. Kyra felt the change with a relief as profound as it was incomplete. The sun had returned, but her goddess had not.

And then, finally, she felt the familiar warmth of the Dawnflower's presence in her soul. It was weak and strangely shaken, as though Sarenrae herself were recovering from a terrible shock, but it was there.

My servant. Heed my call. I need you now.

The words were surprisingly gentle, nothing like the clarion warrior's call that Kyra had expected to hear from Sarenrae. There was no command in them, no compulsion, only an invitation for Kyra to prove that she was worthy in her devotion.

That very gentleness ignited Kyra's determination as nothing else could. To hear the voice of one's goddess directly was an honor that only the most fortunate believers could claim.

Kyra would not disappoint her. Tears trembled behind her eyelashes, and the holy symbol shook in her hand. *Yes. Anything. What would you have of me?*

Golarion faces a danger greater than you can imagine. Not the death of one god alone, but of... everything. Everyone. A shiver of old, remembered terror passed through the goddess's voice. *You must stop it. You, and your friends. I can do no more than aid you.*

The last sparks of Gorum's death had nearly vanished from the sky. One of the final silver motes spun toward them, a shimmering droplet of liquid steel. A sunbeam broke through a cloud as it passed, and it seemed to Kyra that the angle of the spark's fall changed, very slightly, as it tumbled through the light.

It fell not to her, but to Ezren, standing beside her. The wizard's eyes widened in surprise, and he took a step to the side in an attempt to evade it, but the god-spark was falling faster than it seemed. The mote struck him before he could dodge. Silver light blazed across him and flared from the carved eyes of his snake-headed cane. A clap of concussive force, like silent thunder, encompassed him.

Then it was gone.

Kyra gasped, dizzied, and turned a wondering gaze to Ezren. "What... happened?"

The wizard didn't answer. He gripped the snake's head between his interlocked thumbs and spread his hands out to either side of it, staring at the veins and bones along their backs as if he'd never seen them before. His jaw worked, but no words came out. Finally he looked up, shaking his head in mystification.

"I don't know, Kyra. I don't know. But I think I will, soon."

Chapter Ten
OVERHEARD REVELATIONS

Holding her breath, Merisiel eased the manor's window open, hoisted herself up until she could peer over the sill, and then crept stealthily in. By the time she was inside, her muscles were screaming from the strain of moving so slowly, but the satisfaction she felt more than made up for the pain.

No one had seen her, no one had heard her, and once again she'd pulled off a clean trick where few others could. She'd landed in the merchant's private library, with no one to witness her arrival. Perfect.

Meri opened the door a few inches and peeked out. The merchant's house looked much the same as it had the first time she'd broken in, but such appearances could be deceiving. Endio of House Adurguai and his allies had access to substantial magic, and that meant she couldn't take anything for granted. She kept her eyes sharp and her ears pricked as she slipped down the carpeted hall toward Endio's study, where she thought it most likely she'd find some insight into his doings.

There or the master bedroom. After that, if she hadn't found anything, she'd search the rest of the house.

Sculptures, paintings, and gilded curios looked down on Meri as she moved through the halls. No guards, though, and no wards.

Endio's study door was locked, as it had been on Merisiel's previous visit. This time, though, there was an alarm spell nestled into the scrollwork on its front panels.

That's new. The small hairs prickled on the back of her neck. Had the merchant discovered her intrusion?

Crouching in front of the study door, Meri slipped on a glove webbed with lines of silver thread between the fingers. She spread her fingers wide and moved it slowly over the door, letting the threads' vibrations tell her where the magic was strongest. Once she found the alarm spell's anchor points, she'd be able to pick it apart with her other tools.

She was focused so intently on the glove's trembling threads that it took a moment before she registered a soft, irregular dripping sound from farther down the hallway, in the direction of Endio's bedroom.

It sounded like rain pattering from a leaky roof onto thick carpet, but Totra had seen no rain in months.

A knot of tension clenched between Meri's shoulders. *There's been violence.*

She didn't know whether that meant a cracked wash basin or a cut throat, but the sound of dripping meant *something* had broken.

Pulling her hand away from the door, Merisiel removed the silver-threaded glove and moved silently toward the bedroom.

The door had been bashed to pieces. It slumped in the doorway, its hinges torn from their anchors. Bloody claw marks were gouged in the front paneling, but the angle of the marks and the scratches in the doorframe indicated that the blows had been delivered *after* the door was ripped from its moorings, not before.

It wasn't a barrier anymore. Whoever had smashed it so violently had done so for no reason other than the act of destruction itself.

Meri's apprehension rose. She wedged a pry bar around the door's side and levered it away, enough to peer into the room beyond without dislodging it entirely. While she doubted whatever had smashed the door remained in Endio's bedroom, she couldn't be certain, and the door might block it long enough to buy her time to flee.

Inside the room was carnage. A dusting of shredded down from the merchant's silk pillows covered the carpet and furniture. Blood had sprayed over it in a fine mist that stained the downy feathers pink and clumped them together in sticky globs.

The triptych of full-length mirrors in gilded frames that had stood opposite Endio's bed was smashed into wreckage. Shards of glass littered the floor, showing broken bits of images in an indecipherable mosaic. Even the frames had been wrenched apart by clawed hands; dark slashes in the gilt showed where the claws had sunk into the wood and ripped away its gold. The dripping noise came from the merchant's painted porcelain wash basin, which had been hurled against a wardrobe and cracked in two. Water trickled through the armoire's splintered top, plopping irregularly onto wood and carpet.

As for Endio himself...

Meri pulled the door a few inches wider, searching for some sign of the merchant's fate.

When she saw what was left of him, she gagged. The pry bar started to slip out of her hands, and Meri barely managed to keep the door from thudding onto the floor. Turning away from the grisly scene, she eased the door down quietly, slid her pry bar away, and closed her eyes as she leaned against the wall outside.

Merisiel had been adventuring for longer than most humans lived. Over the decades, she'd seen her share of brutality. Death was nothing new to her.

But *that*...

There was nothing left of Endio to recognize. Crushed pink pulp, fragments of bone jutting out from chunks of meat, some wrinkled scraps that might have been skin and might have been clothing.

She wasn't even sure it was him. It could have been anyone. It could have been multiple people. All that Meri could be certain of was that there were pieces of at least one smashed human skull in Endio's bed, and that the entire room had been misted with blood.

Swallowing her gorge, Meri tried to gather herself enough to decide whether she needed to search that room. The wet, metallic stench of blood seeped around the broken door, and all too vividly she could imagine how the damp, sticky down would cling to her fingers and clothes. She'd have to pick it off, bit by bit, for ages.

But she'd been sent there to investigate, and for the sake of Kyra and her other friends, Merisiel felt bound to do a thorough job.

Why was Endio murdered? Was it for something he had, or something he knew? Who'd done it and how?

He might have left clues. Kyra had once told her that people placed under magical compulsion almost always tried to resist having their freedom usurped. Even when they couldn't break free entirely, they'd find ways to sneak lesser assertions of their own wills through. Messages, sabotages. It was part of what made those spells so dangerous for their users: the victims found unexpected ways to fight back.

Maybe the blue jelly she'd seen over Endio's face, and his servants', was some form of magical control. Maybe he'd begun to rebel against it, and that was why he'd been killed. Maybe he'd had time to leave a message behind before he died.

That was a lot of maybes, though, and not much else. She needed real answers.

Grimacing, Meri tightened the cinches on her sleeves. She felt better composed now and ready to deal with the unpleasantness of the task ahead.

Just as she prepared to push past the broken door into Endio's bedroom, she heard voices drifting up from the stairwell at the far end of the hall. Holding the pry bar across her chest in case she needed it as a weapon, Meri flattened herself into the doorway and waited to see who was coming.

There were two voices. Neither was accented like a local's, and neither sounded especially tense. They didn't seem to be aware of the bloody scene they were walking toward. One speaker was male, with a low, smooth voice that Merisiel recognized as Itaguen's. He sounded much the same as he had in Enqatis; evidently he hadn't bothered to disguise his true manner there.

The other voice was so rough and snarled that she wasn't certain it came from a person, or even from a living throat. It sounded more like a beast raking its claws against a stone, or gravel being shaken across a miner's pan.

"—foolish," the rough voice was saying. "Wasting time on this private grudge."

"It is useful," Itaguen replied, sounding both dismissively amused and weary, as though he were responding to a joke already worn thin. "What he asks is a paltry price for what the Salt Cartel is prepared to give us in return."

"Only because they do not know its true value."

Itaguen laughed. "Isn't that how the Salt Cartel conducts all its business? It merely happens that, for once, we're taking advantage of their ignorance. As Master Endio would doubtlessly be the first to tell you, a party's exploitation of superior information does not invalidate a contract under Chelaxian law."

"Cheap the price may be, but it is too much," the snarler responded. "We have no time for this. His trivial grudge is no reason for delay.

We must find Inithyra's Orb. The master demands that we hasten our efforts. He demands it! Earth and sea tremble with the knowledge of what comes. Blood gathers in the heavens, waiting for the storm. When the master holds its secret, his enemies' wails of woe will fill this world and all others."

"As delightful as it is listening to you shriek about the end of all things, I—"

The house jolted underfoot. A series of shudders racked it, as if a giant had seized the entire building in its fist and was intent on shaking it to death. Paintings toppled from the walls. Windows burst in a line marching down the house's length. Tiles rained from the roof.

The bedroom door fell forward. Merisiel thrust the pry bar up, stopping it just before the wooden slab would have crushed her, but its edge hit her shoulder hard enough to bruise her to the bone. She bit back a cry as she wriggled out from under the precariously balanced weight.

The house kept shaking. Crystal and ceramic made a tinkling chorus of destruction as the merchant's treasures fell from their pedestals. Heavier thuds announced the collapse of bookcases, suits of armor, perhaps cabinets and armoires.

Before Meri could decide whether she was safer hiding in the doorway or seeking more stable shelter, the ceiling of Endio's house seemed to dissolve before her eyes. She froze, staring upward in disbelief.

Wood and plaster swirled away in plumes of disintegrating vapor. In the sudden open stretch of sky, the sun on the horizon vanished behind a shadow that had no source. An eclipse cast the world into darkness, yet in that darkness, Merisiel saw Achaekek's serrated blades bite into another god, and she watched the Lord in Iron die. Gorum's body exploded into a fountain of crimson and silver droplets, punctuated by flashing shards of the slain god's armor.

How? It was said that the Red Mantis could not raise a hand against his fellow deities. The Lord of Assassins could kill anyone, anywhere, except other gods. But Merisiel had witnessed him do just that, and she had no doubt that what she had seen was real.

She sank bonelessly against the wall outside the merchant's bedroom, hardly conscious of the movement, or of the ominous creak of the half-toppled door beside her. When the ceiling solidified over her head once more, she scarcely noticed.

A god has died. A god was murdered.

It was only when she heard the laughter that Meri roused out of her stupor.

The laughter was wild, hideous, filled with cruelty. It was a laugh that saw misery, claimed it as victory, and could fathom no other joy.

A few times in her life, Meri had heard traces of that maniacal sadism in other voices: in Skinsaw cultists, among Kuthite fanatics, and in the fevered mutterings of those who had been damaged by coming too close to the unholy powers of the world.

But what she heard now was the distilled essence of what she had only sensed as a lurking influence beneath the surface of the others. This was the pure version, brought to the fore and stripped of any feeling, any consideration, beyond a frantic delight in ruin.

If "delight" is the word. She didn't think it was. Meri was, at best, a casual worshipper of Calistria, but even so, she'd been shown the many ways the Savored Sting found, and gave, pleasure.

What she heard wasn't any of those. It was closer to the relief that an addict feels upon staving off the void just a moment longer. No real pleasure, only a mocking simulacrum of what it might have been, once.

What is *this creature?*

Meri peeked out past the doorway, but it was impossible to see far. Several rafters had collapsed, taking down bookcases and suits of heavy armor in addition to sizable portions of the walls and ceiling. Under a swath of blue sky where the ceiling should have been, a heap of dangerously precarious rubble now blocked the hall.

It hid the two speakers from her, and it hid her from them. At least, she hoped so.

But she wanted to see who Itaguen was speaking to, so she eased her way toward the rubble heap, crouching behind its cover.

"You are amused?" That was Itaguen again. He sounded annoyed, and from the slight strain under his words, Meri guessed he'd been hurt during the manor's quaking. "I'm surprised. If one god can die, so can another. Yours, for instance."

The laughter cut off as abruptly as it had started. "All the power of all the gods of the Great Beyond could not slay my master. But the death of the hollow one? That is a great joke, yes. And now that this joke has been told, we must go. Inithyra's Orb can wait no longer. This changes everything. Our task has become far more urgent. Even you must see this."

There was a silence. Then Itaguen said, "As it happens, I agree. Endio will have to wait on his revenge."

"Yes." The rough voice giggled, a terrible, incongruous sound. Meri paused with one foot poised in midair, unsure she wanted to get any closer to that creature. "He'll have to wait forever. Forever and ever. Forever... "

Itaguen inhaled, a sharp irritated sound. "You killed him. The servants too, I suppose?"

"Yes. Oh yes." There was a thick, grotesque joy in that answer, and a yearning to relive the act. Then a silence, and a shaggy rustling sound, as though the creature were shaking its head as vigorously as a dog might shake off water. "But don't be angry. He was no use to us anyway. He lost the Akithaine map, the fool. So we had no further need for him."

"He... lost it?" Disbelief in that question, and a great deal of anger.

"He warded it against us. Against me. So suspicious, our good friend Endio." Another brief wild laugh, this one accompanied by a wet chittering sound. "He put it in a safe with special precautions against holy souls. Or... the opposite. He was afraid I'd steal it. Funny thought. Very funny. I didn't. But someone else tried and triggered his precious little trap. Now it's gone, all gone. The safe and the map and, alas, poor Endio. But at least our enemies learned nothing. All was destroyed. He managed that much."

Merisiel squinted through a gap between the splintered shelves of a toppled bookcase. She could just make out a shorter, thicker figure next to Itaguen. Female, she thought, although the figure was swathed in layers of rags that made it difficult to tell. The woman's hair hung in a thick gray-brown tangle, and her skin had the rough craggy texture of linden bark. Smooth pink lumps protruded from the fissures of her skin at irregular intervals, like mushrooms sprouting between tree roots.

Curuvrakh? Was this the third conspirator mentioned in Endio's contract? Meri could easily imagine wanting the security of a devil's pact to hold that woman's erratic violence at bay.

If that had been Endio's idea, it hadn't worked out as he'd hoped.

Itaguen seemed to have reined in his temper. He stared flatly at Curuvrakh—if that was, indeed, the unkempt woman's identity—but the coiled, imminent lethality that had tensed him up a moment ago was gone. "Then the Akithaine map is gone, and so too is the man who was going to provide us with a ship. How do you propose we find Inithyra's Orb?"

"Easily. Easier now. Many will have died in the tumult that accompanies a god's fall, and many more will die in the chaos that follows. No one will remark on this man's death. His house is in ruin. And, more importantly, my master has become stronger. Already I feel his voice grow louder in my soul. He comes. He *comes*. Soon, soon." There was another giggle, quieter but no less horrific in its glee. "You are a captain, are you not? In one of your guises, at least. A Free Captain of the Shackles. Though your ship is no ordinary ship, is it? Much faster. So blessed, it is, to have such speed. We will take your ship. Do not bother with a disguise. My master grows impatient."

"Without the map—"

Curuvrakh chuckled. Something stirred beneath her hair. It extended a bristly, chitinous leg from the ropy mass, and a soft insectoid chittering emanated from the tangles. Judging by the length of the leg, whatever was hiding on the woman's shoulders was at least the size of a large house cat. "Gorum's death... changed things. Already, I can feel it. My master will show us the way once we are near. We have only to get close enough for him to guide us."

Itaguen's expression hardened. He'd discarded the hooded cloak he'd worn in Enqatis and now wore a suit of glossy black scales that fitted his form so precisely and moved so silently that Meri knew the armor had to be magic. "It will not be subtle. The *Herald of the Deep* is known to too many. That was half the point of working through the Salt Cartel. We agreed we did not want anyone guessing at our purpose."

"The *Herald of the Deep* is faster than any merchant vessel, and the time for subtlety died with the hollow god. Now we must be swift. As I said: my master grows impatient. We must find the fang."

Merisiel bit her tongue, wondering if the two were about to come to blows. She squeezed closer through the rubble.

The creature in the woman's hair was still moving. Two of its legs caressed her left cheek, over and over. Meri didn't have a clear enough view to be certain, but from the way the legs stuttered and dragged over her skin, she thought the bristles were gouging into Curuvrakh's bark-like cheek.

Then one of the chitinous legs brushed over a smooth pustule in Curuvrakh's face. The softer skin tore apart instantly. Blood and pus erupted from the wound, along with clots of more solid material that Meri couldn't identify, except to feel a queasy certainty that those slime-covered shapes were nothing that should have been in any human body.

The woman wiped a sticky lump from her chin, grunting in strained satisfaction, as the creature that had slashed her retreated back into hiding. Its legs left a streak of wet matter in her hair. "Take what you need from this place. We must go."

Itaguen's lip curled in obvious revulsion, but he turned briskly on his heel, heading back toward the staircase from which they'd come. "We may need to bribe sages and scholars to assist with finding the house. There are baubles downstairs that will serve our purposes. Take the golden ones, Curuvrakh, not the stone. I realize assessing the value of things is not among your strengths."

Curuvrakh eyed the messy smear on her finger and licked it off with a long, prehensile tongue that tapered to a sharp point at its end. "I know the worth of all things, flesh and bone and soul. They exist to be devoured."

Itaguen didn't answer. Soon they were out of sight.

Meri held her breath and waited, listening for every step they took, until she was sure that the two of them had gone.

Then she exhaled, releasing the tension that had built between her shoulder blades from the moment she'd heard the drips in Endio's bedroom. She shimmied back out of the rubble heap and stretched away the stiffness that had tightened her muscles while she hid.

A god had died. The man she'd come to spy upon had been murdered. The one who'd killed him was some kind of monster, and that monster was intent on finding Inithyra's Orb.

She still didn't know how Itaguen fit into the picture, though. He didn't seem to serve Curuvrakh's master, and neither did he belong to the Salt Cartel. And what was the map that Endio had possessed, which Meri had inadvertently led her companions to destroy?

Perhaps Kyra and the others would be able to sift through the pieces of that puzzle and arrange them into meaning. For now, Merisiel meant to ensure that they had as many pieces to work with as possible.

She pulled the teetering door away from the merchant's bedroom and squirmed through the gap beneath. The smell of death met her once more, but this time, Meri's curiosity burned brightly enough to dispel her horror at the scene of Endio's death.

What did you know about Inithyra's Orb? If you had enough resolve to hide a map from Curuvrakh, did you manage to hide anything else?

Glass crunched under her knees as Merisiel crawled into the bedroom. The rug's thick pile squelched beneath her weight, and her palms came up red and sticky. Bits of blood-matted fluff caught between her fingers and in the crevices of her polished leather armor, just as she'd imagined.

She ignored it. Kyra needed answers, and Meri meant to get them.

A chance ray of sunlight fell through the broken window. The room was north-facing, and the sun shouldn't have been able to reach through that window at this hour, but nevertheless, a golden beam glanced through and caught a dented locket buried in the splinters of a side table.

Shifting into a squat, Merisiel picked up the locket. It didn't look like anything special. The silver was plain and tarnished, and the craftsmanship was below the standard of Endio's other treasures. Not enough to make it stand out, but enough that she would have assumed this was a sentimental piece, or else a gift from an unloved relative. Nothing worth paying much attention to.

She flicked it open.

It held a key, and a scratched message in a shaky hand: "Clock. Study."

Chapter Eleven
THE SUNKEEPER'S WELCOME

Do you feel... different?" Kyra asked Ezren, her dark eyes searching him for any sign or symptom.

Ezren shook his head. He didn't, or if he did, it was not in a way that registered over the awe and disturbance that still reverberated through him at the sight he had witnessed in the sky.

Since parting ways with Abadar's faith, he had sworn no allegiance to the gods. It wasn't that he denied their power. That would be foolish, a willful blindness to reality. But the veneration that mortals heaped upon them was seldom warranted, and often held people back from fully exploring their own potential.

Why bother developing one's own ethical and moral compass when one could simply pray to know what was right? Why suffer through the tedium of scientific observation, or the strain and self-doubt of mastering arcane formulae, when magic could be granted on request?

Those who resorted to such devices didn't even know the extent of their dependence. They thought themselves superior for their piety, never recognizing that it left them forever clinging to another's support, unable to stand on their own strength.

Ezren had never wanted that for himself. Let others indenture themselves to the gods if they liked. He would remain beholden to no power but his own.

But the gods, as they said, laughed at the best-laid plans of mortals. Gorum had struck him with a fragment of... something... in the throes of his death, and Ezren could feel it igniting a fire deep within.

Almost as soon as he answered Kyra's question, he felt his answer become a lie.

The blossoming of Gorum's silver blood reminded him of the first moment he'd felt magic spark in his grasp, or the sweet sleepless agony of young love. It was warm as the first rush of wine gilding dull conversations with delight, as potent as black coffee transmuting dull drowsy tasks into electric challenge. The thrill of it was undeniable. *Power.*

Ezren closed his eyes. With an effort of will, he contemplated the effect of the god-spark on his soul and then, carefully, closed it away. He envisioned locking it in a lead-lined casket, as he would bury the corpse of some noxious beast, and dropping it into the dark well of his soul.

I will owe nothing to any god. Not even a dead one.

"I did feel something just then," he said, "but it's gone. Come, we should continue to the Sandfire Catacombs."

As he nudged his camel forward, Ezren looked at Kyra and Amiri. The cleric's eyes were hooded, and the Kellid's face was a grim mask. "Are you... all right?"

Such a feeble phrase, he thought, to convey a question of such weight. Kyra had dedicated her life to her goddess, and she had just seen another deity struck down before all the world's eyes. For all that Ezren disdained the worship of such beings, he understood the import of what Kyra had witnessed, and he grieved for the pain it must have cost his friend.

And Amiri...

The northwoman seemed shaken, having seen what they'd all seen. She had even less reverence for most of the gods than Ezren did. He wasn't certain why she scorned them—they had never discussed the subject—but he knew that her resentment was old and deep.

But she had venerated Gorum, in her gruff, unshowy way, and for the Lord in Iron to be slain by an ambush from behind was a dishonor that would cut her to the bone.

That thought sparked a belated realization. Ezren had been too absorbed by the fact of Gorum's death and the rain of divinity that had exploded from him to see it earlier, but...

"How could the Red Mantis kill him?" Achaekek, the god of assassins, could not harm other gods. He had been created by the deities to serve their will, as an enforcer of divine will and wrath. To prevent their creation from turning against them, they had bound

Achaekek with an eternal, unchangeable injunction: he could not slay gods.

Yet he had. *How?*

"I don't know," Kyra answered. "I don't know... anything. About any of this."

She said it quietly, but in the words, Ezren felt her despair. *She's rudderless.*

He wished Merisiel were with them. But the elf was away, seeking answers to questions that no longer seemed to matter.

Ezren fumbled for some words that might grant Kyra comfort, but nothing came to mind. Consoling those in need had never been among his strengths. No one wanted practical advice in such moments, and anyway, Ezren had none to give.

Unable to think of anything useful to say, and with the god-spark's energy coursing like delirium through his veins, Ezren turned his gaze forward and concentrated only on keeping his balance in the saddle as his camel picked its way through the rocks to the Sarenite sanctuary on the mountainside.

Slabs of stone had fallen across the road in the wake of Gorum's death, and rumblings from higher up the mountains suggested that more might follow, but the camels climbed up the steep path without trouble.

Heat shimmered across the sun-bleached rock, intensifying into wavery columns above the Sandfire Catacombs' blazing golden towers. Ezren glimpsed worn stone plinths, rendered illegible by wind and dust, dotting the turns and landings in groups of four. Some of the plinths still had traces of paint in their grooves, while others had gone bald with age. None were new, or whole.

"They are for offerings," Kyra said, the first time they came to a cluster of carved stones. She dismounted and touched the faded carvings reverently, murmuring a prayer before she went on. "Those who had been redeemed would walk this road on their knees. At each of the prayer stations, they would offer up a token of their past sins, choosing the altar that matched their wrongs. Sins of omission, sins of deliberation, sins of impulse, sins against the self. My translation is inexact, but... that approximates the way that the Sandfire cult divided the wrongs of the world.

"Sarenrae's power would consume these marks of error, purifying the penitent who had brought them. At the top, the pilgrim would be welcomed into the sanctuary and ritually cleansed."

"Is this tradition no longer observed?" Ezren asked. He could see no flames among the plinths, nor even any sigils of elemental magic, though of course that was hardly dispositive where divine power was concerned.

Kyra shrugged, but she sounded a little regretful, or perhaps merely solemn in the presence of such ancient relics. "The practices of the deep desert were never widely known. Too few live here, and too few remain. But they are not forgotten. Sarenrae survives, and this sect survives, and that is all one can hope for in an uncertain world."

No doubt the cleric had said similar things before, but the words carried a different note now, with the aftershocks of Gorum's death still resonating across the peaks and valleys. Ezren nodded, twitched his camel's reins, and fell in behind Kyra for the rest of the ride.

As they ascended toward the sanctuary, fire enveloped them. Spigots worked into the shapes of brass serpents lined the last half mile of the path. Whether by magic or mechanics, they sensed the party's presence, and announced them with twenty-foot plumes of gold flame that rose and fell as Ezren and his companions rode past.

It was like riding through a roaring forge. The camels crowded into the center of the path, rolling their eyes and braying dismay. Sweat soaked Ezren's clothes within minutes, and although he'd meant to drink his water sparingly, he found himself emptying flask and skin in short order. The heat was unbearable.

An insistent tingle spread through Ezren's chest. Power flowed through him, begging for release. *There is no need to suffer. No need for anyone to be in danger. Fire is peril, and safety lies at hand. Only take hold of the power and use it,* use it...

He pushed the temptation away. The fire was a test, not a real threat, and he had no need of dead Gorum's magic.

"Have they no sentinels?" Ezren mopped perspiration from his cheeks and squinted at the golden towers rising from the Pillars of the Sun. From this distance, and with the heat wave of the flames rising on either side, it was difficult to tell, but he didn't think he'd seen a single guard on the entire ride.

"I imagine we would see them soon enough if these fires did not burn gold," Kyra said. She seemed comforted by the blazing walls to either side, despite the murderous heat, and put a gentle hand against her camel's neck to soothe the beast's agitation. "The Dawnflower watches over her temple and marks those who walk the pilgrims' path. If our intentions were hostile or our souls were not pure, her sacred flames would signal that to her faithful."

At the top of the path, the flames died, and Ezren caught his breath at the view that rolled out beneath them. The scorched beauty of the desert unfolded from the mountains, rippling outward in wind-carved loops and whorls of sand and stone. It was harsh and ageless, and seemed to have been washed in new splendor by the ordeal in flame he'd endured to see it.

"Be welcome, travelers," a woman's voice said from behind them. "The Sandfire Catacombs offer you water and rest."

Ezren turned, trying to disguise his startlement.

The woman who'd come from the sanctuary might have been fifty or seventy. It was hard to tell, since the woman had lived most or all her life under the high desert sun, and her light brown skin was deeply lined. Her movements were assured, and she spoke with the gravity of one long accustomed to leadership's mantle.

She wore loose, flowing layers of translucent golden fabric, smoother than linen but not as sheer as silk. Interlocking ornaments of brass, bronze, and gold encircled her neck and chest in an elaborate double collar. A sun-shaped headdress crowned her brow, and a live flame burned in the center of the design. Though the fire was cupped in a bowl of dimpled brass, and the metal rested directly against the woman's skin, she seemed untroubled by its heat.

"Sunkeeper," Kyra said, dismounting and sweeping into a deep bow. Ezren offered a formal bow of his own, while Amiri merely grunted, her arms crossed, and remained in her saddle. "We thank you for your hospitality. We seek—"

"I know what you seek," the woman interrupted. She made a small gesture of apology for her brusqueness, and Ezren saw that, despite her age and authority, the Sunkeeper was shaken. "Forgive me. I should not have spoken so. Today's events—"

"We understand," Kyra assured her. "A god died. A *god*. All of us are struggling to find our footing. Truly, we take no offense."

The Sunkeeper nodded. She beckoned them to the sanctuary's open door, leading the way into the shadowed interior. "The Dawnflower bade us welcome you. Sarenrae said that she had named you as her champion and instructed us to be ready to aid your quest."

An unexpected breath of cool, green air washed over Ezren's face as he neared the entrance, yet he balked at the Sunkeeper's words.

Kyra seemed to share his astonishment, if not his doubt. "She did?"

"Yes. The goddess... spoke to me, after Gorum died." Awe and lingering amazement filled the Sunkeeper's words. "She said that you would come and that you had been charged with a task of the utmost urgency. So I will waste no further time. Please, follow me." The Sunkeeper was a mere silhouette in the sanctuary's dimness. After a second's hesitation, and an exchange of glances with his companions, Ezren followed her in.

Soft, unexpectedly humid air, scented with some exotic flower, enveloped his parched skin. As his eyes adjusted to the sanctuary's gentler illumination, he saw that hanging pots and stone basins held greenery in elaborate arrangements throughout the halls and sitting rooms. Shafts cut into the ceilings admitted light and air, but the sun was filtered through screens that cut its white blaze into geometric lace.

Acolytes in simpler versions of the Sunkeeper's dress came to take the camels. They, too, wore living flames cupped in brass upon their brows. The flames burned in shades of yellow and white, with an occasional tinge of amber or orange, and Ezren noticed that they were positioned so that the wearer could not see the light, but those around them could. He wondered whether they drew upon the same magic as the soul-sensing flames on the pilgrims' path. Was it part of the acolytes' training that they could not read Sarenrae's judgment of their own souls but knew that everyone around them could?

"Sarenrae told us that you would come seeking Inithyra's Orb," the Sunkeeper said as she led them down a spiraling hall into the mountain's heart. Few of the passages that they passed descended, Ezren noted. Most reached back up toward the surface, staying close to the sun. Only this corridor seemed to go down.

"What *is* it?" Ezren asked. "An island, I gather, but I have never heard of it."

"No," the Sunkeeper agreed, "and that is no accident. You will, of course, be familiar with the Windsong Testaments?"

"Of course." The Windsong Testaments, collected by a long line of Masked Abbesses in a centuries-old abbey on Varisia's Lost Coast, represented the shared efforts of myriad religious traditions to parse through Golarion's myths and fables for the true history of the gods. Though imperfectly translated by mortal hands, and subject to endless dispute, the Windsong Testaments represented one of the purest distillations of religious lore in the world.

"Some of the Testaments are better known than others. A few have been deliberately hidden from all but the scholars who work on them. Inithyra's Orb is one of these. We store that story here, in part because its location is believed to be somewhere between Osirion and Mediogalti Island—although, as you will see, there is disagreement on that matter." The Sunkeeper touched a hidden clasp in her collar. One of the ornaments slid out, revealing itself to be a cunningly configured key.

The hallway ended in an oversized door of baked clay bricks embedded in metal mesh. The walls around it were made of the same materials, which Ezren hadn't seen anywhere in the floors above. Runes and holy sigils caught the light of the Sunkeeper's headdress and winked at the party's arrival, as if mocking any notion of opening such an absurdly heavy door. There was a keyhole in the door's center, and Ezren surmised that it was either enchanted or the core of some clockwork mechanism that ran through the entire structure. Otherwise, it seemed impossible that the door could be moved, locked or not.

The Sunkeeper lifted the ornament to her brow, and the flame burning in her headdress spread down a channel carved along the shaft of the key. When she slid the key into the door, lines of golden fire radiated out through the sacred sigils that ringed it.

Within moments, the entire door glowed with holy light. The emblems of every god that Ezren knew, and many he did not, shone on the bricks' faces. He felt an answering throb of power pulse within his own chest—Gorum's dissolving essence, again—and quelled it firmly.

The bricks became translucent, and Ezren realized with a start that what he had taken for a door was, in fact, nothing of the sort. Each of the bricks covered a nook in which a scroll or book had been slotted, like a honeycomb stuffed with lore rather than nectar. There was no reinforced wall, no door within it, and no library behind it. The library was *here*, cleverly disguised.

Withdrawing a bronze-capped scroll case from its alcove, the Sunkeeper stepped back, then smiled at Ezren's surprise. "It *can* be a door, if those who do not know its secrets try to force an entry. But that door is false. It leads only to a labyrinth of traps and illusions, for those who refuse to see the truth of things are doomed to lose themselves in deceit."

The Sunkeeper held the scroll flat across both brown hands and offered it to Kyra. "This is what the Dawnflower bade us give you. You are welcome to study it here, and to make notes if you wish, but you may not take the scroll from the sanctuary, nor may you copy it in its entirety. All we have is conjecture and guesswork, and it must not be represented as a document of holy truth."

"Is that why it was hidden?" Kyra asked, accepting the scroll and gazing down at its sun-marked case.

"No," the Sunkeeper replied. She withdrew the key, and the glowing door went slowly dark. The shadows seemed deeper than they'd been before, the gloom somehow more ominous. Though the flame in her headdress still burned, it seemed small and lonely in its metal cage. "You will see why when you read it."

Chapter Twelve
IN THE SANDFIRE CATACOMBS

For nearly a week, Kyra pored over the Sunkeeper's scroll.

It was tedious, difficult reading. The original script was written in an archaic form that she hadn't studied in decades, and the modern notations were written by a dozen different hands, each more inscrutable than the last.

Although the Windsong Testaments were intended to be a collaborative work bridging all of Golarion's faiths, that cooperative spirit seemed to be more honored in the breach than the observance. From what Kyra could tell, virtually every contributor relied on shorthand and cryptic allusion to drop clues that could be followed only by a fellow believer, and she was fairly confident that the few exceptions were simply doing it so subtly that she hadn't caught them.

Kyra was sufficiently well-versed in the major faiths that she could decipher most of the coded passages. Even so, she knew some of the nuances escaped her. Ezren helped her puzzle out some of the historical references and alchemical codes, but he'd never made a serious study of theology.

Yet, for all her frustrations, Kyra was enthralled by the work. The fragile parchment held centuries of brilliant and painstaking scholarship, drawn from every corner of the world, all aimed at solving the same mystery: what, and where, was Inithyra's Orb?

That question, in turn, went back to one of the oldest legends of Golarion.

The War of Imprisonment. The Devourer's War.

Early in the history of creation, when mortal life was young and the gods were enamored of their wondrous new worlds, Rovagug—the Rough Beast, a monster of raw appetite and destruction—had threatened to consume the entire multiverse in his cruel, titanic gluttony.

He ate whole worlds, glorying in the dying agony of their inhabitants, before the other gods joined in an unprecedented alliance to stop him.

Many of those divine beings died, and those who survived did not win an absolute victory. They could not slay Rovagug. All their might and all their wiles sufficed only to imprison him in an extraplanar dungeon, sealed behind celestial wards, known as the Dead Vault, in Golarion's core.

That much of the history was well known. But in any war of such age and magnitude, thousands of smaller stories were lost.

Inithyra's Orb, supposedly, was a powerful artifact that had belonged to a goddess slain during that war. It had been crafted millennia before Aroden's death, in an age when prophecy and omen could still be trusted, and it was said to foretell the "ultimate fate," or "ultimate fear," of whoever gazed into it. But in the battle against Rovagug, Inithyra died and was devoured, and her orb was shattered. Most of its fragments were lost with its mistress, but one large shard fell into the sea.

Some writers theorized that the shard had become an island, while others argued that it had not, but was hidden upon one. Again the translation was in dispute, and the disagreement was worsened by the fact that no island corresponding with any description of Inithyra's Orb had ever been found.

"That might mean the orb doesn't exist," Ezren said as they gathered in one of the sanctuary's meditation rooms late that afternoon, "or it might exist, but not be a literal island. Or it *does* exist, and is an island, but those searching for it have been looking in the wrong place."

"Any of those possibilities could be true. Or none of them." Wearily, Kyra poured herself a cup of tea, and another for Ezren. She didn't ask whether Amiri wanted one. The Kellid had made it clear that she considered tea a foul-tasting southern abomination and the practice of drinking hot tea in the Osirian desert ludicrous.

"When's Merisiel coming?" Amiri asked, glancing away from the pierced golden sphere she'd been tossing from hand to hand. This meditation room doubled as a sparring chamber, and it held racks of weapons and challengers' tools that staved off the barbarian's boredom during these conferences. After a few days, Amiri would exhaust the distractions available to her in each room, and then Kyra would have to choose another, or else try to ignore the Kellid pacing about the chamber like a restlessly confined tiger.

For now, however, this room's oddities held her interest. The golden sphere's two halves could be filled with alchemical reagents that mixed together when it was thrown, causing it to explode into blinding light. The one Amiri was playing with was empty, but the intricacy of its workings still fascinated her.

"Meri? She'll be here soon, I hope." In truth, Kyra had begun to worry about her wife. It didn't take that long to travel from Totra to the Sandfire Catacombs. Meri should have rejoined them by now, unless something had delayed her, or worse...

"I hope so too. Then maybe you can talk about something other than this orb that might be an island or might just be an orb." Amiri shook her head and tossed the sphere almost to the ceiling. She caught it with a slap against her palm and threw it higher on her next try. "Even if it's not an island itself, our enemies believed it was *on* an island. They wrote it into their contract. But they never said they were after Inithyra's Orb itself, only some 'known prize.' Do we care what or where the orb is, or do we only need its location so we can hunt them down?"

"We don't yet know their intentions," Kyra said. "What prize do they seek? What happens if they obtain it, or if they do not? Sarenrae herself has set me upon this task and instructed the Sunkeeper to give me this scroll. I *must* know what secrets it holds."

Kyra heard her voice harden toward the end, and consciously pushed herself to relax both her tone and her grip on the teacup. Her fingers paled where they pressed against the glazed ceramic. With just a little more pressure, either the cup or her bones might crack.

She closed her eyes and breathed deeply, striving to find serenity, or at least to keep herself from snapping at Amiri. She wasn't angry with the Kellid, not really, but there was so much she needed to do, and she felt so inadequate to do any of it.

Why me, Sarenrae? Why me, when the servants sworn to Sandfire know these scrolls far better than I? How can I be worthy of the trust you've placed in me?

"Tell me about the orb," Amiri said.

Kyra blinked. She'd never heard the northwoman express the slightest interest in Inithyra's Orb, except to mock them for spending so much time on it. "What?"

"This orb you and Ezren have been muttering about all week. You talk to each other about it all the time, but you never discuss it with me. You just send me off to patrol with the guards or spar with the blade sisters. If you can't do that, you try to distract me with toys." Amiri held the golden sphere in front of her face, staring pointedly at Kyra through its piercings, then tossed it back onto its rack with a dangerously hard thud. "You don't think I know what you're doing?"

I didn't. Kyra's cheeks burned with embarrassment that she'd been so transparent, and so uncharitable toward her friend. She had only done it because she'd been under such pressure to serve Sarenrae's command, and because she honestly had not thought Amiri cared. But, if she were honest with herself—and Sarenrae demanded that she shine an unflinching light upon her own actions—then Kyra had to admit that she had also done it because she hadn't imagined that Amiri would have anything to contribute.

She put her teacup down on a brass-stemmed side table, squared her shoulders, and faced Amiri. "I am sorry. I thought... I did not realize you wished to hear our discussions, and I did not wish to impose a subject of no interest upon you."

Amiri didn't blink. "Well, now you know differently."

"I do. Forgive me. I would value your thoughts." Kyra fumbled for her notes and leafed through the hastily scrawled pages without any clear idea of where to begin. *What would be useful for Amiri to hear?*

Off to the side, Ezren cleared his throat but offered no help. He seemed as nonplussed as Kyra was.

A ray of sunlight, falling through the sanctuary's ornately screened windows, bounced off the golden orb Amiri had thrown, and danced across the page.

It might have been chance. It might have been the hand of the divine. Kyra grasped at the hope of the latter and read the passage that the Dawnflower had touched.

"The heretic Formose is the last mortal known to have seen Inithyra's Orb. Four hundred years ago, he wrote that it was in the Arcadian Ocean, that the nearest 'true port' was Oagon, in the drowned nation of Lirgen, and that from there, one must 'chase the Star of Tyrcuval as the kersel drake chases the silver sun.'

"But no one knows where the orb lies in relation to the ruins of Oagon"—Kyra sighed—"because the Arcadian kersel drake died out centuries ago, and no known source records whether it was a diurnal or nocturnal species. Is the 'silver sun' truly the sun, or is it the moon? Is the 'silver sun' a reference to the sun in a particular season or the moon in a certain phase of its lunar cycle? We do not know, and Formose's message remains undeciphered."

Amiri thought it over, running her thumbs across the fur at the edges of her gauntlets. Despite the heat, she'd never taken them off, nor had she exchanged her well-worn boots for lighter sandals. "This kersel drake was a sea creature? Dragonkin?"

"Yes." Art and tales of the beasts still survived, though the animals themselves were gone. Kyra had studied them at length, trying to glean clues.

"They were large? Intelligent? Predatory?"

"So the accounts claim."

"Then I don't think the 'silver sun' is either sun or moon." Amiri waited to let her words sink in, then flashed the grin she'd been holding back. "It's fish."

"What?" Ezren broke in, mirroring Kyra's surprise. He set aside his empty teacup and slid a carnelian-studded brass marker into the book he'd been studying, closing it so that he could focus fully on Amiri's words.

The Kellid nodded. She seemed to be savoring this victory. "Fish. The frost drakes of Glacier Lake hunt in this way. Small fish in the deep waters will gather together into silver balls when clever predators find a way to herd them together. The lesser beasts hunt them as wolves hunt reindeer, chasing their quarry together. But the great predators, like frost drakes, hunt differently. They live so long that they learn the rhythms of the seasons, and they know where and when the big schools of fish gather. Then they terrify the fish into tight balls and feast. My people, and the Ulfen of the Lands of the Linnorm Kings, have learned to watch the great hunters, to know when the silver suns will dawn. Find the island people in those seas, and they will know the same."

"It makes sense," Kyra admitted, after she'd considered it for a moment. "Formose was a seafarer early in his life. He would have seen such hunters on the open ocean."

"The Arcadian Ocean is not what it was, though," Ezren cautioned. "Particularly not around lost Lirgen. Time has changed much in those seas, and the opening of the Eye of Abendego changed more. Just as the kersel drake is gone, whatever fish it fed upon may have vanished as well."

"It's more than we had, though." Kyra folded her notes back into her satchel and pressed her fingers together in a gesture of gratitude to Amiri. "Thank you."

"Then we're going to the Sodden Lands?" Amiri asked, accepting Kyra's thanks with a brusque shrug. A rack of sun-marked halberds was mounted against the east wall, and the Kellid wandered over to study the weapons.

"Once Meri arrives. If we have no reason to believe Inithyra's Orb lies elsewhere."

"Not easy to find a ship willing to sail that way," Amiri grunted, tracing the gold inlay on one halberd's crosspiece with a finger. "Danger on the water, danger on the land. The pirates of the Shackles might be our best bet."

"Do you know one who might take us?" Ezren asked.

Amiri's hand stilled over the halberd. "Maybe. Haven't talked to either of them in a while, but... maybe." She glanced over, chewing her lower lip. "Want me to ask? Last I heard, they were in Port Peril, but that was years back. I'm not sure either one's still alive. If they are, though, they owe me."

"Let us wait for Meri," Kyra decided. "We'll continue our research in the meantime. If we learn nothing that changes our course, then yes: we will go to Port Peril. And I will, once again, be grateful for your aid."

Three days later, Merisiel came to the Sandfire Catacombs. She hadn't reached the sanctuary under her own power; the Sarenites watching the pilgrims' path had seen her collapse at the mountain's foot and had gone down to get her.

Exhaustion hollowed the elf's pale features and dragged the grace from her limbs. She wasn't wounded, but she was badly dehydrated, so much so that Kyra feared for her life. Hours after the sanctuary's faithful had brought her in from the sun and put wet cloths over her desert-scorched skin, Meri could barely muster the strength to open her eyes.

"What happened?" Kyra asked, directing the question with equal urgency to her wife and to those who had carried her in. The Sandfire healers had stabilized Meri, and Kyra knew that the elf's life was in no immediate danger, but that only did so much to relieve her distress.

"It is fortunate Sarenrae guided you to our stronghold," the Sunkeeper answered, entering the sickroom with Meri's battered satchel and backpack in her arms. Before Kyra could ask why the Sandfire Catacombs' leader was personally carrying her wife's belongings, the Sunkeeper laid the items out on one of the patient beds.

It was, Kyra noted, the only bed in the sanctuary that was inscribed with quarantine runes. Enchanted to confine potential plagues so that their carriers could be treated without endangering the healers or other patients, such beds were a rarity, despite their usefulness. The spells to create them were not widely known and were difficult and costly to imbue into wood and metal.

She'd never seen such a device used to hold traveling packs before. "What was she carrying?"

"Something that might have killed her if she had come anywhere but here." The Sunkeeper gestured for Kyra to open the bags. "Please. Your wife uses... unusual locks. I cannot open them, and I do not wish to destroy them."

It was hard for Kyra to take her eyes off Meri, but she nodded and went to the table. The locks and knots that bound Meri's bags were gritted with desert sand. It fell onto the table in little showers as Kyra undid the fastenings, her fingers trembling in a way they never did when she was stitching wounds or extracting arrowheads from her patients' bodies.

What had Meri found? What had done this to her? Why had she brought it with her?

The backpack held mostly papers, along with a few small oddities. Kyra shuffled the pages into stacks, then set the other objects atop them. There was part of a golden crown, set with sea-clouded gems and encrusted with silt; a wooden scroll case adorned with filigreed bands of gold and half covered in barnacles; and an abalone shell bowl filled with opalescent blues, greens, and violets.

In the satchel, Kyra found a handful of crumpled maps; some bills of lading; and a thin, bloodstained book that appeared to be a journal or diary. About a third of the book's pages had been torn out.

Besides the papers, Meri had brought back a pocket-sized spyglass with stars inscribed over its body and red lenses in its eye, a compass with rubies and red garnets embedded at the cardinal and secondary points, and a star chart inscribed on the inner surface of a fish's silver-scaled skin. All three objects were etched or stamped with the same depiction of Sarenrae's winged figure, posed not against her holy sunburst, but against a crimson oval spiked with four bent prongs.

"The Akithaine Heresy?" Kyra murmured, perplexed. It couldn't have been a coincidence that Meri had brought back fragments of the heretic Formose's teachings, but... what did that have to do with her wife's condition?

"That is not what drove her to this state," the Sunkeeper said. The older woman spread her fingers wide around the abalone bowl, lifting it delicately, as though it might scorch her if she held it too long. The flame in her headdress fluttered erratically, blown low by an unfelt wind, and took on a poisoned red cast. "This is."

"What is it?" Ezren had come over to peer around Kyra's shoulder. He murmured a word, and the bowl gave off a pulse of watery phosphorescence, as of some luminous fish glimpsed in the abyssal depths. Its pearly interior grew even more enchanting, mesmerizingly so, enough that Kyra tore her gaze away out of instinctive suspicion.

Even if the Sunkeeper's flame hadn't reacted to it, and even if the Sunkeeper herself hadn't placed it on a quarantine bed to contain its contagions, she would have mistrusted anything so demanding in its beauty.

"The key to our enemies' bargain," Merisiel croaked. She sat up, weakly, gripping the bed's brass rail to hold herself upright. Bruises spread beneath her eyes, and her voice was a dust-dry rasp, but she fought to get out every word. "That's where it all began."

Chapter Thirteen
A LACK OF CONTROL

The abalone bowl bears an insidious curse. Or, rather, two curses," the Sunkeeper said, when it was clear that Merisiel had exhausted herself with her short interjection and could say no more. As yellow-robed healers fluttered around the elf, the senior cleric turned her attention back to the items she'd recovered.

"It manipulates salt and water within its owner's body, draining water and amplifying salt, to create unbearable thirst and dehydration in any creature susceptible to such pressures." Oceanic ripples of blue and green light danced across the Sunkeeper's impassive features as Ezren's magic continued to pry at the abalone bowl's secrets. "The effect might be slow or quick, depending on the whims of its controller, for the bowl retains a connection to the one who created it, and it serves its true master's will while feigning service to another.

"Would you not agree?" the Sunkeeper asked Ezren, raising her eyebrows beneath the gilded whorls and swoops of her elaborate headdress. She sounded brisk, perhaps even irritated at his unwillingness to trust her word and instead using his own analytical spells on the device.

Ezren merely nodded. He regretted the impression of rudeness that he knew he was creating, but he didn't dare interrupt his concentration to answer.

For the first time in decades, the magic was surging out of his control. Gorum's spark thrummed through every strand of his arcane weaving, imbuing it with power that Ezren could barely hold steady.

This was a simple spell. He was only trying to read the enchantments imbued in the bowl. Yet what should have been a cantrip so basic that Ezren could have done it blind drunk had, somehow, erupted into a torrent of arcane power that threatened to burst out of his grasp.

Every filament of energy in the spiderweb of his spell exploded into a kaleidoscope of sounds, images, halos of enchantment, and arcane diagrams. Ezren could glimpse the slow, dull life of the abalone amid the seaweed on its reef. He saw a tentacle lash out and seize the abalone, and watched the jetting silt of its death drift upward as the animal was pulled into the lightless deep.

A blizzard of eldritch formulae and burbled incantations swirled past, and in it he felt the wet throbbing of a profoundly alien mind, and a cold, bloodless hostility to all the short-lived scurrying vermin of the sunlit world. The taste of some nameless entity's contempt, bitter as alkali, filled his mouth so vividly that Ezren nearly choked on it.

There was more, so much more, more than he could begin to comprehend. The strands of magic began to sizzle and burn, scorching his mind as though he were grasping threads of molten steel.

Sweat soaked Ezren's hair and streamed down his forehead. It felt like it should steam from his skin, so great was the heat radiating from him. His eyes stung, but he couldn't blink lest his concentration shatter. He could hear himself panting arcane syllables, but he didn't know what they meant, or whether they were doing anything. All that registered was the breathless terror in his own voice, and the incomprehension.

The spell shattered. The room's lights erupted into multicolored fireballs, streaking soot across the ceiling as the torches went berserk in their sconces. Two of the healers' potion bottles exploded. A wild wind swept through the sickroom and was gone, leaving spilled papers and overturned medicine jars in its wake.

The abalone shell jerked out of the Sunkeeper's hands and floated into the air, then dropped just as suddenly. A yellow-robed acolyte gasped, darted forward to catch it, and then cried out in pain as she tossed it onto the quarantine bed. Blisters bloomed on her singed hands, and wisps of smoke rose from the abalone bowl.

"I'm sorry." Ezren's breath was as labored as if he'd just hauled a calf-sized boulder up a mountainside. Perspiration glued his tunic to his chest and back.

The Sunkeeper lowered her holy symbol, which she had raised defensively with both hands in front of herself. The spectral flame around the emblem dimmed but did not go out. "What did you do?"

"A mistake." Ezren swallowed, wiping the sweat from his brow. "The spell slipped from my control. Forgive me, please. The infirmities of age."

It was a weak excuse, and all the more bitter because it was the best one he had. He'd worked so hard to keep his years from slowing the others, and to conceal any sign of the aches and twinges that it cost him.

But age came for everyone who lived long enough. Incompetence, particularly incompetence in magic, was another matter. Far easier to blame his failings on some passing frailty than admit the truth: because of Gorum's cursed blood, he'd nearly lost control of a cantrip.

He could see that Kyra and Merisiel didn't believe him and was glad that Amiri wasn't in the room to witness his shame. Bad enough that the other two had seen his failure, though neither made any comment on it.

The Sunkeeper inclined her head politely and seemed to accept Ezren's excuse at face value. "As I was saying, and as I hope you will agree: the bowl bears two malign enchantments. The first is its affliction of dryness, which might easily be masked as thirst caused by the desert, or as some related ailment, such as a failure of the kidney. The one who controlled its magic could also control the severity and progression of these symptoms, and might have been able to manipulate more specific aspects. As to that, I am not certain, but it seems possible.

"The second enchantment allows the controller to send telepathic suggestions through the bowl and makes the recipient more vulnerable to such suggestions. I do not believe it is likely that those influences would take hold in one who examines the bowl warily, with care... but I am not certain of the magic's scope. That is why we have it quarantined. Those wards should prevent the bowl's master from reaching us here or eavesdropping on our conversation."

"Then it was not a true contagion you feared?" Kyra asked. She'd absorbed the Sunkeeper's words stoically, with only a single worried glance cast back at Merisiel on her sickbed. "But you said—Meri—"

"The bowl's master tried to kill her before she could come to us," the Sunkeeper said. She straightened away from the malevolently beautiful object, and the golden flame in her headdress returned to its full strength and brilliance. "It drained her body of water and spiked the salt in her blood. But, now that she is in our sanctuary, she should recover swiftly. The bowl has no hold on her here, nor will it again."

"Thank you," Kyra murmured. Ezren nodded in gratitude as well. He'd recovered enough to follow the Sunkeeper's words, though shame still burned his cheeks and the back of his neck.

He tried to focus past the emotion. Embarrassment was nothing but a distraction, one he could ill afford.

I must understand what happened. I must be able to keep control.

Rationally, he knew the failure wasn't entirely his own fault. The spark of divinity in Gorum's blood had caused it. But the god-spark wasn't likely to leave anytime soon, and Ezren had—*should* have had—the skill to maintain his spell despite that distraction.

Losing a divinatory cantrip didn't much matter, at least not where the Dawnflower's faithful could decipher the magic that Ezren could not. But what if he were in the heat of battle? What if he'd meant to conjure lightning or blind his enemies or enhance the lethality of his companions' blades?

He had to master this. He *had* to..

If he couldn't...

No. The thought was not to be countenanced. Ezren forced his attention back to the Sarenites' conversation.

"I understand why Meri brought the bowl," Kyra was saying. "But what was the purpose of carrying the other things? Surely she wouldn't have hauled them such a long distance, under such extremity, without good reason."

"To explain the bargain," Merisiel croaked, waving off a healer who was trying to coax her into swallowing something from a blue ceramic bowl. "Who Itaguen is... or was. Why he put Endio under his control. What he wanted."

Ezren couldn't see what the bowl held, but it had a pleasantly honeyed herbal scent, and wisps of steam rose from its surface. The healer was undeterred by Merisiel's feeble attempts to brush her away, and after a pointed look from Kyra, the elf conceded with a sigh and drank the concoction.

It seemed to strengthen her, for some of the hollowness left her cheeks and temples, and she sat a little straighter in her bed. Her voice remained a whisper, but she could, at least, speak without collapsing. "Papers show expeditions that House Adurguai paid for, and what was recovered from each. Four years ago, the *Merry Mermaid* was blown off course in the Fever Sea. It was thought sunk. I found Endio's insurance claim among his papers. He filed for the loss of the ship.

"In fact, however, the *Merry Mermaid* struck an island undocumented by any of their nautical charts. They were dangerously close to the Eye of Abendego by that point, and none of their instruments worked near the storm, so neither the captain nor the pilot could say with any confidence where they'd landed.

"But they found the remnants of a very strange settlement. I don't know the details. Those papers I couldn't find, not in the short time I had to look. Endio's house was near collapse, and... and our enemies were still there." Merisiel paused, her delicate features twisted by remembered revulsion.

She glanced at the abalone bowl, took a breath, and went on. "A year or so ago, the survivors of the *Merry Mermaid* returned, and Endio's insurers refused to pay, since the ship wasn't lost. I have those papers too.

"They brought back some peculiar artifacts. Those are the ones with the odd Sarenite symbol—the one that looks like the Dawnflower's mark but isn't.

"Some of those finds were so mysterious, and potentially perilous, that House Adurguai had to contract with outside appraisers under the utmost secrecy to assess their nature. I couldn't find all those records, but I took the ones I saw.

"This is where Itaguen and Curuvrakh come in. I'm still not sure what Curuvrakh is, but Itaguen is, or was, a Free Captain of the Shackles. He had an agent in Totra who kept an eye out for certain religious artifacts, and this agent sent word that the *Merry Mermaid* had found something of interest to him. The next time he was in port, Itaguen arranged to meet with Endio."

"And traded him the bowl and these other items for whatever the *Merry Mermaid* had found?" Kyra guessed.

Merisiel inclined her head. Her armor was flecked with sand that had glued to her sweat and dried, and her white hair was tawny with more windblown dust. It fell from her at the small movement, sifting across the sickbed's pristine white sheet. "Soon after that, Endio must have succumbed to their control. I found a note he'd jotted to one of his servants, warning them not to touch his 'healing wraps,' which I think were the blue jellies that I saw him and his servants putting on their faces at night.

"I imagine Itaguen or Curuvrakh told him it would cure the symptoms he'd been suffering. Once they had Endio under their control, it would have been easy to dismiss most of the servants and control those who remained.

"But their control wasn't absolute. Endio tried to resist. That was what the ward on his safe was about—it was aimed at Curuvrakh, not us. Endio was trying to prevent her from using an 'Akithaine map' that he found. We ended up destroying it instead. Curuvrakh was so angry about that she killed him.

"Endio also tried to hide some other things from them. The spyglass, the star chart, and the compass were all among the *Merry Mermaid*'s finds. He hid them inside a secret compartment in his study's clock and scrawled a note about it to anyone, I suppose, who wasn't Curuvrakh. I found the note, and I found the objects he hid, and I brought them here."

Finished with her recital, Merisiel sank back against the pillow propping her up. Kyra went to her side, stroking her wife's dirt-streaked hair. "You risked your life getting these things."

"You needed them," Merisiel replied. She closed her eyes, leaning into Kyra's touch. "What's a life for if not to give those we love what they need?"

Kyra brought her lips low to brush against the top of Merisiel's head, murmuring tenderly. Ezren, feeling like an intruder, turned his attention away from the couple and looked to the objects laid out on the quarantine bed instead.

He didn't want to risk delving into them with magic again, not after what had happened with his last attempt. Instead, after a questioning look at the Sunkeeper, he decided to learn what he could with nothing more than his wits and a magnifying glass.

The three objects that Meri said she'd found in Endio's secret cache were obviously linked, for each of them bore the four-pronged obelisk that signified Akiton, the Red Planet. As one of the nearest celestial bodies to Golarion, Akiton was of great importance to both astrologers and astronomers and could shift the reading of entire prophecies by its position in the sky.

Ezren was not familiar with any association between Akiton and Sarenrae, however, and couldn't imagine why the sun goddess would be linked to the Red Planet's iconography.

Puzzled, he reached for the star chart, hoping to answer the mystery.

The scales on the outer side of the star chart were hard and rippled, with serrated edges that threatened to draw blood when Ezren touched them. Iridescent streaks shimmered deep within each scale, as though each plate was made of paper-thin mica layers trapped inside clear crystals. The scales locked together into flexible armor, rather than overlapping, and no doubt provided considerable protection to whatever fish had worn them.

Ezren didn't recognize the species, though, nor could he glean much of the fish's likely habitat or nature from the section of skin. All he could say was that it had been large, tough, and sufficiently threatened by violence that it had developed its scales into formidable armor.

The star chart inscribed on the inside of the fish's skin was a bit easier to decipher. Ezren had made a better study of astronomy than he had of marine life, and he quickly recognized the map of Golarion's constellations.

It was tilted from the axis that he would have used in his own calculations, however, and the stars had been grouped together in unfamiliar constellations: The Spine. The Bird Mother. Eyes of the Dead.

"These are Lirgeni constellations," Ezren realized aloud. The prophets of the lost nation of Lirgen had been renowned for their ability to read the world's future in its stars. They'd failed to foresee that their empire would be destroyed by the rise of the vast, ceaseless hurricane known as the Eye of Abendego, though, and it was said that the occult order known as the Saoc Brethren, who had once ruled Lirgen, had committed mass suicide upon the destruction of their homeland.

Whether their terrible deed had been an act of despair at Lirgen's loss, or whether they'd glimpsed something unbearable in the last days of their stars that had driven them to it, the Saoc Brethren were no more. The Eye of Abendego had smashed their celestial observatories and drowned their libraries, and almost nothing of their lore survived.

The fragment that Ezren held in his hands was of inestimable scholarly value. As a historical relic, it was priceless.

But it wasn't money that had led Endio to hide it or Curuvrakh to murder him for it. What secrets did it hold?

He put the star chart back. Speculation would not serve him when he had so little information. Better to wait until everyone had time to contribute their thoughts, and Merisiel could tell them more about what she'd observed in Endio's house.

Ezren took up the compass. Its needle wobbled drunkenly, orienting to nothing when he tilted it to and fro. Either it had lost its magnetism, or it was enchanted to find a direction other than true north. Ordinarily it would have been elementary for him to determine that answer, and to decipher whatever magic the compass might have held. But now...

Returning the compass to the table, Ezren picked up the telescope instead.

Superficially, it resembled a navigator's spyglass, but on closer examination, Ezren noted that it lacked the secondary internal mirror that would have reoriented the image for the viewer. This telescope was made to observe the night sky, not the day. Yet its lenses were tinted so deeply that they compromised its function, so either it was enchanted, or it was merely ceremonial.

"It doesn't work," Ezren said, unsure whether he meant the telescope or his own arcane arts. Again he suppressed a pang of frustration. One simple spell would tell him so much, but he dared not reach for the first tool in his arsenal.

An uncharacteristic swell of anger rose in Ezren's throat, and though he swallowed it, the heat lingered in his chest. *Curse you, Gorum.*

Merisiel saved him with a distraction.

"I don't think it's really a spyglass," she said, looking over from her bed. Kyra had moved half a step away to the bedside table, where she was crushing herbs in a mortar for another bowl of the healers' restorative draft. The rhythmic grinding of her white stone pestle punctuated the elf's quiet words. "You're right—it doesn't work. What you might not have seen is that those ornamental bands around the shaft can be detached. They have hidden teeth inside. Unfolded, they look like keys."

"To what?" Amiri asked, appearing in the doorway. The Kellid's skin shone with a light sheen of sweat, and she had the beginnings of a bruise spreading across her upper left arm. Undoubtedly because of that, she seemed in high spirits.

"Glad you made it," she said offhandedly to Merisiel. "I would've come earlier, but the sun sisters didn't want me disturbing you until they were sure you'd survive. I suppose they're sure now, since they let me in. Did it go well in Totra? I see you brought back some loot."

"Well enough," Merisiel said, managing a weak but genuine smile for the Kellid. "It's good to see you too."

Kyra poured hot water over the herbs she'd crushed and strained the steaming liquid into another bowl, then carried it over for Merisiel to drink. "You were telling us about the keys in the spyglass?"

She doesn't want Merisiel wasting her strength before she tells us what she needs to, Ezren thought. From one angle, it might seem like a peculiar sort of protectiveness, but he understood. Merisiel had nearly killed herself bringing these things back. She'd kill herself to explain them to Kyra too. Better if she finished her tale with strength to spare, so that she could rest and recover properly.

"Yes. The keys." Merisiel took the bowl and drank without protest, but it didn't seem to restore her as dramatically as the first draft had. Even with the medicine's aid, she was tiring. "I don't know what they unlock. I couldn't find anything they matched in Endio's house. I hoped Ezren might be able to tell us the answer if they happened to be enchanted."

All their eyes turned to Ezren.

He cleared his throat, conscious of the clammy dampness of his sweat-soaked tunic clinging to the small of his back. The weight of their expectation was crushing. "I cannot. At the moment, at least."

Merisiel gazed at him for a silent moment, her thin elven features inscrutable, then gestured with her drinking bowl to the papers that

Kyra had piled alongside the other objects. "In that case, we'll have to try another path.

"Not everything from the *Merry Mermaid* went to Itaguen and Curuvrakh, nor was it all auctioned to the great houses of Totra. Some went to other dealers. I didn't have time to read all the ledgers, but I took the ones I could find. The cheapest pieces of junk, the things no one thought worth sorting through, were sold in bulk to a dealer named Skrit in Port Peril.

"I've fenced enough goods in my day to feel confident that anything we'd be interested in, if our enemies haven't already claimed it, is likely to have been passed to this Skrit. Rich dealers are meticulous about what they'll handle. They examine every enchantment and test every bit of gilt. But no one looks closely at what goes to a junk dealer."

"Did you not say that your friends were in Port Peril?" Kyra asked Amiri.

The Kellid shrugged. Eying the food that the healers had brought for Merisiel, she reached over and casually took a bowl of oblong, reddish dates. "You don't mind?"

Merisiel shook her head. Amiri popped a date into her mouth and chewed it, then nodded to herself and ate another. "I did say that. If they're still alive, and anywhere on land, it's most likely to be Port Peril."

"Not an easy journey, or a short one," Ezren said. Reaching Port Peril would entail either a months-long trek across northern Garund, alternating between forbidding mountains and harsh desert, or a sea voyage across nearly the full length of the Inner Sea, down Garund's western coast, and around the Eye of Abendego.

"Our enemies have the advantage by sea." Merisiel handed her empty bowl back to Kyra and reclined against her pillows, surrendering to her weariness. "Itaguen has a ship. Fast, maybe enchanted. Curuvrakh seemed to think it would get them to Inithyra's Orb more swiftly than any other vessel they might find."

"Then you must not travel by sea," the Sunkeeper said. "The Dawnflower herself has deemed your task of the utmost importance. You cannot fail. If you cannot reach Port Peril first by ordinary means, then we shall have to find extraordinary ones.

"There is a wizard in Myrissos who can help. He is a recluse, and not friendly to outsiders, but he owes a favor to our order." The Sunkeeper turned to Ezren. "Whether he can help, however, depends on your skill. He has a spell that might bring you directly to Port Peril. I believe he could be persuaded to share it if you are willing to learn. But the casting of it will likely rest on you. And if you cannot control your magic..."

"I will," Ezren said firmly. "I can." *I must.*

Chapter Fourteen
MYRISSOS

A day and a night after Merisiel reached the Sandfire Catacombs, the companions left the sanctuary to seek passage to Port Peril.

Amiri was glad to go. The temple perched in the mountains had begun to feel like a cage. When the furnace wind of the desert flats hit her in the face, it felt like freedom, and the rank smell of her unwashed camel was a welcome return to nature, away from the sun sisters' incense-burning fires and stifling sacred candles.

She kept to herself for much of the journey, refreshed by the solitude and the challenge of pitting herself against the elements, as much as she could within the limits of the soft travel that the others preferred. While they slept in tents, Amiri turned her face up to the sky and stars. While they ate bean-and-sausage stews for dinner and porridge with dried berries for breakfast, Amiri hunted snakes and sand boars for her meals. She wasn't fool enough to let her body weaken for lack of nourishment, and so shared their food as much as necessary, but neither was she going to let her skills rust for lack of use.

Her time in the wilderness was restorative, but she doubted any of her companions felt the same way. They all seemed to be battling demons during their travels, and they each did so alone.

Kyra prayed. The cleric had always prayed at dawn and sunset, and occasionally at noon, but now she prayed even in the hours between, and at night, long after the sun had gone. She prayed for guidance and for strength and to be worthy of the trust Sarenrae had placed in her.

So often did she pray, and for so long, that Merisiel was left to ride in silence beside her for hours. When she wasn't praying, Kyra was as solicitous toward her wife as ever—maybe more so, since Merisiel was still recovering from her ordeal with the abalone bowl's curse and remained more fragile than usual—but Amiri noticed the long and lonely stretches when the elf had nothing to do besides gaze into the wilderness as they rode or pore over the merchant's papers in camp.

Ezren spent the journey buried in his books. He read in camp and in the saddle, wagering that his camel would have enough sense to cover for its rider's lack of attention. The wizard muttered gibberish in his sleep, when he did sleep, and mixed strange potions that seemed meant to augment his arcane abilities somehow or, perhaps, dampen them. Amiri wasn't sure, and he never offered an explanation.

She didn't ask. Let her friends fight their battles in solitude if that was what they wanted. Amiri wasn't one to intrude, at least not in such struggles as these.

As they moved northwest, sunbaked rock changed to sand, and to rock again, and sand again. Shimmers in the distance might have been the legendary Glazen Sheets, a stretch of sharp-edged salt beds that were said to resemble glass, or even to *be* massive sheets of glass left in the wake of some forgotten catastrophe. Or they might only have been heat rising from the sun-scorched wastes, veiling a prosaic danger with wonder.

Kill you just as dead either way.

Too often, Amiri thought, the power of the natural world failed to command the respect that was its due. People cowered before arcane tyrants and feared the fury of the gods, but cold and heat and hunger killed more than any necromancer's skeletal horde.

Even so, she wondered: *Were* those the Glazen Sheets? What would it be like, riding through a landscape where the already lethal sun was amplified by an infinity of lenses tilting into one another? Could anything of this world survive there? If not, was it a place haunted by creatures of pure light and fire?

She stared at the white flashes on the horizon, brooding and wondering, until the last glimpse of what might have been the legendary glasslands—or, then again, might not—vanished behind walls of sun-bleached stone and rolling dunes of sand.

Two weeks later, they came to Myrissos, the hamlet where, according to the Sunkeeper, the hermit scholar who might be able to help them dwelled.

It was a tiny, picturesque village. Just a handful of fisherfolk's cottages, built from sun-faded yellow stone and shaded by billowing white awnings, overlooking a dazzling azure sea. In the market square, a trio of old women played hand drums and reed flutes to an audience of children and sleepy goats.

Despite the dangers of the wild, and the apparent lack of any larger settlement nearby that might have sheltered the village, Myrissos didn't appear to have posted any guards. Amiri and her companions rode straight into the hamlet without even being questioned.

One of the women playing in the square lowered her flute as their camels approached. She had a friendly, toothless smile and an unhurried kindliness that invited trust, despite Amiri's instinctive wariness. "What brings you to our village, friends?"

"The Sunkeeper of the Sandfire Catacombs sent us to seek the wizard Elothain," Kyra answered, nudging her camel over. Her manner was polite, but the cleric couldn't disguise her urgency and didn't try to. "She said we might find him here."

The old woman's smile flickered, then deepened until her eyes almost vanished into the creases of her light brown skin. "Lothi? Yes, you might find him if he wants you to." She put the reed flute back to her lips and blew a series of three high, trilling notes. The sound reverberated through the village, earning a drowsy ear flick from one of the goats.

"Go to the rock wall, there," the woman said, lowering her flute. She nodded toward an old wall of eroded stones that stretched out into the sea. Barnacles dotted the rocks near the waterline, and brown strands of seaweed bobbed along the waves. "He'll come to meet you if he feels like it. If he doesn't, best you move on. Don't try to press Lothi."

"Thank you," Kyra said. She began to turn her camel away, then paused. "Where might we stay in Myrissos? Is there an inn?"

"The widow Osago takes boarders sometimes," the flute player replied, pointing out a nearby house distinguished by the row of large ceramic vessels lined up against its front wall. "Myrissos has no inn. Too small, and Lothi likes being able to chase away anyone whose company he doesn't want to keep."

"I'll deal with the widow," Merisiel said, already sliding from her saddle. "Leave the camels with me. Go talk to your wizard."

"We won't be gone long," the cleric promised, leading the others toward the rocks by the sea.

Amiri didn't see how Kyra could be confident of that. There was no sign of this Elothain. They spread out their saddle blankets and sat in the sun on the rocks, but the wizard seemed to be in no hurry to meet them. The day wore on in heat and stillness, and Amiri soon found herself irritated by the tedium.

Just as she'd begun to get back to her feet, intending to abandon the others to this pointless vigil and find something more useful to do with her time, she spotted a wiry, gray-haired man climbing the slope toward them.

He wore the same simple linen tunic and loose-fitting pants as the other villagers in Myrissos and carried nothing but a bucket and a fishing pole. A conical hat shaded his eyes from the sun, and a utility knife in a plain fishskin sheath was strapped to his waist. He looked a little older than Ezren, but his movements were vigorous and sure. Faded tattoos covered his arms and crawled up the sides of his neck, and he wore a series of fishhooks as earrings in both lobes.

"Mind if I fish?" he asked the group as he ambled up to the rocks.

"Not at all." Kyra drew her saddle blanket aside, brushing away the stray camel hairs it had left on the stones. "We do not mean to be in your way. We're only waiting for someone."

"Oh?" The man settled into the cleared space, sitting cross-legged. He threaded a bit of raw meat onto his hook, stood, and cast it casually into the water. Amiri, peering into the man's bucket, saw that it held several corked jugs and no room for fish.

"Elothain." Kyra watched the man steadily as she spoke the name. "The Sunkeeper of the Sandfire Catacombs thought we might find him here. Sarenrae herself has charged us with our quest, and we need his aid to complete it. Our task is of the utmost importance."

"It does sound that way," the man agreed, gazing out over the shining waves. He pulled his line back in and flicked it out once again, aiming for the calm beyond the froth. "But what if he doesn't care to help you? I've heard this Elothain can be reclusive."

Kyra's smile softened into genuine warmth. "Not that reclusive. The first person we spoke to knew who he was, and where we might find him. Even for a peaceful place, Myrissos is remarkably unguarded. The people seem to trust that they have a protector at hand, should they need one. I suspect the wizard is not quite the hermit that his reputation claims."

The man slid his feet out of his woven reed sandals and stretched his toes in the sun. There were tattoos on the tops of his feet too. He wedged the fishing pole between two rocks, put a small pillow against a tall stone, and leaned back comfortably, as relaxed as if he were entirely alone. Reaching into the bucket, he pulled out a jug for himself and offered another to Kyra. "Perhaps not, where the village is concerned. But to outsiders?"

Kyra demurred with a small shake of her head. "I hope he'll understand that we wouldn't have troubled him if there were no need."

"Your need might not be my need," the man said, tipping the brim of his conical hat up so that he could study Kyra and the rest. He cracked open his jug, and the smell of good beer wafted out. Taking a long swig, he leaned back again on his stone. "But do your best to convince me. I don't think Adira would have given you my name if she believed your cause undeserving."

"The Sunkeeper?" Amiri asked.

"Adira, the Sunkeeper, yes. She always had an overdeveloped sense of duty. I retired to the sun and surf; she retired to... do even more work than we ever did adventuring." Elothain sighed, looking back to the sea. "Well, the luxury of retirement is that you get to choose what makes you happy, even if what makes you happy is taking on more than your fair share of the world's worries. Frankly, I'm content to shirk my share, given the chance. But tell me what you want, and I'll decide whether I care."

"We are racing our enemies to Port Peril." Kyra told the tale of her first meeting with Itaguen in Enqatis, how they'd rushed to Totra to warn Ezren of his peril, and how they'd learned that the danger was greater than they'd feared. She described their meeting with the Sunkeeper and what they had learned in the Sandfire Catacombs.

Elothain listened with interest, sipping his beer. Amiri wished Kyra hadn't declined his offer or that he'd extended it to any of the others after the cleric turned him down. It was hot in the sun, and those jugs had a tempting frost on them. Apparently the wizard wasn't above using his magic for such luxuries. "The dead merchant had Lirgeni constellations and symbols of the Akithaine Heresy among his prizes? Curious. Most curious. I always thought... well, never mind what I thought. Those are mysteries for younger souls to solve.

"Anyway, you've told me what your quest means to Sarenrae, and that's all well and good. But what does it mean to *you*?"

"The Dawnflower's charge is my duty," Kyra replied. "She has instructed us to do this task, and so it must be done."

"You sound so much like Adira." Elothain's mouth quirked in a way that suggested it was, at most, half a compliment. He glanced at Ezren. "You?"

"The Salt Cartel are old foes, and I bear them little love," the white-haired wizard said, "yet what befell Endio of House Adurguai was a fate no one should suffer. The cruelty and monstrosity of our opponents is... troubling. I had hoped that fact, perhaps as well some sense of professional collegiality—if I may be so presumptuous—might persuade you to aid us."

"Mm. But that's about me, not you, isn't it?" Elothain didn't wait for Ezren to answer. He turned to Amiri instead. "What's your reason?"

Amiri shrugged. "Don't let the bastards win."

Elothain tipped his hat back, regarding her more squarely, and laughed. "What?"

"You don't let the bastards win. That's what I've always believed, and how I've always lived my life. Go your own way, let other people live their lives as they please, don't go looking for trouble. But if there's some bastard picking a quarrel or lording it over the weak or murdering people who can't fight back, then you smash his teeth in. Because you don't let the bastards win. Not when there's anything you can do about it."

"Ah. I see. Well, as it happens, I agree." Elothain raised his jug in a toast and tipped the bucket her way.

Amiri didn't have to be asked twice. She grabbed a jug for herself, pulled the cork, and took a long drink. The beer was as cold and refreshing as she'd dreamed. As its glow spread through her chest, the midday sun no longer seemed so oppressive, but welcoming and warm. The sea was a dazzling marvel, the ocean breezes a joy. She understood why a wizard might turn his back on the world to sit here and cast lines into the water.

Elothain collected his fishing pole, which had lost its bait without snaring any fish, and rested it over his shoulder. He finished his jug and dropped it back into his bucket, alongside the two that hadn't been opened. "I won't take you to Port Peril. I don't like that place, and I don't care to see it again. But I will teach your colleague the secret of doing it himself, if that suffices."

"Yes. Thank you. I would be most grateful for the opportunity to study with you." Ezren dug his snake-headed cane into the rocks so he could lean on it as he stood.

"No trouble. As your friend so wisely said: can't let the bastards win."

Chapter Fifteen
ELOTHAIN'S LESSON

I am, truly, in your debt," Ezren said as he followed Elothain along a narrow trail to his home in the bluffs overlooking the sea. It was a steep walk, and though the sun had lowered behind the olive groves, and twilight's shadows spread their welcome coolness across the hills, sweat ran down Ezren's back.

The others had gone back to Myrissos, leaving Ezren to discuss spellcraft with their new acquaintance. None of them could aid him with his arcane studies. This was Ezren's task alone.

"No, you aren't. Perhaps you will be, but not yet. As yet, I haven't given you anything," Elothain replied, amused. Nimbly the other man picked his way through the chalky stones to the unassuming cottage that waited at the trail's end.

It was a small house, simple enough to be a shepherd's or olive farmer's abode, with whitewashed walls covered by climbing flowers in yellows and pinks that faded to white and purple as night fell around them. A donkey grazed on the hillside below the house, and white-necked doves nestled in the tree branches near the front door.

Elothain held open his door. With a casual gesture, he summoned a dancing spark that flittered like a firefly about the room, lighting the sweet-scented oil lamps that dotted the interior. "Shall we begin?"

"Please." In truth, Ezren was so weary he could scarcely drag one foot in front of the other. He would have preferred to begin his studies in the morning with a fresher head, but the urgency of their mission allowed no such luxuries.

And, despite his apprehension about the effects of Gorum's spark, Ezren found himself electrified by the prospect of learning such a powerful new spell as this. Teleportation magic was legendary, but few had the strength or skill to attempt such a challenging spell.

Fewer still had the opportunity to try. Those who had the secret of teleportation guarded it jealously, for it was among the most lethal weapons an enemy could possess, and one couldn't control where knowledge might go once it was released. Ezren had known a few wizards who held the spell, but none who would share it.

Now, at last, he might have his chance to learn. If, and only if, he could maintain control.

Elothain cleared a half-finished taxidermy tray from his kitchen table, then dragged over a second chair for Ezren to sit. "I hope you don't mind working amid clutter. I never could manage a spotless desk, even in my student days. Probably the first sign I wasn't meant for success as a scholar."

"You can't have been that bad. You have a teleportation spell, after all." Ezren sat with a little grunt, casting a curious glance over Elothain's unfinished project. The tray held three small fish formed of stuffing over wire frames. Each had a head made from soft white plaster and eyes of colored glass. They were accompanied by meticulous sketches depicting the fish that would presumably go over each frame, and the knives and hooks laid out in a smaller secondary tray were as precisely arranged as any surgeon's instruments.

"I *have* it. That doesn't mean I can *cast* it. I'm afraid I might have misled your friends a bit." Elothain rummaged through a closet and came back with another tray, this one holding a dozen or so small fish pinned to a cork board under glass, like butterflies.

He fiddled with the bottom of the box. A hidden compartment slid out, revealing parchment sheets so thin and fragile that they were translucent even by the magical lights' dim glow. "It's sometimes advantageous for me to claim to be a better wizard than I am, but the truth is that I have never had the skill to decipher these scrolls, much less master the spells they contain. I kept them as mementos from my adventuring days, and perhaps because the embers of my old ambitions never completely died."

Setting the sheets before Ezren, Elothain gave him a steady, assessing look. "Adira vouched for you, and I trust you won't use the spell for ill. But intent is one thing, and competence another. This is no easy magic. Are you capable of it?"

“I don’t know,” Ezren replied. He felt that he should be nettled by the question’s bluntness, but he was too tired to take offense, and he had wondered the same himself. A month before, if he’d been able to turn his full concentration to mastering the spell’s formulae with as much time as he needed and all the resources of his private library to draw upon, he thought he could have done it.

But with the god-spark assailing his every effort, the weariness of the road blunting his mind, and only these scraps of parchment in a stranger’s house to guide him...

“I must at least try,” Ezren said. He took out his spellbook, turning to a blank page. “I must try.”

“Will you allow me to help?” Elothain asked.

At Ezren’s nod, the other wizard went back to the closet and returned with a book bound in fraying blue fabric. Loose papers had been wedged between its pages, dense with diagrams and notes. Most were in the same neat, even handwriting as the labels on the taxidermy trays, but a few had been pulled from other sources.

“On and off over the decades since I came to Myrissos, I’ve tried cracking that one, along with the other spells I kept from those days. Never succeeded. But I came close, a few times, and there might be something in here that helps you.” Elothain spread the pages before Ezren, summoning another hovering light to better illuminate his notes.

Ezren nodded gratefully at the consideration. Not only at the notes, but that he was spared the task of conjuring his own cantrip to see.

He leafed through the pages. Elothain’s observations were keen and insightful, the work of a brilliant mind. Ezren raised a bushy white eyebrow. “You say you never mastered this?”

The wiry man shrugged. A self-deprecating smile creased the corners of his eyes. “Perhaps I lacked the courage to test my intuitions.”

That was logical enough. The smallest mistake in a teleportation could cause disaster. Yet a wizard capable of making these analyses, then drawing the connections between the arcane filaments in theory, must have been tormented by the uncertainty of never knowing whether his conclusions would actually work in practice.

In that way, Ezren supposed, his arrival in Myrissos might have been a blessing to Elothain: an opportunity, at last, to find out whether he'd been right all along. "May I, then?"

"Please." Elothain's eyes lit with eagerness. "Do you agree with my view on the Gymelen Steps?"

"Yes. I wouldn't have thought to make that connection myself, but once you pointed it out, it seemed entirely intuitive." Ezren tapped a diagram on another page. "And your use of the Veshari-Charthagnion Ring is brilliant."

Elothain dipped his head modestly, unable to conceal the flush of happiness in his cheeks. "You're too kind. I don't ordinarily like to rely on Chelaxian innovations, but—"

"But it's *perfect*. It's an elegant solution to the problem of organizing so many location anchors separately, and without allowing their vibrations to interfere with one another. Again, I wouldn't have thought to apply the rings to this purpose, given they were originally devised for amplifying orchestral sounds, but—yes, it truly does seem a perfect solution." Ezren looked up from the pages to their creator. "If I am able to carry off this spell, it will only be because I had the benefit of your work."

"I shall try not to distract you from further study." Elothain tilted his head at Ezren's satchel, which he'd left sitting next to the door. Papers spilled from the top of the overstuffed bag, and the objects beneath could be glimpsed amid the shadows in its mouth. "Do you mind? It'll keep me occupied as I pretend not to panic at the prospect that I've steered you wrong."

"Not at all. I'd be honored if you chose to share your insights." Ezren saw no reason to conceal his efforts from Elothain. The Sunkeeper trusted the man, and Kyra had already told him everything about their journey. Besides, Elothain had offered to share his precious teleportation scroll with Ezren and his companions, to say nothing of his own personal notes.

It was the smallest of courtesies to permit him, in return, to study the oddities that Merisiel had taken from Totra. If anything, judging by the quality of Elothain's notes on the teleportation scroll, Ezren was getting the best of that bargain.

Elothain took out the objects and arrayed them on the kitchen counter, then tugged at his fish-hook earrings as he surveyed the collection. "Where should I begin?"

"Wherever you like." Ezren hesitated, then admitted, "I cannot speak to the significance of each piece. I haven't delved any of them myself."

"No?" Elothain's eyebrows shot up.

"No." Ezren flinched inwardly. He did trust the other wizard, as much as he could trust anyone on such short acquaintance, but he had no wish to explain Gorum's dubious gift. It felt too private, and too confusing. "I am... cursed." That, he judged, was true, if not the whole truth. "Great power fluctuates through my spells, but I have little ability to control it. None, to be honest. The most minor cantrip threatens to overwhelm me. It has been... difficult.

"It is the reason I have not tried to pry into the secrets those objects hold, though my investigations are hampered without the aid of that magic. But I dare not. The power that floods my weavings is too dangerous to risk."

Elothain studied the pieces on the table. He put the telescope to his eye, traced the lines on the star chart, and hefted the abalone shell that had nearly killed Merisiel. Then he put them all down and looked back to Ezren. "How were you planning to cast the teleportation, then?"

"I had hopes, but not a plan," Ezren answered wryly.

Elothain ticked his short, salt-cracked fingernails lightly against the countertop. "You say the problem is that too much power answers your call, and you cannot hold it?"

"Precisely." Ezren pushed back his chair and rubbed his chest. There was no mark where Gorum's god-spark had entered him, and nothing he could feel as a distinct point of impact in his body, but sometimes he fancied that an ache lingered there, like the memory of a long-healed wound.

"Are you familiar with the strix windriders, or the wave-surfers of Arcadia?"

"No. Neither." Ezren knew that the strix were a race of winged beings who lived among the arid, wind-carved rocks of western Cheliax, where they were invoked as a byword for terror by human settlers in the region, and he knew that the distant continent of Arcadia was connected to his own land of Avistan by a chain of scattered islands, whose inhabitants plied the seas as easily as others rode horses. Though the islanders might not, he supposed, consider themselves to be Arcadians, they were often referred to in Avistan by that name.

But the nuances of either culture were not well known to him, and he had never heard of the groups to which Elothain referred.

"They follow similar philosophies," Elothain explained. "The windriders spread their wings to soar on the gusts that sweep through their skies, and the wave-surfers ride the sea's swells on thin wooden planks. With meditative calm, they skim over these natural forces, which would surely crush them the instant they lost their balance.

"I studied them, and studied with them, because I saw a link between their arts and mine. I never was a very good wizard, as I've told you. But by learning from the windriders and the wave-surfers, I developed an ability to focus on only the most crucial elements of my spells. When attempting great spells, I never tried to harness the full force of the magic. I hadn't the skill or the intuition to weave it quickly enough, and it would have destroyed me. So I played fast and loose. Steering lightly along the surface, as the riders did with wind and wave."

He gave Ezren a self-deprecating shrug. "My masters would have slapped me for such sloppy technique. They would have said, correctly, that such carelessness could easily prove lethal. But it *worked*. When I had no choice but to reach for power that was beyond my control, I could ride it just long enough to get most of what I needed. Good enough, most of the time. Even if it did come with odd side effects now and then.

"Do you suppose you'd like to learn?"

"Yes," Ezren said.

"Let's start with this." Elothain brought over the ruby- and garnet-studded compass from Endio's house. Inscriptions in pearlescent red enamel gleamed upon its inner and outer bronze surfaces, and its glass face was unclouded by any mark of time or seawater. "Just a basic delving.

"Don't worry about controlling all the magic. Let whatever you don't need slip out of your grasp. It'll feel strange at first, since we've been taught from the beginning to control every wisp of arcane energy we call, but it is the essence of this technique. Relax your control without relinquishing it. Hold only what you must, and let the rest flow free."

Ezren inhaled and exhaled, centering his awareness using the meditative techniques Kyra had taught him. They weren't a standard practice in his arcane training, but they felt right for this. When he could feel his breath and heartbeat slowing, and a calmness at his core, he reached for the compass and his magic alike.

Send three strands into Ustagiel's Circle, let them be cast out according to the circle's coordinates, and wrap them about the object to be studied. He could see the words before his eyes, just as they'd been printed in the first textbook he'd studied. The spell was a simple one: three threads of magic gathered into a standard arcane lens-circle, refracted back out again, and extended around the focal object. Each of the refracted strands picked up different nuances and vibrations from the object, enabling a clever wizard to infer much about its enchantments.

That was how it was supposed to work. But when Ezren reached for a wisp of arcane power, a torrent answered his call. The force was so sudden and intense that he was astonished it didn't physically hurl him against the wall. It was as if a waterfall had opened from the heavens, pounding him with its fury.

Hold only what you must, and let the rest flow free.

He needed three strands. Only three strands. With a titanic effort, Ezren separated three strands from the rest, and did his utmost to ignore the power that raged around it.

Send them into Ustagiel's Circle...

It should have been trivial to sketch the circle and its emblems in the air, and to direct the unseen strands into its center with a wave of one hand. Before the god-spark, he'd routinely done it without thinking, as a harpist might play scales before attempting anything that required real concentration.

This time Ezren had to try twice, and dismiss both uselessly deformed attempts, before he managed a passable circle on his third try. Both times he felt magic slipping out of his grasp on the failed efforts and bursting, uncontrolled, into the world. He ignored it.

Trying to recapture the lost energy would have been a fool's errand even if he weren't impaired, and he still had a spell to finish.

Wrap them about the object to be studied.

Catching the strands took another monumental effort. They writhed in his grasp like electrified serpents, thrashing out of Ezren's grip.

When he did grab hold of them, they lashed against him with inconceivable strength. Sweating with the exertion, he shoved three incandescent bolts of energy into the circle and, as soon as they fragmented, thrust them around the compass.

Dizzying images assailed him. There were no subtle vibrations to be interpreted through the shifting sigils of Ustagiel's Circle. A cacophony of foreign cries, shouts, and blurred scenes passed before Ezren's eyes, wrenched from the compass by power beyond anything he'd ever commanded.

He saw a circle of heavily cloaked people with brilliant blue-green wings and iridescent red feathers at their necks. Ezren couldn't tell whether the wings were a natural part of their bodies or merely ornaments fixed to their floor-length robes, and though the figures seemed to stand on two legs, he couldn't be sure of that, either.

They wore featureless masks of silver and skypearl, with bulging, segmented domes of red glass over their eyes that gave them a monstrous, insectoid appearance. Together they chanted before an enormous, red-tinted window, through which Ezren glimpsed a sea of stars far different from those he knew. Scarlet clouds swirled across those alien stars, and Ezren felt a sharp prick of apprehension for no reason he could name.

The image flashed and broke into glittering shards that burned away into vapor. Another spun into view: the same room, empty but for scorched feathers blowing across the floor and bloodstains on the walls. The compass lay amid the wreckage, and Ezren saw that the stars inscribed on its face matched those that had been visible through the window earlier. That view was black and empty now, though, and white cracks splintered across the glass.

The glass shattered. Water poured in, crushing the room's contents, and Ezren felt a resonant pulse of its benthic cold travel through his spell.

Slowly, swirling with clouds of debris that a moment ago had been glass and feathers and instruments, the water settled. The darkness did not lift, but Ezren's senses seemed to shift so that he could perceive shapes and movements as they disturbed currents in the water. He knew, intuitively, that what he sensed was taste and smell and feeling, but his brain still interpreted it, somehow, as sight.

This is not my world. The uselessness of his habitual senses made that clear. Yet still Ezren's spell went on, and he witnessed what he could never have seen with his own eyes.

A slimy tentacle shot from the unseen ocean beyond the broken window. It seized the compass, the spyglass, and other objects that Ezren could not perceive. He felt a malevolent glee radiate from the tentacled scavenger as it withdrew its prizes, and the cruel joy of hostility satisfied.

Again the image flashed and broke. This time, the magic dissipated, and no further visions appeared.

Ezren blinked, looking confusedly about Elothain's cottage. All the windows were tinted red, as were the small glass ornaments that had dangled over them.

The sunbrowned wizard was peering into his coffee cup with a wry twist to his mouth. He tipped the cup toward Ezren. "It's salt. All the water in the cottage has turned to seawater. Happened midway through your spell, shortly after all the glass in the house went red. Even the coffee's turned. I haven't checked the cistern outside, but I'm hoping either the magic didn't reach that far, or you've got some other spell to purify it. I don't fancy having to haul that much water back up here by hand."

"I'm sorry," Ezren said. His throat was rough and dry, and he cleared it awkwardly. "I didn't mean to do that."

"I suspect a lot of things happened that you didn't mean to do." Elothain chuckled, crossing the kitchen to dump his salt coffee out the window. "I've never seen such arcane flaring. But it seemed that you were able to hold what you needed, and that the spell succeeded. Did it?"

"Yes. Not precisely as I intended, but... yes." Ezren rubbed his eyes.

"Do you believe you can try the teleportation?"

"Yes. If I can learn it."

"Then begin," Elothain said, gesturing to the materials he'd laid out on the table.

Ezren picked up the aged parchment scroll that bore the teleportation spell. Though the parchment itself was brittle as a dried butterfly's wing, its rich red ink looked fresh and vibrant, as though the letters had been set to the page mere moments ago. A golden shimmer passed across the arcane inscription as he brought it before Elothain's enchanted light, and he felt the magic's reverberation in his hands.

I can do this. I can.

He closed his eyes, gathering his concentration and extending his senses to encompass the intangible vibrations of magic in the scroll. Then he exhaled in a long, controlled breath, as he'd taught himself when he learned to cast his first, most elementary spells.

Clear your mind. Center your thoughts. There is only the magic, and the magic is all.

Ezren opened his eyes, feeling more like himself than he had in weeks, and dipped a quill into the inkwell Elothain had lent him. Holding it poised over his spellbook, he turned the full force of his intellect to the scroll and began taking notes.

Dawn was softening the sky over a white-laced black sea when Ezren came back to his senses. His back ached abominably, and his eyes blurred with weariness, but elation filled his soul.

He had done it. He *understood*. The spell was his. He had recorded and annotated it in his spellbook, and he was confident that he fully understood the theory. All that remained was to test it in practice.

Elothain was in the kitchen, brewing a pot of intensely dark coffee. By the stained cups dotted around Ezren's satchel, it wasn't his first.

"I suppose I should be sleeping," the wizard admitted, catching Ezren's look, "but I can't. Or I don't want to. Care for a cup? The cistern wasn't affected after all."

"One," Ezren allowed. He stretched his fingers, working out the stiffness of the night's writing. "I should be sleeping too. But I can't either. Or don't want to."

"It reminds me of my student days. The joy of discovery, the thrill of possibility. And the extremely late nights spent trying to cram more information into an overstuffed brain." Elothain brought over a pair of cups, both filled with midnight-black coffee.

Ezren was surprised, when he sipped his, that it was as sweet as it was strong. The taste wasn't unpleasant, but it was nothing he'd tried before. A sap or cane syrup, he guessed. It gave him a welcome buzz of energy, driving his tiredness away.

"You must allow me to thank you for the privilege." Elothain motioned toward the kitchen counter, where he'd laid out the star chart, red-lensed telescope, and other items Merisiel had claimed from Endio's house. "Ever since I settled in Myrissos, I assumed my hopes of making a mark on the world were gone. By choice, mostly. Ambitious wizards generally meet bad ends.

"Of course, as you know, those hopes never died entirely. I'd have sold those spell scrolls long ago if they had. But I never thought I would have the chance to brush against something so profound—so momentous—as this." Elothain shook his head in wonder, struck into silence as he looked upon the objects cluttering his counter. He cleared his throat, unable to keep an awed tremor from his words. "Now I understand why the Akithaine Heresy was stamped out so forcefully. I understand why Sarenrae herself charged you with this task. And I remember why I chose the path of obscurity for myself. I wish you well, my friend, but I fear for you."

Ezren raised his bushy eyebrows. "Is Itaguen that powerful?"

"Itaguen?" Elothain coughed up coffee. Wiping his eyes, he gave Ezren a baffled look. "No, my friend. It isn't Itaguen. Didn't you see the truth in your own delvings? You're on the trail of the Red Fang. The weapon that Inithyra supposedly glimpsed in her orb, the one that was the gods' ultimate fear. The weapon that could destroy the world."

Chapter Sixteen
FORLORN

No one asked why I'm *here.*

Merisiel threw her knife into the eye of a driftwood log thirty feet away, sinking the blade in so deeply she thought she might break it if she tried to pry it out. Nevertheless, she stalked across the gritty sand and jerked the hilt back and forth, taking a perverse joy in the strain she felt through the metal.

She wasn't angry with the wizard. He hadn't even known she was there; how could he have known to ask for her thoughts?

No, what rankled was that Kyra hadn't even seen fit to tell her about their encounter with Elothain when they came back to the village. Merisiel had learned about the wizard from Amiri. Her own wife had barely said a word, deeming it more important to pray for guidance than to spare a moment for Merisiel.

She yanked the knife out of the driftwood, almost disappointed it hadn't snapped, and flipped it over her fingers as she stalked back to her mark. This time, Merisiel spun on her heel and flicked the black knife out so quickly that her blade and hand were a single blur.

Again she pierced the eye with a solid thud. Again it did nothing to lift her bleak mood.

All she wanted was to be able to help Kyra. To take some of the burden away, to be a source of strength for the woman she loved. She just wanted to be *useful.*

For a moment, in Endio's house, she'd done that. Meri had forced her way through that room of horrors, and the grueling desert journey afterward, because she'd known Kyra needed it. Needed *her*.

When they'd reunited in the Sandfire Catacombs, and she'd felt the love and relief in Kyra's embrace and her wife's lips on her sunburned brow, she'd known it was all worth it. She had been happy then, despite the pain of her ordeal. Truly, deeply happy.

In all her decades of life as a Forlorn, Meri had never felt such comfort and belonging as she did in Kyra's arms. Nothing was more precious to her than that.

But as much as Kyra was the center of Merisiel's world, Meri knew she wasn't always at the center of Kyra's.

Her wife was called to serve Sarenrae, and the relationship between cleric and goddess had no place for Merisiel. It was powerful, profound... and exclusive.

Meri had no interest in converting to the Dawnflower's faith. She didn't care about the gods or their games. Her life was hers, free and independent, and she meant for it to stay that way. Kyra had never pushed back against that. They each understood and accepted that Kyra wanted to follow her goddess, and Merisiel didn't, and that was that.

But sometimes that left a space between them, and that space could be lonely.

Meri grabbed her knife and pulled it out again. It slid easily from the splintered driftwood this time, and that annoyed her too. She wanted resistance; she wanted a fight.

There wasn't one to be had. Not with the log, and not with her wife.

Kyra's quest was too important. Meri couldn't and didn't begrudge her that, exactly. She understood the pressure that her wife's duties placed upon her. To be personally chosen by one's deity for a task was an honor that all clerics dreamed of, and feared.

Meri just wanted to have a part in it. To belong and be useful, even if she didn't share the same prayers.

Instead, she'd been forgotten.

Her knife slammed into the driftwood log. Meri stared at the black hilt jutting from the sea-bleached wood, breathing hard, then turned sharply and strode back to the distant lights of the village on the shore.

She left her knife where it had landed. At least she'd make that much of a mark on Myrissos.

Her mood didn't much improve when she found her companions.

They'd gathered in the village coffeehouse, which doubled as its part-time boardinghouse. When there were enough visitors in Myrissos to warrant killing a chicken or hauling down a coil of spiced lamb sausages, the mother-and-daughter proprietors could serve up mouth-watering stews and flatbread for dinner, and it smelled like they'd prepared an exceptional breakfast this morning. Nevertheless, Meri found her appetite spoiled when she realized that the others had assembled without her and were listening intently to Ezren and Elothain. On a table between the two wizards were the curios and papers that Merisiel had retrieved in Totra.

They're talking about my find, and they didn't even wait for me?

Kyra was so enmeshed in discussion with the two wizards that she didn't notice Meri's arrival. The cleric had her head bowed in a semicircle with Ezren and Elothain, all three of them studying the star chart and red-lensed telescope. Not one of them turned to look when the door opened.

Rather than the anger she expected, Meri felt only a dull, thudding hurt. After all she'd endured to bring those things to Kyra, was she really that invisible?

"There you are," Amiri said, looking up from the clay bowl of yellow rice and wrinkled brown beans she was eating. Chunks of tender roasted chicken and dried fruit studded the dish. It looked as delicious as it smelled, but Merisiel made no move to get her own bowl.

"Here I am," she agreed. *Not that it matters.*

She lingered by the door, unsure whether she even wanted to stay in the room. Why, when no one seemed to care?

Calistria, goddess of lust and revenge, taught that caprice was the appropriate response to such stings. A lover's slights were meant to be ignored, or else answered cruelly. Either way, the relationship was broken, and a true Calistrian moved on to the next, aloof and untouched.

For most of her life, Meri had followed that path, dancing lightly from bed to bed without any thoughts of permanence. She'd found only fleeting happiness that way, but she'd also been impervious to hurt. Nothing lasted; nothing mattered.

Now, faced with a fight to keep something that mattered very much, she found herself under-armed. She didn't want to *seem* desperate, but she was, and she had no idea how to make Kyra see that without pushing her away.

But she had to try. However ill-equipped Meri was, she had to try.

Putting on an insouciant air, Merisiel sidled over to the table and feigned a casual glance at the objects she'd collected. "Learn anything?"

"More than I could have imagined," Kyra said, breaking away from their conference long enough to give Merisiel a quick kiss.

It felt perfunctory, and only worsened Meri's hurt, but she reflexively hid her reaction behind a playful toss of her white hair. She dropped her voice to a purr—not blatantly, but just to the coy, teasing level that she knew stirred Kyra. "Oh?"

Her efforts drew no reaction. "These artifacts point the way to the Red Fang," Kyra said, pointing to the red-glassed telescope and the compass beside it. There was awe in her manner, but apprehension as well, even fear. "The Akithaine Heresy was not wrong, after all. It was stamped out not solely because it was blasphemy, but because the blasphemy struck too close to the truth."

None of that meant anything to Merisiel, but the wizards nodded with shared gravity. They were all privy to the same story, and it wasn't one Meri knew. That seldom bothered her—no one expected her to know obscure theological history, least of all herself—but this time she felt her ignorance as an embarrassing lack. "What's the Akithaine Heresy?"

"A sect of astrologers led by the heretic Formose, a former Sarenite disowned by his church. He believed that the red planet Akiton was the true locus of prophesies that had previously been read as revolving around the sun," Ezren answered. "The Sarenites viewed the Akithaine Heresy as a challenge to the Dawnflower's supremacy because it seemed to suggest that Akiton, not Sarenrae's holy sun, was the primary arbiter of these foretellings.

"It might seem a bit academic now, but during Formose's lifetime, the political and economic ramifications of his teachings were substantial. Sarenrae's church in Avistan was at a fragile juncture in its history, and her faith was at risk of losing influential converts who were swayed by the Akithaine Heresy. There is a historical dispute to this day about whether the church had Formose assassinated, or whether it was an isolated fanatic with no formal connection to the Dawnflower's faith who committed the deed.

"Whether or not the church had any hand in it, Formose was murdered, and the Akithaine Heresy was swiftly buried in history's graveyard. Some of their calculations and star charts remained of interest to arcane astrologers, such as the Lirgeni, but otherwise no one, save perhaps a handful of Sarenite historians and inquisitors, has bothered considering their work in centuries. We were fortunate to find any mention of the Akithaine Heresy in the Sandfire Catacombs. Most temples would not have held a word about that fallen order."

"But they matter now?" Meri said, not because she was particularly interested in long-dead heretics and astrologers, but because she was hoping Kyra would take over the thread of the story. *Talk to me. Please, just talk to me.*

Her silent prayer was answered. Kyra nodded, and took one of Meri's hands between her own, clasping it to both give and share comfort. "It does. Here—look." Kyra took out the curved and hooked metal rods that Meri had found concealed in the spyglass's frame, which she had assumed were keys. The cleric fitted them together into a frame and laid it over the star chart, and even Merisiel could see that it connected the constellations in a diagram that then, confusingly, pointed to an empty space on the celestial map.

"The inscriptions on these keys were hidden by magic. Ezren's impairment prevented him from finding them earlier, but Elothain was able to pierce the concealment spell and determine their true purpose. You were right, my love: the spyglass was, in part, a ruse. It has a function, but it was also made to disguise the keys tucked into its frame. They are not literal keys. They're a device that the Akithaine heretics used to decode this star chart."

"To what end?" Meri squinted at the chart again, wondering if she'd missed something. If so, she still couldn't see what. "It just points to a blank spot."

"It does," Elothain agreed, "but if one knows the history of the Akithaine astrologers, it is impossible not to guess that the blank spot suggests the location of a weapon they referred to as the Red Fang. Their heresies claimed that it was a weapon so terrible that the mere glimpse of it in divinations was sufficient to drive prophets mad and cause the collapse of entire cities. It was so fearsome that the gods themselves dreaded it, and that—they claimed—was why Sarenrae falsely made herself the center of astrological readings that should have centered on Akiton instead. She did so in order to prevent anyone from finding the Red Fang."

"And that's why the church of the Dawnflower stamped them out?" Meri couldn't help but laugh a little, although it wasn't exactly funny. "Seems like, if you believed the story was true, you'd want to let that sleeping dog lie. Why would the Akithaine heretics go to so much trouble to uncover a truth that, according to their own beliefs, could cause nothing but ruin?"

"That is disputed," Kyra said, with a trace of regret, "and the truth will likely never be known, since the heretics are long gone. But the prevailing view is that Formose believed Sarenrae should be held to a duty of absolute truth, and that her efforts to conceal certain secrets from mortals were unworthy of her. It is not clear that he knew what those secrets would be before he began his quest to discover them, only that they existed. By the time he uncovered that secret, he was an enemy of the faith, as were his followers. But, in fairness, it is not clear that the Akithaine heretics actually wanted to find the Red Fang. They may only have wanted to prove that it existed, and that their heresy was rooted in fact."

"Well, it looks like Itaguen and Curuvrakh believed them," Meri said, hoping that Kyra would keep holding her close. She pressed her other hand over Kyra's, then let go, not wanting to seem clingy. "But their contract only spoke of Inithyra's Orb."

"Maybe they just didn't want to put the real goal in writing," Amiri suggested. She'd finished her stew and stood up to get more flatbread. "The contract talked about Inithyra's Orb, but it also talked about the 'known prize.' Only reason to be that coy about it is if you don't want other people finding out what the prize is."

"It is the Red Fang, though." Merisiel grimaced as she recalled Curuvrakh's frothing in the ruins of Endio's house. "I'm sure of it. Curuvrakh mentioned it by name. She told Itaguen that they needed to hurry and find Inithyra's Orb, because her master was growing impatient to claim the fang. I didn't know what she was talking about at the time, but now it's obvious. They need the orb to get the fang. That's the 'known prize': a weapon that the gods fear."

"Who's her master?" Amiri asked, around a mouthful of olive-studded bread.

"I think it's Rovagug." Merisiel shuddered. Too vividly, she could recall the disturbing joy in Curuvrakh's voice as she giggled about her master's penchant for destruction, along with the sight of her spiderlike pet slashing its leg across the woman's pustule-ridden cheek. "Rovagug is the one who wants the fang."

Amiri stopped chewing. She squinted at Merisiel, and then at the others. "Why would anyone help her? If she's a cultist of Rovagug, and the Rough Beast wants a weapon that the gods fear... Why would Itaguen be a part of that? He didn't sound that deranged, the way you two described him. What's his angle?"

"He may not believe it is possible for her to succeed," Ezren said. The wizard had, finally, consented to take a plate of dinner, as had Elothain. He didn't seem to have much appetite, though, and spent as much time pushing his chicken and rice around the plate with a torn piece of flatbread as he did eating it. "I'm afraid it is a common delusion among wizards, though hardly unique to us. We can become so convinced of our intellectual superiority that we assume others' schemes must be fatally flawed and our own counterschemes destined to prevail, and fail to accurately credit the chances that we're wrong. Itaguen seems a competent person, and we've seen that he has an extensive mastery of magic. He may be inclined to overestimate his position relative to Curuvrakh's, particularly if she is indeed sworn to Rovagug. The Devourer's servants are easily dismissed as frothing lunatics. Regrettably, that does not always mean they are ineffective."

"Even so. We have the tools to stop them." Kyra drew her hands away and turned back to the table, missing the quick, distraught glance that Meri cast after her. The cleric picked up the star chart and compass, holding them side by side. "The telescope sights Akiton in the sky, lighting the red planet clearly so that it can be discerned no matter the season, the phases of the heavens, or the density of the clouds. The star chart, when interpreted with Akiton at the center instead of the sun, shows an empty spot in the sky, which we believe correlates to a location in the sea near the Eye of Abendego. We don't yet know the full purpose of the compass, but Ezren and Elothain suspect it will activate if we near the object or location that it was enchanted to find. Whether that is Inithyra's Orb, the Red Fang, or some other thing entirely, it must be important."

Kyra wiped at the corners of her eyes. A hint of moisture glistened upon the blue tattoos above each cheekbone, and Meri realized, with a start, that her wife had been crying. "We will not fail. We will not allow Rovagug, or his minions, to obtain the weapon they seek. Sarenrae has given us the tools to succeed, and we will prove that her trust in us is not misplaced."

"Do we still go to Port Peril?" Merisiel searched the others' faces. "Is it still worth seeking out the junk dealer? Chasing the last scraps of the *Merry Mermaid*'s cargo might not be a wise use of our time if our enemies are ahead of us on this trail."

"I don't know that we have much choice," Ezren said. "I believe that I can cast the spell of teleportation, but I am not certain I can do so with great precision, especially if the destination is not known to me. I know Port Peril. I've been there before.

"I know next to nothing about either Inithyra's Orb or the Red Fang. We have a star chart that may or may not give us the general location of one or both objects, and a compass that might help us along the way. But we don't have an actual location, nor do we have any landmarks or identifying features I might use to guide my spell. As far as we know, the star chart points to a region of empty sea—one bordering the Eye of Abendego, at that. I can't even attempt to teleport us there. It'll have to be Port Peril, and then we may as well seek out the junk dealer while we try to settle on our next move."

"All right." Merisiel nodded, satisfied to have a set course of action. The sooner they set out, and did something other than sit around a dinner no one wanted while talking about things they'd learned in dusty scrolls, the sooner she'd be able to do something useful. "When do we leave?"

"I must rest and gather my energy before I can attempt the spell. Tomorrow morning, at the earliest." Ezren stroked his beard, glancing at Elothain for confirmation. "It would be prudent to do this somewhere well outside of Myrissos. There is a considerable likelihood that my spell will produce... unpredictable side effects."

Amiri grunted, wiping grease from her mouth with the back of a fur-gauntleted hand. "Tomorrow morning. We'll meet here and head out to the hillside, so you can terrify Myrissos's goats instead of its people."

"Tomorrow morning," Merisiel agreed.

That night, Merisiel lay on her lumpy pillow, listening to the wind blow through the rattling windows, and watched Kyra pray on the other side of their room.

The cleric knelt on the small, well-worn prayer rug that she carried on all their travels. The Osirian Desert still clung to its knotted fabric so thickly that Meri could see a halo of pale dust ringing the prayer rug in the moonlight.

It stained Kyra's knees as well, but the cleric didn't notice and wouldn't have cared if she did. She was too absorbed in murmuring her quiet devotions to her goddess, and in contemplating whatever answer came to her through the pulses of golden light that shone in the hanging coils of her prayer beads.

That radiance reflected off Kyra's headdress and the smooth brown planes of her cheekbones. In that holy light, she was so beautiful that it made Merisiel's heart ache.

I love you. I love you so much, and I don't know what to do. Tell me, my love. Only tell me how I can help.

She didn't say it. Her words would only go unheard, or worse, interrupt her wife's communion. Kyra was lost in conversation with her goddess, enraptured in something that had no place for Merisiel.

She turned over in her bed, gazing at the cold moonlight as if it could distract from the emptiness beside her.

Uselessly, she tried to sleep.

Chapter Seventeen
PORT PERIL

"You're sure you can get us to Port Peril?" Amiri shaded her eyes with the flat of her hand, squinting against the wind as she studied the gnarled olive trees, white bluffs, and pristine blue seas of Myrissos. Mist pooled in the dips and hollows near the shore, cool and ephemeral as the morning itself.

This land had been cultivated for centuries, and roads were sunk into its identity as deeply as veins in a living body, but there was still a wildness to the wind-bent limbs of its trees and the white slashes of foam on the faraway waves.

It calmed her soul, as being out in the natural world always did. Amiri tried to hold on to that feeling as she contemplated what Ezren was about to do.

What *was* he about to do? Tear a hole through reality and push them through it into a city hundreds of miles away? Dissolve their bodies and send them hurtling through the air as arcane rays, to be reconstituted as themselves—or, maybe, only simulacrums of themselves—in Port Peril?

Amiri didn't know and didn't want to know. She hadn't asked Ezren for any details because she knew they would only upset her. Even thinking about it this much had spiked her heart rate, and she had to take another moment to close her eyes and breathe in the warm salt air before her pulse settled.

All she wanted was an assurance that he knew what he was doing, that the spell would work, and that they'd soon be in Port Peril.

It could even be a lie. Amiri didn't care. She only wanted Ezren to tell her that he had everything under control.

The companions had all gathered in the cool of the early morning, along with Ezren's new friend Elothain, for the wizard to cast his spell. Though Kyra and Merisiel were outwardly calm, Amiri noted the tension with which the cleric kept glancing at the rising sun and the coiled energy that ran through Merisiel's body as the elf paced back and forth across the hilltop. They were nervous too, and probably as eager as she was to hear something reassuring from Ezren.

But somehow the man just couldn't do that.

"This spell is new to me, and I have never tried it before," Ezren said, smoothing a gold-tasseled blue cloth over a flat rock while Merisiel and Kyra looked on from a few steps away. He weighted its four corners with polished spheres of white and pink quartz, then put an iron needle at its center.

After examining his work with a critical eye, the wizard stepped back, inviting Elothain to take a second look at the arrangement. "I believe I can cast it successfully, but I would be lying if I pretended absolute certainty. Particularly given the... additional complications with my magic at the moment."

"Is there anything we can do about it if you botch the spell?" Amiri asked. "You know, like how the camel drovers warned us to cover our eyes if the camels looked like they were about to spit? Do you have anything like that if your spell goes wrong?"

Ezren gave her a grave look, stroking his silver-white beard for a long moment before he answered. "No. If the spell fails, regrettably, there will be nothing you can do."

"Then why," Amiri said, exasperated, "don't you just lie to us about it?"

"She has a point." Merisiel laughed. "Too late now, though."

"Sarenrae will see us through." Kyra clasped her holy symbol, closing her eyes in fierce reverence. "The spell will not fail. We will reach Port Peril safely."

Amiri eyed the cleric sidelong. Kyra had been acting strangely since the Sandfire Catacombs, and she'd only gotten worse since the revelation about Rovagug.

That didn't surprise her in and of itself, since Sarenrae and Rovagug hated each other with a fury that only divine entities could muster. It was Sarenrae who had wounded Rovagug most grievously in their great war, opened the Dead Vault to contain him, and hurled the Rough Beast inside. Though all the gods had played their parts in the Great

Destroyer's imprisonment, Sarenrae had dealt the most direct and painful blows, and Rovagug's faithful had never forgiven her. When their cults and churches clashed, the intensity of their battles was such that the tales reached even to the Realm of the Mammoth Lords.

So Amiri understood why Kyra would take it so ardently to heart that her goddess had chosen her to pursue this quest for the Red Fang. Becoming Sarenrae's agent against the most hated enemy of her faith was, undoubtedly, a heavy burden to bear.

What Amiri worried about was a good deal more prosaic: whether, in her holy haze, Kyra was forgetting to eat, sleep, or do anything else to preserve her sanity along the way.

Or that the rest of them hadn't necessarily signed on to confront a god who devoured entire worlds, and whose minor spawn destroyed civilizations with the ease of children kicking over snow castles.

"In that case," Ezren said, squaring his shoulders as he took a carved driftwood case from Elothain, "I shall begin my spell with the utmost confidence."

He removed two vials of glittering powder, one blue and the other gold, from the case. Carefully he poured them out in sweeping arcs over the stones and the compass needle he'd laid out on the cloth. The powder shimmered and shifted in midair, gathering into finely grained curtains and then separating, seemingly of its own accord, into a network of elaborate looping lines that linked the quartzes in a diagram that superficially resembled a compass rose, but one far more complex than any Amiri had ever seen.

She edged closer. Ezren was wholly focused on his spell, muttering to himself and sweating hard enough that wind-blown powder clung to his arms in sticky sleeves, so Amiri whispered to Elothain instead. "Is it working?"

"Yes," Elothain murmured in reply. "So far. But he hasn't begun the difficult part yet."

The design lifted into the air, solidifying itself into three dimensions. Miniature replicas of mountains and rivers appeared in stipplings of blue and gold upon its surface. The hollow globe revolved before Ezren, and two points began to glow brightly as he wove his fingers through complex gestures and uttered his incantations.

In the center of the globe, the iron compass needle rose up and floated. It spun slowly inside the sphere, sparking whenever its tip or base aligned momentarily with one of the two glowing points on the surface.

Ezren's chanting grew louder, more commanding, and yet more fraught with strain. A wash of desert heat emanated from the globe, blowing back Amiri's short black hair and forcing her to squint against its blaze. Snow materialized above it and drifted down, melting in midair.

The iron compass needle trembled and stuttered as it rotated into alignment between the two glowing points.

"This is it," Elothain said quietly to Amiri. He held his own crooked driftwood wand at the ready, watching Ezren with unblinking intensity.

On the next hilltop, a hurricane gale slammed into an olive tree out of nowhere, whipping its leaves and smaller branches off with a sudden howl. Jellyfish popped from the sky and spattered onto the ground in a wet circle around the storm-tossed tree.

The sky above Ezren curdled into black storm clouds. Lightning fissured down in a stroke that would have struck the wizard straight through the crown of his head if Elothain hadn't lifted his own wand to thrust it frantically aside. The bolt slammed into the ground a few hundred feet away, shuddering the entire hillside and knocking Kyra from her feet.

Blue-white radiance dazzled the sight from Amiri's eyes. Electricity crackled across her metal blades and buckles. She barely had time to drop into a blind crouch before a thunderclap followed on the lightning's heels, so loud that it rattled the sides of her skull and made her teeth dance in her jaws.

Water poured down on her, far too hard and fast to be rain. It was as if she'd leaped into the heart of a cataract and was being pummeled with a force she couldn't hope to withstand. Still unable to see, Amiri opened her mouth to gasp for breath or cry a warning to her friends, only to cough and splutter hopelessly as salt water poured down her throat.

There was, suddenly, no solid ground beneath her feet. She kicked desperately downward, trying to find something to brace herself against, but only swirling water met her efforts. The weight of the giant's greatsword strapped to her back dragged her backward and under, and she fought furiously to hold herself above the surface.

"What—?" Amiri managed to splutter, treading water. Her blindness was beginning to clear, at least enough that she could separate seawater from sky. She blinked a few more times and dashed the back of one hand against her eyes, swirling the other against the waves to keep herself upright.

Her companions bobbed in the ocean around her. Amiri coughed again and spit out more seawater as a wave slapped across her side. She could see, now, that a ramshackle settlement of tall wooden spines and tattered pirate flags rose from the jungle shore to her left, while a motley assortment of ships and smaller craft dotted the water around her and the green isles in the sea to her right. The tar-scented air was warm and humid, and the crescent-shaped harbor was crowded with enough flotsam that Amiri, once she could see again, soon found a bobbing board to support her weight.

They had reached Port Peril.

"Ezren and Merisiel will try to find the junk dealer who bought the odds and ends from the *Merry Mermaid*," Kyra said, once they'd all hauled their dripping selves onto Port Peril's shore beneath the reeking, barnacled overhang of a pier. "I'll go with Amiri to look for her old friends, who may be able to help us secure a ship for our travels from here. If Ezren is correct about the compass's function, our best chance of locating Inithyra's Orb may be to set sail in the direction that the star chart indicates, and then hope that the compass shows us the way once we draw near."

"Fine." Merisiel picked a soggy glob of seaweed from her elbow, regarded it with immense distaste, and dropped it delicately on the rocks. "Anything that stops us from having to travel like this again."

"The spell worked," Ezren said, a bit defensively, as he wiped mud and debris from his own clothing. "We arrived safely and swiftly at our destination."

"Safely, swiftly, and stinking," Merisiel retorted, checking her knives with a baleful air. "I'm going to be cleaning and oiling these for hours to keep them from rusting into scrap. Anyway, you already said you can't teleport us to the orb, so there's no point debating it. Let's just focus on what we need to do now. Should we try for disguises before we move into town?"

"Yes, if you can do them quickly," Kyra said. "We do not know whether our enemies have eyes here, but... we have so little time to spare."

"I don't think an hour more or less is going to decide the fate of Golarion," Merisiel replied, with a touch more acid than Amiri was used to hearing from her. The elf opened her satchel, made a face, and then tipped it over to pour out half a gallon of seawater. "I might not have much left to work with, though, after Ezren's resounding success of a spell."

Kyra regarded her wife with a blank look that didn't quite conceal the hurt and bafflement that betrayed itself in her brown eyes. "Do what you can."

Irritably wiping away a dribble of filthy water, Merisiel pulled a case from her satchel and cracked it open. She dipped a slim finger into a pot of paint, then beckoned for Amiri to lean forward and close her eyes. "I always do," the elf muttered, too quietly for Kyra to hear, as she began smearing oily-smelling paint across the barbarian's forehead.

An hour later, the disguised companions emerged to infiltrate Port Peril. Merisiel and Ezren headed to the mercantile district of Scrimshaw, distinguished by the curved pillars and yellowing ornaments of salt-weathered whalebone that advertised its inhabitants' wares, while Amiri led Kyra toward the grisly stone arch known as the Dead Man's Dance Hall.

She'd heard rumors that the pirates' new Hurricane Queen, Tessa Fairwind, had softened some of the excesses of her predecessor, the notoriously sadistic Kerdak Bonefist. If that was true, however, the Dead Man's Dance Hall didn't offer much evidence of it.

North of the impoverished sprawl of the Beggarbriar district, the natural stone arch carved by wind and time stood high above the glittering waters of Jeopardy Bay. Once it must have been a landmark of breathtaking beauty. Now it was still breathtaking, but for a vastly grimmer reason.

Metal cages crusted with decades' worth of grime and salt spray creaked from long chains anchored in the stone. Each cage held a condemned victim, living or dead, who'd been consigned to rot in the Dead Man's Dance Hall either by the Hurricane Queen herself, or by one of Port Peril's assassins, who paid the Hurricane Queen a fee to put especially impressive victims on display as advertisement for their skills.

Carrion birds perched on the arch in a croaking chorus of black feathers and beady eyes, occasionally flapping down to test whether a likely-looking morsel still had enough fight to be troublesome or was ready for them to feast. Other scavengers swirled in the waters below, breaching the waves to seize their prize whenever the birds knocked loose a sizable bone or chunk of gristle.

"Why are we here?" Kyra asked, taking in the sight. The wind turned, bringing the cages' stench to their nostrils, and the cleric gagged as she covered her nose with a fold of her cloak.

"Figured it was the first place I'd check for my friends." Amiri had already scanned the cages and was confident she didn't know any of their current inhabitants. She planted a hand on a low wall and vaulted over it to the path beyond, heading toward the rust-stained wooden bridge that led to the Dead Man's Dance Hall. "If they're in the cages, or their names are on the dance list, then we can stop looking."

Kyra trailed reluctantly behind. "The dance list?"

The condemned people in the cages had noticed their approach. Some of the stronger ones began to call to them. Amiri couldn't make out most of their cries, but she assumed they were pleading for water, or medicine, or a quick death. One man, with a distinct rattling lisp to his cries, shouted over and over for rum. Amiri ignored them, but she could see that the cleric was having more difficulty turning a deaf ear to their pleas.

"They write down the names of everyone who's been consigned to the cages," she told Kyra, hoping to distract her. "That way, when the faces have rotted off the skulls and the bones have fallen into the water, Port Peril can still know who was sent to die there. The old Hurricane King started the tradition so he could boast of the enemies he'd sent to the Dead Man's Dance Hall, and the new queen kept it because those who pay for the cages will pay to have the names recorded too."

"Where is this list kept?" Kyra asked. The prisoners' cries were growing louder as they got nearer. The cleric's mouth tightened, and Amiri began to fear that she might be foolish enough to bring them water, or heal their wounds, or do something else that would invite the Hurricane Queen's wrath upon them.

"It's over there." Amiri pointed to a series of bronze tablets that had been embedded in a red-and-white stone edifice near the base of the bridge that led to the cages. A handful of empty rum bottles, candles fixed in skulls, and other tokens of remembrance were scattered about the memorial stones. "We're looking for Boskrag the Fiddler and Sir Osmund of Westcrown."

Kyra nodded, but she was barely listening. "There's something wrong with them."

Amiri blinked. "My friends? Probably, but that isn't very nice to say."

"No. The people in the cages." Kyra held up a hand, motioning for quiet. "Listen."

Dubiously, Amiri tilted her head into the wind. As she opened her ears to the cries she'd brushed aside earlier, she realized Kyra was right. There *was* something wrong with the prisoners in the cages.

They weren't begging for water or mercy, as she'd assumed. They weren't begging at all. Their shouts were threats, filled with unhinged rage and vile descriptions of what they would do to her and Kyra. The man shouting for rum wasn't asking them to bring him a flask, but instead swearing that he'd drink his own from the sockets of their bloody skulls.

How do they have the strength to be so angry? Amiri had watched people die in gibbets. They died of thirst, exposure, and cold; they baked in the sun or froze in the wind. They grew weak, gave up, and succumbed.

She had never seen or heard a prisoner in a cage who'd had the strength to scream after the first day or two. The smarter ones never tried, conserving their energy for survival.

But all these prisoners, even the ones that looked so close to death that the crows were sitting on their top bars, still had enough in reserve to howl threats at two women who had done nothing to harm them. They clawed through the gaps in their cages, trying to tear at Kyra and Amiri, and spat their hatred uselessly into the sea.

One man gnawed so furiously at his filthy bars that his teeth cracked and his lips split into bloody pulp against the salt-roughened steel. He just stared at them, wild-eyed, and gibbered incoherently through the red froth that dribbled into his beard.

Amiri shivered. In the worst of her rages, she'd never been as mindless as this. "What's happened to them?"

"I do not know. But clearly something has." Kyra regarded the prisoners with solemn pity, then shook her head. "Given their condition, the cages may be the safest place for them at the moment. Certainly the other citizens of Port Peril are likely safer with them confined, and we can do nothing to aid them until we learn what is amiss. Let us see the tablets."

"Right. This way." Stepping around the makeshift memorials scattered around them, Amiri led her friend to the red-and-white stone carvings that held the bronze tablets. Each tablet was three feet high and two wide, and bore names hammered into its face in long, amateurishly uneven lists. Port Peril didn't lack for skilled metalsmiths, but it did apparently lack for people willing to pay them to emboss the names of the condemned.

The stone carvings that housed the tablets were, by contrast, so skillfully done that their sculptures appeared to breathe with life. They were sculpted from a red-veined stone, smoother than marble, that couldn't have been quarried from any of the islands nearby. Each and every one depicted a scene of gruesome sacrifice being performed by, and sometimes on, towering figures with single eyes in the centers of their foreheads. They wore paneled robes and carried elaborate, wavy-bladed knives, and on their altars they cut apart birds and beasts that had long gone extinct in the world.

"They say these islands were once inhabited by monsters," Amiri offered by way of explanation. "The Chelaxians who first came here thought the islands were cursed and pulled their ships away without trying to settle any of them. That's how the pirates took Port Peril. No one else would come near. Made it a good place to hide, and eventually to build."

"Could that be what cursed the prisoners?" Kyra asked.

Amiri shrugged. "Maybe. But it's been centuries since pirates came to Port Peril. If the islands really were cursed, you'd think they'd have succumbed long ago. Anyway, do you see my friends' names on the tablets?" She'd been looking herself, but reading wasn't her strong suit, and the amateurish lettering on the lists made for hard going.

"No," Kyra said, after spending nearly half an hour in careful study of the plates. "I do not see either Boskrag or Sir Osmund among these names."

"That's a relief." Amiri hadn't been terribly worried about Boskrag. The half-orc could be supremely irritating, especially when he got drunk enough to try fiddling, but he had enough sense to keep himself out of the kind of trouble that got people killed. Sir Osmund, on the other hand, had once been a crusader at the Worldwound, and he had an unhealthy tendency to insist on fair play and moral rectitude from the sorts of back-alley degenerates who slept with bottles under their pillows and named their favorite knives after their mothers.

She had been at least half expecting Sir Osmund's name to appear on the list of invitees to the Dead Man's Dance Hall. It was good to be disappointed.

Something else about the tablets had caught her eye, though. She leaned down, tracing a line of hammered letters so new that the exposed bronze at the edges was still sharp and bright. "A lot of these were added recently. Very recently. And hammered in hard enough that the chisel broke through the plate again and again." Amiri straightened and moved down the row, squinting at another plate. "They're all like this. Someone was swinging that hammer like they were trying to bash in a dragon's skull."

"Yes, I noticed that as well." Kyra frowned at the tablets. "I wonder whether it's related to the rage that consumes these poor prisoners."

"Maybe." That was an ugly idea. Bad enough that the cages' occupants had lost themselves to hatred. Amiri didn't like to imagine the possibility that those who had imprisoned them had done the same. The violence embedded in those raw metal gouges was hard to ignore, though.

"Where do we look next?" Kyra asked.

Amiri thought it over. "Let's try the Locker, since it's close by. There's a good chance Sir Osmund might have made himself known to the local law. If we can't find any leads there, Eastwind's likely our best bet for both of them."

"Very well." Kyra cast one last look at the prisoners dangling in their gibbets, tormented by crows and vermin and whatever strange demons gnawed at their souls. The wind was rising, and the creak of their chains drowned out their awful cries. "Let us hope, too, that we can find some answer to this curse."

Chapter Eighteen
STEW MEAT

Is Port Peril always like this?" Merisiel crossed her arms as she looked down the shuttered street.

Ezren could only shrug. He hadn't been to the pirates' haven in years, and he had never stayed for long. But the raucous, vibrant port he remembered was a far cry from this sullen, suspicious place.

The last time he'd been in Port Peril, the streets had been crowded with sailors newly released on shore leave, quartermasters rushing to resupply, buccaneers looking to spend their ill-gotten gold before the law or a bounty hunter found them, brothel masters eager to help them spend it, and rum, rum, rum everywhere. Some of it was genuine, much of it was cheap counterfeit swill dyed with burned sugar, and all of it fueled a never-ending bacchanal. Every dockside door had been flung open to the revelry.

Now those doors were barricaded, and the few people out on the streets hurried past with lowered heads and averted eyes.

Gone were the fiddlers and drummers playing merrily on each corner in hopes of earning a few tossed coins for their hornpipes. Gone, too, were the vendors hawking meat pies and fried eels, the luck sellers offering pierced coins and fraudulent dragons' teeth as charms for good fortune, and the pawnbrokers waiting to snap up sailors' finds in exchange for just enough gold to buy another kiss or flagon.

"I've never seen it this quiet before," Ezren said, uneasy.

"Do you think there's a plague in town?" Merisiel lifted her head and sniffed the wind. "No, I don't smell anything. No lime, no pyre smoke, no rot. If death's come to Port Peril, it's not sweeping people away in masses."

But what else could it be? What, other than a plague, inspired such widespread fear? Ezren didn't ask aloud. He could see that Merisiel was on edge, wondering the same thing.

"How are we going to find a junk dealer if no one's open for business?" he asked instead. "There isn't even anyone we might ask for directions."

"Let's find a tavern," Merisiel suggested. "Whatever's happening, this is still a port. There are ships in the harbor, and pirates with heavy pockets and hungry mouths. Someone will have a kitchen open to solve that problem for them."

Ezren nodded, searching the streets for a painted sign or plume of smoke that might signal a likely option.

It was Merisiel who found one first, though. The elf pointed out a ramshackle hut, its front door propped a few inches ajar by a cracked half brick. No sign hung above the door, but the savory smell of a meaty stew wafted from the interior, and faded smudges of white and blue on the exterior walls suggested that at some point it might have been painted with a public house's designs.

Merisiel pushed open the door and strode in, radiating absolute confidence. Ezren followed behind her, squaring his shoulders and trying to look imposing. The elf had disguised him as a scarred, heavily tattooed tough, doubtlessly her idea of a joke.

She herself was disguised as a wildcat bawd, with her sleek white hair transformed into a ratty black tangle and her close-fitting armor carefully hidden beneath colorful rags that revealed nothing while suggesting everything. Gaudy brass caps, midway between weapon and ornament, covered her fingers. She cut a memorable figure, but everything that distinguished her was something that could be cast aside as soon as she needed to disappear.

The tavern's patrons looked up as the two of them entered. It was a grimy, dingy place, with a grimy, dingy clientele. Only a few of the tables at the periphery of the room were occupied, as if the customers, like dust balls, had drifted into the corners and been forgotten. Though it was only midday, the filthy windows and smoky fire cast the interior into a false twilight and lent a sinister aspect to the bowlegged pirates and squint-eyed drifters who sat about the commons.

A female goblin with a large burn scar across her stubbly scalp squatted on a stool behind the bar, spilling spirals of rotgut liquor around cockroaches on the counter and lighting them on fire.

Whenever one of the insects dashed through the burning rings to escape, she chortled, pinned it down with her thumb, pulled off one of its legs, and tossed it back into the innermost circle. By Ezren's estimation, she had about a dozen cockroaches in varying stages of dismemberment trapped upon the bar.

Merisiel betrayed no trace of disgust as she swaggered to the counter. "I'm looking to sell a few odds and ends somebody recently gave me," she said, with a wink that was half leer. "Nothing too valuable, I reckon, but it's sparkly junk at least. Know anyone who might handle such wares?"

The goblin looked up, taking a swig from the bottle she'd been using to draw her fiery rings. "Conversation's for customers only. Everybody else gets—" She punched a clawed green thumb down on the head of a three-legged cockroach that had dragged itself across a burning line, ending the poor insect's misery with a crunch.

"We can be customers." Merisiel jerked a thumb at Ezren, who took the cue and came closer, looming over the elf's shoulder as best he could. "I'm hungry, he's thirsty. Give us your best of both." She pulled out a gold coin, clamped it showily between her teeth, and spun it across the bug-stained counter toward the barkeep.

With a flick of one wrist, too quick for Ezren to follow, the goblin made the gold coin disappear. Just as swiftly, she pulled a cloudy, cracked glass from under the bar and filled it halfway with the swill from the bottle she was already holding. She slid it over to Merisiel, knocking a wounded cockroach along with the glass.

"Thanks," Merisiel said dryly, flicking the dying bug away.

"Don't mention it." The goblin tossed a wooden bowl at Ezren. It was crusted with unidentifiable pasty globs, some dried into rock-hard crusts and others damp enough to squish under his fingers when he caught the vessel. "Help yourself to the pot over the fire."

Ezren cast a dubious look at Merisiel, but she nodded to indicate that he should play along, so reluctantly he trudged to the cauldron bubbling over the tavern's central fire.

Up close, the smell that had seemed vaguely appetizing from the street had a rancid, off-putting odor. Streaks of brown goo, blackened where they fell into the fire's reach, burbled down the cauldron's sides.

Having seen the rest of the tavern, Ezren didn't doubt that whatever meat was in that pot would have turned a vulture's stomach. Nevertheless, he reached for the ladle that leaned against the poker and ash broom in the soot-crusted tool rack. *I don't have to eat it. Merisiel only needs me to pretend.*

Using the ladle's handle as a pry bar, he lifted the cauldron's lid.

Hands floated in the scummy brown broth. Human, orc, dwarf, all tangled together like a wrack of nightmarish seaweed. Some had cooked so long that the skin and muscle melted off their softened bones. Some were fresh enough that Ezren could still make out the lines and colors of the tattoos on their weatherbeaten skin. Greasy bubbles caught in the knuckle hair of an orc's hand, and the fingernails were beginning to float free from a woman's dissolving hand.

Trying to keep his composure, Ezren set the lid down and backed a step away.

The goblin cackled. "Don't care for my cooking?"

"I'm not very hungry."

"No? Too bad. I am." She hopped onto the bar counter, splashing liquor and cockroaches underfoot, and grinned wide. Her teeth were sharp, shiny, and red as holly berries. "And if you're not a customer, well, I reckon that makes you stew meat. Boys?"

The bar's other patrons pushed back their chairs, cracking knuckles and baring teeth. They didn't all have the goblin's polished crimson fangs, but most of them had at least an eyetooth that was stained scarlet, and those who didn't bore some other mark: red-rimmed nostrils, crimson clouds in the whites of their eyes, or spittle that looked half blood.

"Don't suppose we can talk you out of this," Merisiel said, sounding equal parts bored and resigned. Without waiting for an answer, she hurled her liquor glass full into the goblin's face, then grabbed the smaller creature by her enormous ears and smashed her head into the flickering remnants of her cockroach fire.

The goblin howled and beat her fists clumsily backward, but Merisiel used all her weight to hold the bartender's face down in the spreading flames. "I just wanted some directions. You give me directions, I'll let you up."

Ezren couldn't make out the goblin's answer. The bar's customers were converging on him, led by a barrel-shaped man with snakes tattooed across his chin and cheeks, and a gaunt aiuvarin, or half-elf, woman who resembled a skeleton wrapped in paper for skin. The aiuvarin's mouth was smeared with garishly bright red lipstick that, Ezren realized with a belated shock, wasn't paint, but rather the raw, bleeding flesh beneath her peeled-off lips.

He was still holding the ladle. Raising it across his body like a quarterstaff, Ezren reached for one of the simplest spells he knew. The magic surged into his grasp, powerful but contained, and the ladle split apart into long, shivering steel darts. With a discordant metallic wail, they hurtled into the snake-tattooed man's torso, impaling him against the tavern wall.

The man grabbed the bladed needles and pulled them out of his body. They grated horribly against his ribs and sliced his hand down to the bone, but he didn't seem to care. Wrenching them from his chest and side, he tried to throw them back at Ezren, but the magical darts dissolved into shimmering dust. The ladle reappeared, intact and seemingly untouched, in Ezren's hand.

"We will eat you," the gaunt aiuvarin crooned, burbling the words through her skinned lips. She smiled, and the spaces between her teeth were full of blood. It welled from the corners of her eyes and trickled from her left nostril. "You'll not be wasted. We will chew your flesh and drink your blood. We need you. The sweet meat of your death... "

She swung at him with her nails outstretched like claws. Ezren pulled back, barely evading the blow, and was astonished that her scraggly, flaking nails tore through his sturdy traveling clothes as easily as if they'd been wet paper.

The needles hadn't taken the barrel-chested man out of the fight, so Ezren tried a slightly more challenging spell. Raising a hand to the ceiling, he gathered moisture from the air and condensed it into a ray of elemental cold.

This time, the magic flared into its own living fury. Instead of coalescing into the tight, controlled line Ezren tried to draw, it followed the lingering echoes of his last spell. The energy splintered into a blue-white imitation of his needle spray, each bolt cloudy and shagged at the edges with hoarfrost.

The bolts screamed across the room, splitting and splitting again into a blinding fountain of ice shards and snowflakes. As they broke and multiplied, they picked up other impressions, other resonances: disembodied mouths filled with glass-needle teeth, a six-legged spider with gnashing jaws in place of its body, an eye fringed with lashes made of bleeding fangs.

They tore apart the bar's patrons, ripping into their bodies with unholy hunger. Icy teeth and bladed hailstones shredded the patrons' flesh and pulverized their bones. And through it all, in the center of the frozen maelstrom, Ezren felt a glow of red joy.

Who were these wretches that dared attack him? He, who had the power of a god at his fingertips? Destruction would be a kindness. These were monsters, cannibals, torturers of helpless insects—and they deserved to be tortured a thousand times worse in return.

Yes. Ezren felt his lips curl back in a monstrous smile. It wasn't his own smile, and the shock of feeling his face twist into someone else's expression snapped him out of the crimson haze.

No. He put his fingers to his forehead, his eyelids, his cheeks. He felt the contours of his own face, and the familiar roughness of his beard. Relief washed over him.

When he drew his hands away, he was astonished to see them dripping with blood.

It wasn't his. The entire interior of the tavern was washed in red. Nothing was left of its patrons save a pink pulp smeared across the windows, and a few odd fragments here and there. A clump of hair stuck to the back of a chair, the stump of a leg bone thrust up from an oozing boot.

"Merisiel?" Ezren cleared his throat, fearing the worst.

"I'm alive." The elf's head popped up from behind the bar. Her tan makeup had rubbed off her forehead in streaks, exposing the paler skin beneath, and some of her brightly colored rags were lacerated and dripping with melted ice, but she didn't seem to have been hurt. "What did you *do* to them? I've never seen a spell like that. It was like a blizzard of ice demons."

"Yes. It was... like that," Ezren said, striving for calm. Rationality. Sanity in a world washed with blood. "I believe I have some insight into what has befallen Port Peril."

"I saw the monsters in the blizzard. It's not hard to guess. Not many things have such ugly faces." Merisiel lifted a hand to plant on the bar so she could vault herself over, saw the morass of pulverized flesh that coated the counter, and thought better of it. She stood up, brushed off her clothes, and walked around the bar. "Rovagug?"

"Rovagug."

"We need to find Kyra. If the Rough Beast is somehow influencing the people of Port Peril, that's a problem." Merisiel fell quiet for a beat, her sharp, bright eyes lingering on Ezren. "Are you all right? You looked strange, for a little while, in the middle of that blizzard. Not quite like yourself."

"I'm fine." He said it too quickly, and then shook his head. "I am now, that is. I felt a malign influence come through the magic. It tried to take hold of me. Perhaps, if I had held the spell longer or tried to cast another, it might have succeeded. But it did not."

"That's still not good. You have a god-spark. If Rovagug touches your mind... "

Ezren nodded grimly, wishing he hadn't told Merisiel what had happened to him. "We will discuss it with Kyra."

Merisiel regarded the slumped form of the goblin bartender. Smoke still sizzled from the scorched stubble around her wide green ears, but nothing else moved. "Do you still want to look for the junk dealer? This attempt seems to have come to a dead end."

"We should. It's all connected. The more we know about the *Merry Mermaid*'s travels and her cargo, the better our chances of unraveling how and why the Devourer has extended his taint so deeply into Port Peril."

"Well, all right." Merisiel blew out a breath as she considered the problem. "I might have another idea. No more taverns, though. And we'll have to change your disguise before we leave. This one's soaked in blood."

"Yes." Ezren wiped his hands clean, as best he could, on the inside of the tattered tunic Merisiel had dressed him in. He stripped off his outer layers, grateful that the cheap disguise had absorbed much of the gore and left his own clothes relatively untouched. Ordinarily, he could have used a cantrip to clean his garments, but that carried more risk than he wished to court at the moment. "Where should we look next?"

"If this junk dealer hasn't already succumbed to the Worldbreaker's influence, he'll have reached the same conclusion we did: the best protection against one god's influence is another's. We'll go to the temples."

Ezren nodded. He crumpled his soiled garments into a loose ball, turning them inside out so that he could wipe his hands one last time as he discarded the gore-spattered pile. "We must be careful in our approach. It's likely that Rovagug will have pushed his corrupted creatures to attack his old enemies' strongholds. Particularly Sarenrae's."

"I know." A bleakness came over Merisiel's face, and her shoulders dipped before she gathered herself and squared them. "For that reason, too, we need to find Kyra."

Chapter Nineteen
SANCTUARY

There was a fight here," Amiri said, crouching to pick up a bloody bottle fragment from the rubble-strewn street as they drew near the Inheritor's Harbor. She examined the red-streaked glass and flicked it away. "Not professionals. Brawlers. Maybe just a drunken mob."

Kyra could see that for herself. Wooden shingles and clay tiles had been knocked from the surrounding buildings; flower boxes and flags had been torn from the houses nearby. The small temple of Iomedae in Eastwind appeared to have been hastily barricaded behind makeshift fortifications of overturned carts reinforced with lumber scraps, but those barricades had failed, for the main doors had been breached and torn from their hinges.

No one had tried to repair that damage, and the street was empty and still.

Foreboding gripped Kyra as she and Amiri walked toward the ransacked temple. No drunken mob would attack a temple of Iomedae. One maddened by the rage of Rovagug would, though.

This was where the records in the Locker said that Sir Osmund of Westcrown could be found, but it didn't look likely that they'd find anyone in the Inheritor's Harbor. No one living, at any rate.

Kyra didn't know how much more horror she could take. The Locker had been bad enough. Port Peril's prison had long been infamous for the callousness and corruption of its guards, and for the notorious Tidal Cells, where unruly prisoners were submerged with each turn of the tides and sometimes devoured by the jigsaw sharks who swam in with the rising waters.

No, the Locker had never been a pleasant place, but it had become something far worse in the plague of violence that swept Port Peril. Kyra prayed that someday she would forget what she had witnessed as she walked through those cold, dripping halls, hearing the distorted howls of guards and prisoners alike bounce off the gray stone walls.

They'd found bodies, and things that might once have been bodies, and the remnants of sacrifices that told them the Rough Beast had devoured the minds of those who had committed those deeds. They had not found anyone alive, though the cries from the depths suggested that there were still souls in torment below.

Neither Amiri nor Kyra had suggested that they should try to find or help those souls, and while the Kellid seemed at peace with her decision, Kyra couldn't help second-guessing her own. *I might have done something. I might have saved one.*

But she might also have died, and then she would have failed Sarenrae's charge. Her duty to the Dawnflower had to take precedence. Everything else came second.

In the Locker's records room, they'd found ledgers that mentioned Sir Osmund of Westcrown. He had apprehended a handful of minor criminals over the past two years and had brought some of them to the Locker to face what passed for Port Peril's justice. The entries gave his address as the Inheritor's Harbor, a charity chapel in Eastwind, and so Kyra and Amiri had gone to the temple to look for him.

As they picked their way across the trampled mud, and then through the smashed barricades around the front door, Kyra ventured a cautious call. "Is anyone here?"

"Don't bother." Amiri slid past her, stalking forward in a hunter's crouch. The Kellid moved silently over broken glass and floorboards, never drawing a creak from the damaged chapel. "About a dozen people left this place after the fight, so there were survivors. Many of them were wounded, but they didn't have to fight their way out, so they must have won and driven off their attackers. After they left, though, they didn't come back. No one did, except maybe a scavenger or a would-be patient. Whoever that was, they didn't go deep into the chapel, and they left quickly."

Kyra stepped over an arc of blood sprayed across the floor. Someone had died there. "There's no one inside?"

"No one we want to talk to. But they might have forgotten to finish off an enemy or two. And from what we've seen so far, Rovagug's corrupted don't die like normal people." Amiri drew a long knife, better suited for close-quarters fighting than her greatsword, and stalked deeper into the chapel.

Past the battered foyer and blood-spattered waiting room, they found a treatment room with linen-draped patient beds and a wheeled operating table. Beds and table had been overturned and pushed into a barricade against the door. This one didn't appear to have been breached, however.

Kyra opened one of the creaky wooden cabinets. The bandages and wound ointments were gone, as were all the medicines with sedative or tranquilizing effects. Other syrups and tinctures remained on their shelves, untouched. "The violence didn't get this far."

Amiri straightened and sheathed her knife. "Osmund was here. He left a trail sign." She moved to an alcove in the treatment room's east wall, where a white ceramic vase held a trio of wilted white roses. The vase was painted with Iomedae's holy sword. A smudge of soot crossed over the sword, making a sort of V shape.

The Kellid lifted the vase out of the alcove and looked under it, then peered at the bottom of the vessel. "This is the message that the trail sign meant for us to find, but I don't know what it means."

Emptying out the dead roses, she flipped the vase over and handed it to Kyra. Several inscrutable symbols had been etched onto the white ceramic.

"It's a code of faith," Kyra said. She brought the vase over to a south-facing window, murmuring a prayer as she held it up to the sun. A sunlit spark danced across the letters, confirming that it had been written by a blessed hand and was no trick meant to deceive her. "There is a sanctuary in the Knotworks where people may seek the protection of holy faiths against the corruption that consumes Port Peril. Whoever wrote this message went there and invites those who can read the script to join them."

"That's Osmund. Can you find the place?"

"If you can take me to the Knotworks. It will be somewhere in the eastern portion of the district. We should look for a cavern facing the sea. There will be a stone lion near the entrance, and a lantern burning with a yellow flame."

"All right." Amiri glanced out the window, grimacing at the sun's position in the sky. "We'd better hurry. Searching the Knotworks might take a while, and I don't want to be out in Port Peril after dark."

"No." Kyra put the vase back in its alcove and replaced the wilted roses as well. Should their enemies return to this place, she didn't want them finding Sir Osmund's message. "I only hope Merisiel and Ezren find safety before sundown."

"They will." Amiri glanced out the window at the devastated city. Crows squabbled over a heap of clothing slumped in the rubble. Their croaking cries carried harshly over the empty streets, filled with an anger and cruelty that no animal should have. "You know they will. They'll probably beat us there. With their junk dealer too."

"Yes." Kyra forced a smile as she moved to the door. The cries of the crows rang in her ears. "No doubt."

Please, Sarenrae, let it be true.

They moved swiftly through Port Peril, avoiding the few people they encountered on the desolate streets. The handful of passersby they saw eyed them with equal mistrust, but that brought Kyra a certain reassurance. It meant that not everyone had succumbed to the unholy rage that had seized the Locker and assailed the Inheritor's Harbor. Ordinary people still lived there, and if the curse could be lifted, they might soon restore Port Peril. The pirates' haven had always had a resilient spirit, and she hoped that it might survive.

If we can find an answer in time...

It was midafternoon when they reached the Knotworks, the network of labyrinthine tunnels that dug into the high bluffs beneath the pirates' city. Amiri had chosen a circuitous route, believing it safer to stay in the open as long as possible before descending into the Knotworks' tangle. She'd warned that it was easy to be ambushed in the maze, and as they climbed down a rickety bamboo ladder toward the first ledge, Kyra understood what she meant.

A chaotic web of ladders and rope bridges spanned the face of the bluffs, connecting ledges and caverns to one another. Oversized buckets and lifts, cranked by hand or by harnessed mules, enabled transport of large goods and less mobile visitors. Those mechanisms stood idle now—the ones that hadn't been smashed at the froth-washed bottom of the cliffs. Other than the crash and churn of the waves below, Kyra heard nothing from the once bustling Knotworks as she climbed down.

"This is the east entrance," Amiri said, helping Kyra off the ladder. A wide ledge led to a large, shallow cavern divided into multiple wood-framed booths, each covered by a bright striped or patchwork awning. Onion skins and fish scales blew about the abandoned stalls. Small flags fluttered at the crosspieces and along the frame posts, but nothing else moved.

In the deepening afternoon light, Kyra studied the walls of stone and wood. She found what she was looking for on the side of an overturned apple crate, almost lost amid the lengthening shadows: a childish drawing of a butterfly with a circle of stars on its upper right wing. One star was blue, the rest white. "Second tunnel to the right."

"How many people would recognize that code?" Amiri asked as she took the lead into the Knotworks. They soon left the sunlight behind them, and the Kellid lit a torch to continue into the stone tunnel. Watery mud coated the floor, causing their footfalls to slap wetly in the smoky dark.

"Any Desnan, and most servants of Shelyn and Sarenrae," Kyra said softly as she followed Amiri. Rats peered at them from smaller holes burrowed into the Knotworks, revealing no more than a bald tail or a pair of beady eyes in the torchlight before they vanished. "It is a commonly used marking, and not among the protected secrets of the Radiant Prism. It is meant to be widely recognized by lay followers and anyone else who might benefit from the goddesses' guidance."

Amiri grunted. She stooped low with the torch, sweeping it over the tunnel floor. "There are a lot of tracks in this mud, and they mostly head the way we're going. I'd say the mark's drawn a healthy share of followers. Whoever's protecting this place better have some security, because with this level of traffic, Rovagug's corrupted must have noticed it too."

"I am certain they have not left themselves unguarded." As they passed through the Knotworks, accompanied by the squeak and scurry of unseen rodents, Kyra noted more Desnan signs scrawled upon the walls. They led the reader onward through the maze, signaling a right turn here, a left there, a dangerous chasm ahead.

For someone who could not read the signs, she guessed, the tunnels would be far more hazardous, though probably not deadly. This did not seem like a labyrinth meant to kill, although it could easily have been altered to become one. It was only meant to hide its people, and it did that well.

After about half an hour, the tunnel widened, and Amiri's torchlight fell over the stone likeness of a regal male lion. It had been carved from golden marble in the imperial Taldan fashion and had likely been looted from some naval fort by pirates long ago. A warm yellow glow emanated from the cavern behind it.

Upon rounding the bend, Kyra could see that the yellow light came from a lantern that hung on a mount worked to resemble a fanciful, multicolored songbird with long, curling tail feathers.

The cavern appeared to be a dead end, but Kyra suspected that was a ruse. Approaching slowly, with her hands in plain view in case any hidden guard was watching them, she knelt in the light of the songbird's lantern. "Sarenrae, show me the way."

Even before she spoke, the lantern's flame began to change color. Its yellow shifted to green, then deepened to turquoise. In the wavering azure glow, Kyra saw the outline of a hidden door with a pull ring in the wall five feet away. Whether it had been concealed by magic earlier or had been painted with some alchemical compound that reacted only to this light, it had been invisible a moment ago but stood out now.

She took hold of the ring, glanced back to make sure Amiri was with her, and pulled.

The door swung open on oiled hinges. It led to a wire-walled cage of the sort that smugglers and fences sometimes used to hold new customers at a safe remove. Beyond the cage's walls, Kyra could see nothing but darkness.

"Do we go in?" Amiri whispered hoarsely behind her.

"Yes. The Dawnflower would not lead us to harm." Feigning a confidence that she only partly felt, Kyra strode into the cage. After a tiny hesitation, Amiri followed, gripping her knife.

The door closed behind them. A sudden gust of wind blew out Amiri's torch, casting them into absolute blackness. The Kellid snarled, throwing the torch aside to clang loudly against the wire walls. "What is this?"

Just as Kyra raised her holy symbol to invoke Sarenrae's illumination, a brown-haired man emerged from the darkness, wearing a shining pendant upon his chest. Broad-shouldered and of towering height, he was easily one of the largest humans Kyra had ever seen. A red-trimmed white cloak flowed from his shoulders, and he wore plate mail inscribed with Iomedae's holy sword and sacred sigils, adding to his stature.

As his light fell over them, the man started. "Amiri? Have you come to fight with us?"

The Kellid ran a hand through her short black hair, unable to keep from grinning despite their circumstances. "Not exactly. It's good to see you again, Osmund. This is my friend Kyra. We need to ask for your help."

"Can your need be greater than Port Peril's?"

"Yes, actually." Amiri jerked a thumb at the cage that enclosed them. "Do we have to talk here? You'll want to hear this story, and it's not short."

Sir Osmund hesitated again, long enough that Amiri noticed it and narrowed her eyes. "Don't you trust me?"

"I do." He took a key from a ring at his belt and unlocked the cage's far door. "Forgive me for greeting an old friend so shabbily. These are trying times. But I'm glad you came. Have you been here long?"

"No. We arrived just this morning," Amiri said, following the armored Iomedaean away from the cage and down a narrow corridor tight enough that Sir Osmund's plated shoulders came within an inch of scraping the stone on either side. Kyra walked behind them, quietly observing.

"Ah. If you had been here from the beginning, you'd understand my caution. But I can explain that, if you like, after you've told your tale." Sir Osmund ushered them to a small cavern where weatherbeaten chairs, softened with frayed and mismatched pillows, sat in a circle. Boxes against the walls held spare clothes, blankets, utensils, and toys.

"Right. Well, let me tell you why we came," Amiri began, with a glance at Kyra. "It started in Totra... "

"So you need passage out of Port Peril?" Sir Osmund asked when Amiri had finished. A younger man, black-haired and blue-eyed, coughed politely as he came to the patched curtain that served as the door to the sitting area. At a nod from Sir Osmund, he brought in a platter with a hunk of cheese, a pile of small salt-cured fish, and several fist-sized lumps of bread that were half scorched and half dough. After setting the platter and a pitcher of water on the table, he left again.

Kyra was surprised to realize how hungry she was and tore into the modest meal with as much eagerness as decorum would allow. "Yes. Though it seems we may have some difficulty finding a captain, or a crew, capable of setting sail."

"Perhaps." Sir Osmund fell quiet. He gazed at the platter but ate nothing. "How much of our troubles do you wish to know?"

"Everything," Kyra said before Amiri could interrupt to ask for the abbreviated version. "We do not know what might be relevant to our own task, or what might allow us to help the poor souls of this city."

"As best I can tell, it started shortly after the Godsrain," Sir Osmund said, leaning back on his chair while his guests ate. It creaked alarmingly under his armored bulk but did not give way. "The Eye of Abendego often sends storms to Port Peril, but in the days after the Godsrain, those storms were of unusual frequency and fury. Many old hands said that the hurricane itself seemed to be growing larger and angrier and was pulling in ships that would have been on safe courses before.

"Be that as it may, one thing I can say for certain is that two nights after the Godsrain, we saw the first of the red storms."

"Red storms?" Amiri asked around a mouthful of half-chewed fish. She'd been even hungrier than Kyra, or at least less restrained about showing it.

"After the Godsrain, the sea storms that blow in from the Eye of Abendego began to carry a swirling red mist," Sir Osmund said. "They are the source of the contagion that has consumed all that was good in Port Peril. Those who are exposed to the red storms lose all semblance of decency, mercy, self-control. Their behavior becomes increasingly erratic, their thoughts confused and prone to paranoia. Over time, and more rapidly with repeated exposure, they become monsters. Those worst afflicted are altered in body as well as soul, and they become fully Rovagug's creatures. I have slain many, and grieved each one, for none chose the fate that the Great Destroyer inflicted on them." He paused, staring down at his interlocked hands. "I regret to say that this fate befell our old friend Boskrag. I pray that his soul has found peace."

"Is there a cure?" Kyra asked.

The knight shook his head. "Not one that works for the entire city. Our prayers can hold it at bay here in the tunnels, where the red storms do not yet reach. The more powerful clerics and champions among us can lift the curse from individuals. But, as you doubtlessly know from your own experience ministering to the needy, that method is not sufficient in the face of a major contagion. We can't hold back the tide with bare hands."

"If everyone outside the tunnels is tainted, how can we get a ship?" Amiri asked. "You seemed to think there was a way, but I'm not seeing it."

Sir Osmund managed a slight, lopsided smile. "Amiri. Always relentlessly focused on your own needs. I missed that, believe it or not. To answer your question: we have a few ships, and some smaller vessels. A few crews managed to find sanctuary before Rovagug seized them. They brought their ships in safely when they could. Other ships were abandoned in the harbor, close enough that we could rush out and bring them in before they foundered.

"Whenever we have enough skilled sailors gathered in the sanctuary to crew a ship, we wait for the weather-readers to find a break in the red storms. Such respites have become fewer and farther between as the Eye of Abendego intensifies its wrath, but they do still come. Then we send a ship out to sail away from here with as many passengers as it can carry. It is a slow, hazardous, piecemeal evacuation, but it's all we can offer."

Amiri cracked open one of the burned bread balls. It was speckled with weevils, but after a second's pause, she bit into it anyway. "Can you give us a ship?"

"I can ask for volunteers," the knight replied. "Some might be willing to risk it. You and your companions are formidable, and Kyra's presence, in particular, is likely to reassure some. On the other hand, your quest is likely to lead you into danger, and it is possible that the red storms or their victims may target you specifically. In the early days of the violence in Port Peril, many worshippers of Sarenrae were the victims of seemingly random attacks. We didn't realize the connection until later, when the corruption had gone far enough that the mark of Rovagug began appearing upon those it had claimed."

"What if we offer to pay them?" Amiri finished her roll and took another.

"You'd probably get more volunteers," Sir Osmund conceded. "Most of them were pirates before they came here. Offer them a pouch of gold to take to the seas, and you're speaking their language."

"Very good," Kyra said. She could no longer resist asking the question that had been tormenting her since their arrival. *Merisiel...* "Have you heard anything of—"

An unseen chime rang through the room, melodious but penetrating. Sir Osmund stood, his demeanor grave. "Please excuse me. We have another visitor."

"Should we go with you? In case there's trouble." Amiri was already pushing back her chair, one hand on her greatsword's hilt. She looked eager for a fight, and Kyra could see that the eagerness troubled their host.

"Amiri... you should know that those who succumbed most quickly to the red storms were the ones like you. People who channeled their rage in battle. I think the taint exploits that. One and all, they fell, swiftly and badly, in the very first days. We could not save any." Sir Osmund shrugged uneasily even as he strode toward the entry cage. His pendant ignited with holy white light as he entered the darkened tunnels, casting a halo about his armored form. "I welcome your company, but I must ask you to stay out of any fight that might result. Please. Above all, I implore you, do not give in to your battle rage here."

Amiri blinked, visibly startled. She looked to Kyra, as if she might be able to confirm or deny what Sir Osmund had said, and then turned back toward the knight with a wounded scowl. "Fine."

Ahead, Sir Osmund's light fell upon the wire cage. As he drew nearer, it illuminated two figures—two dear, familiar figures.

Kyra's heart leaped for joy. "Merisiel!"

"Kyra." The elf's black-armored shoulders dipped minutely in what would have been a heaved sigh of relief from anyone else. "How long have you been here? What did you find?"

"An hour, maybe two." Kyra wasn't certain. Without the sun to guide her, she couldn't tell how much time had passed. "Sir Osmund is one of Amiri's friends and the man we sought in Port Peril. Did you find the junk dealer?"

"Skrit? No. We followed codes and trail signs to get this far, guessing that he might have done the same. Rats are survivors, they say. But we haven't found him yet." Merisiel studied Sir Osmund, who was unlocking the cage. "I was hoping maybe whoever guarded this sanctuary could tell us where to look."

The knight shook his head as he turned the key and stepped aside, holding open the door with unsmiling courtesy. "I do not recognize that name."

"I think he does," Ezren said. The wizard pointed to a crevice near the ceiling, where a coarse-furred brown rat was watching them with an uncommon intelligence in its round eyes. It opened its mouth and let out three distinct squeaks, then disappeared back into its crevice.

"Did we see that rat earlier?" Amiri asked Kyra.

But she could only shrug. Rats all looked the same to her. They'd seen no shortage of rodents in the Knotworks, but she couldn't have said whether this one was among them.

A moment later, the rat returned, bearing a yellow pebble. It flung the pebble down to Ezren, who picked it up with a bemused expression and held it out to Sir Osmund's light. Black letters had been painted on the stone.

"Follow me," they read.

Chapter Twenty
GIFTS OF THE MERRY MERMAID

The companions exchanged a look.

"I could write a note back," Ezren suggested, "and the rat could bear that to its master."

"We don't know how far it would need to go, and rats aren't exactly fast travelers over distance." Merisiel eased her aching shoulders. Their travels through Port Peril had been fraught and exhausting, and she had only just found Kyra again, yet it seemed they had no choice. "If we're going to follow it, we should just follow it."

"Then let's go," Amiri said. The barbarian's relatively relaxed air suggested that she and Kyra, at least, had been given a meal and a chance to rest a bit.

"Lead on," Merisiel told the rat. To Sir Osmund, she added, "We'll be back soon."

Then, wearily, she turned around in the cage and went back out to the Knotworks, following the brown-furred rat.

It led them through the tunnels with uncanny confidence. The rat pointed out secret entrances hidden behind piles of debris and stacked crates, stood on its hind legs and squeaked to warn them about simple but lethal traps rigged against intruders, and once ushered them into a concealed side cavern as something large and wet squelched past, leaving an odor of curdled swamp gas in the air.

Finally the rat scampered up a wall and scrabbled at a wooden object out of sight overhead, which unrolled a rope ladder that led to a gap in the ceiling. Its head poked out of the hole, and it chittered at them before disappearing again.

"Fine." Merisiel eyed the darkness. Grabbing the swaying bamboo rungs, she hoisted herself up the ladder. "Follow me after thirty seconds if you don't hear screaming."

She clambered into another tight, twisting corridor, this one seemingly excavated by claws and teeth rather than handheld tools. Using her elbows and knees to pull herself along, Merisiel wriggled through the tunnel until she came to an abrupt drop down a hole in the floor at the other end. The rat stared at her from the edge, twitching its whiskers, and then darted through in a flash of oily brown fur.

Suppressing a grimace, Merisiel followed. She could hear her companions making their way through the tunnel and knew they'd soon be behind her. Cramped as it was, there was no time to hesitate.

She grabbed the stone lip and swung down. The drop was about seven feet, not difficult. Merisiel landed in a crouch and moved aside, clearing the way for the next person to come through.

A smoky oil lamp burned in the cavern she'd just entered. It illuminated a cluttered room, perhaps twenty feet long and ten wide, although there were so many boxes and bundles piled up against the walls that Merisiel wasn't sure of the precise dimensions. Rusting bits of junk, tarnished scraps of wire, and unidentifiable miscellany spilled out of every container. The air was heavy with stale smoke of oil and the musty, animalic odor of woolen clothes that had been stuffed into storage without being washed.

The rat was nowhere in sight, although that wasn't surprising given the jumble that crowded the room. Just as Amiri dropped down the hole, joining Merisiel, a hatch opened in the floor, jostling aside a pile of disassembled gears and stained alchemical beakers.

A hunched figure in a tattered brown coat emerged, blinking myopically at Merisiel and Amiri through wire-rimmed spectacles with mismatched lenses. He looked like a bipedal brown rat, perhaps four feet tall. A patched and stained violin case teetered across his back, and on his shoulder perched a smaller rat, presumably the one that had guided them to this place.

"Oh, you're real," the ratfolk said, sounding vaguely surprised. He blinked at them again, whiskers twitching around his large pink nose. "I wasn't sure you were going to be real."

"Are you Skrit?" Merisiel asked. "We were told you might have dealt with some wares from the *Merry Mermaid*, a trading ship out of Osirion. This was a while ago, and you might not remember—"

"Yes, yes. I have them all... Where was it? Give me a moment. Around here." Skrit bustled through the clutter, picking up boxes and peering into sacks before tossing them aside, no better organized than they'd been before. Several times, he checked the same place twice, having apparently forgotten that he'd already looked there. He barely twitched an ear as Kyra, and then Ezren, came down the hole to join the rest of the group.

"I was told you'd come," the ratfolk said without turning around. "I had a dream. Well, I had several dreams. I ignored the first few. Why should the gods talk to me in my sleep? I don't talk to *them*. No business in that, none at all. Gods never pay for what they want. Terrible customers.

"But the dreams kept coming. Wouldn't leave me alone. Then the red storms hit, and I realized the warnings were real. Not just bad fish and indigestion. No, the gods really were trying to tell me something. And that was... *this*!" Skrit hoisted a shabby velvet bag out of a larger sack. He held it up to the companions as though he were showing them some legendary hero's sword, not a threadbare, moldy-smelling bag of unidentifiable lumps.

"What is it?" Amiri asked.

Skrit's round ears dipped. He blinked at the Kellid, clearly annoyed that she wasn't in awe. "What's left of what I bought from the *Merry Mermaid*. The dreams said you'd want it."

"Sarenrae spoke to you? What did she say?" Kyra pressed forward, knocking over a heap of crockery.

Skrit clicked his teeth disapprovingly and hurried over to straighten a pile of chipped saucers. "I don't know if it was Sarenrae. It might have been some other god. It was a dream, not a conversation. The dreams warned me that the red storms would come, and that I should take shelter deep in the Knotworks. They said that you'd come too, sometime after the storms did, and that you'd want the leftovers from the *Merry Mermaid*. So I bundled them up for you, and here they are."

"What's in there?" Amiri reached for the bag.

The ratfolk snatched it away, waving his forefinger at the Kellid. "No grabbing. No, no. The dreams said to give you all of it, but they didn't say I had to give it up for free. It's yours for a price."

Merisiel crossed her arms and tilted out her hip. "What price?"

A shrewd look crossed Skrit's furry face. His tongue peeped out briefly through his large orange incisors. "I want out of Port Peril. Safe passage for me, and for Ratty."

"You named your rat Ratty?" Merisiel managed to twist her laugh into a cough at the last second.

The ratfolk gave her a reproachful stare. "He's a rat. Why shouldn't I call him Ratty? It's what he is."

Merisiel looked at the others, offering a shrug. "We're hiring a ship out of Port Peril anyway. Why not bring him along?"

"I don't want passage on a ship," Skrit interrupted, tail twitching. "No. The dreams said that if you got here at all, it would be by magic. Teleportation. That's much safer than a ship sailing through the red storms, going gods know where. So that's what I want. I give you the things from the *Merry Mermaid*, you teleport me and Ratty somewhere safe. Then go away and leave us alone. I don't want anything more to do with gods. Terrible customers. The worst."

"Can you do it?" Kyra asked Ezren.

"I'll do my best," the wizard replied. "Tomorrow."

Late the next morning, in the sanctuary that Sir Osmund and his fellows had carved from the Knotworks, Merisiel and Kyra stooped over the collection of odds and ends that Skrit had sold them. Ezren had returned to the ratfolk's lair to fulfil their end of the bargain, and Amiri was out patrolling with her old friend.

Kyra and Merisiel were alone, for the first time in what felt like ages, and Merisiel felt all the pent-up emotions of the last few weeks crowd against the back of her throat in a choking welter. She couldn't focus on the detritus from the *Merry Mermaid*.

It was all worthless junk anyway: a dented brass toothpick or scarf pin with a red glass gem; an oversized monocle with a badly scratched lens; a ceremonial stone dagger too large for any human to wield, which might have been worth something if it hadn't been worn down to a nub by waves and sand.

There was a chunk of beautifully carved red-and-white marble that had probably been part of a collar necklace at some point, and another chunk that bore the likeness of a phoenix. Those and a few other pieces, carved in a similar style and likewise broken off from larger items, were the only things that looked like they might have any value. A jeweler might be able to cut out the images and smooth their edges to set them as cameos in new pieces, but at best they were raw materials in their current state.

Meri was supposed to study the objects with an appraiser's eye, picking out trick pieces or forgeries, but so far she hadn't spotted anything noteworthy. She couldn't fathom why Sarenrae would have come to Skrit in his dreams and told the ratfolk to set these things aside.

Kyra seemed to have no such doubts. She bowed her head over each piece, cradling it in her hands as she prayed. "Sarenrae, guide me. Is this what we are meant to take? Is this the key to our quest?"

Each time, sunlight blossomed between her hands and surrounded the object in a halo that dwindled into nothingness. Each time, Kyra put the object down and moved to the next. She worked with seemingly infinite patience, but Meri knew her wife well enough to read the dejection from each failure, and to see the increasing desperation with which she picked up each new possibility.

Though Meri ached to interrupt, she didn't interfere with Kyra's prayers. She'd seen the misery and terror that the red storms had inflicted on Port Peril. Both Kyra and Sir Osmund seemed convinced that this was merely the beginning of some greater disaster, the full scope of which they could not yet grasp.

Compared to that, what did Meri's feelings matter?

So she swallowed her heart and held the pieces of junk up to study by Kyra's holy light, and tried to find something, anything, that might help her wife fulfill Sarenrae's charge.

"I have it," Kyra said beside her. Relief filled the cleric's voice, and with it a tremble of fear and awe. "This is what Sarenrae meant for us to find."

She held out a chunk of red-and-white marble. It was one of the carvings that Meri had looked at earlier and passed over as insignificant. This one depicted two overlapping circles, with a partial view of stars behind them that suggested it represented a solar or lunar eclipse. In the heart of the eclipse was a ring of sigils, and at the base of the carving was a round gap where some curved part or object was missing.

"I'm not certain," Kyra admitted. She'd borrowed the Akithaine artifacts from Ezren before he'd left to meet Skrit. Taking the compass out of its case, she fitted it to the marble carving. "I can sense only that there is an unholy reverberation in its core. This carving was broken from an item of great evil, and it retains a connection to that power. It may be a pass token, or a key. But I think... "

The compass slotted into place with an audible click. A fiery needle sprang from the compass's center, orienting northwest. Kyra exhaled in satisfaction, and relief. "That's it. That's the piece we were missing. Formose must have made this compass to show his followers the way back to Inithyra's Orb. I would wager that the marble carving is connected to the orb somehow—perhaps it's a fragment of the orb itself, or it was quarried from the island that holds it—and the compass uses that resonance of belonging to orient toward the whole."

"What will we find when we get there?" Meri asked. It was a hollow question. What she really wanted to ask was: *When will I have you back? When will there be space in your heart and mind for me?*

But she couldn't ask that without sounding like she was begging, and Merisiel refused to beg for attention. "If Inithyra's Orb is, or comes from, a place of such desecration that you can sense it from this fragment, why would Sarenrae send us there?"

"I don't know that either, but I cannot know everything in the Dawnflower's design. The nature of faith requires us to accept the unknown and trust that our actions are guided by a wisdom we cannot, and need not, comprehend. Sarenrae sent us to find this object. We have it. We may learn its purpose later if that is part of her design. If not, it may remain a mystery forever. But I will have served as I was bidden, and that is all that matters." Kyra wrapped the stone in a handkerchief and tucked it into a pouch. "Let's find the others. It's time for us to leave Port Peril."

It took less time than Merisiel expected to make their departure arrangements. Given the increasing danger of the red storms, Sir Osmund's people had developed a highly efficient system for launching their escape vessels whenever a lull in the red storms allowed. Merisiel soon discovered, however, that this was not the reason she and her companions were able to leave so expeditiously.

The night before they were to leave, Sir Osmund called them to the small waiting area where he'd spoken to them when they first arrived.

Only a single day and night had passed since Kyra found the chunk of carved marble in Skrit's bag. Ezren had attempted to delve the piece, with little success. All he'd been able to tell them was that it had been carved by giant hands, that it had been broken from a temple on a jungle island, and that the temple had not originally been built to serve unholy ends but had been corrupted by a profound malevolence that bubbled up from below.

But whether it was a part of Inithyra's Orb, he could not say. Nor could he tell them what to expect at the compass's destination, beyond those vague warnings.

Perhaps they would find out soon. There was a decent chance, Merisiel guessed, that the compass, telescope, and star chart might lead them back to wherever the *Merry Mermaid* had landed. Once they had a ship, they might soon know the answer to that question.

The companions gathered in the sitting room as bidden. Merisiel was nearly the last to arrive; the others were already seated on the chairs when she walked in. Ezren looked drawn but alert, energized by the challenges ahead. Amiri paced restlessly around the chairs, eager to be gone.

Kyra sat with her back straight and her hands folded serenely in her lap, but Merisiel could see how much her wife's cheekbones had hollowed and how heavy the shadows under her eyes had become. The flame of her devotion was burning her to nothing, and Merisiel didn't know how much more she could withstand.

Sir Osmund came in last. The towering knight was accompanied by two other people, whose faces Meri had glimpsed around the sanctuary but whose names she did not know.

"Please allow me to introduce you to Samo and Nahoa," Sir Osmund said, gesturing in turn to the woman and man who'd come in with him. "They'll be your crew. Samo, Nahoa, please meet Amiri,

Ezren, Merisiel, and Kyra. They're the ones who need your help sailing out of Port Peril."

"Our crew is two people?" Amiri asked, raising her eyebrows. "To sail a ship?"

"You'll be taking a boat, not a ship, and you won't need anyone else. Samo and Nahoa were touched by the Godsrain, and they have been gifted with extraordinary power. Losing them will be a blow to our efforts here, but they insist that they must go with you."

Merisiel looked the two over. Samo was a woman of about fifty, clad in reindeer furs and woven bark, with a feathered club at her side and a bone pendant dangling over her chest. A wide-brimmed hat shaded her features. She had a reserved, otherworldly mien, but radiated calm and acceptance rather than judgment.

Nahoa was much younger, probably not far over twenty. He was a bronze-skinned, powerfully built warrior whose broad chest and shoulders were covered in black ceremonial tattoos. Pierced claws clattered about his neck, and his curly black hair was partially held in a bone-threaded topknot. He carried a serrated bone fishing spear that thrummed with power.

"The waves will bear us to your destination, and the winds will hold the red storms at bay," Samo said. "You will need no other crew. The sea itself will carry your boat." Her lilting voice carried an accent Meri had never heard, but Amiri seemed to recognize it, for the Kellid stopped pacing and cast a penetrating look at the older woman, which Samo appeared to ignore.

"That is a great gift," Kyra said. "Why do you offer it?"

Nahoa shrugged, his claw necklace clattering, and shifted his spear to the crook of his arm. He ran a hand sheepishly across the top of his head, smoothing down the long black curls. "It's what we're supposed to do. I don't know how to explain it. When I was struck by the Godsrain, I heard a call. I... I wasn't able to do what it asked of me. It went away after I tried and failed, and I thought that was the end of it. But when you arrived in Port Peril, it came back. I don't know where you're going, or why, but we are meant to go with you."

Doubts flickered across Kyra's face, but the cleric voiced none of them. She raised a questioning eyebrow at the others.

"Should we not take some of Port Peril's refugees with us?" Ezren asked Sir Osmund. "If we're taking a boat out of here, with such a small crew, there would surely be room for others."

The knight shook his head. "I do not know your destination, or how perilous it may be, but I do not believe you are headed in any direction I could justly send a civilian. There were some buccaneers and adventure seekers who might have been willing to follow you into the unknown, but Samo insisted that no one else be permitted to go."

"Why?" Suspicion crept into Ezren's voice. Merisiel shared his wariness: why were these two strangers so eager to isolate them on the open sea?

If Sir Osmund hadn't vouched for them, she'd have considered this the prelude to an ambush, and she still wasn't sure that was wrong. How well did the Iomedaean know them, really? How well did any of them know *him*?

"Because you carry a god-spark," Samo answered, leveling a stare at Ezren. "We can sense it. Anyone who has been touched by the Godsrain can sense it. Nahoa was struck by one of fallen Gorum's sparks, and the spirits came to me as I brought him back from death's brink. Those of us who have received this power are drawn together across the world, as if by some design of the gods, and when we are close, we know one another. Perhaps you have not yet encountered others, but you will.

"Some may offer aid, but most will only try to enlist you in their own causes. Even more will try to destroy you, for they believe that by killing you, they can claim your divine power. Gorum's nature permeates his gift. The god of war left a legacy of conflict embedded in the shards of his divinity, and that violence will follow wherever you go."

Beneath the brim of her red bark hat, Samo's golden eyes were unblinking, willing them to accept the truth of her words. "The reason we do not wish to bring anyone else with us, wizard, is because no one else will be safe. You are touched by Gorum, as are we. Death follows in our wake."

Chapter Twenty-One
CARROWAY

Do we accept their offer?" Merisiel asked. Samo and Nahoa had excused themselves, allowing the companions to discuss the matter in private, but the elf sounded tense, as if she didn't quite trust that they weren't listening in.

Kyra lifted an empty hand, as if to signify that she had tried to weigh the answer and had found nothing. "I do not know."

"Your goddess didn't give you the answer?" Amiri snorted. She'd been in a foul mood for the past two days. Ezren was glad they'd be leaving soon; the Kellid was spoiling for a fight, and it would be poor repayment for their hosts if she found one.

"No. Sarenrae cannot see the future any more clearly than can we," Kyra said patiently, and probably for the thousandth time. "Prophecy died with Aroden, and that is true for the foretellings of gods as well as mortals. The Dawnflower can see what has happened, and what is happening, across the world. Thus she can warn us of what our enemies have done and can inform us of matters of known significance. But she cannot tell us what *will* happen, and so she cannot advise us in this. Too much is unknown for Sarenrae to grant counsel."

"Fine. If Sarenrae won't tell us what to do, I will. I say we accept." Amiri bit a frayed end off one of her gauntlets' laces and spat the scrap of leather across the room. "They seem like they can handle themselves in a fight, which might be useful. I didn't smell any treachery on them, but if I'm wrong, it's two of them against four of us. I like our odds."

"Two who possess considerable power," Ezren cautioned. "However, I agree with Amiri. I would like to talk to them and learn more about... my condition. Their experiences may help me learn to better control this power."

Merisiel stood up, stretching each of her legs in turn. When she was finished, she slid her newly sharpened knives into close-fitting sheaths tucked into the hardened leather plates that protected her thighs. "That's three in favor, then. I'm not sure I buy the story about some mysterious 'call' telling them to join us, but I didn't get the sense that they wanted to betray us, either. Maybe they're just fanatics. I'm fine with that. I've had profitable partnerships with fanatics."

"Make it unanimous," Kyra said. She rose with a gentle rustling. The cleric had found a cache of incense somewhere in the Knotworks, and the odor of sweet smoke clung to her robes. "I have no reason to doubt them. If you trust them, that is enough for me to do the same. I will tell them now that we are honored to have their company on this voyage."

⚔

They left early the next morning, taking the *Carroway*, a modest fishing boat that hardly looked capable of withstanding a voyage across a calm ocean, let alone the Eye of Abendego. There was barely enough room to store essential supplies, or for them to sleep in shifts, yet Samo and Nahoa seemed untroubled by the craft's limitations.

"The sea will provide," Samo said, and once they set sail, Ezren understood what she meant.

When Samo whispered to the water, it rose in a swell that carried the *Carroway* through storms and lulls alike. When she spoke to the wind, it parted around them, even as it lashed the ocean into white froth on either side. Though their course steered them ever closer to the Eye of Abendego, the *Carroway* ran on a smooth path between fifty-foot waves and abyssal troughs.

"This is what the god-spark enables you to do?" Ezren marveled one evening, standing beside Samo as she guided the *Carroway* westward, into the eye of the setting sun. It was a scene of striking and terrifying beauty, with the waves around them cresting red in the sunset and crashing down in showers of splintered diamonds.

It would have been awe-inspiring enough if they had been on solid ground, witnessing the thunderous majesty of a waterfall. But they stood on a tiny boat in the midst of a roaring sea, and every instinct Ezren had cried out that they were doomed.

Instead, in defiance of all the laws of nature, they floated in a cup of cradled stillness. The sea around the *Carroway* shone like a road of polished topaz, swirling into amethyst and sapphire in the boat's wake.

"It is one part of my blessing," Samo answered. If controlling the magic taxed her, Ezren could see no sign of it. She didn't fight to force her spells into shape, as he did. Her magic flowed effortlessly, drawing wistful envy from him. Once, it had been so for him too.

"I admire your mastery of the god-spark," Ezren told her, trying to keep the pain of his own loss from his words, as he gazed across the wonderment of the waves. "May I ask your secret? Magic has been… a difficult thing for me since I received my god-spark."

"You cannot master what you do not accept," Samo answered. The sunset cast a ruddy glow on her reindeer furs and made fiery gems of the salt crystals that had dried on her woven-bark hat. "To control the god-spark, you must accept that you are one with it, and it is one with you. It is no longer a shard of dead Gorum in your soul. It *is* your soul.

"Only when you cease fighting this phantom of a dead god and understand that the shadow you've been warring against is your own, will you regain the harmony you have lost. Until then, you are doomed to struggle needlessly against yourself."

"I see." The sunset was fading, the waves deepening from sapphire to ink. Ezren looked up, but there was nothing to be seen of moon or stars. They were close enough to the Eye of Abendego that its storm clouds dominated the sky. By day, the sun broke weakly through from time to time, but the lesser lights of the night had no chance. Without the enchanted spyglass from the *Merry Mermaid*, they would have been wholly unable to navigate using the heavens. "I will consider your counsel."

Samo's eyes were lost in the shadows of her hat, but Ezren could feel the animist—or spirit-speaker, as she called herself—staring hard at him. "Consider quickly. I do not offer my words out of kindness, wizard. You *must* master your gift, or else your quest will surely fail, and all of you will likely die. Do you have any idea what you are challenging?"

"I thought I did. But it sounds like you believe otherwise."

"I have seen your star chart. I have read the signs, both those written on the parchment and those you cannot yet see." Samo breathed a sigh, which melted into the wind around the *Carroway* and was swept away by the storm outside. "You are no astrologer."

"I've made a study," Ezren replied, nettled.

"No. You have made a study of astro*nomy*. The science of it, yes. What can be measured with scope and chart, you know. But what must be felt in the dance of the celestial bodies, what is only known through intuition and emotion... to that, you are blind. This is why you do not apprehend the danger into which you walk." Samo stared off into the lowering night again. How she knew where to guide the *Carroway*, Ezren couldn't fathom. Stars and moon were gone behind storm clouds, and any subtleties of current were lost to the thrashing waves. She never looked at the Akithaine heretics' spyglass. He did, to check her course, and found it unerring each time. But how the spirit-speaker managed to keep them on the path, he could not guess.

Ezren might have been inclined to dismiss her words as mystic meanderings were it not for the very real evidence that Samo did, in fact, see and sense more than he could.

"What danger do I not see that you do?" he asked.

"The conjunctions in your star chart do not exist in this world," Samo said slowly. Ezren had the distinct sense that the spirit-speaker was measuring her answer, searching for words that could encompass ideas never meant to be contained in that medium. "What we are sailing toward is... a real place, which exists in this world, but also a possibility that can only be glimpsed from here. A warning. It is not true here, not yet, but it holds a vision of the future that will break this world, and all others, if it comes to pass. And it holds the key to making that vision true."

Ezren's chest clenched. "'Break this world and all others'... Rovagug. Do you mean that the star chart shows what might happen if the Rough Beast breaks free of his prison? Or *where* it might happen?"

Samo nodded, her bark hat dipping into and out of darkness as she moved through the light of the *Carroway*'s lamp. As night descended around them, an enchanted glow filled the lantern's glass, making it seem even more that their boat was its own island of tranquility, apart from the rest of the world. "It is a vision that drove entire civilizations to devolve into senseless mayhem. Sects that sought to guard the secret destroyed themselves by learning too much of it."

"Inithyra's Orb, yes. Is this the danger we face?" Ezren knew well the risks of exposing one's mind to forbidden lore. Any properly trained wizard was aware of that hazard, and of the myriad ways in which proscribed knowledge could warp and infect its holders.

"It is a part. It is not the whole."

"What is the whole?"

Samo stepped squarely into the lantern's light so that Ezren could not mistake it when she turned away from him and faced into the wind, gazing at the storm toward which they drove. Her dismissal could scarcely have been clearer. "Apprehend a part of it and survive. Then we can discuss the whole."

As they sailed closer to their unseen destination, following the star chart and the guidance of their fiery compass, the sea below them took on a red glow of its own. Faces swirled in the crimson brine, staring upward with empty eyes and imploring mouths. Some had glowing motes swirling in the dark whirlpools of their maws, which spun like broken galaxies or held shards of incandescent ice for teeth. They had one eye, or two, or dozens. They were human, animal, monster. Rage twisted them, or agony, or grief. Ezren couldn't read the emotions bubbling up in the phantom faces, but he could feel the echoes of those feelings rising from the water. When the waves swept the faces away in blurred ripples, their misery lingered, roiling like steam over the sea.

"We near the island of the dead," Samo said, standing alongside Ezren. Her face was masklike beneath her hat. Red froth spat up from the waves and clung to her hands, dripping like blood from her fingers. The water lost its light as it parted from the sea, but it remained red. "The dead, and the corrupted."

"What do you mean?" Amiri asked, coming up with Nahoa to join them. The Kellid had streaked her face with war paint in a fashion Ezren had never seen before, with dots and spirals inked in black across her brow and cheekbones.

The young warrior, normally good-humored, seemed even tenser than Samo. He wore war paint in a similar style, though the patterns differed. "You'll soon know. But that discovery is one you must make alone."

No one said anything else. Merisiel and Kyra joined them too, gazing alternately at the nightmarish sea of faces or into the crimson storm ahead. The *Carroway* shuddered and bucked as the waves hammered into their boat, breaking through Samo's protective spell with increasing force.

The waves began to slam into the boat with real fury, spraying red mist across its length. One jolt knocked Kyra from her feet, and then the entire boat tipped vertically as the wave continued to lift the *Carroway*. With a cry, Merisiel dived to help her wife, but the suddenness of the change had surprised them all, and none had thought to secure themselves with ropes. The two women slid together across the storm-slicked deck, streaking the wood with a wide red smear of poisoned water.

Amiri grabbed them as they were about to go over. Gripping the railing with one hand and Kyra's clothing with the other, the Kellid hauled them back up, her wiry muscles straining. With every step up the steeply slanted deck, she let out a noise that was half grunt, half growl, until the wave dropped the *Carroway* and Amiri fell back.

Ezren braced himself for the next wave. If the last was any warning, another might break their boat in two. Samo's spell seemed to have failed almost completely. Just enough of her magic remained to keep the storm from tearing them apart outright.

He closed his eyes, feeling the red spray run down his face, and wondering whether he was destined to join the phantoms in the sea.

Then the *Carroway* shot through a gap between swells and into a sudden calm. Caught unawares, Ezren rocked forward against the rail. It struck him hard in the chest, and he opened his eyes with a grunt.

Deep gray fog surrounded the boat, sheathing it in silence. The crimson storm was gone. Only a small radius was visible around their vessel, but within it, the sea had taken on the aquamarine hue of a tropical bay under clouds. There was no trace of the faces in the water, nor of the red stain on the waves.

Through the mist, Ezren thought he could just make out the shapes of tall buildings rising above a rocky shore. They had an alien cast, as if the dimensions and geometries hadn't been made for human use, but he could make out little more than ghostly silhouettes wavering in the fog.

"You must go ashore alone," Samo said as the *Carroway* bumped against a piling of red-and-white marble. Behind it, a pier stretched away into the fog. It, too, was built of the striated stone, and was broader and wider than any Ezren had seen before. Each of the pilings had an ornamental carved cap, so worn by time that its original shape was lost and only a pitted knob remained.

"You're not coming?" Merisiel asked, turning her head sharply. A lock of white hair fell over one eye.

"I will safeguard the boat," Samo replied. Her voice reverberated strangely in the fog. It seemed to carry too far, and Ezren had the irrational fancy that this wasn't accidental, that there was some malign consciousness in the mist that wanted them to be heard by the island's inhabitants. "Else it will not be here when you return, and you will be unable to leave."

"And I must safeguard Samo," Nahoa said. His hands rested on the haft of his spear, but the ease of his stance didn't conceal the wariness with which he watched the shore. "Besides, there is no need for us to witness what this place holds. We have already seen enough of it with our own eyes. This island's warning is for you."

"What is it? Where are we?" Amiri scanned the pier and the half-visible buildings behind it.

"Ghol-Gan," Ezren realized aloud. The red-and-white stone, the elaborate carvings, the inhuman dimensions... "This place was built by the cyclopes of Ghol-Gan."

Samo nodded. "It was a temple. It was sacred to them, and it destroyed them. Now you must go to it and see what they saw. We will wait for your return. One day, and one night.

"If you do not return by then, we will go, for we will know you are lost."

Chapter Twenty-Two

THE RUINS OF GHOL-GAN

Mist swirled about Kyra's feet, clinging to the hem of her robes as she stepped from the *Carroway*'s boarding plank to the fog-shrouded docks of the nameless island that Ezren claimed was a piece of lost Ghol-Gan. The plank's uneven wood creaked beneath her weight, but on the stone dock, her steps made no sound at all. She had expected the smooth marble to be slippery, but it felt secure underfoot despite the condensation that glistened across its breadth.

Can it be? The ancient empire of the cyclopes was little more than a legend in Golarion. Supposedly it had flourished during the Age of Legend, millennia ago, and had reached a pinnacle of artistry and sophistication unrivaled in its time. The one-eyed cyclopes were said to have been peerless in foretelling, able to see farther into the future with their single-focused gaze than could any other creature.

Then their empire collapsed within the span of a few short centuries, crumbling into a shambles of cannibalism and blood sacrifice on altars of grooved stone. Most of the cyclopes died. The few descendants who still survived to this day were brutish, dull-witted monsters who dwelled in caves and terrified local villagers.

Nothing of the cyclopes' present circumstances suggested that they could once have been capable of constructing buildings and boulevards of the grandeur that rose before Kyra in the mist. Yet the proof was too spectacular to be denied: ziggurats and archways of red-swirled white marble, all built to giants' proportions, in stacked colonnades that emphasized the natural curve of the island's bay and harmonized with the jungle greenery of its interior while drawing the wilderness into order.

The structures' soaring dimensions made Kyra feel as insignificant as a mouse in a castle, and their subtly alien geometries left her dizzied as she stood beside the sea, trying to absorb what she was seeing. "Where do we go?"

"I was hoping you'd tell us that," Amiri grunted. The Kellid eyed their surroundings warily, keeping her knees bent and her hands always close to her weapons. "Where's the storm? Why's it gone suddenly?"

It *was* gone, Kyra realized. She'd been so struck by the wonderment of finding herself in the ruins of Ghol-Gan that she had momentarily failed to notice how strange it was that the heavens were calm here.

The serenity wasn't like the bubble of safety that Samo had conjured for the *Carroway*. On the boat, they'd all been aware of how small and fragile their magical shelter was. The rage of the Eye of Abendego had never been far from view and had nearly shattered their boat before they'd made landfall on this island.

Here, though, only the softest lap of waves against the pilings reached Kyra's ears. Not a breeze from the perpetual hurricane seemed to penetrate the fog. As close as they were to the continent-swallowing storm, the sky should have been a solid mass of thunderclouds, yet when Kyra looked up, she saw gentle mist lit by a diffuse glow. It might have been sunlight, but she felt nothing of Sarenrae's warmth in its sterile whiteness.

Sea-foam lapped at the pier's pilings. That was the only sign Kyra could see that they remained in their own world, and that the Eye continued to boil outside these sheltering clouds. Only those crimson bubbles, clinging to the stones by the sea.

"I don't know," Kyra admitted, ill at ease. She took a few steps down the pier, then hesitated again.

"The compass points that way." Merisiel held up the device for all of them to see. Its flaming needle wavered like a candle in the wind, then steadied and spun toward a tall, narrow ziggurat perched on a green-crowned cliff half a mile away.

Swallowing her discomfort, Kyra nodded. She still couldn't sense Sarenrae here, and it unnerved her. She stole a last glance back at the *Carroway*, already missing Samo's remote but steadying self-assurance. "Then I suppose we go there."

Together the companions walked up the spiraling streets. They were made of interlocking stone tiles in some sort of repeated geometric motif, so vast that Kyra couldn't see the pattern. The tiles were irregularly cut, and each was at least two feet long and three feet wide. The largest ones were six or seven feet across.

Ugly red blotches spattered across some of them, apparently at random, as if a flock of gigantic birds had passed overhead and strewn the ruined city with droppings of half-digested meat. On closer examination, Kyra realized that the scabrous matter had burbled up through cracks between the paving stones, like water welling from a spring, and that it always emerged where three or more stones touched. She couldn't tell what that foulness was, but it was unmistakably unholy. "There is a corruption here. Avoid it."

"It almost calls to mind the Worldwound, before that blight was sealed." Ezren mused aloud. "But there, the land was rife with demons. Everything is peaceful here."

"Everything is peaceful," Kyra agreed, but her unease only grew.

Jungle greenery spilled down the walls of the nearby buildings as Kyra and her friends moved farther from the shore. Flowering vines hung from the archways in heavy drapes that had been left wild and untrimmed for so long that past decades' vines had not only died and been entombed by more recent growth but had fully decayed into dirt from which additional vines sprouted. The tangle was so dense that in places it had brought down entire arches, toppling giant-built stone under its weight.

Yet despite the lushness of the vines and the rich perfume of their gold-streaked white flowers, there was something disconcerting about their dominance of the landscape. Kyra couldn't quite put her finger on what it was, until Amiri solved the mystery for her: "They're all the same plant."

"The same species?" Ezren asked, looking over from his examination of the red splashes on the tiles.

"No. The same *plant*. Like an aspen grove. There are many stems, but they all come from the same roots. So it is with these." Amiri pulled apart a tangle of vines from a clump of decayed wood to show them how the strands were interconnected. "It must be able to produce seeds too, or else it wouldn't flower, but everything we've seen so far looks like the same plant to me. Even when the colonies have been separated by one of these rockfalls, you can see that the vines were connected at one point, before they tore apart. And it is the only plant I've seen on this island thus far. There's nothing else. Only this one."

"That's... odd." Merisiel frowned, tugged at the lobe of a pointed ear, and then shrugged. "But there's no sun here, and the air is calm, even though we're within spitting distance of the Eye of Abendego, so the entire island having only a single plant isn't the only oddity in this place."

"Suppose that's true." Amiri brushed the dirt from her hands and off her curved leather shin guards. Straightening, the Kellid loped back to the front of their little group. "I like it less than the lack of sun, though. What if the reason there's only one plant is because it's killed all the others, and everything else here too? What if it's watching us? What if we're next?"

"What if you stopped talking?" grumbled Meri, stalking after the barbarian.

Kyra cleared her throat to hide a smile, knowing her wife would hear her amusement. It was good that Meri was joking again. The elf had been alternately remote and irritable for the past few weeks, and although Kyra had a good guess as to why, she hadn't been able to do as much to repair the damage as she would have liked.

She hadn't had the time or the energy. Everything she had was given to fulfilling Sarenrae's charge. And though Kyra knew that wasn't fair to Merisiel, who after all had never sworn to serve the Dawnflower herself, it was an unfairness that she was, at least temporarily, powerless to rectify.

She was a servant of her faith. Her first duty was, and had always to be, to her goddess.

Forgive me today. I will make it up to you tomorrow.

It was a wish that she'd made before, on other missions, and one that Meri had always honored without quarrel.

But "tomorrow" had rarely felt so far away, or so uncertain.

Breathing out a silent sigh, Kyra turned her attention back up the path. Here, too, the red blight burbled up from between the paving stones, though the splotches weren't as large or as frequent on the cliff road.

The compass's fiery needle was blazing so brightly in Meri's hand that it turned the elf's white hair to molten gold and painted her sharp cheekbones red. The green gem on her forehead appeared to be black, its heart lit by a tiny, reflected flame. It made her even more beautiful, but also unnerving: like an eldritch creature of elemental fire, not the woman who held Kyra's heart.

"We must be near," she said, simultaneously relieved and in dread, as she mounted the first steps leading up the cliffside to the ziggurat.

The steps were carved for giant feet, each one higher than Kyra's knee. Amiri and Merisiel scrambled up them without difficulty, but it was considerably harder for Kyra, and she worried about Ezren's ability to climb to the top. After the first few steps, the wizard had to resort to hoisting himself up with his elbows and knees as often as walking.

"Do you have some spell that would make this easier?" Kyra asked quietly, after helping him up another step.

Ezren shook his head and mopped the sweat from his neck. A vein pulsed across his forehead. "None I dare use. Not for something as trivial as this. Don't worry about me, Kyra. I'll be slower than the rest of you, but I'll get to the top."

"Of course." Nonetheless, Kyra stayed by Ezren's side, offering a hand whenever she could. There was no way to do so unobtrusively, but he never complained of her aid and never turned it down. By that, more than anything, she knew how difficult the ascent was for him. The wizard's pride was a prickly thing, and for him to swallow so much of it must nearly have choked him.

When they reached the top, Amiri and Merisiel were already there, eating dried figs and honey-smeared hardtack. Behind them, the ziggurat cast a hulking shadow across the path. The crimson upwellings barely reached up here, but she spotted two dotting the road ahead.

As Ezren joined the other two, catching his breath under the pretense of sharing their meal, Kyra walked over to examine the ziggurat's doors. "Is it safe?"

"It's not trapped," Merisiel said. "Not the same as 'safe,' but it's all I can say."

"Understood." Kyra craned her head back to take in as many of the doors' carvings as she could. Like the rest of the marble city, it had been built by and for giants, and she hoped that some hidden magic or mechanism would make it easier to open the doors, because otherwise she couldn't see how they'd manage.

Enormous figures had been carved about the ziggurat's base. Each stood alone, separated from the others by bas-relief columns etched with the same white-flowering vines that climbed over the nameless city, and each had been depicted in vivid detail. Though the cyclopes were identifiable as unique individuals by their garb, positioning, and the staves that each held, they also had peculiar commonalities.

All of them held their mouths wide open, showing that their front teeth were missing and only the broad rear chewing teeth remained. Every cyclops's single eye had been either covered by a curious contraption made of stone disks interwoven with ropes or vines or removed and replaced by a faceted orb. The lines of ritual scars had been carved with painstaking fidelity around each of the missing eyes to make it clear that they had been cut out, yet the figures were depicted in rich clothes and ornate jewelry and were plainly of high status.

Above the door were two gilded spheres, one in gold and the other in silver, which hovered against a carved representation of a clouded sky. The spheres were mounted on articulated stone arms that changed the background as they swept across it, transforming the clouds to either a starry night or a clear sky dotted with tiny birds.

Everything about the ziggurat's design and decoration said that it was a holy place, but Kyra didn't recognize the iconography. She knew, vaguely, that the cyclopes of Ghol-Gan were said to have followed a celestial religion oriented around the sun and moon as paired, benevolent powers, and that they had, shortly before the empire's collapse, abandoned their old faith to follow a path of blood-soaked atrocity and sacrifice instead.

But which did these maimed figures represent? What did the vines between them signify? The temple itself showed sun and moon, but were they being swept aside or honored?

Dawnflower, guide me.

"Cover one eye," Ezren said, coming to stand alongside Kyra.

"What?" Kyra blinked, then put a hand over her left eye and studied the carvings again.

They looked different. Only subtly so, but the images seemed flatter, and she had to rely more on the elaborately etched backgrounds to get a sense of perspective. The most notable change, however, was that several images she'd originally taken to be blended together had become distinct and separate.

"There's a gap, or... something... in that one's eye covering." Kyra pointed out one of the carvings. The cyclops had a short beard, a missing eye covered by a stone plate, and a staff crowned with a pair of overlapping disks, perhaps meant to represent an eclipse. One of the red spatters dripped down his cheek. "Meri?"

"On it." Merisiel climbed up the carving, finding toeholds in minute crevices and bracing her weight against the sides when they drew close enough to hold her. She stopped when she got to the cyclops's face. "It's not the original. Part of this carving was broken out, and this piece was slotted in to cover the damage."

The elf wiggled it free and tossed it over to her wife. "Take a look. As for the original gap..." Meri stretched up on her toes, bending with impossible flexibility to peer directly into the cyclops's vacant eye socket. "I think this might have been the source of that chunk of rock we got from Skrit back in Port Peril. Looks like it was broken out of here, and then covered over."

"Should we try fitting it back in?" Ezren asked.

"Yes," Kyra said, hoping it was the right answer. She reached into her satchel, took out the compass, and popped the brass circle out of its marble housing. With a quick underhand, she tossed the stone to the elf.

Meri caught it and fitted it into the cyclops's socket. It clicked into place and sank into a previously hidden recess. Above her head, the sun and moon began to whirr on their arm mountings.

Quickly the elf sprang away from the wall, landing in a crouch and retreating to rejoin the others. The four of them watched as stone sun and stone moon ascended to the center of the artificial sky, sweeping stars and birds up in their wake. The alternating views of day and night collided in the middle, with the moon stopping directly in front of the sun in an imitation of an eclipse. In the eclipse's center, a red spark flared, casting nightmarish shadows across the overlapping stones.

The ziggurat's doors parted with a heavy groan. Darkness yawned between them.

Merisiel held up the compass. Its fiery needle had gone out when Kyra removed the marble piece, leaving the instrument's face inert and dull in the ziggurat's shadow. "Nothing more from this. I hope we've arrived."

"We'll soon find out," Kyra said. She lifted her holy symbol, taking comfort in the blessed golden light that surrounded her as she stepped into the gloom.

A deep, cool silence enveloped Kyra and her companions as they entered the ziggurat. Kyra's light seemed a small thing in its vastness, unable to reach the walls and brushing only dimly over the faces of the cyclopean sculptures that towered over them in alcoves. The companions' steps made little noise in the cavernous interior and were soon lost in its endless hush.

"How big *is* this place?" Merisiel whispered as they moved in. Enormous as the ziggurat had been from the outside, it nevertheless seemed impossible that it could stretch so far, or be so empty, within. There weren't even any supports, as far as Kyra could see. Only vacant space, reaching toward infinity.

"There," she said, relieved, as a glowing pinprick appeared in the emptiness ahead. It emanated warmth and comfort, and Kyra felt certain, somehow, that the light represented safety in this place of the unknown. Her holy symbol's radiance pulsed in her hand, as though it, too, recognized a kinship with that distant luminance.

Quickening her step, she moved toward the glow.

It resolved into a pair of cyclops statues facing one another, each holding a crystal sphere over its head. One was translucent gold, the other smaller and flecked with motes of silver. Weak light pulsed in each of the spheres, illuminating the statues down to the knee before surrendering to the dark.

A human woman in blue-and-gold robes knelt between them. Her long, flowing golden hair was gathered loosely in a halo that spilled over her light brown shoulders and curled into her lap. As Kyra and the others approached, the woman raised her head.

Her eyes were liquid fire. Holy light wreathed her neck and wrapped itself about her arms, emanating from her palms as she lifted her hands in greeting. Her bronze features were perfect, inhumanly so, yet in her smile was all the mercy and understanding humanity could hold.

Kyra let out a gasp and fell to her knees, touching her forehead to the floor. She was barely conscious of the alarmed looks that her companions exchanged around her, or of how strangled her own words sounded. "*Sarenrae.*"

"Yes." The goddess stood. She was no taller than Amiri, the shortest of their group, but the divinity of her presence could not be mistaken. "Kyra, my precious servant. Merisiel, Ezren, Amiri. You have done well to come so far. I am grateful to you. But more will be asked of you, very soon, and that is why I am here. The message of the gods must be delivered directly."

"What message?" Ezren's eyes narrowed. He might have been as awed by the goddess in their midst as the rest of them, but Kyra knew the wizard was not likely to show the immediate deference of a servant as she had. He bristled like a tomcat spotting an unfamiliar dog in its territory—overmatched, and knowing it, but determined not to cede ground without at least assessing the situation fully.

"That we need you. The Rough Beast stirs. You have felt this yourselves and have seen the violence of his presence reach out through the red storms of Port Peril and the increasing fury of the Eye of Abendego. You have seen the stain of his touch even on this isle, which was once sacrosanct against him. But there is more you do not know, and which you must learn before you can stop him. For that is, ultimately, what we will ask—that you stop Rovagug from escaping the Dead Vault and destroying this world and all others in his rage."

Silence greeted the goddess's words.

Kyra was too stunned to speak. She sat up on her heels, looking to her companions, but they were all as dumbfounded as she was.

Sarenrae *wants us to stop* Rovagug *from breaking free of his prison?*

It was impossible—too immense a task, with too much at stake, for her to even comprehend. Her mind reeled from accepting its reality.

What could she possibly do that the gods could not? What could *any* of them do?

"You can act directly, my servant, where we cannot. Ancient bargains bind us, and the price of magics woven long ago. But there is another risk, a graver risk, as well." Sarenrae's fiery eyes dimmed. The radiant glow in her left hand coalesced into a scimitar of flickering fire, then dissipated back into light as she shook the weapon away.

The goddess raised her palms toward the two crystal spheres held by the cyclops statues looming over her head. Their stuttering light steadied and brightened, filling the gold and silver orbs. "The seers of Ghol-Gan were truly among the greatest produced by this world, and the prophets of this island were the finest that their civilization ever knew. Here they held a shard of Inithyra's Orb, and their visions pierced the veils of futures unknown.

"Unlike so many others, their foretellings did not fail in the wake of Aroden's death and the Age of Lost Omens. The futures they saw before that time were accurate. Events that would have occurred after Aroden's death came back to them as murky and unknowable. But the cyclopes of the Peacebound Isle never had a false reading."

"Is that where we are? The Peacebound Isle?" Somehow, Kyra managed to ask the question in an approximation of her normal voice, not an awe-strangled croak.

"Yes. At least, that is the closest approximation of its name that your language permits." Sarenrae bent and took Kyra's hands, lifting her to her feet. The goddess gazed into her eyes, and Kyra trembled in terrified rapture.

Never, never had she imagined she would behold Sarenrae in any manifestation, let alone anything this personal. Never had she thought that the goddess would take her measure so directly. Kyra could *feel* Sarenrae examining her soul, testing its strength and resilience, and probing gently but unmistakably for flaws.

Sarenrae released her hands, and Kyra shivered in loss and relief. She didn't know what her goddess had seen, but she hoped it was enough. Tears streamed down her cheeks, but she didn't dare brush them away. She didn't dare move at all.

The goddess smiled and reached out to wipe them for her.

"If you allow, I will tell you what the prophets of the Peacebound Isle saw, and what brought Ghol-Gan to ruin. It impelled them to build this sanctuary and place such harsh strictures upon their own island that it became a place of death. I will show you, also, what they could never have glimpsed, because only the gods themselves could have withstood the witnessing of those events. And, finally, I will tell you of the future that they never knew, because it happened long after the collapse of their empire and the destruction of their order, and after Aroden's death obscured their scryings.

"They did not know why their prophecies failed to reach past that point in the future, but they had one guess. It was wrong then. It may not be wrong now. But if you will let me show you what I have said, perhaps you can avert the course of that calamity."

"Please," Kyra whispered. "Show us."

Chapter Twenty-Three

THE DAWNFLOWER'S GIFT

They were such brave mortals.

Sarenrae had examined each of their souls, and in them she had found such courage and resolve that, once again, she was left humbled by mortals' capacity for heroism.

They were so... ordinary, and yet extraordinary. Other than the wizard, who had been struck by Gorum's death, they hadn't a fraction of the power that the least of her servants in Everlight possessed. And even the wizard had no idea how to control the divine essence that surged through him. He was like a child with a magic sword, and Sarenrae could only hope he learned to use it before someone took it from him.

No, none of them had any prayer of prevailing against the forces that awaited them. They all knew it, too; she had seen the secret despair that lurked at each one's core.

But it didn't matter. They were determined to try, even if it meant their lives, even in the face of near certain failure. Each one of them was steeled for a hopeless fight, trusting that the sacrifice must be worth *something*, or the gods would not ask it of them.

It touched her profoundly. The heroes of every age always inspired reverence in Sarenrae. These were people who had so little, comparatively, and yet were possessed of a fierceness that would not be denied. They didn't have the weapons of gods, but they fought as if their empty fists were mightier than Iomedae's sword.

And they believed in the righteousness of their fight. That was the key, the crucial element. It was why Sarenrae had chosen them as her own champions in the battle to come, and how she had persuaded the other gods to permit her the choice.

None of Asmodeus's servants could have succeeded in the task before them. None of Gozreh's could have done it, none of Calistria's. Only ones who had a core of purity had any hope of success. For this task, the gods needed servants who would choose virtue over temptation, patience over anger, and self-sacrifice over expedience. But it had to be a *choice*, a true one, not the blind obedience of a soulbound lackey or the ingrained nature of a celestial servitor.

Only a mortal could make that choice.

Sarenrae hoped, desperately, that she'd correctly identified the mortals who would.

"Come," she told them, as she reached out to the long-dormant magic of Ghol-Gan, "and I will show you where this tale began."

The statues raised their glowing orbs, silver in front of gold. As the spheres aligned as if in eclipse, the light of the enchanted sun shone through that of the moon and split apart into dazzling refractions. Rather than forming a simple rainbow, however, the enchanted light played out in unfocused images that, under Sarenrae's guidance, sharpened into the vivid semblance of a forest glade that filled the entire sanctuary.

"So that's why they made it so big," Merisiel noted, watching the scene fill the cavernous space.

"Yes. The Peacebound Seers' vision chamber was built to accommodate any vision they could summon through Inithyra's Orb," Sarenrae agreed. "But what I will show you now is not one they ever saw."

At a curl of her fingers, the image shifted into moving life. Dappled sunlight spilled through the perfect leaves of the trees that ringed the glen. Pale pink flowers dotted their branches, while purple trumpets bloomed around the trees' trunks. White-and-yellow star-flowers spangled the lush green grass.

A lithe, blonde elven woman, clad in yellow and black, slipped lightly through the trees. Though the image reproduced by the cyclopes' statues lacked the full force of Calistria's presence, the goddess remained unmistakable. Her beauty was extraordinary, and every movement she made was its own dance of allure, but her presence was edged with a waspish, mercurial danger. Even as an illusory phantasm, she projected lust and threat in equal measure, so strongly that Sarenrae herself felt stirred at the sight.

Just as Calistria came to the edge of the glade, she slipped on something unseen in the grass and fell with a cry. For several moments, she writhed on the ground, gripping her thigh, and when she finally came up, her leg bore a bloody wound.

"This was the beginning of our ambush," Sarenrae explained, as the elf in the image pulled herself up against a tree and spent a moment visibly struggling to gather enough magic to coax the tree into growing a low branch she could break off as a crutch. "The Rough Beast had turned his attention to three worlds in that epoch so long ago, but this world was the youngest. By staging our ambush here, we hoped to contain Rovagug's potential devastation to minimize loss of life. We knew Calistria's beguilements were unsurpassed, but her usual methods were unlikely to work on Rovagug. So she pretended to quarrel with Kist-Aurek, a vengeful god of ambushes and snares, and he set this trap for her."

The trees at the glade's edge rustled. Calistria looked up, her perfect face freezing into a terrified mask, just as a spiny long-tailed beast sprang from the brush. It was a skeletal thing, just pale slick skin stretched over ribs and claws and nubby vertebrae. Three bulbous eyes sat in a pyramid at the center of its doglike face.

Torn grass and ruined blossoms showered from the creature's claws as it leaped at Calistria. The wounded goddess flung herself to the right, flicking a long knife like a wasp's stinger up at the creature's underbelly as she did. She opened a vicious gash across the length of its abdomen. It squealed in agony as it landed in the meadow, claws churning through grass and dirt.

Both combatants panted for breath as they squared off, neither one able or willing to press the attack, for a minute that seemed to stretch to infinity.

"We feared, for a moment, that our trap had failed," Sarenrae said. "Calistria and Kist-Aurek had wounded each other, but their entire fight was staged. The purpose of it was to leave them both so vulnerable that Rovagug would be tempted to devour them. The greater the victim's suffering, the greater his delight, and the only thing he loved more than eating a world was eating a god.

"This gave him the opportunity to eat two at once. We knew he was watching, for we knew Calistria had caught his attention before setting this snare. But we did not know whether he would take the bait, until—"

The earth erupted in a fountain of slime and blood, as though the world itself were giving birth to monstrosity. Trees exploded around it in a fifty-foot radius, their heartwood bursting into gory splinters.

A swarm of gibbering, malformed mouths spewed from the earth, surrounding Kist-Aurek. The skeletal god hissed and struck with blinding speed, not at any of the mouths, but at a talisman of bone and crystal that had been hidden among the trees and now lay in the fouled dirt.

The talisman shattered, and a fanged trap of diamond and rune-inscribed bone sprang into being around the churning mouths. It was incalculably complex, and so vast that it encompassed not only the mouths but the unseen bulk of the abomination below them.

Its spearlike diamonds bit in, drawing ichor and blood. A chorused howl of pain and rage roared from the mouths.

The creature in the earth heaved itself into view.

Rovagug. Even in this spectral image, the sight of her ancient adversary filled Sarenrae with a burning, bitter hatred. She was a goddess of mercy and redemption, one who extended compassion to any enemy who would accept it, but there was no forgiveness for the Rough Beast.

Not then, not now, not ever.

Rovagug was an incomprehensible abomination. He looked as if some twisted celestial sculptor had stripped a thousand creatures down to their digestive systems—teeth, mouths, gullets, intestines—and then smashed them all together like so much raw clay, leaving some pieces recognizable and others reduced to squirming pulp.

Claws and pincers protruded randomly from the mass, ripping at anything they could reach, including each other. Mucous bubbles rose to the surface, swelling and popping in slimy bursts as they birthed new appendages. Whenever any part of Rovagug was wounded beyond repair, it was shredded by the others, or else spontaneously exploded into geysers of caustic effluvia that melted everything nearby.

The Rough Beast could not be contained by Kist-Aurek's trap. After his first furious roar, Rovagug laughed in terrible mirth.

A shudder racked his body, undulating through his enormous mass and all his thrashing appendages. The cage of bone and crystal shuddered, trembled, and broke apart as though it were no more than gossamer trying to contain a raging bull.

Instantly Rovagug's mouths seized Kist-Aurek. One needle-toothed maw snapped off the lesser god's hindquarters. Another sucking mouth, ringed by flapping folds of drooling, acidic lips, engulfed Kist-Aurek's upper limbs and melted them away from the rest of his body before slurping them down. A third pair of jaws wrenched off and swallowed his head. The rest went down in smaller pieces.

But Kist-Aurek's sufferings did not end there.

After they'd been swallowed, each piece burbled up in a membranous swelling, where it floated in a bubble of Rovagug's digestive juices. The membrane was thin enough that it could easily be seen through, and so it was evident to all that Kist-Aurek was not dead. His dismembered body twitched and spasmed as Rovagug slowly digested him, and the eyes in his decapitated head rolled over to stare at the rest of his body being consumed.

Even as Rovagug dismantled the lesser god, he chased after Calistria. The elven goddess had fled the glade, sprouting translucent wasp's wings that bore her away with unearthly swiftness, but Rovagug pursued her with equal speed. Smashing the forest to either side, he raced after the goddess. The image did not follow them, and both gods were soon out of view.

"Once we'd focused his attention on your world and a single target," Sarenrae said, "Calistria lured Rovagug into the field where the rest of us waited, leading to the battle that ended with his imprisonment in the Dead Vault. Calistria survived, so her name is remembered. Kist-Aurek did not, and so both his name and his sacrifice have been forgotten.

"For his bravery, Kist-Aurek suffered terribly. It took him millennia to die. But it was he who struck the first blow in the war, he who dealt a wound painful enough to compel Rovagug to pursue Calistria into our true ambush. Many gods stood against him in that battle, but the chance to confront and defeat him existed only because Kist-Aurek landed that first blow and drew off that first portion of the Rough Beast's power. The site where Rovagug's blood spilled is also the scar of the Dead Vault, a place far from here remembered today in your world as Gormuz.

"The legacy of this deed is crucial to the events that now unfold." With a gesture, Sarenrae dismissed all but a small section of the image. The vision narrowed to a shard of bloody diamond that had been thrust into a long bone and then gummed about its base with gore and gristle, creating a macabre knife.

"This is the Fang of Kist-Aurek. It holds the memory, and the magic, of the first blow in our war. It holds, too, the power that Kist-Aurek stole. Not enough to save its creator, regrettably, but enough to turn the tide of our war and enable our alliance to defeat the Rough Beast.

"Kist-Aurek meant for that siphoned power to be destroyed in the second stage of his trap, but he himself was slain before he could finish the work. The fang has been a constant torment to Rovagug, both because it holds the memory of his great defeat, and because it is a key to escaping his prison. Should it be stabbed into the Dead Vault's scar, it would return the power that Kist-Aurek stole from him and strengthen him enough to allow him to wrest free of his bonds."

Sarenrae paused. She did not wish to repeat the mistakes that the gods had made in the past, and yet these mortals needed to understand the gravity of what was at stake.

"The vision of Rovagug's freedom helped bring down Ghol-Gan," she told them. Miniature reflections of ruin danced across the image of the Fang of Kist-Aurek. Those, Sarenrae judged, were sufficient to accompany her warning; she neither needed nor wished to enhance the mortals' view. "Their seers looked through Inithyra's Orb and saw a future that they could not abide. They witnessed a disaster, born during an unnatural eclipse, that would result in the death of gods.

"In that darkness between sun and moon, where neither of their celestial gods could aid them, they glimpsed the truth at the center of their world—your world—and a future that they could not hold back with all their prophets' wisdom or warriors' strength. The cyclopes knew, through that vision, that their civilization would not be able to restrain Rovagug's fury, nor would they survive it. That knowledge cast them into a despair from which they never recovered and created a bleakness that they sought to obliterate by following new paths paved in blood.

"That is what they saw in this temple. That is the doom that Inithyra's Orb brought to Ghol-Gan. I do not wish to break you as the cyclopes were broken, and so I will not show you what they saw. Know only that the sight was so terrible that it drove their empire to ruin—but know also that what they saw need not be what happens. Aroden's death meant the death of prophecy, and the liberation of this world from the shackles of destiny.

"Already, reality has unspooled away from what the Peacebound Seers foresaw. They did not witness Gorum's death by Achaekek's hand, nor did they know that the shards of his divinity would fall across the world. In this, there is an opportunity to change fate by breaking the fang... but also a great and grievous chance that the disaster that plunged Ghol-Gan into embracing oblivion will, indeed, come to pass."

"Why didn't you just break the fang?" Amiri asked. Light from the reflected scene washed the Kellid's face in stark contrasts of red, black, and white, emphasizing the wild spikes of her hair and the sharp planes of her face.

"Breaking Kist-Aurek's blade ourselves would have exposed us to Rovagug's essence, and even the gods fear that." Sarenrae touched the cyclopes' device with her will again, and the image of the bone-and-crystal blade dissolved.

In its place rose a different picture: a brutish orc, clad in scraps of rough hide armor streaked with blood and soot, hacking out a tunnel with a pick made from the skull of some draconic beast, which spit golden sparks with each blow. He did not dig through ordinary earth, but some warped black crystal that emitted ear-piercing wails of misery every time the dragon-skull pick bit in.

"This was Verex the Despoiler," Sarenrae said. "I do not know what he sought in burrowing through the walls of reality, but I can tell you what he found."

As Verex's pick swung down again, the black crystal cracked suddenly and deeply, as though he had struck a hidden flaw in the stone. Foul red mist swirled up from the crevice, rapidly filling the tunnel. The skull at the end of his pick turned on its wielder, snarling and biting, as its empty sockets glowed crimson. Verex dropped the pick and stamped the skull to flinders with two hard kicks, but his wounds bled into the mist. The blood evaporated into wet red fog, and its coils wrapped around him.

Sarenrae gestured, and the image went still. "He dug too close to the Dead Vault, and Rovagug took him. I will not show you how he was consumed. Know that it was ugly and that even a creature as wretched as Verex did not deserve such agony. Know, also, that this is what all gods fear would become of us, were we to release the power in the Fang of Kist-Aurek and expose ourselves to Rovagug's corruption.

"What happened to Verex, and what would happen to any god seized by the Rough Beast, is worse than you can imagine. Verex was not utterly devoured, as Kist-Aurek and so many others were, but transformed. Rovagug warped him in soul and purpose, partly for the sheer pleasure that such cruelty brought him, but also so that Verex might become powerful enough to serve as a useful agent in this world.

"His own thoughts and goals have been stripped from him. All that remains is Rovagug's pawn, thoroughly subjugated to his master's whims. Now Verex's sole purpose is to seize the Fang of Kist-Aurek, bring it to the scar of the Dead Vault, and use it to free his master."

"How do we stop him?" Kyra asked.

Sarenrae's heart sang at her servant's courage, even as she felt a fresh pang of worry for these mortals. *So brave, so fragile.* "You cannot attack Verex directly. Other champions, gifted with god-sparks of their own, have tried and failed. They were lucky to escape with their lives. Should he slay and consume you, he would gain your god-spark and grow stronger."

"If we can't kill Verex, then all that remains is to prevent him from taking the blade," Ezren said, his eyes on the frozen image of the orcish god ensnared in tendrils of poisoned blood. "We must destroy the fang ourselves."

"Yes," Sarenrae said. "You must finish Kist-Aurek's work. Shatter the fang into the dead god's trap. That will dissipate its fraction of Rovagug's power permanently, weakening the Rough Beast enough for his prison to contain him securely once more."

"It's not so easy to decline a god's gift." Ezren turned away from the image and toward the radiant goddess. The murky red glow of Verex's transformation cast the wizard's eyes into deep shadow beneath his bushy white brows, but darkness was no barrier to Sarenrae's vision, and she saw that the wizard did not flinch in meeting her gaze. "If I could have refused Gorum's, I would have. I could not. I was powerless to reject the god-spark.

"That was but one tiny fragment, and Gorum was in no state to care what I did with it. What makes you think any of us would be able to resist the full force of Rovagug's will?"

"He will not be able to exert his will upon you, not directly. Kist-Aurek severed Rovagug's connection to his magic when he contained it within his trap. But, of course, the Rough Beast's corruption is formidable even when he does not intentionally command it, and holding such power is its own temptation." Sarenrae regarded each of the mortals in turn, hoping they understood the full gravity of her warning. "You were chosen, in part, because you do have the strength to resist. But it will not be easy. You must be absolute in your conviction."

"And if we're not?" Merisiel asked.

"Then your companions must be prepared to do what must be done to ensure Rovagug does not reclaim his power."

"Kill the corrupted one, you mean," the elf pressed. Her eyes were black and unreflective in the ugly red light, revealing nothing.

"Yes." Sarenrae would not lie to these mortals. They needed the truth, and they deserved it.

"If it must be done, it will be done," Kyra promised, touching her brow, lips, and heart in an oathkeeper's salute. It was an old form, one that had fallen into disuse centuries ago, but perhaps her servant thought Sarenrae was unlikely to notice the passage of so little time.

"I hope it will not be necessary," the goddess replied, "but you must be prepared for all contingencies."

"How do we find and destroy the knife?" Ezren asked.

"Long ago, the Fang of Kist-Aurek was brought here, to the Peacebound Isle. The details of its journey matter not, but the seers built this sanctuary to protect it as Ghol-Gan crumbled around them. When all else plunged into brutality and despair, they held fast, at the cost of their order and their lives. Their seals kept it hidden for long ages. When you remove it, those seals will be broken, and your enemies will be able to sense its presence in the world. You have seen Rovagug's corruption already seeping through the island. It will not take him long to find this place, once the island's wards are gone. At that point, you will have to race to finish your task before his servants intervene."

The wizard's brow creased. "Where's the scar of the Dead Vault?"

"In one way, that is a difficult question to answer. For eons, it lingered below Gormuz." Sarenrae paused a moment, and a flicker of regret and sadness flashed in her eyes before she continued. "I would rather not speak at this time of what became of that place, but since then, the scar has shifted as Rovagug writhed within the vault. Whenever he tested his bonds anew, the scar found a new place in reality. The last time this happened, the scar settled here." One last time, Sarenrae gestured to the statues, and the light of their sun and moon shifted once again. Verex's frozen image melted into overlapping pools of silver and gold radiance, then reformed into the semblance of a gargantuan hurricane twisting over open water.

Amiri squinted at the vastness of the storm, and at the tiny fringes of shoreline just visible beyond its reach. "The Eye of Abendego?"

"Yes. The upheavals that shook reality at the time of Aroden's death gave Rovagug another chance to send his howls up into the world. They emerged from the Dead Vault and echoed through the boundaries between realities here, creating a storm that has no end. I fear that they may have called a shard of Gorum's power to them as well.

"Now, with the Lord in Iron's death, what began on that dreadful day has continued. Just as an infection in the flesh causes swelling, so too did the world swell. The sea itself churned and gave way to a new isle. At the heart of the Eye of Abendego, you will find this island, and from there, the scar through which you must travel. The reality contained within is where Kist-Aurek first struck Rovagug, where we ambushed him, where we caged him. Today, that is where the boundary between your world and the Dead Vault is at its most fragile. It is also where Rovagug's own servants will seek to free him if the fang falls into their hands."

"Then everything comes down to this scar." Amiri flexed her fists, swung her arms across her body, and tightened a hide gauntlet that had begun to come loose. "Does it have a name?"

"Desna called it the Godsgrave," Sarenrae answered, "and I suppose I came to think of it that way as well. But it never had a name agreed upon by all, because those who survived that battle seldom spoke of it. We felt that the memory, like the scar itself, was best left buried."

"The *Carroway* might be able to take us there, but Samo was barely able to fight through the storm to get us to this isle," Ezren said doubtfully. "If we're to reach the Godsgrave, we'll need something to bolster our ship."

"I will give you that." Sarenrae moved toward Kyra and lifted her hands to either side of her servant's face. The holy light in her palms cast a doubled glow across the cleric's features, illuminating the blue tattoos beneath her eyes, the tears that trickled down her cheeks, and the slow, determined breaths that puffed almost silently through her lips. "My servant, my daughter, my cherished friend. Will you permit me to place my power in you, so that you may do my work in this world?"

Kyra nodded. "Yes," she whispered. "Yes. I accept."

"Then it is yours." Sarenrae closed her eyes and intoned a single high, clear note. The light in her hands intensified, growing brighter and brighter until a small sun filled the cyclopes' sanctuary, obliterating the lesser light of their orbs and the image of the Eye of Abendego. The world became gold and white and warmth, and then the sun passed from Sarenrae's hands and into Kyra, where it dwindled into a spark that the mortal could hold.

The spark lingered over Kyra's chest for a moment, pulsing in time to her heartbeat, and then it melted into her chest and was gone.

"I will not dishonor your gift," the cleric said hoarsely. She touched her chest with uncertain fingertips. "I swear it. I will defeat Rovagug."

It was not a lie. Sarenrae sensed the truth in her servant's vow. The mortal honestly believed she would prevail, so strong was her faith in Sarenrae and her gift.

If only she knew what she faced...

But was that, too, not one of the mortals' secret strengths? There was so much the gods had seen that they had not, and these mortals were thus undeterred by that knowledge. Kyra had only heard stories of the Great Devourer, and though she had encountered his cultists and creatures, she had never beheld the terrible might of the dread god himself.

So it was possible for her to believe in her vow, and in the certainty of Sarenrae's victory. And in believing, she could make it so.

"I am grateful for your faith, my servant." Sarenrae drew back her hands and turned, letting her light fade. She could feel the magic of the cyclopes' sanctuary ebbing around her. It would have failed already, had she not filtered her own divine power into their wards to bolster them, but she could not sustain that much longer. If Rovagug sensed her here, he would know she was protecting the fang, and he would direct all his strength to destroying these mortals and claiming their prize.

They had so little time. "Now, please, come. I must show you to the Fang of Kist-Aurek."

Chapter Twenty-Four

THE FANG OF KIST-AUREK

As her friends followed Sarenrae out of the cyclopes' vision chamber, Amiri felt an irritating tingle flush across her person. It was as if she'd been brushed by invisible nettles over every inch of her body, and the venomous annoyance of their sting had somehow inflamed her emotions along with her skin.

She looked about suspiciously, bristling at the possibility that an unseen sorcerer had crept up on them while they were distracted, but there was no sign of any such enemy. The cyclopes' sanctuary was as hushed and empty as it had been a moment earlier. Nothing had changed except that Amiri could see the walls and ceiling soaring high overhead once they'd moved out of the vision chamber.

Intricate carvings covered the walls, depicting constellations interwoven with long scrolls of geometric runes that Amiri couldn't read. Mosaics of glittering glass tiles, separated by broad wedges of silver and gold, reflected Sarenrae's light across the ceiling. They were worked into spiraling, kaleidoscopic patterns that made Amiri dizzy and obscurely angry, as if they were taunting her with words she couldn't read and equations she couldn't solve.

The cyclopes' designs weren't merely decorative. They were intended to make her feel small and stupid. Probably they were meant to have that effect on anyone who wasn't one of these oh-so-special Peacebound Seers, but the seers were all dead and Amiri wasn't, so she supposed the last laugh was hers.

Even so, they made her angry. Everything here seemed to make her angry. She rubbed her forehead, trying to settle her temper, but it didn't work. Nothing worked. She wanted to hit something, and she didn't know why, and that made her want to hit something too.

"Are you all right?" Ezren asked, catching her motion. He looked concerned.

Amiri shrugged. She cracked her neck to one side and then the other, trying not to look at the ceiling mosaics as she did. The sound of popping joints soothed her, but only for a second. "The idea of facing Rovagug..."

"It is... worrisome, yes." Ezren looked ahead to the radiant figure of Sarenrae, and then back to Amiri. "But a goddess trusts us with this task, and I cannot doubt her wisdom. If she believes us capable, then it must be so."

"Gods can be wrong. Gods can *die*, Ezren."

"I know. Nevertheless, they are wiser than we. That may be a small reassurance, but it does reassure me."

Not me. Amiri stared at Sarenrae's back, feeling something stiffen and bristle deep inside her. Who *was* this goddess to treat them like pawns? Kyra's goddess, not hers. The Dawnflower had no claim on Amiri.

They were still talking, the cleric and her goddess. Amiri loped a little closer, lightening her step so that she moved as soundlessly as if she were stalking prey. Whatever plans they were making, she wanted to know.

"—and so the Peacebound renounced violence completely," Sarenrae was saying. "Not only did they forswear all manner of fighting and weaponry, but they pulled out their incisors and left only their molars, to make a public show of their refusal, and indeed their inability, to eat meat as their kin did. The most venerated among them put out their own eyes, which had witnessed too much of the world's cruelty, and replaced them with sacred stones from this isle, where only peace was permitted.

"Even at the height of Ghol-Gan's enlightenment, the Peacebound Seers were considered extremists, and truthfully, they were. Once Ghol-Gan began to descend into decay, they were truly isolated in their practices. But their extremism served a purpose.

"They knew that the Fang of Kist-Aurek could free Rovagug, and they could surmise that the Rough Beast's servants would try to seize it. When they attempted to learn whether that attempt would succeed, however, their divinations failed, for—unbeknownst to them—that day would not come until after Aroden's death, in an age without prophecy.

"What they did know was that Ghol-Gan would fail to keep the fang safe. Worse, they foresaw that the despair brought on by this truth would cause their empire's collapse into chaos and savagery, and they saw that Rovagug's pawns would try to exploit that to obtain the Fang of Kist-Aurek. Already, in the waning days of their order, they saw the signs of corruption spread to their once-sacred isle."

"The red splotches?" Kyra asked. "We saw them welling through the paving stones outside."

"Yes." Sarenrae's fiery eyes never blinked. It was a small sign of her inhumanity, but one that fascinated Amiri. "Legacy of the blood sacrifices that their kin committed, and a means by which Rovagug could reach through to this place. When the Peacebound Seers saw that manifestation of blood and destruction seep through the bedrock of their island and taint the sacred stones of their high roads, they knew their end had come. Their people had fallen too far to be saved and would soon turn against them.

"The last great act of their sect was a ritual that placed the Peacebound Isle under a seal of absolute pacifism. Their sanctuary was made invisible and inviolable to creatures of violence. Anyone, or anything, who committed an act of violence upon the Peacebound Isle would be struck dead immediately."

"But how would anything survive?" Kyra asked, mystified. "Birds of prey, the fish in the sea, even the insects—"

"They died." Sarenrae said it softly, and with great sorrow. Her radiant mantle shifted from gold and white to a somber, soot-edged orange, like a flame blown low. "They all died. Even the violence of birth or mating caused the Peacebound Isle's curse to strike innocent creatures down, for nothing is born without blood. That is why nothing lives on this island except for a few plants that can propagate themselves without insects. Even the seers could not long survive their own spell. Either they left the island as soon as it was completed, or they remained as caretakers until the eventual day that they, too, succumbed.

"Most chose to die here. They did not wish to remain in the world their kin had created. But none were left to bury them, and their bones are long gone."

"Stupid," Amiri blurted. Kyra and her goddess turned to look at her, the former with open-mouthed shock, the latter with an arched eyebrow of curiosity.

She shrugged, but she didn't back down from what she'd said. "What were they going to do if someone broke through their spell? Peace doesn't last long without force to protect it. You're saying they had a key to Rovagug's cell, and instead of defending it properly, they just... lay down and died? Stupid. It was stupid."

"Their sacrifice—" Kyra began, but she cut herself off with a frustrated shake of her head and a sidelong glance at Sarenrae.

"It was not in vain," the goddess assured her. Sarenrae resumed walking through the cyclopes' gigantic hall, moving faster than she had before, as though some secret alarm had spurred her to hurry. "It bought them time. Perhaps more importantly, it prevented their cannibal kin from finding or using the Fang of Kist-Aurek. I have little doubt that if the inheritors of Ghol-Gan had been able to locate Kist-Aurek's blade, they would have released the Devourer from his prison, for creatures lost to impulse and rage are easily lured to his call, and still more easily bent to his whims.

"But you are not wrong," she said to Amiri. "The Peacebound Seers are dead, and their island is nearly so. No one guards it any longer, and Rovagug's influence spreads rapidly from the core of the Eye of Abendego. His power, and his need, have eroded the ancient safeguards to the brink of failure. You have seen the marks of his presence all across the island, and they have even reached to the exterior of this holy sanctuary.

"I have lent my own power to shore up the Peacebound Seers' wards, but their spells are weakening swiftly. Even with my aid, they had faltered enough that you could find this place. Soon, they will fail altogether, and then he will be able to find it too.

"Were it not for you—and, yes, your willingness to use the weapons that the Peacebound Seers forswore—the Rough Beast would find and claim the fang. So you are correct, young Amiri: there are times when peace will fail, and violence must answer."

They had come to a great door at the end of the hallway. Sarenrae stopped a few paces from its archway, sunlight pooling about her semihuman form.

Bands of gold and silver, etched with blocky sigils and braided into knots and webs, reflected her holy light away from the cyclopes' gigantic door. Glass mosaics flowered between the metallic bands, mimicking the patterns that had followed them along the ceilings all this way and intensified Amiri's vague but inescapable sense that this place was somehow mocking her.

To either side of the archway, twenty-foot-tall stone cyclopes looked down on them with inscrutable marble faces. Like the ones outside, they were depicted as missing the teeth from the front halves of each jaw and sacred stones replacing their eyes.

"The Fang of Kist-Aurek lies beyond this door." Sarenrae gestured toward it, and then she folded her hands over her heart. The goddess's sacred light pulled inward, gathering around her like a reversed shadow. At its core, her figure began to fade. "I dare not be exposed to it, so I must leave you now. Once you open the door, the wards will fail. The fang is yours, and the hope of this world lies with you."

In a twinkling, the goddess was gone. Her presence had begun to annoy Amiri in a way that she couldn't articulate—and, she thought, was probably not fair, since what was *really* irritating her was the condescension mortared into every tile of those infernal mosaics—but she still felt strangely bereft when Sarenrae's golden glow faded away.

"She was real," Kyra breathed, pressing both hands to her heart. Wonder filled the cleric's voice. "She was *real*. She touched me with her hands and charged me with her duty."

"Do you feel all right?" Merisiel asked, oddly tentative. The elf came forward almost apprehensively, as if she wasn't quite sure what to expect from her wife, or even whether Kyra still was the person she'd known as her wife.

"I feel no different. Only blessed to have the Dawnflower's trust." Kyra looked up at the cyclopean runes that scrolled down the door's face. The guardian statues seemed larger and sterner in the gloom that had replaced Sarenrae's light. "Are we prepared to open it?"

The gods themselves fear this Fang.

Curiously, the thought didn't frighten Amiri. She felt only eagerness to behold the weapon. What would it be like to wield such a blade? It had been crafted by all the skill and cunning of one god and had tasted the blood of another. More than blood. It had captured the essence of no mere demigod or demon lord, but the Rough Beast himself, slaughterer of pantheons.

"Open it," Amiri said.

Kyra placed her palms flat where the lines of silver and gold crisscrossing the mosaics met. She closed her eyes, murmuring. A spark ignited in the center of her holy symbol, brightening until its light enveloped the entire door. Amiri had to shade her eyes with a hand and look away, and even then tears wetted her lashes.

The mosaics collected Kyra's light, igniting in chains that spread across the door, one tiny glass block after another. When the entire design was aglow, the door shone for the space of a long, tense breath, and then it was gone as if it had never existed.

In that instant, the irritation that had been plaguing Amiri vanished. She felt suddenly liberated, possessed of an exultation that cried out to be expressed in violence.

Not now. She could wait. If Sarenrae's warning was to be heeded, they'd find their enemies soon.

But it was hard to push away the impulse, even without anyone in sight to strike. Harder than it should have been, somehow.

Kyra's light spilled through the archway to reveal a chamber that had likely been small by cyclopean standards but seemed immense to Amiri. It measured perhaps thirty feet long, thirty wide, and nearly as high. Other than a single ten-foot-tall plinth of red-veined white marble, it was empty.

A long crystal-bladed knife rested atop marble supports on the plinth. Its handle was a length of gristly bone, knobbed and discolored by ancient gore. Murky red energy swirled within the blood-smeared crystal, pulsing with a power that called to Amiri.

"I'll get it," Merisiel said, strapping on a pair of climbing gloves with rough black palms. Amiri had seen those before. They were enchanted to cling to any surface, enabling the elf to scale smooth walls and concave surfaces that no one else could climb.

It should be mine, Amiri thought, but she clamped the thought into silence. Let Merisiel retrieve it first. She could take hold of the fang once they had it.

Kyra nodded, and her wife was off. Slapping her hands from hold to hold and swinging her body weight from side to side, Merisiel hoisted herself up the plinth. In the blink of an eye, she'd reached the top, and with one victorious hand, she took the Fang of Kist-Aurek from its mount.

A calamitous shudder racked the sanctuary. Mosaic tiles shivered from the ceiling and fell like bladed raindrops. One slashed Ezren's cheek, drawing a thin line of blood that ran into his beard. More pattered against Kyra's clothing, clicking on her headdress and the enameled ornaments across her chest.

Amiri covered her head with her gauntleted forearms, running forward to Merisiel. "Throw it to me and come down!"

"Don't need to throw it for that," Meri answered. She bent forward to tuck herself around the fang and sprang off the plinth, landing in a nimble roll and popping out of it with the weapon still gripped firmly in one hand. Even before she was fully upright, the elf was bolting for the archway. "Let's get out of here."

Amiri didn't need to be told twice. The place was collapsing.

As they fled through the vision chamber, she saw that the red stains from the sanctuary's exterior were spreading through the entire structure like blood in water. They weren't isolated splotches anymore; they joined together into an expanding net, with tendrils that stretched out quickly toward the companions.

The seal of peace has shattered, and the Rough Beast wastes no time.

Wherever the fingers of corruption touched, mosaics shriveled and crumpled inward into slimy black fragments, and carved marble went spongy and treacherous as moldy bread. As the carved cyclopes' hands liquesced into rot, Inithyra's Orb fell from the statues' grasps. It vanished beneath their melting forms, buried in the temple's dying throes.

"Sarenrae, shield us from our enemy's hand." Kyra gripped her holy symbol. Divine light surrounded her in a fifteen-foot radius, wide enough for all four of them to crowd into her protective sphere. It pushed back the reaching tendrils and solidified the decayed marble underfoot, at least for the moment. Amiri saw how the red stains pushed against Kyra's sphere and how the light dimmed and smoked at any prolonged contact. They had to move fast, or they were dead.

"The boat," Amiri grunted, running for the exit. "We need to get to the boat. Samo can take us from here."

Kyra nodded, and Ezren wheezed assent. Together, the four of them ran from the crumbling sanctuary, pieces of blackened mosaic and rotten stone tumbling around them.

Outside, the white mists of the Peacebound Isle had taken on an ominous red cast. The sun hadn't been visible through the fog before, but now Amiri could make it out as a glowering crimson presence beyond the clouds. A sulfurous wind stirred the isle's vines and rattled dead leaves along the abandoned boulevards, and though Amiri couldn't see the ocean, she could hear the crash of angry waves reverberating through the mist. The noise seemed louder and more hostile as Kyra released her protective spell.

"Rovagug is coming." Amiri could feel the Rough Beast's awareness drawing near, drumming in her soul like the hoofbeats of a distant stampede shaking the earth.

"The boat," Ezren gasped. The wizard was neither as athletic nor as young as the others, and he was badly winded.

Amiri wasn't strong enough to carry him, not while running herself. She didn't know what to do, and worry for her friend cut through the haze of annoyance that had gripped her since they'd entered the sanctuary.

"Come on, Ezren," she urged, falling back to run by his side. "We only have to get to the boat. It's all downhill from here. Just lean forward and let yourself fall. Don't try to stop it. Let gravity do your work."

He grunted, having no breath to waste on words, but he seemed to take heart from her encouragement. The wizard ran as best he could, and Amiri stayed with him. Kyra and Merisiel didn't slow and were a hundred yards ahead by the time they reached the cliffs and began their final descent toward the harbor.

Red splotches marred the marble paths around them and blighted the flowering vines that climbed over the ruins of Ghol-Gan, but these were more widely scattered and didn't pursue the companions with the intentional fervor of the manifestations in the sanctuary. For an instant Amiri let herself feel a surge of relief, until the fog parted below them and she caught sight of the harbor.

There was another ship at the dock. It would have dwarfed the *Carroway* had the smaller boat been in view, but the vessel that had brought them to the isle was gone. Only the stranger's ship floated by the pier, and Amiri bristled at it instantly.

It was no ordinary ship. Its sails looked like fins of such a deep turquoise that they seemed almost black, stretched over bony spines sheathed in fine-grained scales. The hull was not built of wood or iron; it might not have been built at all. It was the same inky blue-black as the sails and masts, and had the sleek, efficient lines of an oceanic predator. So vibrantly organic did the ship seem that Amiri wouldn't have been surprised to see its ballista ports open to reveal eyes.

She pulled up, dismayed. "Where's Samo? Where's the *Carroway*?"

Laughter met her question. It was wild and hateful, a shriek of rage that could be called a laugh only because it erupted in pulses.

Mist blew away from the cliff path, revealing a shaggy-haired woman dressed in clumps of rags that seemed to be adhered to her body rather than held by straps or buckles. Her face was almost wholly obscured by the gray-brown knots of her hair, and her skin was fissured with rough, pitted plaques that looked more like tree bark than anything human. Pink swellings bulged between the scabrous plaques.

She seemed to be alone, yet Amiri was more afraid of this lone, laughing woman than she would have been of a phalanx of giants.

Anyone who stands alone in battle is to be feared, the elders of her people had told her, and she'd learned it to be true. Loners in the wilderness were likely to be sick or starving, and therefore unpredictably dangerous, or else were so formidable that, like the white bear, they needed no companions.

This one is both.

"Be careful," Amiri called to the others. "The island's seal is gone. They may attack."

They'd let some of their lead slip, but Kyra and Merisiel were still about twenty yards ahead of Ezren and Amiri. "Curuvrakh," the elf snarled, taking a step back as she recognized the shaggy woman.

"You know my name?" The woman in rags pushed her hair behind her shoulders, revealing more of her face. Amiri couldn't see clearly from this distance, but whatever she'd shown Merisiel and Kyra made the other two recoil. "That's funny. I don't know yours. I know who you are, though. A wizard who can't use magic, and a servant of a coward god. She didn't stay to fight, did she? She was here, and she ran, tail between her legs. My master tastes her terror and laughs.

"Then there's you," Curuvrakh added, tilting her head at a grotesque, broken-necked angle as she studied Merisiel. "Whoever you are. Not important. But you have the Fang of Kist-Aurek in your weak little soft-thing hands. That can't be allowed." She laughed again, harsh and malevolent. "Give it to me."

"Meri, don't," Kyra interjected. She thrust out her holy symbol. Sunlight glowed through her fingers, intensifying into a twisting blast of gold-white fire that struck Curuvrakh squarely in the chest.

The shaggy woman screamed, but there was laughter in her scream, and when she emerged from the fiery torrent, her grin cracked through the blackened skin of her face. Even Amiri could see the red slash of Curuvrakh's smile amid the char. Something seemed to be wriggling under or inside her burns, visibly repulsing the other two.

"Give me the fang," Curuvrakh ordered Merisiel, punctuating her words with another cackle. She held out a blistered hand, the sun-scorched skin sloughing from it in ribbons.

To Amiri's horror, Merisiel complied. The elf was stiff as a corpse, trying to fight whatever magic was in Curuvrakh's command, but her arm shot out with the Fang of Kist-Aurek gripped in one white-knuckled hand.

"Stop her," Ezren gasped. The wizard leaned heavily on his walking stick. Arcane energy crackled around him, but it was shapeless as static before a storm, not the thunderstrike they needed. Even if he did manage to form it into a spell, Amiri doubted it would be in time to stop Curuvrakh.

I'm the only one left.

She vaulted forward, sprinting at full speed. Leaping over piles of rubble and gaps in the cliff road, she raced toward the half-paralyzed Merisiel and the cackling woman who held her in thrall. As Amiri closed in, she pulled out her knife, unsure whether she meant to gut Curuvrakh or hack Merisiel's hand off at the wrist if that was the only way to stop her from handing over the fang.

Either seemed equally reasonable, and only the smallest part of Amiri voiced any protest at the thought.

When she was ten feet away, just a step or two short of striking distance, she saw Curuvrakh's face full on. The sight made her stumble mid-stride.

Worms and misshapen bones and squelching gobbets of wet, pink flesh squirmed together in Curuvrakh's spell-charred face. Spiders' legs twitched in place of her cheekbones, causing the scraps of skin over them to shift and bulge obscenely. Her left eye was gone, and the sucking mouth of a lamprey rose from the socket, gobbling at the air. It was as if Kyra's spell had torn away the crust of a rotten meat pie full of maggots, exposing the hungry corruption beneath.

Curuvrakh laughed. Something squirmed in her hair; Amiri glimpsed a hairy, chitinous leg that looked as if it belonged to a spider as big as a cat. "Who are you, little one?"

"The one who's going to stop you," Amiri spat back. She recovered her footing, shoved away her knife, and yanked her greatsword from its sheath.

"Are you?" Curuvrakh reached forward and plucked the Fang of Kist-Aurek from Merisiel's hand. The elf's face twisted in agony, but she offered no resistance. "That's not what this looks like to me."

Looking past Merisiel, Curuvrakh fixed her good eye on Amiri. It widened slightly, and the nightmare worm squirming in her other socket exhaled a grotesque, burping laugh. "Did you think this would be yours? You did, didn't you. You've been touched by my master. Poor little soft thing. Who *are* you? The old man's nursemaid? Not a warrior. You're barely even worth killing. You—"

The tip of a bone spear punched out of Curuvrakh's throat from behind, cutting off her words in a wheeze of pink-tinged air. Clutching at the weapon, the woman staggered around in a slow spin.

Nahoa, painted for war, stood on the slope behind her. The young warrior's face was grimly set, refusing to give in to horror. His black curls blew wild in the breeze. He raised a hand into the air, and the barbed bone spear rematerialized in his grip. As he drew his arm back for another throw, Curuvrakh snarled and hurled herself, along with the fang, off the side of the cliff.

Tattered, batlike wings sprouted from Curuvrakh's back as she plummeted through the air. Parts of them were transparent and veined like wasps' wings; other patches were pulsing liquid blobs, like blood coagulating into fresh scabs. They held together, though, and they bore the monstrous woman through the fog toward the blue-black ship at its pier.

"We must go," Nahoa said, slamming the spear's end against the ground in frustration.

"I gave her the fang." Merisiel sounded sick. The elf swayed as if choking back nausea, her hands balled into impotent fists. "I *gave* it to her."

Amiri growled. She was angry at Merisiel for surrendering the weapon, but angrier at herself for failing to land a single strike, and still more furious at Curuvrakh. *I'll show you a nursemaid.*

Nahoa gripped the elf's shoulder to shake her out of her self-condemnation. It was enough to rouse Merisiel back to her senses. She shrugged his hand off testily, and he let go at once, raising a palm in apology.

"We must go," the islander said again. "Samo hid the boat so our enemies would not find it. I'll take you there."

"He's right." Kyra squared her shoulders. She was as distraught as the rest of them—perhaps more so, Amiri thought, since she'd just failed the charge that her goddess had personally given them—but already the cleric was moving past disappointment and shifting back to steely determination. "We must reach the *Carroway*. Then we must go to the Godsgrave so that we can take the fang back and break it as Sarenrae instructed."

"Right." Amiri nodded, as did the others.

But in her heart, she thought, *I'm not breaking* anything *until I've used it to cleave that witch's taunting face in two.*

Chapter Twenty-Five
OVERDUE CONVERSATIONS

"I failed."

Merisiel was only muttering to herself, and hadn't meant for anyone to hear her, but the *Carroway* was a small boat and Samo's calming of the waves hushed much of the sea's noise. Ezren looked up from his spellbook.

"We all failed," the wizard said. He put a beaten bronze marker on the page he'd been reading and closed the book, then got up from the folded blanket he'd been sitting upon and joined Merisiel at the railing.

Around them, the sea glowed through a golden haze. Kyra had threaded her divine power into Samo's incantations, strengthening the spirit-speaker's magic until it could bear them into the Eye of Abendego. The *Carroway* cleaved through waves that towered twenty feet taller than the boat itself, and skated between gusts that would have smashed its hull to kindling. All the storm's fury raged just beyond them, but nothing reached the boat except an occasional spray of salt foam.

Merisiel almost wished she could feel the storm, though. She would have welcomed the battering of wind and wave as a replacement for the turmoil in her soul. "At least you tried. Gorum's curse prevented you. You all had reasons, and you tried. I just... gave her the fang."

"You fought her magic as long as you could. I was there, Merisiel. I saw it." Ezren touched the back of her arm lightly, offering friendship without pressing it. He knew her well enough to respect her distaste for being touched.

Right now, though, it was all Meri could do to keep from throwing her arms around him in a hug. She held on to her dignity, but barely. Staring woodenly over the railing at the gold-washed sea, she said, "You have the power of a god. Kyra does too. Even Amiri seems stronger than usual. She has since Port Peril. But me? What do I bring to the group? All I've done is give up the key to Rovagug's cell.

"I don't belong here, Ezren. I can't fight these foes."

"We wouldn't have found the fang without you." Ezren faced the sea beside her and put his arm around Merisiel's shoulders. She didn't shrug it off. "You're clever and resourceful and fierce, and we *do* need you. I know I do, and Kyra does too."

"Does she?" The words slipped out, bitterly, before Meri could hold them back. She cursed herself for that failure too.

"Of course." Ezren gave her a shrewd sidelong look from beneath his bushy white brows. "Have you talked to her about this, Merisiel? Really talked to her?"

"I don't want to trouble her. She has so much to do, and there's so little time. We're nearly to the Godsgrave." Meri made a small, helpless gesture with one hand. A wave slapped against the side of their little boat, spraying her with salt. It tasted like tears.

"That's why you should talk to her. Now, before we arrive. You're right that there isn't much time, but that's true for all of us. We may not survive the battle ahead. What if you do, and she doesn't? What if she does, and you don't? What if you leave these things unsaid, and then there is never a chance to say them?"

Meri glanced at the wizard. Weariness shadowed his eyes and deepened the lines around his mouth, but that only seemed to enhance the wizard's air of hard-won wisdom.

Being around him calmed her, much as being around Kyra calmed her. Measured by years, the wizard was far younger than Merisiel, but he had taken more from the years he'd had.

Raised apart from her kin, among people whose lives flickered and burned out just as she was beginning to know them, Meri had learned to keep a wall around herself. Calistria's teachings had reinforced that instinct. Friends died, lovers vanished. No one could be relied upon. Opening up to them only caused her pain—and them too, sometimes.

So she hadn't. Not for years, decades, even the better part of a century.

But now, facing the prospect of losing her friends and her own life, she felt the emptiness of that approach.

Death was a frightening prospect, but worse was contemplating the possibility that she'd wasted her life in loneliness. *What are the years for if they must be empty?*

"You're right," Merisiel said. "I'll talk to her."

Ezren nodded, still gazing at the unnaturally gold-hued sea. "About Amiri..."

"Yes?"

He fidgeted with a fleck of sea spray on an embroidered blue sleeve. "You mentioned that she's seemed different since Port Peril."

"Don't you think so?" Merisiel looked at him questioningly. She turned away from the railing, wiping half-dried foam from the green gem on her forehead. The salt itched, and she didn't want it clouding the jewel. "Perhaps I'm imagining it."

"No. I don't think you are. I've noticed it as well. Do you remember what her friend the knight said? That the red storms tended to affect people like her more strongly. I started seeing a shift in her then, and I believe it became more pronounced on the Peacebound Isle. Especially once we reached the Fang of Kist-Aurek."

"What are you saying?" Merisiel narrowed her eyes. She hadn't noticed Amiri's temper getting worse on the Peacebound Isle, but she also hadn't really been paying attention. All her energy had been focused on the fang and on Sarenrae's charge to Kyra.

"I don't know. Perhaps only that I'm concerned about her. I don't want to believe that it's possible the Devourer might be influencing her, but..."

"But you can't rule it out, either."

Ezren locked eyes with her for a steady, unsmiling moment. "Can you?"

"No," Merisiel admitted.

"Maybe you should talk to her too. I will. If nothing else, perhaps we'll be able to lay our fears to rest."

"All right. But only after I talk to Kyra."

She found Kyra in Samo's cabin, where the two of them, along with Nahoa, were seated on the floor around a low table, sharing honey-colored tea in carved bone cups. A censer smoked in the table's center, filling the small room with pungent smoke that made Meri feel lightheaded.

"Meri." The cleric looked up with a wan smile, warm but exhausted. Smoke curled around her face, but Meri didn't think that was why Kyra's eyes were reddened. "They were just telling me about their encounter with Verex-That-Was, the orc god Rovagug corrupted."

"He almost killed us," Nahoa said. The young warrior said it with simple fatalism, as if he had told this tale enough times to have accepted its reality but still hadn't reconciled himself to the loss. "I would have died if Samo hadn't pulled me out of there. She nearly had to burn out her spirit-gift healing me."

"The wounds were not so difficult. The taint was what taxed me. I think, if Nahoa had not been so stubborn, and so strong in his sense of self, I might not have been able to do it." Samo frowned as she reached out to adjust the kettle that sat on a glowing stone next to the censer. It seemed to gather and condense the smoke, as if they were drinking that as much as their tea. She nodded toward a tray of empty cups beside the door, inviting Merisiel to take one, but she declined with a small shake of her head.

"We're worried that something similar might happen to us at the Godsgrave," Kyra said. "Especially to Amiri."

"You too? Ezren said something about that." Meri hovered in the doorway. She didn't want to interrupt, and she hated to be so obvious in her vulnerability, but... "Kyra, when you have a moment, could we talk?"

"Yes, of course." The cleric gathered her robes and stood, nodding politely to the others. "Please excuse me."

"It doesn't have to be right now," Meri said hastily. "You're busy, and—"

"No," Kyra said, serenely but with great firmness. She put her teacup down and joined Merisiel at the door, touching the back of Meri's hand and letting her fingertips rest there for a second. Her hand had been warmed by the teacup, and that warmth flowed into Merisiel like borrowed strength. "You have not had enough of my time these past weeks. I do not know how much of that time remains. Let us talk."

Meri nodded and swallowed, taking a moment before she trusted herself enough to speak. "In our room?"

"In our room."

Kyra led the way to the small cabin they shared with their companions. It was only a few short steps, yet to Meri it felt as long as a condemned man's walk to the gallows. All the way there, she wondered what she would say to Kyra, and what words she could find to say it.

I need you. I need you to need me. I'm so afraid of what might happen, and I do not want to be alone. I was alone for so long before you. I can't do that again.

It sounded so pathetic in her head. So desperate, so obvious. No Calistrian would say any of those things.

Before now, Meri wouldn't have said them either.

But on the brink of the Godsgrave, how could she stay silent?

Together they entered the cabin. It was a cramped little space, just a bunk for the two of them separated from Amiri and Ezren's half of the room by a hanging curtain. Kyra's prayer rug was rolled up neatly at the head of her bed, doubling as a pillow, and her amber-and-gold prayer beads hung from a nail on the frame.

She'd made their half of the cabin a home, as she always did. No matter how far they traveled, or how light the cleric had to pack, she found ways of bringing her roots along. A tiny stub of candle filled their space with a hint of sandalwood, oud, and incense, the fragrance of Kyra's temple.

Next to her prayer beads, she'd hung a lapis lazuli necklace that Merisiel had "liberated" on one of their early adventures and given to her at the beginning of their courtship. That necklace was stolen, and Kyra knew it, so she'd never worn it. She had, Merisiel knew, later gone back to pay the merchant its rightful price. But she'd never discarded it either and had carried it with her all this time, always placing it somewhere near her bed.

In her medicine case, she kept a perfume bottle that they'd purchased while shopping in Absalom.

They hadn't been looking for cosmetics that day; they'd been trying to find an armorer who could affix Meri's thigh sheaths back onto her armor after they'd been torn off by an irate troll. Meri still remembered how they'd laughed when the shop assistant coaxed the two of them into trying on all manner of oils and unguents that neither of them could imagine themselves wearing. They weren't courtesans or idle baronesses; they were adventurers who lived on the road and had no time for such fripperies.

But they'd had fun pretending, that sunny afternoon in Absalom, and there *had* been one scent that stirred Merisiel. She wasn't versed in such things and couldn't explain why it had such an effect on her when Kyra put it on, but her wife had seen the look on her face and had purchased it at once.

Kyra only wore that scent to bed, and she still sometimes blushed when she dabbed it on. That had always charmed Merisiel, that her wife was still a little shy about admitting her own allure.

As she studied the perfume bottle nestled among Kyra's tinctures and ointments, she realized that she didn't have any similar mementos of her own. It wasn't anything she had done intentionally. She just had never thought to collect any keepsakes, though she could have.

Now she regretted that choice. *Why* don't *I have anything of hers? Of* ours? *Why was it so important to pretend I was unfettered, when all I ever wanted was to be forever bound?*

She shook her head and sat on the edge of Kyra's bunk.

The cleric closed the door. "What's the matter?"

"I failed. With the Fang of Kist-Aurek. I gave it up to Curuvrakh without a fight, and I've hated myself for it ever since." Merisiel saw Kyra's face twist in pain, saw the denial begin to take shape on her wife's lips. She held up a hand to forestall it. "I know you're going to say it's not my fault, and... all right. Maybe it wasn't. I'm not sure I can believe that now, but maybe I'll be able to believe it later. I don't want to fight about it, anyway."

Merisiel dropped her head into her palms, digging her fingers into her long white hair. A tiny part of her mind protested, reflexively, that this pose was not remotely seductive, but at that moment Meri could not have cared less. She didn't *want* to put on a show for Kyra, not if they were about to sail into Rovagug's maw. She wanted to confess the truth. "I just... I don't feel like I'm contributing. You have Sarenrae's blessing. Ezren has a god-spark. I'm only me, and it doesn't feel like that's very much, compared to what we're facing. I want to be more, Kyra. I want to be able to help you. I want to *matter*.

"I'm not sure I do, right now. But I need to. I can't—I can't be alone again, Kyra. I can't go back to the life I had before you. I only... I need you to see me. To hold me. To *need* me, the way I need you."

Kyra didn't answer for a moment. Finally, apprehensive, Merisiel looked up through the tangled veil of her fingers and hair.

Her wife was crying. Tears cut bright lines across Kyra's brown cheeks. "Oh, my love," she managed at last, her voice hoarse and shaky. Kyra reached out, tenderly, to twine her fingers through Merisiel's. "You are my world, my heart, the water of my life. I am so sorry if you've felt that you do not matter. Nothing could be less true. You are *everything* to me, Merisiel.

"I must ask you to forgive me. I've been so lost in my own fears that I neglected yours. But, oh, my dearest... I am so afraid." Kyra took in a trembling breath, gazing at Merisiel with so much love and anguish that Meri's own eyes began to shine with mirrored tears. "What if I can't live up to Sarenrae's trust? What if I fail? What if fulfilling her charge costs your life? Mine—yes, very well, that is the oath I took. But *yours*... I couldn't live with that, Meri."

"You can't say that," Meri whispered. Kyra's words filled her heart to overflowing, but she shook her head anyway. "If that's what it cost, I would give my life gladly. A thousand times. If I could have chosen to die rather than lose the Fang of Kist-Aurek, I would have. I won't... I *can't* be the reason you fail. Please."

Kyra nodded. She brought their intertwined fingers to her lips and kissed Meri's hands, formally and tenderly, three times. Then she sat back, released her grip, and wiped away her tears. "You won't be. I might be, but you won't. I have faith in you, Meri. But I fear that Sarenrae chose the wrong champion in me."

"Why?" Meri had never heard her wife express any doubt in her faith.

"I could not stop Curuvrakh. Sarenrae gave me the power, but I failed to use it. I relied on the spells I knew, instead of drawing upon the full force of her divinity. If I had done that, if I had trusted her gift fully, I might have stopped the witch. Instead, I only proved myself unworthy of the Dawnflower's blessing."

Kyra leaned back heavily, slumping into her bunk and shutting her eyes. "You blame yourself for our failure, but the failure was mine.

You had no one but yourself in that moment, Meri. I had my goddess. All the strength I needed was there, waiting, and I was too blind or foolish or cowardly to use it."

"That's not fair. You'd only been given her blessing a few minutes before," Merisiel protested. She reclined next to Kyra on the bunk, caressing her wife's brow as she might have soothed a sick child. Then, after a moment, she rose on one elbow. "Could... could I help?"

"How do you mean?" Kyra looked at her curiously.

"Maybe I could share the burden with you. Maybe... maybe Sarenrae chose *us*, not just you. I know I've never asked to be involved in your faith before, but we've never been faced with a task like this either."

"Oh, my love." Kyra's smile was tremulous. She touched Meri's temples reverently, then the gem on her forehead, and finally her chin. "Yes. That would be the Dawnflower's wisdom: to see that I am only strong because I have you beside me. Would you really want to share this with me?"

The knot in Meri's throat tightened. "Yes. If I can."

Kyra brought her holy symbol up between them, pressing the cool metal between her forehead and Merisiel's. She leaned forward, fanning her fingertips out to touch both their temples, and whispered a quiet prayer in the warm, secret space they shared. It was not a formal prayer; Meri supposed it couldn't be. What ritual could cover this?

A glow emanated from the holy symbol, encompassing them both within Sarenrae's holy luminance. Kyra's words softened into a reverent hush.

Music filled the silence. It was not real; it never touched Meri's ears. But she felt it in her soul, and she saw a vision of golden light behind her eyelids that left her awestruck at its beauty. Her breath skipped a beat, then started again, faster and shallower. "Oh."

"Oh," Kyra agreed wryly. She lowered her holy symbol, tucked it back into her robes, and brushed a hand over Meri's snowy hair. "Thank you. For everything. I am sorry we've let these struggles create distance between us."

"It's my fault too. I should have come to you sooner." Meri sighed. She nestled against Kyra, drawing comfort from their closeness. "I wish we could stay like this forever. Or at least until we come to the Godsgrave. I've missed it. Just being with you."

"I've missed it too." Kyra relaxed against Meri, but only for a moment. All too soon, as Meri knew she would, the cleric drew herself up again. "But there is much to do before we reach the Godsgrave. Samo and Nahoa have told me all they know about the cursed thing they fought, and now that I've seen Curuvrakh with my own eyes, I have some thoughts about her as well. We should discuss tactics with the others as soon as possible. And you must learn to use Sarenrae's gift."

"All right, all right," Meri groaned, exaggerating it slightly in hopes of amusing Kyra. She sat up, raked her fingers through her hair, and shoved it back behind her pointed ears. "I'll get Amiri. Ezren wanted me to talk to her anyway."

Kyra nodded, reaching over to brush away a lock of white hair that Meri had missed. Then she stood, adjusted her headdress, and smoothed the wrinkles from her robe. "About her temper?"

"That, and the possibility that it's influenced by Rovagug's taint. I don't think it'll be an easy conversation." Meri vaulted herself off the bunk with a thrust of both hands, springing to her feet. She felt lighter than air, despite the unpleasant prospect of having to broach the group's suspicions to Amiri. The talk she'd truly dreaded had been the one with Kyra, and that had ended in more wonder than she'd dared dream. She could still feel the ember of holiness in her chest, marvelous and discomfiting. "But that's all right. I can work miracles now."

Amiri was with Ezren. In order to give Kyra and Meri some privacy, or because they wanted their own, the two of them had sequestered themselves in the cramped side shed where the *Carroway*'s food and other essential supplies were stored.

Meri slowed as she came to the door, listening for the tenor of their conversation. She wasn't trying to eavesdrop, exactly, but she did want to get a read on Amiri's mood before she tried to interrupt.

"—nothing to talk about," Amiri was saying, her voice sharp and short. "I'm fine. So I use my anger to fuel my fighting. What of it?

You never had a problem with that before. Is it because you and Kyra get to be gods now? You don't want any of us little people doing anything that might interfere?"

Ezren's reply was too soft for Merisiel to make out. His tone was conciliatory and patient, as calmly reasonable as he could make it, but Amiri responded with an impatient, disbelieving huff.

Meri crept closer, her ears pricked.

"I *do* value your friendship, Ezren. Really. But you're wrong. I don't know how to say it any more nicely than that. You're wrong. I'm fine, and I won't let you down again when we get to the Godsgrave. We don't need to talk about this anymore."

Meri backed away on cat-quiet feet. Then, all but whistling to signal her oblivious innocence, she sauntered toward the supply shed, making sure her footsteps slapped the deck loudly. "Amiri? Ezren? Kyra wants everyone to gather to discuss tactics."

"Very well." The wizard emerged from the supply shed, brushing dust and packing straw from his clothes. His mouth was set in a thin line, and his shoulders bowed under an invisible load. "I shall see you there."

"Amiri?" Merisiel peered into the shed.

The Kellid sat cross-legged on the floor, hemmed in by sacks and barrels. She'd propped her greatsword on a crate in front of her, with the scorpion stinger she'd taken from the desert outside the Sandfire Catacombs next to it. The dried husk of the stinger's poison sac looked fouler than Merisiel remembered, as if the residue inside the organ had curdled into something between blood and venom and had swelled enough to coat the sac's entire interior. A rancid stench permeated the cramped little room, and Meri suspected it came from Amiri's prize.

"I killed this beast," Amiri said, gesturing to the stinger. Her eyes were red-rimmed, as if something had recently irritated them, but she didn't seem to notice. "It was a monster of its kind, and I killed it, alone. The witch didn't recognize me as a warrior, but she will. This I swear, Merisiel, on the bones of my ancestors. She will."

"I don't doubt it." Merisiel crouched in the doorway to bring her face level with Amiri's. She didn't crowd in, though. The Kellid's gaze was glassy, and while she'd always been a bit disheveled and wild-haired, Meri had never seen her this unkempt. "Amiri? Will you tell me something?"

"What?" Amiri cocked her head at Merisiel, but her eyes remained unfocused.

"How do you get out of your rages? When the fight's won, and all our enemies are slain, how do you calm yourself down? I've always wondered that."

"I just..." Amiri blinked. She put a hand to one temple, then to the hilt of her greatsword, looking as confused as if she'd woken from a troubled slumber and found that the monsters she'd dreamed were real.

The barbarian looked at Merisiel again. This time, there was recognition in her eyes, and a lost, wondering fear. She stared at the scorpion's stinger apprehensively, as if she'd never seen it before. "I don't remember. I *should* remember. I know how to do it. I know that I know this. But it's gone. Why can't I remember?"

"Perhaps it'll come back to you," Meri said, concealing her worry. "Do you want to go and meet with the others?"

"No." Amiri closed her eyes and inhaled deeply. The foulness in the air seemed to strengthen, and Meri could have sworn that she saw vapor from the coagulated residue in the scorpion's stinger swirl up and hiss out through the cracks in the dried sac, like incense smoke. "I don't need to talk about tactics. I know my tactics. Find my enemies and kill them. Just get me to the Godsgrave, Merisiel. I'll take care of the rest."

That's what I'm afraid of, Meri thought as she left.

Chapter Twenty-Six
ACCEPTANCE

You cannot master what you do not accept.

Samo's words echoed in Ezren's mind as he stood by the *Carroway*'s gunwale, resting his elbows on the railing and gazing out to the gold-hazed sea.

Their meeting on tactics had, predictably, borne little fruit. They knew too little about their own capacities, let alone their enemies', to make meaningful plans. Kyra didn't know the full range of powers that Sarenrae had bestowed upon her, and Ezren was still struggling to cast the spells he'd mastered ages ago, let alone enhance them with the god-spark's surging power.

And their enemies...

Ezren had shared his hypothesis that Curuvrakh was, as Amiri had guessed, a witch. In the beginning, she might have been an ordinary cultist of Rovagug, or perhaps even some unknowing innocent who had stumbled into the dread god's grasp. Then the Rough Beast had chosen her as a channel for his divine power, and whatever humanity had remained within her had been obliterated.

That gave them some insight into what she had become but little information as to her capabilities. Most witches were conduits for far lesser beings, and neither Ezren nor any of his companions could guess what monstrous gifts Rovagug might have granted his personal puppet.

They knew even less about Itaguen. The available evidence suggested he wasn't human. Ezren's arcane analysis of the items they'd recovered from the *Merry Mermaid*'s trove, Merisiel's observations in Endio's house, and the glimpse they'd caught of his ship at the Peacebound Isle, suggested that he had a considerable mastery of magic, and that his true origins lay in the deep sea.

But beyond that? All they had on Itaguen was guesswork and conjecture, and trying to base any strategy on that was beyond foolish.

The only one of their enemies that they had real intelligence on was Verex-That-Was, the orcish god who'd been warped into a spawn of Rovagug. Samo and Nahoa had confronted and tried to slay that one, serving the call of another power that, like Sarenrae, had hoped to forestall Rovagug's escape. They had failed after a hard-fought battle that had nearly killed them both.

They had full control of their god-sparks, and they failed.

Moreover, they'd all agreed it was reasonable to surmise that as Rovagug neared freedom, his pawns would become stronger as well. As terrible as Verex-That-Was had been when Nahoa and Samo fought him, he was likely far worse now.

We have no chance if I cannot do this. Too much depended on Ezren's control of the god-spark.

In Elothain's house, he had learned to let go of what he couldn't control. That had granted him some ability to channel the energies of the arcane, but it was far from the mastery he'd once had. Merely holding on to a fraction of his power, while allowing the rest to spin off into chaos, would not suffice against the challenges ahead.

Ezren took a deep breath, focused on an imaginary point on the horizon, and raised his hands to trace the spiraling sigils of Avrayul's Torqueri against the clouds.

I accept it. The power of divinity is mine. It is part of me. It is not Gorum's gift or Gorum's curse or anything of Gorum's at all. He is dead and gone. This is me, and only me, and I must be the master of myself.

Electricity crackled about Ezren's fingers and flickered across the silver embroidery of his robes. The god-spark pulsed within him, threatening to overwhelm his senses.

His vision blurred, and his hair stood on end as the magic rose in answer to his call. His staff tingled against his palm, spitting blue motes that turned the air to ozone. Energy crackled around him, and his feet lifted off the ground.

He didn't fight it. *This is mine. This is me. There is nothing to resist.*

Ezren steadied his stance in the air, widening his feet slightly, and began twisting the glowing runes of the torqueri into a long, thin spike. "*Esdri ovryan, esdri althun.* Lightning, be my spear."

⨯

Two days later, or as near to that as Ezren could determine, given the time-distorting glow of the magic that shielded the *Carroway*, a red mountain rose on the horizon.

It was a curved, clawlike spike, so tall that it soared above the Eye of Abendego's most ferocious waves. Foam frothed about the raw rock of its base. Its crimson peak was lost to the storm clouds, but when the fiercest flashes of lightning struck, so hot that they burned through the clouds' black bellies, Ezren could glimpse the mountain's tip impaling the heavens.

"This is a new wound in the world," Samo said, craning her neck. The bone necklaces threaded around her throat clicked against one another, their song muffled by the dense fur of the spirit-speaker's garb. "It was not here before, and it causes pain to all it touches. The waves and the sky cry out at its abomination. This should be the center of the hurricane, a vortex pulling all comers down to be crushed beneath the sea. But now Rovagug emerges, and his grave is risen from the depths."

"How long until we reach it?" Kyra's holy symbol pulsed with a reflection of the cleric's agitation as she studied the looming spike. Ezren had noticed that such manifestations were becoming more common, and more pronounced, as Kyra developed greater confidence in wielding Sarenrae's power.

Samo lifted a hand to the wind, then dipped her fingers toward the salt spray that slapped against the *Carroway*'s side. "A few hours. Three, four. Perhaps less. The vortex at the heart of the Eye of Abendego is gone, but the current still pulls strongly toward the spike. It smashes the ocean against that poisoned rock with all the viciousness of its master."

"Is there anywhere we might land?" Ezren asked. "Curuvrakh and Itaguen are traveling by ship. Unless they found a way to make that ship fly, they must have some sort of port. Surely Rovagug would not be so foolhardy as to risk sending the Fang of Kist-Aurek to the bottom of the sea or smashing it uselessly against his mountain."

"I will look." Samo lowered her hand toward the sea again. "Spirits of the troubled sea, come to me. See where this foul intruder is weak, and speak to me the secret of where I might strike. Let me aid you, wounded sea. Show me where to go."

White foam, tinged gold by the *Carroway*'s protective nimbus, gathered in her palm and rose into the air in three shimmering streaks. Each streak shaped itself into the distinctive W-shaped silhouette of a frigate bird. Spreading their enchanted wings wide, each of the birds rode the winds in a different direction, circling toward the red mountain ahead.

Samo leaned back on the railing. Opaque white fog swirled in her eyes, and her features were composed in an otherworldly calm. Only a few minutes after her birds had departed, the spirit-speaker spoke, her voice distant and emotionless. "There is another danger in the water. A tribe of athamaru fell victim to the Devourer's red storms, which tainted the ocean waters as they tainted the winds above. They have become Rovagug's creatures, and they await his chosen ones on the mountain. They will not let you pass unchallenged."

Amiri let out a laugh that was half a growl. Her breath had become noticeably fouler, as if she'd been eating carrion and had let it fester between her teeth, though as far as Ezren knew she'd only had the same salt fish and stewed carrots as everyone else on the *Carroway*. "How dangerous are they?"

"Less so than any other adversary near the Godsgrave," Samo replied, "but there are many of them, and they have called other corrupted beasts to their host. Their numbers will make them formidable."

"Good." Amiri grinned. "I'm not interested in easy prey."

Ezren exchanged a look with Kyra and Merisiel. Their shared concerns about the Kellid had only grown with each passing hour. She hardly seemed like herself anymore, and Ezren feared that her increasing thirst for blood could make her a liability in a fight where they couldn't afford to lose any edge.

Samo raised her hands to the sky, whispering an incantation that caused the *Carroway* to lurch in the water and speed forward, altering its angle as it went. The spirit-speaker's eyes remained white and seemingly blind. "The birds have found their mark. There is a cleft in the mountain where the athamaru await their emissaries. Itaguen's ship has not yet arrived, but it comes, and the spirits of the sea dare not interfere. We must race to arrive first."

"How close are they?" Kyra asked.

"They are ahead of us but moving more slowly. Their ship is a living thing, and though it swims strongly, it cannot match the speed of the sea. We can overtake them. We cannot, however, do it without being noticed. Our destination is the same, and our paths must cross shortly before arrival."

"Then we'll need to prepare for a fight as soon as we land. Or sooner." Ezren's grip tightened on his snake-headed cane. Whether in eagerness or terror, he wasn't sure. One way or another, the moment of truth had arrived.

Kyra set her jaw. "What of Verex-That-Was?"

"The spirits do not see him," Samo said, "but they sense his presence as a wave of dread moving over the cold seafloor. He, too, comes to the Godsgrave. Be ready."

Swiftly they drove through the angry sea. Within the hour, Samo's magic began to falter against the increasing fury of the Eye of Abendego. Kyra bent her head in prayer to shore up the animist's spell, and Sarenrae's aura grew stronger around their vessel.

It was impossible to pretend anymore that the *Carroway* was sailing under its own strength. Samo's spirits, surging up from the water like a pack of seals whose tails and flippers melted into froth, carried the ship above the waves on their translucent backs. Kyra's magic shone within and around them, armoring the spirit-seals in golden motes and swirling through the seawater of their bodies.

As they neared the red spike of the Godsgrave, the ocean churned crimson. The waves were laden with flecks of dissolved rock, or whatever spiritual manifestation Rovagug channeled into that material, and Kyra's light burned brighter as it pushed away the taint.

"Almost there," Nahoa urged, standing near the prow.

Samo nodded, but she scarcely seemed to be listening. The spirit-speaker was as still as a carved image beneath the shelter of her wide-brimmed hat. Only thin trickles of sweat at her temples betrayed the immense strain she was under as the seals bucked and heaved beneath their boat.

The red mountain loomed over them, ugly and crooked as a skinned claw. Its heights were slick and smooth, glistening in the hurricane's lightning as though wet with fresh blood. Veins bulged out of the rock, and Ezren could have sworn that he saw them pulse with the heavy heartbeat of the monstrous god buried beneath it.

The base of the mountain was a chaotic, tortured mass of red spews and spirals knotted around spikes of pale bone and rock. It was as if the pulverized corpse of some enormous beast had been torn apart, its intestines spilled around broken ribs and organs flopped between cracked bones, then petrified in all its gory color and hurled into the sea. As the *Carroway* reached the wave-wracked outskirts of the Godsgrave, Ezren saw that the resemblance wasn't as fanciful as he'd imagined. There really *did* seem to be loops of viscera and raw, bloody bone, all on a scale of such vastness that he could hardly conceive of it, embedded in the mountain's base.

"Dead gods' remains," Kyra breathed, staring at the mountain's base in fascinated horror. "These are Rovagug's victims. His prey. He kept them with him, as he kept Kist-Aurek."

"Are they dangerous?" Merisiel ticked her fingertips over the hilts of her knives. Her eyes stayed on the shore, scanning for danger amid the grisly slopes.

"I expect everything here to be dangerous." Kyra cinched the bands that held her sleeves tight against her forearms, preventing them from billowing over her hands in a fight. "Where is Itaguen's ship?"

"Below the waves, not above," Samo answered. "It swims as a shark, hidden in the water. It will be here soon."

"Let's go, then," Kyra said. "Before they arrive to stop us."

"I would go with you, if you will have me." Nahoa shouldered his bone spear and tied back his unruly black curls, which had been tugged loose by the wind during the *Carroway*'s final, frantic rush toward the mountain. "I have faced this beast once before."

"I'll take all the help we can get." Merisiel knotted her own hair back with a few quick, practiced jerks.

Samo lifted her hands, and five of the spirit-seals broke away from the pack beneath the *Carroway*. Ezren was about to ask whether they should untie the vessel's single lifeboat when Nahoa leaped onto a seal's shimmering back. Seawater splashed up around the young warrior, but he straddled the spirit-seal easily and waved an arm for them to join him.

Amiri and Merisiel sprang off the boat with equal ease, landing astride their own seals. Kyra followed less confidently, one hand slipping, but her seal caught her and bore her back up before the cleric could slide into the sea.

"I'm afraid I'm a bit too old for those acrobatics," Ezren demurred. He raised his staff instead, inscribing a circle in the air with its serpentine head, and then deftly drew three arcane sigils stacked in a line within the ring.

Magic came to him, flooding through his mind and body in a surge that he no longer feared or fought. *I am the master of myself.*

Rather than resisting the power, Ezren embraced it, bending his spell fluidly around its energy instead of trying to force that energy into an inflexible shape. He pulled the lattice of his arcane weaving about the power, and then he released it into its new form.

Ezren flew. Wind tugged at his robes and whistled past his ears as he soared up through the golden nimbus of the *Carroway*. More than the freedom of his flight, Ezren gloried in the sureness of his craft. He felt like himself again, once more in control, and that was a greater boon than any spell could grant.

Below him, Merisiel laughed in surprised delight. Amiri raised a hand in a rude salute. Ezren was already looking past them, though, to the host that awaited them on the shores of the Godsgrave.

He had met athamaru before. The ones he had known had been peaceful farmers of oysters and seaweed, however, and bore little resemblance to the creatures who swarmed over the coils and bones at the mountain's base.

These were monstrous, and they were caught in monstrous suffering. Superficially, they resembled bipedal fish, with wide frills framing their flattened faces and thin limbs that ended in finned fingers and toes. The outline of those original forms could still be seen in these athamaru, but their bodies had been broken and reshaped by Rovagug's touch.

Their scales had roughened and warped into jagged hooks that bit into the flesh beneath, trapping each athamaru in a torturous suit of spikes. Blood, darker and more blue than human blood, ran in the grooves between each scale, dripping from their fins and footsteps. Their ornamental head fronds had been eaten away by large, inflamed sores, and many had exposed wounds that ran so deep that Ezren could glimpse raw bone and sinew as they moved.

Some rode enormous eels. Their mounts had been altered as they had, and Ezren couldn't help but feel a pang of pity for those poor animals, who could not possibly understand what had happened to them.

He wasn't sure how much the athamaru understood either. They scarcely looked sentient. Blood sheeted over their eyes like secondary lids. More dripped from their gills, nostrils, and bruised, fish-lipped mouths. They dipped their barbed spears in their own blood, as if it were poison, and hurled those spears at Ezren as he flew overhead.

None struck. He answered with another surge of arcane energy, this one shaped into a wave of force that called upon all the elements to lend their fury to his attack.

Earth and fire burst against the shoreline in a furrowing explosion. Seawater boiled into steam before it transformed into scalding jets of superheated air. Athamaru and armored eels went flying, their scales ripped apart and their blood sizzling into cooked streaks on the mountain's red coils.

A second later, Kyra hurled her own blast of fire into the fray. Incandescent golden energy erupted from the cleric's hands as she rode up on the back of her seawater steed, landing in a splash of brine as the spirit struck the land, and its corporeal form dissolved. Kyra's spell exploded into a blinding fireball, finishing off a dozen wounded athamaru and hurling the survivors farther from the landing zone.

In the steaming space that their spells had cleared, Amiri, Merisiel, and Nahoa leaped ashore. Shards of coral sizzled and popped around them as fresh waves washed over the fire-baked stone.

"Quickly," Nahoa cried. A twisting path wound up from the beach, through the tortured bones and veins of the Godsgrave, toward the storm-swallowed peak. Shells jangling about his neck, the warrior sprinted up the steep incline, sweeping aside injured athamaru with his spear.

Behind him, an immense black shape surged out of the sea. Itaguen's monstrous ship had collapsed its sails and masts, taking on the streamlined shape of a great barracuda as it swam undersea. The living ship lunged onto the baked stone of the Godsgrave and anchored itself in place with black claws, opening a fanged mouth to vomit out Itaguen, Curuvrakh, and another horde of warped athamaru.

Curuvrakh brandished the Fang of Kist-Aurek in a hand that was more scars than skin. Her wild hair tossed in the storm winds, revealing glimpses of a cat-sized thing latched onto the back of her neck like a gnarled tumor studded with malformed spider legs.

"What fools you are to have come here," she cackled. "Did you dream that you might stop us? No. My master comes to reclaim this world, and you will be his first meal."

Itaguen, at her side, seemed far less pleased to see Ezren and his companions. The bald man dropped into a crouch, brandishing a pair of long, curved blades that seemed to have been cut from iridescent fish scales. Unfamiliar glyphs blazed on the flats of each blade in hues of oily, opalescent silver and violet.

Those aren't knives for fighting, Ezren realized. *Those are spellblades.* Like his own snake-headed staff, they were a wizard's tools.

He swooped down, thrusting a hand before him with fingers spread wide. Arcane power crackled in his grip. Sketching the essential elements of Thewtigar's Principle of Polarity with a few strokes of his staff, Ezren coaxed the raw magic into a bolt of blue-white electricity. As he finished the final rune, he swung the staff wide, hurling the lightning at Itaguen, Curuvrakh, and their lackeys.

With inhuman speed, Itaguen dashed forward to intercept the bolt and vaulted himself up in a flip. He crossed his blades in midair, slashed them through a series of protective glyphs, and landed on his feet. Eviscerated by Itaguen's counterspell, Ezren's magic dissipated into a shower of harmless, twinkling sparks.

The athamaru, emboldened, rushed up the slope after Amiri, Merisiel, and Nahoa. They licked the heads of their spears as they ran, splitting their tongues against the edges, then threw the blood-and-spittle-streaked weapons at their foes. Nahoa took a grazing wound to his left biceps and shouted in surprised pain. "Poison!"

"They have worse than that," Kyra cried. The cleric ascended into the air on a fiery golden spiral, riding the winds alongside Ezren. As she rose to the sky, she pointed to the white-capped water beyond Itaguen's ship.

A hulking, hideous form burst through the waves. It was so massive, and so torturously broken, that Ezren's mind recoiled from accepting the sight.

Verex-That-Was. The orcish god, consumed by Rovagug, had become a nightmare in flesh.

Seawater poured off his swollen, misshapen head, which had been brutally caved in. Fragments of Verex's skull poked through his bleeding skin, and his lower jaw had been cracked down the center. One damaged eye squinted through a heavy overhang of macerated flesh. The other had been split into six or seven smaller orbs that floated around in his head like diseased bubbles. All of his eyes bulged horribly, as if they were being squeezed out of his skull by inconceivable pressure.

He had four arms and two legs, the latter so damaged that he heaved himself ashore on stumps of splintered bone. Vestigial limbs sprouted from Verex's back and sides, tearing mindlessly at his own flanks in undirected rage. Ribs and spikes, indistinguishable from one another, jutted from his torso. Some were covered by skin. Others had torn through.

Verex-That-Was roared through his mangled jaw and lifted a forelimb to drag himself ashore. He brought his clawed hand down on a cluster of athamaru and their eels, crushing his own allies heedlessly. Pulp squirted from between his fingers and washed into the sea.

A second forelimb crushed Itaguen's sleek black vessel into splinters. Shards of the ship's fins punched through Verex's palm. He lifted the injured hand to his face, licked at the wound with a grotesquely long tongue, and then flicked his hand out at Amiri, Nahoa, and Merisiel, flinging the scraps of Itaguen's ship, and gobbets of his own torn flesh, in a contemptuous arc.

Merisiel flattened herself to the ground, narrowly escaping the barrage. Amiri and Nahoa were caught out of cover. A chunk of bloody wreckage slammed into the Kellid, crushing her against the mountainside. Bone shards riddled Nahoa, who fell and did not rise.

Ezren did not descend to help his fallen companions. There was too little he could do, and too much risk if he tried. Instead, he willed himself higher, knowing that there was no escape from Verex-That-Was. Not by air, not by water.

There was nowhere to run. All that remained was to fight.

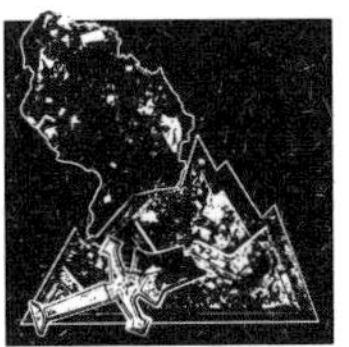

Chapter Twenty-Seven
GODSGRAVE

Amiri's vision went black as the back of her skull cracked against the mountain wall. A mangled mass of metal, bone, fish skin, and bleeding meat had rammed into her chest. She grunted, pulling out pieces of fin spine that had impaled her chest and abdomen. The thinnest shard was thicker than her thumb. Some were as wide as her wrist and grated against her bones when she tried to jerk them out.

I should be dying, a part of her protested, but mostly she ignored that thought. Wounds or no, Amiri *wasn't* dying. She felt stronger than she could remember feeling in a very long time.

The battle fury was in her, promising to take away her pain and drown her fears as it always did. She would crush her enemies, shatter their skulls, exult in their dying whimpers. All she had to do was embrace her anger and let it guide her sword.

This monster was a fool if it thought she would die that easily.

Amiri opened herself to the adrenaline rush of her rage.

She stood up, shoving off the wreckage of Verex's attack. A spine from the ship's fin jutted from her chest at an irritating angle. Amiri grabbed it and squeezed. The steel-hard spine crunched between her fingers, and she pulled it out, taking a twisted pleasure in the noise it made as it ripped through her skin.

Shifting her grip on the dripping spine, she hurled it back at Verex. Her strength was incredible. Never had Amiri felt so powerful, so vital, so intensely alive. The warmth of her own blood, pouring from the lacerations across her face and torso, was refreshing as a summer rain.

The spine struck the monstrosity right above his sagging eye.

He roared, and Amiri laughed in answer.

"I am no mouse," she shouted down the slope. Drawing her greatsword, she held it over her head in both hands. "I am no nursemaid. I am a warrior. I am Amiri! Fight me, and die."

Ezren wasted no time mourning the loss of his lightning spell. He wove another, more complicated and more powerful, and sent the full force of his god-spark into the creation. *Try counterspelling this one, you false-faced pretender.*

Chain lightning exploded from his staff, streaking toward Curuvrakh. The witch vanished in the blinding flare of blue-white electricity. It leaped away from her and struck Itaguen with equal force, then hammered into the vastness of Verex-That-Was.

It ended there, snuffed out prematurely by the corrupted god's massive bulk, but Ezren was satisfied with the damage he'd done. Itaguen was reeling, his black armor smudged and smoking, and Curuvrakh was bent double as she strained to regain control of her lightning-clenched muscles.

Even Verex bore a nasty scorch mark across his grotesque hide, and two of his vestigial limbs had burst under the force of Ezren's spell. One hung from his side like a storm-snapped branch, its clawed fingers twitching, while the other was a ruin of stripped skin dangling from a bony core.

Ezren's satisfaction didn't last long.

Verex's wounds healed with astonishing speed. The less damaged of his two injured arms twisted sickeningly as its bones knitted themselves into an uneven spiral, leaving the limb visibly mangled but able to claw as viciously as it had before.

The other arm exploded. Three athamaru warriors who'd been thirty feet away from Verex disappeared into puffs of red mist and scales. The spawn of Rovagug merely grunted. A new arm began to squirm out of the slime that dripped from his self-inflicted wound. Bony shrapnel dribbled out of the oozing hole as the new arm wrenched itself free.

"You cannot hurt a god," Curuvrakh chuckled, shuddering through one last spasm as she recovered her balance. "Not for long. And this is but my master's pawn. Scarcely a true god at all."

"We'll see about that." Kyra brandished her holy symbol. Fire fell from the heavens in a twisting barrage aimed at Curuvrakh. The roar of the flames held a celestial music, and their golden fury left a whiff of incense that, for an instant, dispersed the carrion stench of Verex-That-Was.

Itaguen rolled to the side with inhuman speed, evading the holy blast. Verex lumbered almost deliberately into it, perhaps to show his contempt of Sarenrae, or perhaps because he didn't deem Kyra's spell any threat.

If the latter, it was a miscalculation. The holy fire scoured Verex. His blood boiled in the open cauldrons of his wounds, and his flesh burned to the bone. He screamed so terribly that four serrated teeth, each longer than a man's leg, dislodged from his ragged gums and fell to the earth. One struck an athamaru, snapping the warrior's neck instantly.

These wounds, unlike those caused by Ezren's lightning, didn't heal. Verex's flesh bubbled where it had been seared, but the burns remained.

"We can kill him," Merisiel exclaimed.

"We can hurt him," Ezren corrected. Killing might be another matter altogether. It often was, with beings of such power.

Itaguen brandished his blades again, carving burning lines into the air. Ezren caught the fiery forms of sigils that suggested Thassilonian runes of power, but he knew enough about that ancient and once obscure form of magic to recognize that whatever school Itaguen had trained in, it was not Thassilonian.

A fiery tornado roared up from the circle of glyphs Itaguen had cut. It extended to a thirty-foot height, engulfing Ezren in a swirl of cinders and furnace-hot smoke.

Coughing, Ezren covered his face with a sleeve, fighting to breathe through the searing air. It was impossible to see through the smoke. Opening his eyes in that heat was only inviting them to be baked. Blind and unable to find his bearings, he spun helplessly in the sky.

Curuvrakh was chanting below. The burning winds rushing around Ezren were deafening, but he heard enough of the witch's incantation to recognize similarities to a spell that he had once seen a druid use to walk between trees.

This was different, though. The words were fouler and cruder even than the corrupt speech of demons. There was a flare of magic, and then—

"She's gone. I'm going to chase her," Kyra called from the sky.

You're the only one who can hurt Verex, Ezren wanted to protest, but he couldn't get the words out through the flaming vortex.

He couldn't do anything but burn.

Merisiel watched Kyra fly off in a spiral of golden sparks, vanishing behind the tornado of fire that had swallowed Ezren. She understood why her wife had gone—Curuvrakh had the Fang of Kist-Aurek, and they couldn't allow her to use it—but that meant they'd split their already small force and had lost their most powerful member.

Well, it's not the first time they've needed me to pull them out of the fire. Drawing her knives, Merisiel hurled a barrage of blades at Itaguen, Verex, and the athamaru around them. She chose her targets opportunistically, throwing at whatever she could hit: the side of an athamaru's unguarded neck, Itaguen's face as he concentrated on his blades, and anything that looked like it might be a weak point in Verex's heaving mass.

At the same moment, she sought out the power that Kyra had lent her on the *Carroway*. She did so clumsily, not sure how to use it—but Sarenrae's blessing chose its own shape, and golden light flashed into each of Merisiel's knives, leaving her hands as glowing darts.

Each blade exploded on impact. The athamaru collapsed, his head torn almost completely from his body. Itaguen dropped a blade and clutched one hand to his face. Blood ran from between his fingers. It was red, at first, but quickly changed to an oily blue-black substance with a strong fishy odor. As the false human struggled to hold his disguise, his fiery tornado fell apart, releasing Ezren.

Verex tilted back his malformed head and let out a bellow that shook the mountain. Blood and teeth fountained from his maw, raining over the battlefield. Cysts boiled up from the spawn of Rovagug's flanks, swelled, and burst. Each of them birthed a different abomination.

Deep-sea eels with bite marks torn from their bodies, hulking earthen figures coated in bloody mud, other things Merisiel couldn't name... *They're all his past meals, aren't they? All the creatures he's eaten, or that his master has.*

All the regurgitated creatures were partly digested. They reeked of bile and worse. Meri wasn't sure if they were alive or undead, real or facsimiles animated by Verex's malevolence.

What she did know was that there were far too many of them for her to take down with knives, even blessed ones. Too many to fight on the open shore, either, where they could easily be surrounded.

"Retreat!" she shouted, backing up the slope. "We need a narrower choke point!"

To her astonishment, however, Verex-That-Was didn't press the attack. The brutish god froze, then suddenly began digging into the red rock of the Godsgrave with all six of his primary limbs. He sank into the stone as if it were soft mud, and it closed over him with a stinking burp.

"You're too late," Itaguen said, covering his face with an ichor-smeared hand. His words were slurred, as if he were forcing them through a mouthful of slime, but his laughter was clear enough. "They've found the seal."

"What's your angle in this?" Meri asked, keeping her weight light and balanced on the balls of her feet as she retreated up the mountain path. Coils of semipetrified viscera squirmed in her peripheral vision, but she couldn't let them distract her. She just needed the man to drop his guard for an instant or lower his hand a few inches... "You're no cultist of Rovagug."

"I serve no god," Itaguen spat. He shifted his grip on his remaining knife, raising it to trace a new sequence of runes. His fingers parted over his wounded face—not enough to give Merisiel the shot she wanted, but enough to reveal glistening blue-black skin around the right eye socket. The eye itself was round and yellow, with a side-slitted pupil like a goat's. "Let them all kill each other, as they deserve. Let the Rough Beast devour as many as he likes before the rest bring him down."

"What if they can't?" Merisiel pressed. "They nearly failed the last time." The athamaru were edging closer. She flipped a few knives at them to hold them at bay, but the fishlike warriors weren't her real target.

Keep him talking. Keep him talking, and unwary.

She could see that Itaguen had the same idea. He talked to distract her as he cut the runes of his spell. "They know their enemy now, and the Rough Beast's weaker than he was. They'll kill him this time. But not before he kills enough of them for us to finish off the rest and claim our rightful place as rulers of this world and all others."

"Oh. So you're in this because you want to be a god. Or you're upset that you aren't one already. That seems reasonable." Meri snorted, baiting Itaguen shamelessly.

His lip curled just the tiniest bit, but it was all the reaction she needed. She threw another knife at Itaguen's wounded eye, guessing that he'd flinch, and that he'd likely overreact when he did. This was not a creature who'd been injured often, or recently, and he was both furious and frightened that he was hurt now.

She'd read him right. Itaguen flinched at the knife, and then he overcorrected in blocking it with his own blade. His stroke rose too high, knocking Meri's sunfire-imbued blade aside harder than necessary, and left a clear path to his throat.

Meri didn't waste the shot. She called upon all the Dawnflower's might, channeling it into her next throw, and she hurled her knife unerringly into Itaguen's neck.

Sunfire burst from the blade. It burned him from the inside out, flaring within his black armor. His mouth opened in a scream, but only light poured from his lips.

Itaguen fell to the ground, blazing, but when the light of Sarenrae's fury died, the corpse lying on the Godsgrave's red stone wasn't human at all. It resembled nothing so much as a thick-bodied eel, perhaps nine feet long, with mucus-coated skin and long, thin tentacles trailing from the back of its six-eyed head.

"What *is* that?" Meri gawked at the alien carcass, but her mystification didn't last long.

Ezren swept down, patting the last of Itaguen's cinders from a smoldering sleeve. "We must go up. The seal's in danger. Gather near."

Amiri snarled as she heard Ezren's call.

She'd been ready for a fight. Had, in fact, been desperate for that fight. Her enemies had been arrayed before her, ready to be slain, and then... they'd fled, or died, before she'd had the chance to strike a single blow.

It was as if she'd been dying of thirst in the desert, and someone had offered her a drink of cool water, only to snatch it away from her lips as she was about to swallow.

I could kill the athamaru, she thought. There was some solace in that notion. But she could kill them just as easily later, whereas Curuvrakh and Verex-That-Was might escape her wrath.

Lowering her greatsword, she joined the others reluctantly.

They were worried about her and afraid of her. Amiri saw how Ezren's eyes widened beneath his bushy brows when he saw her condition and how Meri's lips pressed together before she gathered the courage to ask: "Are you all right?"

"I'm fine. Let's kill these monsters." It was only half true. Amiri felt weaker as the fight moved away from her. Her battle rages didn't normally work that way, and she wondered whether the aura of the Godsgrave might be to blame.

It wasn't worth puzzling over. The effect was what mattered, not the cause. If she wanted to keep her strength, she needed to stay in the fray.

Ezren held his staff out over their heads and, chanting, spun in a circle to encompass all of them within its snake-headed reach. Wind whirled up from the ground, lifting Amiri and her companions aloft in an eye-watering rush.

Red winds howled around them as they flew upward. There were faces in the wind, phantasms with vacant eyes and hollow mouths that moaned soundlessly as they spun. Most looked human, or nearly so, but Amiri spotted a three-tailed fox among them and an antlered creature that resembled a reindeer with a runic mark between its eyes.

Lightning flashed from the storm clouds, striking so close that it lifted Amiri's hair off the nape of her neck. Below, she could see Curuvrakh's hunched form on the flat top of the red spire and Kyra flying in gold-sparked spirals around the witch.

From this vantage point, it was evident that the flat area was not as level as Amiri had assumed earlier but was uneven and cluttered with peculiar debris. She could make out bones, broken weapons, growths of monstrously warped coral, and mats of venomous, choked seaweed. Barnacles and mussels, distorted by the malignancy beneath them, dotted the red stones. They looked like partially fleshed skulls hanging from the rocks, their muscular bodies protruding from the shells like swollen tongues.

Between them, the red plateau was fissured with cracks and furrows. Thick, pebbled tongues reached out of some gaps, while others were fringed with suppurating gums or mismatched teeth. Eyes bulged from the flesh. Most were intact. A few had been crushed between tongues and teeth and dribbled jelly in gooey pools.

There was no sign of Verex-That-Was.

Ezren brought them down on the flattened area, only twenty feet away from Curuvrakh. The Fang of Kist-Aurek, clutched in the witch's hand, had begun to emanate a sullen red light from its crystal blade. When that light touched the hanging, skull-like shells, the misshapen shellfish chattered and shuddered on the rocks, trying to turn away. The faces in the wind cringed from it, their moans growing more frantic, until their mouths stretched so wide that they ripped in half and blew away.

The witch looked up as they landed. Her tangled gray-brown hair flapped in the gusts, revealing the creature crouched on her shoulders: a mangled assemblage of spider and scorpion parts, crowned by a heap of oozing red eyes, with several lopsided mouths chittering within the crevices of its body. Two of its legs were buried in Curuvrakh's neck, and when they twitched, she moved jerkily in obedience to its unspoken commands.

"Begone!" she shouted, slamming the Fang of Kist-Aurek into a glowing rift at her feet. Fiery sparks flared up from the ground, transforming into multicolored butterflies as they cascaded down and dissipated. She struck it again, and a second shower of sparks exploded into sulfurous hellfire.

"I am not a *nursemaid*," Amiri growled. She slapped her palms against her greatsword's hilt, drawing strength from the steel. The blade was already bloody, though she couldn't remember hitting anything with it since they'd come to the Godsgrave.

It was strangely hard to remember anything. Past and future seemed as amorphous as the faces stretched on the whirling winds, or the eyes oozing up between the teeth in the plateau's pits. *Doesn't matter. Not important.*

The fight was all that mattered.

Raising her greatsword overhead, Amiri charged.

Curuvrakh screamed in frustration and lifted the Fang of Kist-Aurek to block her. Amiri's greatsword crashed against the blade of crystal and bone, slamming against it so hard that the force of impact numbed her arms up to the shoulders.

Snarling, Amiri heaved her sword back and swung again. Blood frothed on her breath and dribbled down her chin. Her entire body felt hot, and she was dimly aware that her sword's hilt was smoking where she gripped it.

"No," Curuvrakh spat. Her monstrous face twitched in fear and anger. The wormlike mouth in her left eye squirmed, its concentric rings clamping at the air. "I am the master's avatar. Mine is the hand that will free him. Not you. Not yours!"

"Need hands for that," Amiri grunted. She struck, twisting her hips to angle her blow.

Her greatsword sheared through Curuvrakh's forearms. The witch's hands, and the fang clutched in them, fell free in a double gout of blood.

Tossing her own sword aside, Amiri dived for the fang, just as the chitinous abomination on Curuvrakh's shoulders jerked its forelegs out of the witch, knocking her to the ground, and leaped off her to do the same.

Amiri grabbed the fang first. A torrent of vigor filled her as her hand closed around the haft, obliterating any sense of pain. Her wounds sealed behind craggy, plated scabs, armoring her in blood and iron. Her jaw cracked audibly as her teeth elongated into thick, sharp tusks, pushing her lips open into a beast's grin.

I am unstoppable. She laughed, delirious and delighted.

The chitinous thing jumped at her, bladelike forelegs extended, shrieking through all its mouths at a high, shrilling pitch. Words pulsed in Amiri's mind. *Give it to me. Give it to me!*

With the command came a pulse of magic, pushing her to obey. But it was easy to resist, ridiculously so. It was easy even to ignore her fleeting desire to smash the abomination with the fang. If she broke the crystal against this creature, it would seize the power—and it had already proven itself unworthy of any such honor.

"You were weak. You failed. You die." Amiri caught the creature squarely with a punch, knocking it to the ground. It lay there, half-stunned, as it thrashed to get its legs back under its body.

Amiri lifted a boot and smashed it down, crushing Curuvrakh's spider. She ground her heel into its carcass, enjoying the squelch and crunch of its body.

Standing in the mess she'd made of the witch's familiar, she leaned forward to loom over Curuvrakh herself. "Do you know my name now?"

"Yes." Curuvrakh coughed and laughed. Blood pooled around her, more from the wounds that the spider had left in her back than from Amiri's cleaving of her arms. She was dying fast, but she no longer seemed to care. The worm wriggled in her eye. "You are Amiri. The master's new pawn."

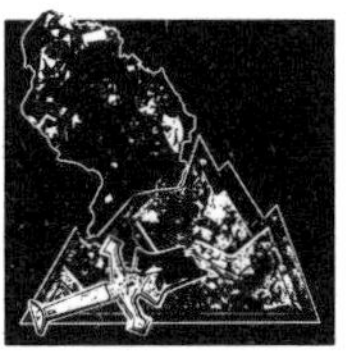

Chapter Twenty-Eight

THE FANG AND THE SEAL

The seal is nearly shattered. Kyra, riding the Dawnflower's celestial winds, looked down into the rift that Curuvrakh had hammered with Kist-Aurek's Fang. Flakes of red stone crumbled and fell into its maw. A shimmering dome still covered the crevice, sealed by the golden icon of Abadar's key, but the seal was tarnished and acid-eaten, and the silver sigils that swirled behind it were splotched with clotted red.

How many gods remain? It couldn't be that many. Several of the gods who had originally lent their strength to Rovagug's seal were dead. Dou-Bral, who had been instrumental in imprisoning the Rough Beast, had been transformed into Zon-Kuthon, a mutilated perversion of his prior self, and Kyra wasn't certain that his works—great pinions nailing the vault shut, called Star Towers—had survived his alteration. Other deities, such as Iomedae, Cayden Cailean, and Norgorber, had emerged only after the Godsgrave was buried, and might never have been asked to touch it.

She'd seen Curuvrakh smash through Desna and Asmodeus's seals. How many more could be left? Perhaps Abadar's was the last.

And then the Rough Beast will be free.

"We must find the second part of Kist-Aurek's trap," she called to Ezren, circling above the plateau in the opposite direction. "Amiri has the fang. We need only find the second half, and we can shatter it safely."

If we can trust Amiri. The Kellid's transformation upon gripping the fang had been shocking. Her wiry build bulged with new muscles, many of which had torn through her skin like an undersized shirt. Slabs of dried blood crusted her body in plates of grotesque armor. Her face, distended into a bestial muzzle by too-large teeth, was all but unrecognizable.

Ezren flew alongside her. "Do we strike her down?" the wizard asked, echoing the question that tormented Kyra.

"No." Sarenrae's warning echoed in her mind, but... "This may be Rovagug's ruse to turn us against each other and deny us victory at the brink. Amiri has not struck at his seal. I won't believe she's corrupted until she uses the fang to aid him."

"Are you certain? If Abadar's seal is the last... " Ezren didn't finish the thought. There was no need.

If Abadar's seal was the last, a single strike from the fang would end it all.

But Kyra had to make the gamble. She had to believe in her friend.

The Dawnflower teaches that in every person is a secret strength, a secret will, that can be turned to good. Even in Rovagug's creatures, if not the Great Destroyer himself.

They had to give her that chance. They had to hold faith in Amiri. And if that hope were a trap, and the very weakness that the Rough Beast intended to exploit, knowing that Kyra and her companions would hesitate to slay Amiri as they would not have hesitated to slay Curuvrakh or her familiar...

It didn't matter.

Sarenrae help me, I can't kill Amiri. Not unless I'm sure.

"All I am certain of is that we need to find the trap." Kyra veered off to scout the plateau.

It truly was a graveyard of gods. Among the bones were relics of dead faiths: a withered crown of flowers, a staff of colorful crystal strands twisted together around gems of incalculable value, a wooden mask painted with black trapezoids and triangles that clicked together and separated in complex, repeating patterns. There were bare skulls larger than mammoths on the plateau, and bones so fine they could have belonged to mice.

Seaweed clung to the debris, masking much of it beneath dried sheets of kelp and sargassum, and deformed shellfish further obscured various objects' natures. Gaps in the plateau belched irregular gouts of malodorous red smoke, obscuring Kyra's view.

Those troubled her less than the rifts that emitted haunting songs, snatches of archaic conversation, or detailed illusions of serene glades and astrological observatories laden with complex arcana. Each and every one of those rifts fed into one of the monstrous mouths that seethed just beneath the plateau's thin skin of stone, and Kyra was distressingly certain that the maws used fragments of the gods they'd devoured as lures to draw in fresh prey.

How can we find it in this? Seconds ticked away into minutes, or possibly an eternity. Kyra landed, searching on foot, but had no better luck. Sweat ran into her eyes as she squinted through the crimson vapors, trying to find one god's leavings among the remains of hundreds.

"I have it!" Ezren called. The wizard alighted on the plateau. He bent, pushed aside a barnacle-weighted mat of seaweed, and held up a hollow crystal ring and disk connected by silver chains. It had clearly been made to fit over the fang's diamond-like blade, though little else in its construction resembled the fang in its current form.

Hope gave Kyra new strength. "Amiri! We have the trap! Bring us the fang!"

Amiri turned toward them stiffly, as if she weren't sure she'd heard them correctly. Her jaw sagged open and then clenched shut. She blinked, and blood ran from her eyes, dripping from her scabbed chin.

She took a step toward them, then another. The haft of the fang smoked in her hand.

"I—" she began, but she never finished the sentence.

The earth ripped open at her feet. Gore and gristle fountained up, along with slabs of shattered rock. The explosion threw Amiri backward, and Kyra couldn't see what became of the fang.

Verex-That-Was heaved himself up from the devastation. The spawn of Rovagug roared in victory and challenge, lowered his heavy head, and charged straight at Ezren.

I cannot stand against a god, Ezren thought, but he did not run.

He watched his doom thunder toward him with a frozen, clinical detachment. Every mote of spittle that splashed from Verex's maw, every gibbering mouth and swollen protrusion, stood out in high relief.

It was a problem to be solved. Ezren had to protect Kist-Aurek's device long enough for Amiri to use it on the fang. Therefore, he had to prevent Verex-That-Was from seizing or breaking the device. But he could not simply flee with it, because they needed it to remain near the fang.

Killing Verex, based on his prior observations, was not a likely possibility.

Kyra was thirty feet away, and in the air. Merisiel was fifteen feet away, running toward him. He couldn't see Amiri and surmised she was behind Verex's obscuring mass.

All these thoughts flashed through Ezren's mind so quickly that he didn't consciously parse them. He merely raised his staff and, trusting in the god-spark to bridge the divide between what he knew to be true and what he deemed theoretically probable, tried to weave every arcane discipline he knew into a single, united defense.

It had to be illusion as much as reality, for he couldn't hope to hold Verex-That-Was at bay for long if the spawn of Rovagug could direct his full wrath against Ezren. Only if Verex was so confounded that he wasted much of his energy chasing feints did Ezren have any prayer of staving him off long enough for help to arrive.

I can't kill him, but I might be able to buy us time.

Ezren summoned a spark of pure arcane force, then split it into the full spectrum of possibilities: air, fire, earth, metal, water, wood. Reality and unreality, magnetism and repulsion, reactions exothermic and endothermic.

A kaleidoscope of effects sparked from the head of his staff. Ordinarily, Ezren would have flung them at his adversary, but instead he tried something he'd never done before.

Relying on the god-spark to guide his calculations, he bent the beams of magic into a shimmering shield. Opalescent light surrounded him as, working too fast for calculation, he knotted the rays into loops. Stars and flames coruscated around him, alongside the dizzying shimmer of warped time and the fun-house mirrors of bent space. His armor looked fragile as a soap bubble as Verex bore down on him, but Ezren stood tall and unafraid in its center.

He held up Kist-Aurek's device in a wordless taunt. Then, deliberately, Ezren moved it behind his back. At the same time, he used a tiny spell, just an apprentice's rudimentary flicker of magic, to wink the device out of his hand and onto the ground ten feet behind him, directly in Merisiel's path.

It was the simplest of ruses, so simple and stupid that it couldn't possibly fool a god.

But Verex was expecting world-shattering spells of the sort Ezren had visibly wrapped around himself. He wasn't expecting him to then toss away the prize they'd all sought. The spawn of Rovagug's bulging eyes never strayed from Ezren as Merisiel dived in, grabbed the crystal ring, and sprinted away in unfeigned terror.

Outside the shield of spells, the spawn of Rovagug reared up on his hind limbs, bones splintering into marrow-specked shards beneath his bulk, as he prepared to demolish Ezren and his spell alike.

Inside, Ezren offered a silent plea to his friends.

Hurry. Hurry, and break the fang.

The trap was more complicated than anything Merisiel had ever seen.

She hadn't dared to study it until she'd bolted away from Ezren and had taken cover inside an enormous, shattered skull. Boxed in by teeth taller than she was, she crouched and examined the assemblage of crystals and chains that was supposed to disperse Rovagug's stolen power forever.

The device consisted of two primary pieces: a crystal hoop and a saucerlike disk of the same material, connected to one another by silver chains. The chains were anchored to the disk by fixed rings but had lobster-claw clasps on the ends that connected them to the crystal hoop. Almost all of the clasps were unattached, such that the chains dangled freely from the disk and were unconnected to the hoop.

Both hoop and disk were inscribed with archaic runes in a language Merisiel didn't fully comprehend, though it was one that bore ancestral similarities to the sigils that she'd seen used on other arcane traps throughout her career. The runes on the hoop were matched to silver and bone rings that, presumably, the lobster claws were meant to lock into.

Kist-Aurek's faithful must have kept his work going after he died. I wonder how many of the trap runes I know were his creations.

Wonder if there are any of his believers still around. Hope so. Hope they're proud that his legacy still has teeth to bite his final prey.

Merisiel fiddled with the trap, trying to ascertain whether she needed to reconnect the dangling chains and, if so, where. They could be woven through and around each other into complicated designs, but she wasn't sure whether that was necessary.

An earthshaking roar made her jump. She stole a glance through the skull's vacant nostrils to see how Ezren was faring, and winced.

Verex swiped a gigantic claw across the wizard's many-layered bubble of a shield. The sphere went opaque, turning to a sphere of stone veined with metallic ores, and the spawn of Rovagug's paw took on a chalky gray cast. Ribbons of earth wrapped around his fingers. His talons stiffened into immobility, and Meri let herself hold a second's hope.

Then Verex clenched and released his fingers. Dirt and dust crumbled away. He struck at the sphere with a second raw-knuckled paw, but this time Merisiel didn't wait to watch what happened. Ezren's spell was running out too fast for her to waste any more time.

She ran her fingers over the runes on the crystal ring. *Poison. Burn. Paralyze.*

They were trap effects. *Do I link the chains to the desired outcome? Is that how this works?*

Disintegrate...

Meri squinted at that last rune, unsure she'd deciphered it correctly. It could be "disintegrate," or "dissolve," or "evaporate-obliterate."

Whatever it was, she couldn't see any better option. They didn't want to poison Rovagug's stolen power or paralyze it. "Evaporate-obliterate" seemed like the best course.

She rushed to attach the hooks to the ring that pierced the hoop next to that rune. The first two clasps locked in easily, but her hands were getting sweaty, and another roar from Verex shook the skull around her. She dropped the chain, cursed, and fumbled to hook it alongside the others.

Three done. Four to go.

Come on, come on...

Kyra missed Ezren's surreptitious throw to Merisiel, but she guessed what had happened as soon as the elf scrambled to hide inside a cast-off skull. Her wife would not have abandoned the fight lightly, nor would she have given up searching for Kist-Aurek's device. If she'd run away from Verex-That-Was, it was because Meri had something that the spawn of Rovagug could not be permitted to find.

There was only one thing that could be. And if Meri was hiding Kist-Aurek's trap, rather than taking it to Amiri at once, that meant she needed time to study it or repair it or... something.

Which meant, in turn, that Kyra needed to help Ezren distract Verex-That-Was.

She swooped toward the monstrous god, trailing golden sparks. She deliberately cut a path over Verex's head so that the falling fire would sting him and was gratified to see his bulbous eyes blink in irritation as Sarenrae's cinders fell into them.

Verex snapped his split jaws at Ezren in a vicious bite. The shield dimpled inward, then rebounded with amplified force, slamming the spawn of Rovagug with a wave of his own kinetic energy and snapping his head backward. His teeth shattered in a chorus of bloody pops. Two of his smaller, rheumy yellow eyes exploded.

But Ezren's shield was dwindling swiftly. It wasn't even a full bubble anymore. Only a few coruscating rings of energy remained.

Kyra raised her holy symbol. "Sarenrae, smite this foe."

A sunburst engulfed Verex-That-Was, along with all the plateau around him. The bones of dead gods burned in its heat. Stones cracked and broke. Verex roared in agony as his skin sloughed off blasted muscle and his cysts burst into steam and boiled ichor. The unholy vapors of his body dispersed into clean air, their taint obliterated by Sarenrae's blessed light.

When the radiance dimmed, the dread god was badly hurt. His big eye was sealed behind an overhang of baked flesh, and the smaller ones were white and blind as boiled onions. Blisters massed on his tongue.

He let out a long, low growl, shredding the blisters against his teeth and spitting their fluid at Ezren. The entire body of the spawn of Rovagug shuddered, and his unseeing eyes rolled upward. A terrible tension radiated across the plateau as psychic energy gathered around Verex-That-Was. Twenty feet away, amid the seaweed drifts, some dead god's artifact let out a keening wail among the bones and spontaneously shattered.

A shockwave of retributive pain thundered outward from Verex-That-Was, smashing everything in its path. It passed through Ezren's shield effortlessly and slammed the wizard against a rocky protrusion with a nauseating crack. The skull that Merisiel was hiding in burst apart, crushing the elf with heavy chunks of bone even as Verex's psychic assault hammered her.

The concussive wave struck Kyra in midair and sent her reeling to the ground. She hit the plateau hard, narrowly managing to take the fall on her hip and shoulder instead of her head. Even so, she thought she'd broken her upper arm. It was all she could do to push herself up to a sitting position, and her vision blurred from the pain.

Verex lumbered toward her. He didn't rush; he didn't need to. The spawn of Rovagug was so immense that he closed the gap in two steps. He looked down, seeming almost amused by the tiny, pitiful woman clad in blue and white. Her divine aura had gone out when the shockwave hit her. She looked only human now.

"It is fitting," he said in a thick, tortured voice garbled by his shredded tongue and broken teeth, "that you should die here. My master will devour you, as he has so many others, so that you can await your puling goddess in his belly."

Kyra turned her head shakily away from the monster. She saw Ezren push himself off the rocks, bleeding from the head and leaning on his staff, and she saw Verex's sides shiver convulsively before the god-that-was spewed a gory flurry of bone shards at the wizard. Ezren went down under the grisly assault, and he didn't get up again.

Merisiel was creeping away from the wreckage of the skull. The elf was hurt, favoring her left side and moving with a stiff hitch instead of her usual feline grace. But she still had the strength to crawl, and she was doing so with purpose. Something crystalline glittered in her right hand.

She has the device. She needs to get to Amiri.

Kyra didn't answer Verex's taunts. That would have been too obvious. But she groaned, as if he'd struck a nerve.

Verex-That-Was reached down with surprising delicacy and pincered two claws around Kyra's head, picking her up as a malicious child might have lifted an ant.

He carried her over to a tooth-lined rift in the plateau and dropped her beside the bleeding gap in the ground, pressing her face toward the crevice. The stumps of rotten teeth, emerging from the plateau like carrion-cored stalagmites, ground into Kyra's cheek. "Look. See your fate. This is the only future left to you, your goddess, and the wailing meat-lumps you've brought my master today."

Kyra didn't want to look. She closed her eyes, trying not to breathe in the wet stench that rose from the depths. But a soft female voice moaned despairingly from within the rift, and horrified curiosity made Kyra glance down.

A wan, mournful face looked back up at her. The woman's moon-pale features were lovely, and the sky-blue hair that floated about her face was radiant with divine light, but all the life and vivaciousness had been drained from her. Only suffering was left. Her neck ended in a ragged stump, and tooth marks marred the visible stub of her spine.

In the next instant, the woman's blue hair dissolved into a matted, acid-slimed tangle. Her eyes and nose shriveled into half-digested nubs, and her flawless skin became a chewed ruin. A snake's nest of tongues emerged from the fleshy walls of the rift around her, burrowing into her flesh from all sides. But her voice stayed the same, impossibly melodic, and weighted with more pain than Kyra could bear.

"There are hundreds of these godlings in my master's belly. Thousands. The Great One ate her, and now she is his. Forever. Soon you will be too, and your goddess with you, and when the Great One grows bored, you can sing together to amuse him from within his belly."

"No," Kyra said, but it came out as a whisper, and she knew no one heard.

No one but Verex, who laughed.

I should break that seal.

Amiri couldn't say where the impulse had come from. It wasn't anything her companions had suggested. Breaking the seal wasn't why they had come here. Was it?

She didn't think so, but she wasn't sure. It had become very difficult to be sure of anything once she'd taken hold of the fang.

The only true certainty in Amiri's world was that she was unbearably angry, at everything, and that smashing the fang into that seal promised to relieve some small part of her irritation. The weapon *wanted* to crush that feeble, flickering magic. She could feel the intensity of its desire smoldering in its red crystal heart and all through its bone-and-sinew haft, and she could not help but share it.

The magic was so weak. So annoying. It deserved to be destroyed. Her hands trembled with how badly she wanted to swing the fang into it with every ounce of her strength.

But there was something, some reason, why that wasn't the right thing to do...

Wasn't there?

"Amiri!"

She looked over, confused. Merisiel was crawling toward her, injured, with a stolen diamond in her hand. No, not a diamond. Some crystal contraption tangled up in silver chains. "What?"

"I have the second half of Kist-Aurek's trap." The elf thrust her crystal bauble forward, her black eyes filled with pain and desperation. A trail of blood smeared across the red plateau behind her. "Please. The fang. Shove it through. I fixed the chains. It's ready. We can destroy the fang. Quickly!"

Why would I destroy this? Without thinking, Amiri clutched the fang against her chest, tightening her hands on its haft. A rumbling growl filled her chest.

"Please, Amiri, you have to destroy it. You have to destroy it *now*." Meri turned her head to the side, terrified. Amiri followed her look to the hulking shape of Verex-That-Was. The brute loomed over Kyra, whom he held pinned to the ground beneath a colossal claw.

It looked as if he were shoving the cleric's face into a rift, to be eaten by the mouths inside. Amiri's rage rose at the sight. "I'll kill him."

"No. Amiri, it's a trick. The fang isn't a weapon. Please, just—"

Amiri stopped listening. Brandishing the crystal blade, she stalked toward the spawn of Rovagug menacing Kyra.

The spawn of Rovagug turned toward her and, contemptuously, slapped Kyra with his enormous tail as he dropped her by the rift. Gristly bone and knotted scars slammed into the cleric, knocking her ten feet across the plateau. She hit a pile of barnacled debris and lay still.

"Fight me!" Amiri shouted at the corrupted thing. She spun the Fang of Kist-Aurek over her head. Crimson light streaked from the blade, creating a looped red aura about her. Its power cascaded around her, making her feel invulnerable.

This wretched spawn might threaten her friends, but it was no match for Amiri. Not while she held the fang. "Come and fight. I am not afraid. I'll slay a god."

"Amiri, no." Ezren tottered up from the gore-blasted heap of bones where he'd fallen. The wizard was dazed, barely standing. His robes were a shredded mass of filth, their colors lost under a caked, dripping layer of Verex's spewed bile. "Please. We're your friends. Trust us. Destroy the fang."

"I must slay this demon." Amiri turned her eyes back to Verex. "Look at you. You're all dying. You need me to kill it, just like always."

"*No.* It's different this time. You have to resist the rage. Amiri, we wouldn't lie to you. Please. This anger comes from Rovagug. It's not you. It's a trap. It's—"

Verex swung a vestigial limb at Ezren. The malformed arm ripped off the spawn of Rovagug's body, disintegrating into chunks of skin and cracked bone. Ezren tried to dodge, but he was too badly hurt, and could only stumble uselessly. The volley took the wizard in the left side, ripping him apart. He fell, and all he held fell with him.

Ezren's satchel fell open as it struck the ground. Bottles and jars of esoteric materials rolled out, along with the wizard's inkwell and pen case. The coins of a half-dozen realms tumbled across the plateau in a tinkling cascade.

So did a small jewel-like bird, perhaps a phoenix and perhaps a peacock, perched on a branch of green cut glass and amethyst.

Amiri stopped short. She cocked her head at the little bird. *He bought that? He carried it all the way from Totra? For me?*

A memory came to her: a sun-warmed desert bazaar, the two of them side by side. Her momentary relaxation at knowing she had a friend, that she wasn't alone in this frightening world.

Someone who noticed her reaction to a small thing in the market, and who considered it important enough to buy it for her, though she had never asked.

She blinked. Verex was thundering toward her. The spawn of Rovagug's grotesque, knotted forelimb came down on the bird, crushing it into oblivion. A single glass leaf rolled away, sparkling on the red plateau.

This rage destroys everything.

What was the purpose of the fight if all that was left at its end was ruin?

Suddenly apprehensive, Amiri whirled toward Merisiel. "Where's the device?"

The elf spun the crystal object across the ground to her. It clicked against the obsidian-black femur of some nameless god and came to a stop ten feet away.

Verex was closing on her. The reek of his presence washed over Amiri, and the furnace heat of his breath steamed across her skin. Every step he took rocked the plateau.

All of Amiri's instincts and experience screamed at her to face her enemy.

He has killed my friends... or will kill them. He will kill me.

But she turned her back on Verex-That-Was, and she ran from him to seize Kist-Aurek's trap instead.

Amiri shook the tangle of crystal and chains out with a growl of frustration. She'd thought she'd be able to shove the fang into the contraption and be done, but this was as infuriatingly finicky as any fine lady's jewelry.

The rage was there, begging to be used. *I could slay a god. I could kill him!*

No. Merisiel wouldn't have bothered latching all those stupid little chains into place if they weren't important. Trying to ignore the thunder of Verex storming toward her, she fitted the fang's blade into the crystal ring, and then twisted it to catch the silver chains in its grooves without breaking their latches. It was slow work, and it had to be done carefully, and it threatened to drive her mad.

Verex's claw swept in from her peripheral vision. If she dodged, she'd ruin the device.

There was only a split second to decide.

Amiri made her choice. *I do not need to fight to win.*

Bracing against the blow, she shielded the fang with her body.

The claw was bigger than she was. Verex lifted Amiri off her feet and hurled her to the brink of a rift twenty feet away. She felt a hip crack, and her vision blacked out for an instant.

Eyes rolled toward her from between the teeth that fringed the gap nearby. Amiri snarled at them as she squirmed away on the ground, unable to stand. But she hadn't dropped the fang or its crystal cage, and the corrupted vigor that flowed through her kept her conscious.

I need the rage. Amiri had never been hurt this badly without the haze of battle fury to shield her from the pain before. She was dying, fast, and could feel it.

But if she invited the rage in now, she wouldn't be able to concentrate on threading the fang's blade into the chains. It was almost in—*almost.*

Her hands shook with the unaccustomed difficulty of trying to rush through such a task with an enemy at her back. *I can do it. I* will *do it. I don't need rage to be strong.*

Verex was closing on her again. Amiri's time was nearly gone.

But she needed no more.

Entwined in glimmering metal chains, the Fang of Kist-Aurek slid neatly from the crystal hoop into the crystal disk. As soon as its tip struck the disk, the blood-smeared diamond blade shattered.

The disk flared into multihued brilliance. Incandescent white light spiraled out across the silver chains, melting them instantly, and then vaporizing the liquid metal a second later.

A great weariness descended upon Amiri. Her false vitality had evaporated along with Rovagug's power. She was suddenly cold and weak and very lightheaded. Slumping to the ground, she leaned her head against the rock behind her and let the broken remnants of the fang and its crystal cage fall limp into her lap.

Verex had reached her. He raised his earth-crushing claw again.

Amiri looked up from beneath its shadow, unafraid. She twitched a finger, rattling the shards of crystal that spilled across her thighs, and managed a wan little smile.

"I win," she said, as the claw came down.

Chapter Twenty-Nine
SACRIFICES

Light engulfed the Godsgrave.

Kyra, lying face down on the plateau, squinted her blood-gummed eyes against the stark white flare that shot up to the sky between Amiri and Verex. A high crystalline peal sounded, like a church bell of the gods, and the white light burst into prismatic brilliance that enveloped a third of the plateau, completely obscuring the Kellid and the spawn of Rovagug.

A murky red ball of energy hovered at the center of the spiraling white light. Ghostly silver chains wrapped around the smoldering energy and pulled it apart. The red vapor was caught up in the tornado of light and, with a fading phantasmal roar, was obliterated.

The light faded. Verex was gone—or at least the gargantuan form of him was gone, though a smaller heap of slumped flesh lay where he had been. Kyra could see nothing of Amiri.

The red winds around them had died, and the distorted faces that had spun in their grip were gone as well. The mouths in the rifts were mostly silent, though some still muttered and gibbered softly to themselves. Otherwise, the Godsgrave was quiet save for Kyra's own ragged breathing and faint moans from her companions.

Everything hurt. Her clothes were soaked with blood, and worse. She could barely budge her limbs. But her friends were wounded, perhaps even dying, and there was no time to rest.

Kyra forced herself into a sitting position and fumbled open a potion bottle. The draft tasted of herbs and honey, and it banished the worst of her injuries. She exhaled in relief, permitting herself one breath of respite, and then stood unsteadily to check on the others.

Ezren was easy to find, since she'd seen where he fell. Hurrying to his side, Kyra stepped over the trampled remains of the belongings that had spilled from his satchel. The wizard lay at the end of the trail, unconscious and pale from blood loss.

His wounds were grievous, complicated by blood-filled boils around each injury. Kyra could feel the unholy corruption emanating from the swellings and drew on Sarenrae's power to purify them. "Dawnflower, I beg you, heal my friend."

Warmth flowed from Kyra's hands into Ezren's body, restoring and reviving him. The bloody boils receded, and his lacerations mended into new pink flesh. His breathing steadied, then grew deeper, and after a moment he sat up groggily. "Thank you."

"There is work yet undone," Kyra said. She clasped Ezren's shoulder and moved on. Others needed her care.

Merisiel was standing on her own strength, patching up a cut on her upper right arm with ointments and bandages. Other bruises and slashes were already mending under thin layers of yellowish paste. "I'm fine. Fine compared to everyone else, at least. I'd like you to look at these scratches later, but I'll be all right for now."

"Good." Kyra meant it. She hated having to heal her wife. Though she had full faith in Sarenrae's power, tending anyone's injuries meant seeing them devastated and in pain.

But it was more than that, really. Before beginning work, a competent healer had to assess the nature and severity of the injuries being treated, and that meant studying someone's hurts while doing nothing, in the moment, to help them.

She could manage that clinical detachment with strangers, or even her friends. It was much harder to bear those stretches of agony with Merisiel.

Even that, however, would have been preferable to what Kyra found when she reached Amiri.

The Kellid was dead.

Verex had crushed her thoroughly. It was a small mercy, at least, that she no longer looked like a monster. The little of her that was left was too badly damaged for her final corruption to show.

But that was a bitter consolation. Their friend had deserved better than this. She had been no willing creature of Rovagug's, but a brave warrior who had fallen to a corruption she never wanted. Amiri had fought back as long and as hard as she could, and in the end, she had wrested a hero's death from the jaws of disaster.

It is not fair. It is not right. Kyra thought of the horrors she'd glimpsed in Verex's grip, when he'd forced her face down to the window of Rovagug's prison, and shuddered.

Had their friend been consigned to an eternity of such suffering?

"Oh, no," Merisiel breathed, coming up beside her. "Oh, Amiri."

Ezren, grim-faced and solemn, joined them a moment later. He had rigged a makeshift sling from a tool belt and a torn piece of his cloak and had his right arm bundled close to his chest. A half-healed cut along the wizard's scalp continued to ooze a trickle of blood, but he ignored it as he gazed upon Amiri and the monster she had slain. "We could not have succeeded without her sacrifice."

No. Kyra looked over to what was left of Verex. He seemed a much smaller thing in death. The corpse that lay on the plateau was less than a fifth the size of the spawn of Rovagug who had burst from the water below. Gone were the vestigial limbs, the swarm of eyes, the crimson vapor that had swathed his every movement.

He just looked like an orc. An old, tired, toothless orc, who had succumbed to a wasting disease that left him collapsed in the rusted shell of armor he could no longer carry.

Even as they watched, Verex's body stiffened and lost its color. It turned to a likeness in rust-red ash, then crumbled into the rest of the debris on the Godsgrave. Only a heavy bronze torc and a scarred leather armband remained.

"Is it done?" Merisiel asked, shielding her face against the blowing dust. "He's gone."

"Verex-That-Was is no more," Kyra said, "and the Fang of Kist-Aurek is broken. But no, our work is not yet done. The seal over Rovagug's prison remains thin. Curuvrakh weakened it to the brink of failure before she was killed, and the Rough Beast can reach through more easily than ever. Unless we can restore what was lost, it will only be a matter of time before he finds another way to break free. Even now, the same misery that he visited upon the athamaru and the pirates of Port Peril threatens to extend across the entire world."

Ezren nodded in weary agreement. "We must strengthen the seal, as best we can. Come."

Together, the three of them walked toward the rift where Rovagug's seal lay. Curuvrakh's corpse sprawled a few feet from its lip, motionless in a pool of congealing blood. The witch had dragged herself closer, to die in the presence of her god, but it didn't seem that she had been rewarded for her final act of faith. Her face was contorted in a rictus of absolute horror, and she had recoiled so violently from the rift's edge that she'd cracked her skull against a sharp rock at its side.

Meri made a sound of mingled pity and disgust when she saw the witch's body. "What do you think she saw?"

"Her final fate." Kyra had no doubt about that. "She saw what becomes of the souls that Rovagug consumes and realized she was destined to be among them. The Rough Beast has no mercy for his worshippers. They suffer as much as his enemies."

"Well, it's what she chose." Merisiel shrugged. "Don't ask me to feel sorry about it."

"No one should have to suffer so." But it was Amiri that Kyra was thinking of, not Curuvrakh.

She tried to push the thought away as they came to the rift's edge. The task at hand would demand all her concentration; she couldn't afford to let her mind wander.

Whatever peace had settled upon the plateau had not reached the seal. It roiled with greater agitation than ever, and the symbols that shimmered upon it were stretched thinner, their enchanted colors bleeding into one another. Beneath that fragile ward, an infinitude of furious energy roiled like lava, rising up in fanged mouths and misshapen eyes that devoured one another and burst in endless waves.

"Let me heal you before we begin." Kyra laid a hand on Ezren, renewing Sarenrae's blessing. The vile energy within the rift roiled even more fiercely as the Dawnflower's holy magic glowed above it, and Kyra had to concentrate to maintain her composure. *That* was what they meant to challenge. "You must not be weakened or distracted, and I would not have you do this task with any mark of Rovagug upon you."

The wizard closed his eyes gratefully, flexing the fingers of his right hand and then the arm itself as he released it from its sling. "Thank you."

Putting the sling aside, Ezren carefully laid out his remaining ritual aids. Many of his materials had spilled and been ruined during the fight, but he seemed satisfied that enough was left for this task. He put out a thin wand of aspen wood, three bottles of colored sand, and a device that resembled a silver-and-bronze gyroscope with a center disk of intricately etched white jade. "I am ready."

Kyra lit a cone of sacred incense and placed it within a pierced bronze holder to shield it from the crimson winds. She knelt in its fragrant smoke and raised her holy symbol in both hands. "Sarenrae, guide your servant. Help me heal what was broken and restore the shield that the gods forged for our world."

The smoke wafted past her shoulders, taking on a golden tinge as it spread across the faltering seal. A tattered image appeared of Asmodeus's scarlet Archstar on a field of black, as it had appeared before Curuvrakh smashed the archdevil's seal with the Fang of Kist-Aurek. The image was broken into eight jagged shards, but all the pieces were there.

"Now," Kyra urged Ezren. "The seal was forged equally from the arcane and the divine, and both must work in unity to restore it."

"I dislike touching Asmodeus's work," Ezren muttered, but he took up the wand and a bottle of ruby-red sand. Carefully he spilled thin lines of the powdered gemstone across the image's torn edges, as though he were using it to stitch together a banner that had been rent on the field of battle. As each ruby line sifted down over the seal, Ezren flicked the aspen wand through arcane diagrams, intoning the words that would bind the magic in place.

The seal steadied. Asmodeus's insignia shone darkly on its face, whole and strong, and then vanished as other emblems resumed their eternal swirl over the rift. But the Archstar was among them again, and Kyra felt the crushing malevolence of Rovagug's presence recede slightly from the plateau.

As if in response, the red winds intensified. Kyra's clothes flapped about her, and Ezren had to hold his sand bottles tightly against his chest to keep the wind from snatching them away and smashing them against the rocks. The gyroscope whirled wildly, the runes etched on its jade face smoldering.

"Quickly!" Kyra cried. She stretched a hand toward the rift, closing her fingers in the air as she exerted her will to pull another set of fragments together. Gozreh's dewy leaf floated up to the surface, split into a dozen fragments like the Archstar before it. "Bind it!"

Ezren nodded, uncapping a vial of powdered blue sapphire as the winds lashed his hair against his face. He poured measured lines of gemstone dust over the broken symbol of Gozreh, and they fell cleanly, guided by his magic rather than being diverted by the howling gusts of Rovagug's rage. The leaf was made whole again, a vibrant midsummer green against its lake-blue background.

Once restored, Gozreh's symbol slipped back into the seal as Asmodeus's had before it.

Other gods and symbols followed, so many that Kyra soon lost count. She had never fully appreciated the size and fury of the War of Imprisonment. What mortal could? Only legends survived to their day, and so few among those who walked Golarion had ever seen the face of a single godling. How could any of them imagine a war of thousands?

Curuvrakh had cut through dozens. For hours, Kyra and Ezren worked, painstakingly, to restore what the witch had so nearly destroyed. Specks of jeweled sand stung tears from Kyra's eyes, and her fingers grew numb around the Dawnflower's symbol, but together they worked on and on, despite their wounds and weariness.

At last they were almost done. Only one emblem remained: Sarenrae's ankh, with its ring of wings.

As she drew the broken symbol's pieces together, though, Kyra glimpsed the faces of tormented souls bubbling up in the rift behind them. Curuvrakh's monstrous likeness bobbed up from the murk, let out a single mute scream, and was gone. A blue-feathered tengu with three eyes rose next to a gnome whose face was a patchwork of obscene tattoos, apart from the bleeding hole where her nose appeared to have been bitten off.

And then there was Amiri.

Amiri!

The Kellid was monstrous. Not the proud warrior she'd been for most of her life, but the bestial thing that Rovagug had made of her at the end. That hurt Kyra almost as much as seeing her among the rift spirits did.

She isn't far. I could reach her...

Kyra didn't realize that she had actually extended a hand toward Amiri's spirit until Ezren shouted: "No!"

She recoiled with a start. "I didn't—"

"If you reach through—"

"Then what?" Kyra blurted the question without thinking, but then she wondered what the answer was. She looked at Ezren, eyes wide at her own temerity, and the sudden flaring hope that it might work. "Can I pull her out? Will the seal hold back Rovagug's taint as her soul passes through?"

"I don't know. Maybe. Maybe not. But Kyra, we can't risk it. I hold Amiri dear as well, and mourn her as much as you do, but *this is Rovagug's prison.*"

"She gave her life for this cause. I cannot allow her to give her soul as well."

Dawnflower, tell me I'm doing the right thing. Kyra prayed with all her devotion, but her goddess gave her no sign either of approval or warning.

This is my choice alone, she realized, and plunged her hand through.

Amiri grabbed her wrist. The Kellid's mouth moved, but the grotesque tusks that swelled from her jaw made it impossible to guess what she was trying to say.

Her grip was real, though. Kyra felt the desperate strength of it as a shock. In the same instant, she realized that Amiri was trying to pull her into the rift as much as Kyra was trying to pull her out. *Rovagug still holds her. Amiri, be strong. I will get you out.*

"Sarenrae, help me redeem this soul," Kyra pleaded, pulling harder. The heat on the other side of the seal was unbearable; even without Amiri dragging her down, she couldn't withstand the strain for long.

Golden light enveloped Kyra, coruscating where it intersected with the seal. The nimbus spread to encompass Amiri, but it struggled to do so. Like a candle guttering in the wind, the radiance faltered.

"Please. Amiri! Resist the corruption!" Kyra braced her legs and hinged at the hip, using as much leverage as she could get from her angle.

Slowly, painfully, she pulled Amiri up.

When the Kellid's spiky black hair touched the seal, the magic flared and spat. A layer of filthy red slime appeared on Amiri's hair, then her scalp, and was scoured off of her as Kyra hoisted her through the layers of divine magic. The crusted, armor-like scabs broke off Amiri's body, and the yellow tusks loosened in her jaw. Her eyes lost their crimson tint and stopped bulging from her head.

The corruption is *held back.* Kyra's heart sang at the sight, and she redoubled her efforts to pull Amiri out. She could almost taste her friend's freedom, sweeter than honey.

The Kellid's forehead came up through the seal. Her nose, her chin. Then her neck, then the tops of her shoulders. She opened her mouth. A look of panic came over her, and she gagged, shaking her head frantically.

"What's wrong?" Kyra leaned in.

Amiri's mouth gaped even wider, and her tongue shot out, thicker than Kyra's wrist and monstrously long. It wrapped around Kyra's neck and yanked her forward, to the edge of the rift. Only Ezren grabbing her around the waist kept her from falling in.

Miniature mouths opened along Amiri's tongue. Some laughed at Kyra in wild, vengeful hysteria. Others bit her with burning needle teeth. A few had eyes inside, or skinny, multijointed arms, or tiny swirling echoes of the rift that had birthed them.

YOU CANNOT TAKE A SOUL FROM ME.

The words came from no mouth. No mouth could have voiced them. They were the roar of a god, and though that god was distant and imprisoned, his rage was unbearable.

Kyra's ears bled. Ezren staggered back, doubled over in horror and agony. Amiri's body thrashed like a marionette being jerked by an angry child, and the tongue spewing from her throat pulled tighter.

JOIN HER. JOIN HER FOR ETERNITY.

Black fireflies swarmed Kyra's vision. A static buzzing filled her ears. She could feel the tongue's teeth chewing at her flesh and blood running down her chest and back, but nothing else. The rest of her body was numb, meaningless.

Then, suddenly, the pressure released. Kyra gasped for air. Her windpipe felt as if it were full of shattered glass, but it was the most welcome pain she could imagine.

Merisiel, wearing Verex's immense bronze torc, had pulled Amiri away. The elf's slight figure bulged with muscles she'd never had before. She let out an unexpectedly guttural, almost orcish-sounding grunt, and hauled up on the Kellid's shoulders. Amiri was bucking in her grip, but she couldn't break Merisiel's unnaturally strong hold. Bit by bit, the rogue tugged her through the seal, and with each inch that passed through the gods' ward, more of Rovagug's taint was forced out of her.

The barbarian's tongue slapped at Merisiel, hitting her hard enough to split her lip and bloody her nose, then wrapped around her face, suffocating the elf. Its hideous little mouths gnawed at her, the air, and each other.

Meri set her stance and pulled harder, and Kyra could see from the concentration on her face that she was contesting her friend's fate with every fiber of her own being and every shred of the strength she'd claimed from Verex.

With one final hoist, the elf freed Amiri from the rift. As the Kellid's feet came through the seal, the last clinging wisps of foulness were purged from her. The monstrous tongue shriveled into dust and blew away, cut off from the power that had sustained it.

Amiri stood on her own two feet at the crevice's edge. For a moment, she was real, as solid and tangible as she had ever been in her life.

"Thank you," she said. She smiled at each of them, almost bashfully, and lifted empty hands in gratitude. "Thank you, my friends."

Then she was gone, and only the rift remained.

Slowly, using both hands, Merisiel took off the torc. She slumped to the ground and let the heavy piece fall beside her. Shaking, she wiped her hands over her face where the vile tongue had closed around her. "I couldn't let him take you."

"My love. You saved us." Kyra stroked Merisiel's head and ran her hands over the elf's shoulders, both as a caress and to check for wounds. She found nothing serious, only bruising and minor cuts.

There was no time for more. "We must finish the seal."

"Summon the next sign," Ezren said. He collected his bottles from the ground, where they'd fallen when Rovagug's voice had struck him down. The aspen wand had cracked underfoot during their struggles, but at a word and a touch from the wizard, the slender wooden rod mended itself. "I am ready."

Kyra turned her toppled incense holder upright and relit the cone. "Sarenrae, allow us to finish this task, in your name and by your hand."

The Dawnflower's ankh reappeared, accompanied by a shower of stars. Kyra steadied the image, and Ezren poured powdered opal over its cracks, wafting the aspen wand through the dust.

The emblem solidified, shining with renewed magic, and folded back into the rotations of the seal.

The last of the red winds died out. A calmness settled over the plateau as the torments of the endless hurricane drew back, returning to the stillness at the eye of a storm, a silence that felt near deafening after they'd spent so long enduring Rovagug's rage.

"We have won," Kyra breathed, scarcely able to believe it. "The seal is restored."

Ezren capped the vial of opal dust and studied the ward once more. "We could do more."

"How?" Kyra had reached out to snuff her incense cone, but she paused with her hand poised above the smoke-smudged holder. "We've restored the seal. The red winds and red tides are gone. Rovagug is barred from Golarion once more."

"The divine seals are intact," Ezren agreed, "but we might add one more: a seal of mortality.

"Why should the gods be the only ones responsible for holding the Rough Beast at bay? This is our world too. I have never liked relying on divine protectors, and I like it less now that I've seen them up close. We won this battle, and we've proved our worth. I believe we have every right to leave our mark, and I believe we have the power to do so in a way that bolsters the works of the gods."

Kyra hesitated. She did not wish to trespass upon the domains of the divine, and she wasn't certain that they did, in fact, have the right to alter the Rough Beast's seal by virtue of their victory at the Godsgrave.

But if they could make the seal stronger, that was the only thing that really mattered.

"How?"

"I can guide you through the spell. You need only give your power to the cause." Ezren paused, his eyes bright beneath his bushy eyebrows. "But it would mean giving up all of it. If we do this... it'll drain my god-spark, and Sarenrae's gift. And even that might not be enough."

"What else?" Merisiel asked, moving closer to Kyra in a protective stance. "What more can you ask of her?"

"We must give something of our vital essence to the spell. For the gods, that price means little. They are immortal, truly immortal, and have an infinitude of years to spend. But for us... if we have any immunity to time, it is only by virtue of the god-spark and your divine power. Once that's gone, the cost may prove heavy. You may lose decades of your life to this. Even all of it. I cannot say for certain. No mortal has ever done such a thing."

"Does it have to be her?" Merisiel stepped forward, intent. "I can do it."

Kyra shook her head. "Meri—"

"Hush." The elf regarded her wife fondly, but she remained steadfast. "I want to do it. I want to help. It's all I've wanted since we started this quest. Besides, I can pay that price more readily than either of you. I'm an elf; I have years to spare. I wouldn't want to lose a single day with you, and Ezren would, I'm sure, like to keep the time allotted to him.

"But for me? Kyra, I don't *want* to live decades without you. I was alone before I met you. So alone." Meri shivered as she said this, a quick little movement like a cat flicking water from its paw. "I don't want my future to look like that past. So if you can take those lonely years from me, do it. I would ask you to do that even if it helped nothing else. But if you can take those years and use them to bolster Rovagug's seal... you must. Of course you must."

To that, Kyra could say nothing. She only nodded, tightened her hand around Meri's, and tried not to let the tears fall from her eyes.

Ezren cleared his throat. "Then let us begin."

Uncapping each of his bottles in turn, the wizard traced a sequence of lines and circles over the glowing seal. It was an arcane diagram, but not exclusively so. In the small spaces between the quadrants, and on the periphery of each circling ring, Ezren added the marks by which Golarion's peoples identified themselves.

He drew the scarab of Osiriani resilience, and the royal lion of Taldan pride. The stout dwarven emblems of Highhelm's clans marched in a column down one side of the diagram, matched by the graceful lines of Kyonin's elven families on the other. Between them, Ezren sketched the hunter's mark of the Kellids, and the flaming swords of Mendev, and even the symbols of those who had bravely accepted the final sacrifice, defending mortals against immortal threats: the blind eye of the Peacebound Seers, the broken shields of Lastwall, and others Kyra did not know.

As Ezren added each emblem to the whole, Kyra felt a tug deep within her soul. She surrendered Sarenrae's gift willingly, bit by bit, offering it up to the magic as the strands of Ezren's design came together. She could see the wizard doing the same, burning through the last of his god-spark to fuel the ward he was building.

When it was nearly complete, he beckoned to Merisiel, indicating that she should stand on the far side of the rift, at the head of the seal he had drawn. "Are you ready?"

"Yes." The elf stood with her arms crossed, her face drawn but resolute. The energy of Ezren's spell lifted her white hair in a billowing cloud behind her shoulders and reflected off her black armor in multicolored beams.

"Prick your finger, and let the blood fall onto the seal. Three drops."

Merisiel nodded. She drew a knife and cut her thumb in a quick, small movement, pressing her forefinger against the nick to measure out the drops.

Three red beads fell in, one after another, and vanished into the magic. Meri pulled her hand back and pushed her cut thumb hard between her fingers.

Tendrils of magic rose toward the elf, embracing her in a complex, twining pattern. Meri gasped and stiffened as she lifted up onto her toes, but she did not resist, and she didn't seem to be in pain. Kyra held her breath as she watched, at once afraid for her wife and in awe of her courage.

The magic receded. Meri sank back onto her heels, trembling and breathless. "Is it... am I... ?"

"Yes." Ezren's shoulders sank down and back as he released the tension he'd held throughout the casting. His bottles of crushed jewels were empty, and the aspen wand had charred down to a cinder core as he'd finished the ritual. Shaking the useless ashes from his hand, he looked at Kyra. "My god-spark is gone. Your gift?"

Kyra searched inside herself, seeking Sarenrae's presence. She had grown used to the glow of the divine over the past few days and expected to feel hollow without it, but the loss troubled her less than she'd imagined.

Her faith was still present. The Dawnflower hadn't abandoned her. All that had changed was that her goddess's presence was quieter, less overwhelming, as it had been before their visit to the Peacebound Isle.

But it was not gone. Sarenrae's *power* was gone, but not her presence.

Instead, as Kyra looked within, she felt a tiny flicker of renewed connection.

My servant. Sarenrae's voice was warm and filled with endless gratitude. *You have done all that was asked of you and more. You and your friends have given so generously of yourselves: your courage, your blood, your lives.*

I would offer you one small gift in return, as token of my thanks, and that of all the gods whose work you have done today. Take what is left of your blessed incense, and place it on your dead friend's chest.

"I am... as I was before," Kyra answered Ezren. "But Sarenrae remains with me." She picked up the incense holder, cupping her hand around its window to prevent an errant breeze from stealing the tiny stub that remained, and carried it to where Amiri lay. The other two followed her, with open curiosity but respectfully silent.

When she reached the fallen barbarian, Kyra took the smoldering scrap of incense out of the holder and placed it on Amiri's chest. She tried to ignore the bones jutting out where they shouldn't, and the limbs twisted into agonizing angles. *This is not Amiri, merely her mortal shell. Her soul is free, and this is only the flesh she discarded.*

The incense ignited into golden flame. It spread over the Kellid, shrouding her in sunbright fire. In that purifying pyre, the marks of Rovagug's corruption burned away from Amiri's body, just as they had been forced from her soul as her friends dragged it through the seal.

Her limbs righted themselves. Crushed ribs straightened over regenerated organs; torn sinews stitched themselves back together and then bound new muscle to bone. The Kellid's skin, purged of foul scabs and perpetual wounds, sealed back over her body.

The flames faded away. Overhead, the clouds parted, and a ray of sunlight fell through.

It touched Amiri's face. She opened her eyes.

"I would like," she said, looking to each of her friends in turn, "to go home."

EPILOGUE

"Where do you wish to go?" Samo asked.

They had reunited on the *Carroway* and were sailing north on seas that no longer required the spirit-speaker's magic to quell. Rather than a haze of golden mist, Kyra could look out over the boat's bow to cloud-striped skies and the ocean's endless blue.

Behind them, the storm wall of the Eye of Abendego remained. It had churned there for over a century, and none knew how long its winds would continue to blow. A new isle dwelled within the hurricane's eye, which doubtless still harbored horrors and dangers within its craggy shores or amid its freshly risen peaks, but these were not the horrors and dangers of a god. In time, other heroes might be called to face these threats, and the winds of Abendego might lessen in those days, but for now, the sight of the hurricane was strangely comforting.

Gods had perished, and the world had nearly ended, but for now, at least, the fury of Rovagug's wrath had abated.

Kyra turned away from the prow. "I don't know," she admitted, looking at her companions. "There is still the matter of the Thurible of the Dawn, which Meri and I were charged with finding. Itaguen gave us some leads, before this all began, but we had no time to pursue them. And now that so much has changed, I do not know whether the faith still wants that artifact or would prefer that we be reassigned to other duties."

"Like the Godsgrave," Amiri muttered. The Kellid looked to the boat's stern, where their wake trailed off into a blue-gray infinity of water. The red spire of the Godsgrave was far behind them, nestled deep in the eye of the storm, but Kyra could feel its malignance lurking even past the storm wall.

"We did all we could," Ezren said. The wizard's tone, however, hinted at his uncertainty, and Kyra shared those doubts.

Luckily, Nahoa's god-touched powers had allowed him to recover quickly, even from Verex's grievous attack. He and Samo had slain the rest of the corrupted athamaru while protecting the *Carroway*, but that only meant they'd dealt with the warriors who had come to the Godsgrave. If others remained, deep undersea, they might yet return to undermine Rovagug's seal.

As might others.

Kyra had felt a deep foreboding as she'd left the red plateau on its spire. Even when his seal was buried beneath the sea, Rovagug had reached out to touch the world. Now the Great Devourer was held back more firmly, but the island that had lifted from the sea remained. A new path to the Dead Vault had been forged in the world, alongside the gulf that was the Pit of Gormuz. And even though the way had been sealed and this new land lay well-hidden within the maelstrom of the vast hurricane, there was a forbidden allure to the island that Kyra somehow knew would be known as Godsgrave Isle from this time forward.

People would come. Perhaps not soon, and perhaps not in any great numbers, but once they learned of Godsgrave Isle's existence, people would come. Rovagug's cultists would embark on unholy pilgrimages to free their god, of course, but others would come as well, drawn by curiosity, adventure, or a desire to loot the relics of the dead gods littered about the site of their ancient war.

She doubted that these ventures would go unopposed. Traditions of guardianship and legacies of watchful eyes had endured centuries to the modern day along the rim to the Pit of Gormuz, and in time, new traditions and legacies would doubtless form around, and within, the Eye of Abendego.

Unless the Dawnflower instructed otherwise, however, guarding it was no longer Kyra's duty.

"Ezren is right. Our part in this is done," she said aloud.

"Then I'd like to go to Absalom," Amiri said. "Valeros might still be there. I want to tell him how I faced down a god and won. Figure that ought to be good for a few drinks."

"Valeros? You could tell him you faced down a rabid mouse and he'd buy you drinks," Merisiel snorted.

"So? Free drinks are free drinks."

"Point." Meri looked at Kyra. Her white hair tossed in the wind, and the green gem on her forehead gleamed in the afternoon sun. "Do you have any objection to Absalom?"

"I do not." Ezren steadied his staff against the boat's gentle rocking. "My experience with the god-spark has left me with many questions. I should like the opportunity to conduct further research in the libraries of the Arcanamirium and to consult with my colleagues there."

"That's nice, Ezren, but I wasn't asking you." Meri raised her eyebrows at Kyra. "Well?"

I am so fortunate to have these friends. To have my wife. To have this day and this horizon of calm.

Kyra didn't regret the loss of her power. It had never been hers anyway. Sarenrae had lent it to her for a single task, and Kyra had discharged that task. She had fulfilled her goddess's trust and honored her purpose and now...

Now she was grateful that burden had been passed to others, and that she could have the luxury of a little time for everything else she loved.

"I agree," she said, going over to take Meri's hand. "Absalom sounds wonderful."

ACKNOWLEDGMENTS

This book would not exist without the patient and enthusiastic support of Mark Moreland, who made the whole thing possible. I owe him an infinity of gratitude and thanks.

I am also indebted to everyone at Paizo, past and present, including Erik Mona, James Sutter, Pierce Watters, and Dave Gross, each of whom was a great friend in doing the Pathfinder Tales. All of the Tales authors were, and are, an inspiration and a joy to work with.

I am grateful to James Jacobs, James Case, Luis Loza, Eleanor Ferron, Mark Seifter, Michael Sayre, Scott Keim, and everyone else who let me keep adding small bits and pieces to Golarion here and there.

I would also like to thank Marlene Stringer, my lovely agent, who has made all my scribbling possible.

I'd like to thank the office Pathfinder gang: Pete Andrews, Ellen Corrigan, Jennie Doran, Julia Jacovides, Katerina Krohn, Virginia Manoyan, Dave Napiorski, Anthony Salzetta, Michael Scalera, Megan Sprance, Erin VanBuskirk, Sara Walenta, and Laura Zipin.

And, of course, the OGs: Joseph Duffy and Cole Stevens.

I'll get you guys someday. YOU CAN'T SURVIVE FOREVER.

I would also like to offer special thanks to Wanda Zimba, who brought clarity and structure to this ungainly pile of words with her editing skills, and did so with great speed.

Finally, thank you to the readers and fans of Golarion, who made this and so many other fun projects possible. I owe everything to you.

ABOUT PATHFINDER

Godsrain takes place in the world of the popular Pathfinder Roleplaying Game. Launched in 2007 as a series of adventures for the contemporary version of the world's oldest RPG, Pathfinder grew from a monthly adventure magazine into a self-sustaining roleplaying game of its own. Now in its second edition, Pathfinder has sold 18 million books since its debut, becoming one of the world's most popular tabletop roleplaying games. Pathfinder has been translated into 8 languages and been adapted into the bestselling Pathfinder Adventure Card Game, a variety of board games, multiple computer games, and over three dozen novels, comics, and other accessories and merchandise.

For more information about Pathfinder, visit **paizo.com/pathfinder.**

THE WAR OF IMMORTALS

As part of the rich narrative of the Pathfinder world, *Godsrain* is just one of several Paizo releases comprising the War of Immortals publishing event. In the War of Immortals, one of the world's most influential and powerful deities—Gorum, god of war—dies, throwing the entire multiverse into chaos, both as other gods struggle to fill the vacuum left in his wake (all while ensuring they're not the next to perish) and as mortals race to recover the god-sparks that fall from his rent corpse. These shards of armor and rain of blood, called the Godsrain, imbue those who touch them with the power of divinity and leave a trail of war in their wake.

The event is anchored by the *War of Immortals* rulebook for the Pathfinder RPG and plays out over the course of multiple Adventure Paths, standalone adventure modules, fiction, rule supplements, setting gazetteers, and more over the course of several months, and redefines the status quo of the Pathfinder world going forward.

If you'd like more fiction dealing with the characters from *Godsrain* or the Godsrain itself, be sure to check out the supplementary prequel e-books, *The Godsrain Prophecies* by Erin Roberts and *Before the Godsrain*, both available now.

For the full slate of War of Immortals tie-in products, please visit **warofimmortals.com.**

ABOUT THE AUTHOR

Liane Merciel lives in Philadelphia, where she practices law and spends altogether too much time frying in the sun while running in big pointless circles. She lives with two delightfully odd children, a very patient husband, and Crookytail, the world's best and nicest old mutt.

THE PATHFINDER FICTION LIBRARY

Since 2007, exciting fiction set in the dynamic world of the Pathfinder Roleplaying Game has inspired Game Masters, players, and fans of high fantasy alike. Find any of the listed titles and more at paizo.com or wherever you buy your digital fantasy literature.

Tales of Varian Jeggare & Radovan
by Dave Gross
"The Lost Pathfinder"
Hell's Pawns
Prince of Wolves
"A Passage to Absalom"
Husks
Master of Devils
"A Lesson in Taxonomy"
Queen of Thorns
"Killing Time"
King of Chaos
"The Fencing Master"
Lord of Runes

Tales of Rodrick & Hrym
by Tim Pratt
"A Tomb of Winter's Plunder"
"Bastard, Sword"
Liar's Blade
Liar's Island
Liar's Bargain

Tales of Salim Ghadafar
by James L. Sutter
Death's Heretic
"Faithful Servants"
The Redemption Engine
"Boar and Rabbit"

Tales of the *Stargazer*
by Chris A. Jackson
"Stargazer"
Pirate's Honor
Pirate's Promise
Pirate's Prophecy

Novels
Godsrain by Liane Merciel
Operation Hellmouth by Chris A. Jackson

Winter Witch by Elaine Cunningham
Plague of Shadows by Howard Andrew Jones
The Worldwound Gambit by Robin D. Laws
Song of the Serpent by Hugh Matthews
City of the Fallen Sky by Tim Pratt
Nightglass by Liane Merciel
Blood of the City by Robin D. Laws
Called to Darkness by Richard Lee Byers
The Wizard's Mask by Ed Greenwood
Stalking the Beast by Howard Andrew Jones
The Dagger of Trust by Chris Willrich
Skinwalkers by Wendy N. Wagner
The Crusader Road by Michael A. Stackpole
Reign of Stars by Tim Pratt
Nightblade by Liane Merciel
Firesoul by Gary Kloster
Forge of Ashes by Josh Vogt
Beyond the Pool of Stars by Howard Andrew Jones
Bloodbound by F. Wesley Schneider
Hellknight by Liane Merciel
Starspawn by Wendy N. Wagner
Shy Knives by Sam Sykes
Reaper's Eye by Richard A. Knaak
Through the Gate in the Sea by Howard Andrew Jones
Gears of Faith by Gabrielle Harbowy

Novellas
The Compass Stone: The Collected Journals of Eando Kline edited by James L. Sutter
Dark Tapestry by Elaine Cunningham
Prodigal Sons edited by James L. Sutter
Plague of Light by Robin D. Laws
Guilty Blood by F. Wesley Schneider
The Treasure of Far Thallai by Robin D. Laws
Light of a Distant Star by Bill Ward
The Shroud of Four Silences by Liane Merciel
The Godsrain Prophecies by Erin Roberts

Anthologies
Before the Godsrain edited by Mark Moreland
Tales of the Zoetrope by James Case and Simone D. Sallé

Turn the page for a sneak peek at

OPERATION HELLMOUTH

By Chris A. Jackson

Available November 2025

Chapter One

HELL ON WHEELS

Cover!" Harsk bellowed, as only a dwarf can bellow.

The sonorous warning rattled Valeros's ears even more than the clamor of the battle that surrounded them. Heeding the warning, as he always did whenever the sharp-eyed dwarf announced danger—unless, perhaps, the danger of too much ale—he dragged Seoni down behind a sizeable boulder. Chips of shattered stone battered his shield before they hit the ground, the consequence of a near miss by a Chelaxian ballista bolt.

"Sorry!" Val hauled himself off the sorceress and risked a peek over the top of the boulder. The battlefield was chaotic, but to his practiced eye, it made sense. Andoren soldiers and combat engineers fought to dig protective trenches in zigzag tracks up the incline to the citadel, while Chelaxian forces rained missiles, arrows, and magic down on them from the walls and defensive trenches. They'd been at it for some time by the look of things.

"Better bruised than skewered," Seoni replied, brushing debris from a livid contusion on her thigh. The injury hadn't damaged her runic tattoos, at least. An arrow zipped past close enough to flutter her hair. "I feel like they don't *like* us or something!"

"They're Hellknights! They hate everyone equally!" Valeros ducked again as a sling stone rang on his shield. "I didn't expect things to be so... lively!"

Something exploded nearby, causing dirt, rocks, and bits of bloody armor to rain down on the trio.

"Ya mean *deadly*, don't ya?" Harsk growled, hunkering his stocky frame behind their boulder, which would have sheltered two people nicely.

"Fair point," Valeros admitted.

"'Twas *your* idea," Harsk accused "It's a bloody *war*! Did ya think we'd be sittin' down for tea and biscuits?"

The point was more than fair; Andoran's incursion into Isger in an attempt to capture Citadel Altaerein—or Hellknight Hill as the locals called it—was a bold tactic and bound to ignite the tinderbox that was Andoren relations with Cheliax. If they controlled the ancient elven portals beneath the citadel, Andoran could transport troops, dignitaries, and assassins all over Avistan and Garund. The incursion might indeed start a war, but it could also win it. Lending aid to the effort seemed the right thing to do.

"I'd rather be on the *right* side than the *safe* one!" Valeros countered.

They lived in a changed world, after all; one where gods of war were slain by gods of assassins, and the shattered remnants of divine flesh and armor rained down as warshards, granting god-like powers—and sometimes curses—to any who claimed them. Cheliax was striving to claim as many as possible, and Andoran saw the crimson light of Hell dawning on the horizon. When the devil-worshiping empire gained enough power, they would lay siege to all of Golarion.

A deep-throated roar interrupted his vehemence or perhaps emphasized the point that this wasn't a safe place.

"What the unholy hell now?" Harsk groused, scanning the sky instead of the ravaged battlefield.

This new threat, unfortunately, proved hard to miss.

A vast shadow swept through the smoke and dust, huge crimson wings hammering the air like a ship's sails amid a gale. The creature banked and swooped low over the battlefield, fire lancing from its cavernous maw. Screams filled the air, but hundreds of arrows and bolts of magic flew up from the Andoren forces. Most of the projectiles clattered harmlessly against the beast's iron-hard scales, but several punched holes in its wings and a few even drew blood.

"A bloody *dragon*? Are you *kidding* me?" Harsk sounded about ready to abandon this fool's errand, but Valeros wouldn't have it.

"Hellknights, dragons, devils... what did you expect; dancing girls and a feast in our honor?"

"Not just *any* dragon!" Seoni said. "That's the diabolic dragon, Kierothax!"

Val had heard the name and cursed under his breath. The dragon had been active in the region for the better part of a year, appearing wherever it could advance the cause of House Thune. This was, however, its first appearance in a full-scale battle. "What's that monster doing *here*?"

"Hell if I know, but they're obviously supporting Cheliax!" Seoni pointed as the great beast wheeled, and dove again, this time low enough to rake an Andoren trench with their massive claws. Bloody, shredded armor rained down in the dragon's wake. "Diabolic dragons don't generally engage in open warfare."

"They look ta be doin' a bang-up job of it!" Harsk observed.

Val risked another glance and saw that the Andoren forces were rallying to counter the new threat. Ballistae were being hauled up over the edges of trenches to aim skyward, and spellcasters were venturing from their protective bunkers. The dragon wheeled and swooped low. "The beast's coming in again!"

"Right at the main siege trenches!" Harsk added.

"Not this time!" Seoni stood as the dragon swept past them toward the primary Andoren offensive, runes flashing around her hands, her tattoos crackling with arcane energy.

Val expected lightning or some other destructive magic, so he gaped in surprise as the low-flying beast suddenly plummeted to the ground. The dragon roared in rage, wings billowing and legs extended to soften its landing. Claws like swords gouged the earth, flinging up dirt, felling small trees, and raking deep furrows. The creature skidded to a stop, unhurt, but their attack was foiled.

The Andoren response was swift and devastating.

Ballistae cracked, a storm of arrows flew, and magical energy crackled and arced through the dust-laden air. The dragon howled in impotent rage as the barrage pummeled their unyielding scales. Too far from the lines to retaliate with tooth and claw, they vaulted back into the air, banking hard to avoid a second onslaught.

"Nicely done!" Val pulled Seoni back down behind their boulder.

"Didn't put it out of commission, but surely gave it somethin' to think about." Harsk risked a look. "It's takin' up a perch on the battlements!"

"They'll attack again." Val took a good look at the beast, noting that several of the ballista shots had hit their marks. The dragon glowered there like a vulture looking for their next meal. "But the Eagle Knights hit it hard."

"We need to support the main offensive, and that's over there!" Seoni pointed, and Valeros could see she was right, then ducked as a projectile blasted more chips from their boulder. "And I think we need a bigger rock!"

Valeros scanned the field—a ragged landscape of upturned earth, corpses, wounded soldiers, and downed trees—and immediately saw another advantage to repositioning. "Well, at least the conflict there is so close to the enemy that the dragon can't roast the Andorens without killing their own soldiers."

"Always ignoring the mastodon in the alehouse!" Harsk snapped. "There's three-score Hellknights between us and them!"

"Give me a moment." Seoni lurched up to her feet again, runes and electricity flaring in her hands and along her skin. The resulting spell raked the hillside with a jagged track of lightning that arced from one Hellknight to the next. The armored knights thrashed and jerked as their metal accoutrements sparked and popped under the barrage. "That calmed them down! *Now*, can we get closer to the Andorens? We can't support them from here!"

"I love it when you take charge!" Valeros reassessed the field of battle with a glance. He might not be able to read a book without getting a splitting headache, but he could read battlefields like maps in his head. The Chelaxian forces held the high ground and were using it to their advantage. The citadel was fortified with siege engines, but the Hellknights were making sorties to break the Andoren advance. The latter were still advancing doggedly, leapfrogging in daring dashes from trench to trench, covering each advance with deadly fire and blazing spells.

"There!" He pointed. "That downed tree! I'll cover Seoni! Harsk, you dissuade any curious Hellknights."

"Bloody hell!" Harsk peered over the top of the boulder, took aim with his arbalest, and fired. "Curiosity dissuaded! Go!"

"Stay with me, Seoni," he said.

"Keep up, then!" The sorceress dashed forth, nimble as a cat on the uneven ground.

"Damnable long-legged woman!" Valeros ran after her, trying to stay between her and the battle proper and hoping they wouldn't come under friendly fire from nervous Andoren archers.

Seoni wore red, which drew attention, especially when the Andoren forces wore blue and silver, and Cheliax wore crimson and black. No Andoren soldier with two eyes would mistake her for a Chelaxian upon close inspection, but someone might at a distance. Val wore his signature bronze-painted half-plate and had picked up a shield emblazoned with the golden eagle of Andoran from an injured soldier, so he hoped his proximity to her would send a message. He heard Harsk's livid cursing and pounding feet behind them, then another crack of his arbalest. The dwarf was loading and firing the ponderous weapon as they ran. Valeros concentrated on incoming hazards, and more than one arrow shattered on his shield before they took cover behind the downed tree.

"Well, we're closer," Seoni announced with a sideways smile.

"Piece of cake, right?" He grinned back at her, then risked a glance over the log as Harsk arrived.

"Cake?" The dwarf huffed and panted from the run, working the lever that cocked his heavy weapon and loading a bolt. "Yes please! And a nice cuppa tea!"

"I forgot my teapot!" Valeros quipped back.

"Use that bloody tankard at yer belt, then!" Harsk stood, took aim, and fired. "Looks like the hell spawn are upping their game," he added as he ducked back behind their cover.

"More than a damned dragon? What next?" Valeros started to look, but a bellow from a nearby Eagle Knight officer answered his question.

"War wagons! All units, take cover!"

"Best advice I've heard all day!" Harsk added, hunkering lower behind their log.

Valeros ventured a peek over the lip of his shield and grimaced. Three wagons, each drawn by six armored warhorses mounted by equally armored Hellknights, plunged down the hill. The sides of the wagons were walled with ironbound oak, studded with spikes, and fitted with firing ports. Atop each conveyance stood a siege ballista and more knights, archers, and spellcasters.

"If the dragon supports that sortie, we're in for—" He gaped in shock as Kierothax turned on its perch and dropped down behind the citadel's wall. "They retreated into the fortress!"

"Good! Now all we gotta deal with is them war wagons!" Harsk observed.

The lead war wagon roared through the foremost line of Andoren soldiers like a bull through a picket fence. Many dodged to avoid the reckless charge, but some didn't and perished.

"Strike Team V!" an officer bellowed. "Lieutenant Rorque, take that damned thing down!"

"Yes sir!" a young woman cried out.

Rorque? Valeros felt startled at the familiar name, knowing the chances that it was the woman he'd known in his youth were miniscule. She'd been a farmer, not a warrior. In fact, she'd tried very hard to dissuade him from becoming one. When he saw the officer more closely, he was taken aback.

The young woman led a team of six from the security of a hastily dug trench. They wore the livery of Eagle Knights and wielded a diverse array of weaponry. She was raven-haired and olive skinned, brandished two swords, one short and one longer, just as Valeros used to wield. They immediately encountered resistance, enemy soldiers and Hellknights lunging up from cover.

The young woman—Rorque, he assumed—met the opposition with reckless lightning attacks, whirling and slashing at two opponents simultaneously, her blows finding chinks in the Chelaxians' armor. Three of her foes went down before her compatriots even arrived to help.

"*Damn*, she's good," Seoni observed, casting Valeros a glance. "She fights like *you* used to."

"She does," he admitted, watching rapt as she whirled and slashed with abandon, her face alight with battle glee. "Reckless."

"Aye," Harsk agreed, "but I think that war wagon might dampen her enthusiasm."

Valeros started to move before his conscious mind caught up with his actions. His only thought was to aid the small troop before they were run down by the massive war machine. Intuitively, he knew he was too far away to get there in time, but his instincts never did listen to reason.

As he watched the young Rorque fight, however, he saw himself in her style and ferocity. For her age, she demonstrated astounding skill and awareness, countering attacks that a lesser warrior wouldn't even see coming and shaking off blows that would have staggered most seasoned veterans. Someone called his name, but Valeros charged on, if not to get there in time, to witness from close range how they fared against the onrushing war wagon.

"Vitalia!" one of the woman's compatriots bellowed. "Upslope!"

She downed another foe and whirled toward the charging war wagon. "Fan out! Cut the traces! And disable that ballista!"

As she turned, Valeros caught a good look at her face, and his heart skipped a beat. This wasn't the woman he'd known in his youth, of course, but by Cayden's cups, she bore a striking resemblance. A vision flashed in his mind of his first love, the tears in her eyes as he told her he had to leave.

"I can't live like this," he'd said. *"I can't give up my dreams... even for you."*

The Eagle Knight contingent obeyed their lieutenant's orders like the seasoned veterans they were, three breaking left and three right. An archer among them fired a gleaming shortbow, and another cast a volley of shimmering projectiles, both at the siege engine mounted atop the wagon. The soldier behind the weapon fell to the onslaught, sparing their young lieutenant the fire of that heavy machine.

"Move, damn it!" Valeros urged, as the lieutenant stood firm before the rumbling war machine.

The two knights mounted on the lead horses bore lances, and lowered them to skewer her, but the instant before they struck, she leapt, not at them, but aside. As the lances passed close enough to ruffle her cloak, she rebounded off a boulder beside the track, leaping high, and struck. Her swords clove not armor or flesh, but the leather traces that bound the massive warhorses to the wagon. As she launched herself over the mounts and into the clear, the tongue of the wagon, released from the lead pair of horses, fell to gouge into the earth like a plow's blade.

The result was jaw-dropping.

Although the lead pair of warhorses charged on unhindered, the tip of the stout oak tongue of the wagon struck something solid. The impact knocked the second pair of horses and their riders into the air. Two tons of horses, riders, armor, and hardwood tumbled head over heels in a catastrophic chaos of destruction. The final pair of horses fell with their legs broken, the riders flung forth into the mayhem. Then the wagon itself struck the tangle of flesh, steel, wood, and bone. The ironbound wheels didn't shatter, but the forward axle of the conveyance snapped. The leading edge of the wagon struck the ground and the entire conveyance flipped end over end.

Valeros roared in triumph at the masterful maneuver, thrusting his sword into the air in salute.

The young lieutenant, recovering from her roll, glanced his direction and her eyes went wide. For an instant in time, they stared at one another, and the familiarity in her features smote his heart.

Maybe...

"Val! Incoming!"

Seoni's cry, followed by the crackle of lightning, whirled Valeros around in time to see a second war wagon bearing down on him. The sorceress' spell raked the side of the wagon, but it rumbled on, warhorses' hooves churning up earth like the prows of ships.

Valeros had no time to leap clear, no time to dodge. He raised his shield, and the impact of a Hellknight's lance struck it so hard his feet left the ground. His last thought before the war wagon ran him down was, *Oh, this is gonna hurt.*

To his astonishment, it didn't. There was nothing but impact and blackness and silence.